The Lady and the Loyalist

1774

HEART OF THE REVOLUTION
BOOK ONE

STEPHANIE MCRAE

for Cory
for your love
for your loyalty
forever yours

Master, go on, and I will follow thee
    To the last gasp with truth and loyalty.

— WILLIAM SHAKESPEARE

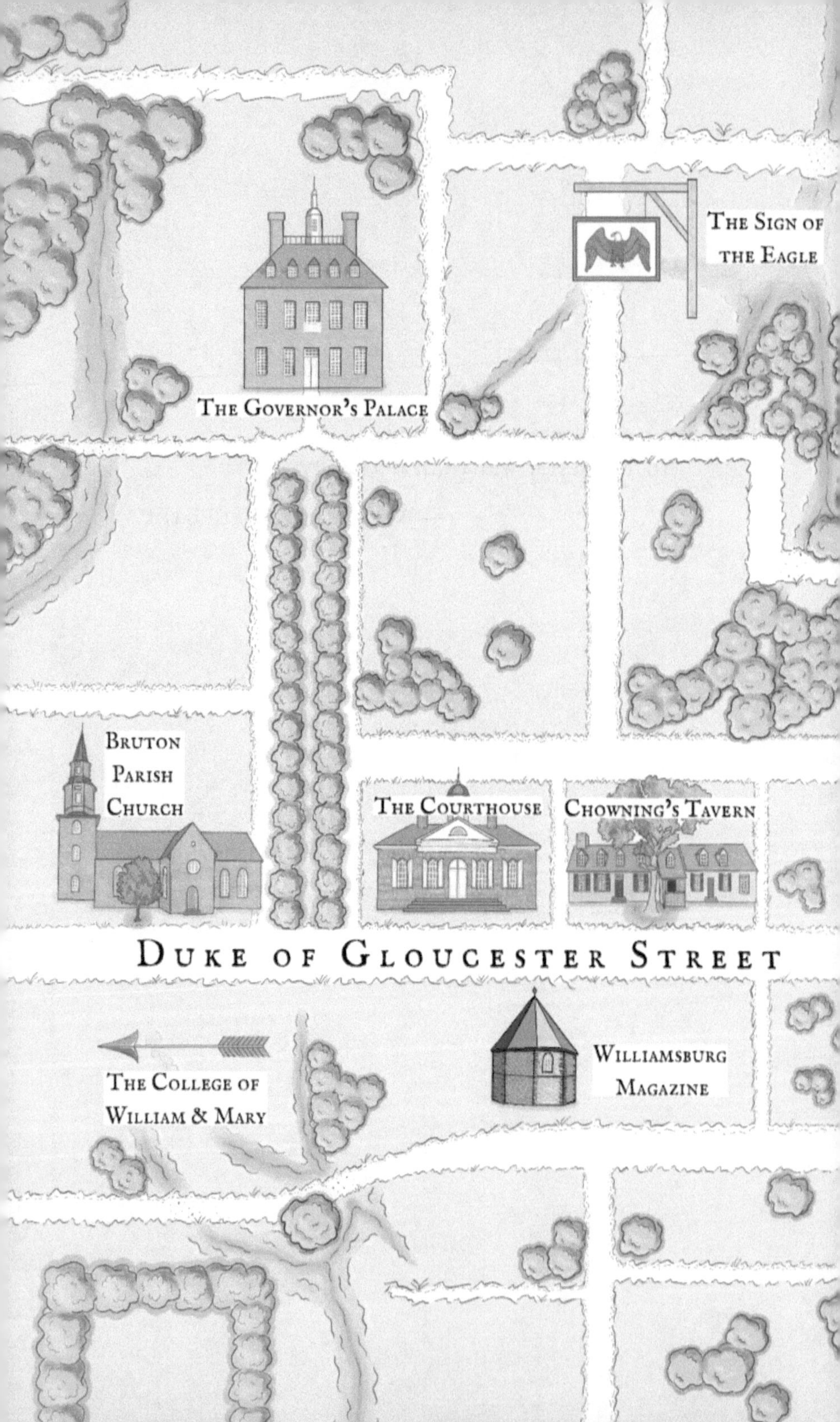

THE GOVERNOR'S PALACE
THE SIGN OF THE EAGLE
BRUTON PARISH CHURCH
THE COURTHOUSE
CHOWNING'S TAVERN
DUKE OF GLOUCESTER STREET
THE COLLEGE OF WILLIAM & MARY
WILLIAMSBURG MAGAZINE

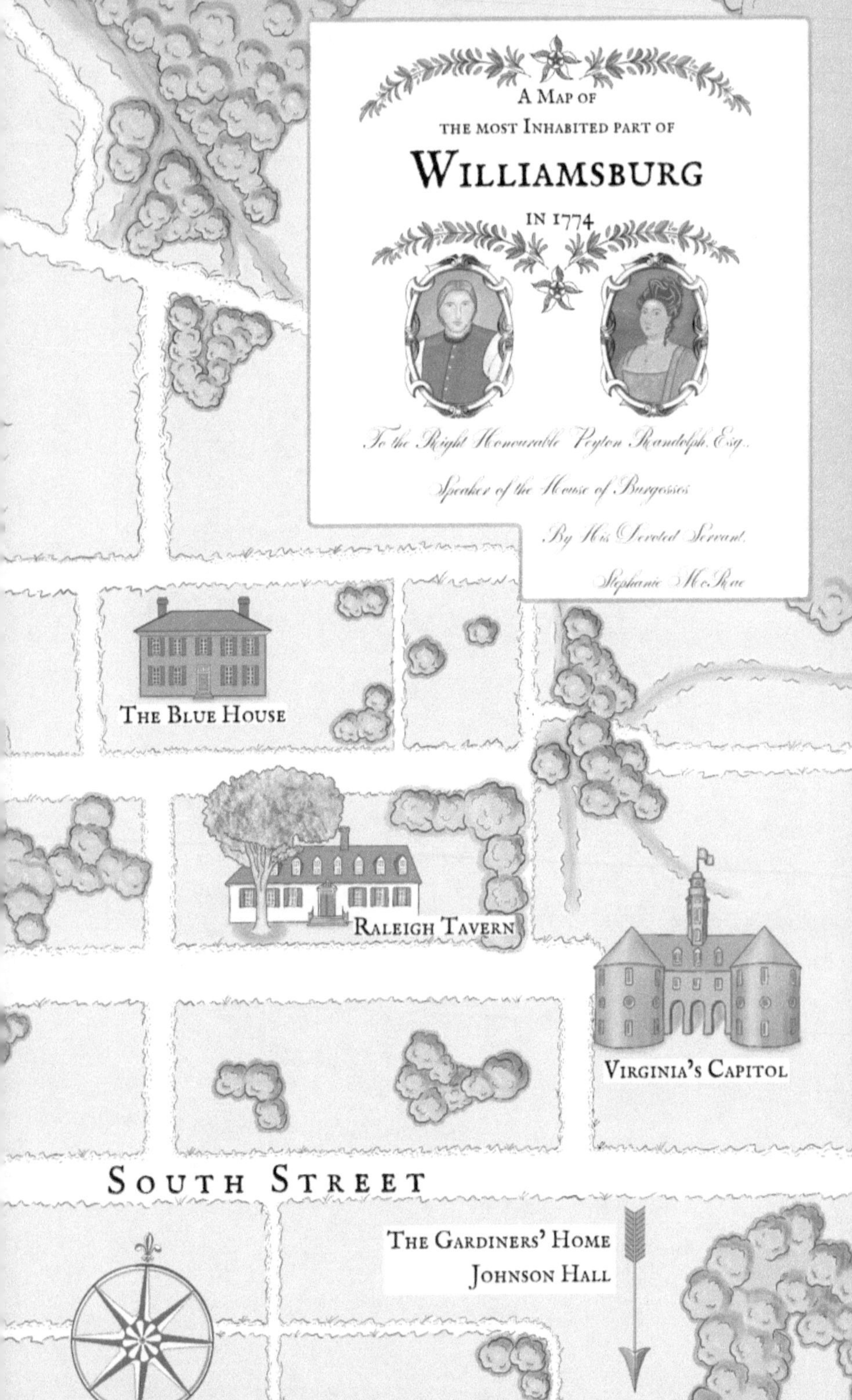
A MAP OF
THE MOST INHABITED PART OF
WILLIAMSBURG
IN 1774
To the Right Honourable Peyton Randolph, Esq.
Speaker of the House of Burgesses
By His Devoted Servant,
Stephanie McRae
THE BLUE HOUSE
RALEIGH TAVERN
VIRGINIA'S CAPITOL
SOUTH STREET
THE GARDINERS' HOME
JOHNSON HALL

Glossary

This glossary is provided for the convenience of readers who like to know the exact meaning of every word within a novel. Like any respectable writer, I have endeavored to present these words within their proper context so their approximate meaning can be easily understood by readers who prefer not to reference wordlists that remind them of school assignments. Please note that some compound words were not standardized in the eighteenth century (1700s) and may appear different in other books including some original sources.

Active service—active duty (military service)

Afore—before

Banyan—a man's leisure garment worn only at home. A wealthy gentleman's banyan would be made of a luxurious material, such as silk. The garment was inspired by clothing from the East Indies. It was more tailored than a wrapping gown

Barrister—a courtroom lawyer

Bedgown—a t-shaped garment similar to a shortgown that could be worn over a nightshift

Bill of Rights—in 1774, when Americans discussed the Bill of Rights, they referred to an Act of the English Parliament in 1689. That act included the right to free elections, the right of

Protestants to bear arms, and the right to free speech in Parliament. The bill also forbade standing armies in times of peace and "cruel and unusual punishments." It was signed by King William and Queen Mary as part of the Glorious Revolution

Breeched—in the eighteenth century, little boys wore dresses. Sometime between the ages of four and eight, a boy would stop wearing dresses and begin wearing breeches or trousers. In the language of the time, he would be *breeched*

Brief—a court case

Cabbage—scraps of fabric

Cabinetmaker—a woodworker who specializes in making furniture

Clothespress—a large piece of furniture for storing clothing. Often, this is a tall cabinet with shelves

Confidence—secret

Constitution—the word *constitution* was used frequently in the *Virginia Gazette* in 1774. In that time and place, the word could refer to the Magna Carta, the 1689 Bill of Rights, or the collection of laws and traditions that make up the English government

Delft—a city in Holland that became famous for its fine pottery—delftware—which was typically white with a blue design like china

Diet—the house special

Ensign—a flag

Feme sole—a legal term for a woman who owned property

Fichu—French for neckerchief

Fortnight—two weeks

Great house—the master's house on a plantation (as opposed to the outbuildings and slave quarters)

Haversack—a large cross-body bag, often made of canvas, used by soldiers and travelers

Hire—rent

Hoecakes—cornmeal pancakes

House of Burgesses—similar to the British House of

Commons, the House of Burgesses was colonial Virginia's lower legislative body. Each county sent two burgesses who had been elected by the county's male landowners. The House created Virginia's laws, but those laws were subject to veto by the council and the royal governor

Indented—indentured

Ken—know (Scots dialect)

Kerchief—a large, triangle of fabric that wrapped around the neck and covered the chest for modesty and sun protection. Also called a fichu or neckerchief

Livery—the uniform worn by a footman or other household servant

Magazine—a building to store ammunition and other provisions for use by the militia

Mantua-maker—dress-maker

Mayhap—possibly, maybe, perhaps

Miasma—a strong, unhealthy odor, believed to cause illness

Mitts—fingerless gloves

Naught—nothing

Panniers—made of hoops and worn under the petticoats, panniers made the hips appear wider and were essential to a fashionable silhouette

Petticoat—a skirt. During the eighteenth century, it could refer to any skirt, not just an underskirt

Portmanteau—a bag made of stiff leather

Provincial—colonial

Queue—the classic hairstyle of the founding fathers: hair gathered back into a low ponytail or braid

Roman pearls—large glass beads that look like pearls

Save—except

Sennight—one week

Settee—a wooden bench, sometimes padded; a sofa

Shortgown—the eighteenth-century equivalent of a woman's t-shirt. The shortgown was a t-shaped garment that ended between the hip and mid-thigh. It was worn over a petticoat, often with an apron and kerchief. This was the daily uniform of lower-class women. It was sometimes worn by women of the middling and upper classes when they weren't expecting company

Stays—similar to a corset, stays were a foundational garment that gave the torso a conical silhouette. Stays were stiffened with cords, baleen (from whales), or reeds and would hold their shape whether they were laced tightly or loosely

Sultana—a relaxed gown that wrapped around the figure and was tied with a sash. This loose-fitting garment could be worn without stays

Sweetgum burrs—also called gum balls, the spiky clusters about the size of golf balls contain the seeds of the sweetgum tree

Tester—the canopy of a four-poster bed

Tobacco notes—used as colonial currency beginning in 1730, a tobacco note represented ownership of a certain number of pounds of tobacco from a warehouse stock

Toilette—washing and dressing

Tricorn—a hat cocked in three corners

Tulipiere—an ornate delftware vase for tulips

One

THE LADY OF BAILEY MANOR

MARCH 18, 1774, EVERSLEY, ENGLAND

Miss Susan Bailey crooked her elbows as her maid, Lucy Pryor, tied an organza apron over her silk petticoat. The apron was trimmed with yards of lace, more valuable than some dowries. But the apron wasn't simply decorative. It displayed Susan's rank, a little shy of a titled lady, and her responsibilities at Bailey Manor.

"Pretty as a picture," Lucy said, handing her a gilt-framed looking glass and tidying the room in her brisk, precise way.

The glass reflected a plump face, freshly rouged, with no circles under her eyes from dancing into the night. She had encouraged Papa to leave the assembly at ten. By then, she had danced with several gentlemen and heard the concerns of all her neighbors. She patted the sausage curls securely clipped to her hair. Lucy had pomaded and powdered the dark hair into something from a fashion plate. It was high enough to command respect and low enough to avoid Isaac's teasing.

"Thank you, Lucy. That will do," Susan said. She rose from her toilette and crossed the hall. A maid holding a breakfast tray waited beside the tall double doors. She curtsied. Susan nodded in greeting and opened the doors. "Mama?" Her voice echoed in the gloomy chamber. White smoke rose from a silver perfume burner. She pulled back the heavy bed curtains. "Good morning, Mama." A shaft of light cut across a jumble of pillows and illuminated the wan face of her mother. Her eyes squeezed against the light, and she rolled away, disrupting the pug who slept at her feet.

The maid set the tray on a table beside the bed. The pug released an irritating series of yips, then scampered across the bed, snagging the coverlet with a claw. Mama sat up as slowly as a daffodil unfurling its petals. An avalanche of pillows tumbled to the floor. Pug the Undeserving continued yipping until Mama offered him a juicy slice of ham. He dragged it across a pillow before gobbling it up. Susan frowned. The bed linens would need to be changed again.

At last, Mama's languid gaze fell on Susan. "I'm feeling rather poorly this morning. I could use some laudanum." All Mama cared about was laudanum and her lapdog.

"You had some yesterday. The doctor said no more than thrice a week. You can have more tomorrow."

Mama collapsed on the feather bed. "I didn't know you were so cruel. You know where it's kept." Her voice was accusing. She never thanked Susan for assuming all the responsibilities in their home and community that belonged to the lady of Bailey Manor.

Susan's voice was calm and commanding. "You can speak with the doctor about it next week. Until then, I must follow his orders."

"Until then, do turn away all my callers. I'm in no state to receive them."

"But, Mama, your dear friend, Mrs. Langley, promised she would call this morning. You always feel better after a visit from her."

Mama waved the suggestion away. "Tomorrow. Tomorrow, when I've had my laudanum, then I can see her."

"She can't come tomorrow. Remember, her niece had a baby.

She's leaving this afternoon for a visit. She'll be gone for at least a fortnight. If you don't see her today, you won't see her for weeks."

Mama stroked Pug. "Then bring her up here when she calls. I don't have the strength to manage the stairs."

"As you like." Susan opened the clothespress and pushed aside the shapeless sultanas. "You should wear something nice." She pulled out a bright yellow petticoat and a floral jacket and draped them over the dressing chair. "Yellow is such a cheerful color."

Mama frowned and turned to the spread on the breakfast tray: another slice of ham, a boiled egg, cheese toast, a sweet bun, a slice of fruit tart, and a pot of tea. "What does Hill expect me to do with so much food? I scarcely have the appetite of a sparrow." She propped herself on an elbow and tore a piece of a bun as dainty as a rose petal. "If I continue to feel so low, I won't be down for meals."

"I'm sorry to hear that. That reminds me, the cook sent up next week's meals." She pulled the folded paper from her pocket and set it on the bed where Mama could see it. "I was on my way down to discuss it with her. What do you think?"

"I don't know why you trouble me with this." She considered the paper as she savored the sweet bun. "I don't have the constitution for such delicacies, but if I did, I should prefer a meal of venison to dining on turkey three days in a row." She hesitated over the fruit tart. "I wonder if this might disagree with me." She carved out a bite the size of a berry.

"I'll let Hill know." Susan pocketed the paper and left her mother to pick at her breakfast. She swept down two flights of marble staircases, her hand skimming the gilded balustrade, through the painted hall, the vestibule, and into the kitchen.

Hill was rolling pastry dough. She saw her mistress, dusted her hands on her linen apron, and curtsied. "Morning, my lady."

"Good morning, Hill."

"Is the menu to your liking, miss?"

"I switched Thursday's rice pudding out in favor of gingerbread. The reverend loves your gingerbread."

Hill flushed. "Thank you, miss." She resumed rolling the pastry. "Is there anything else?"

"If there's any fresh venison, my mother would prefer that for Wednesday. And Henry Keats broke his leg." He was one of the Bailey's tenant farmers, so Susan was responsible for his care. "Put a basket together for his family. They have three young children. I'll deliver it this afternoon." She would go during her walk with Anne.

Isaac entered the kitchen in bare feet and a brocade banyan. His dark hair hung about his face. "Susan. There you are. Have you seen my shirts? I'm missing five of them."

She shooed him out of the kitchen before he interfered with dinner preparations. "They went out with yesterday's laundry."

"The laundry went out yesterday? But I need to pack." All Isaac could talk about was his upcoming trip. In place of a grand tour of the continent, Isaac would visit their aunt in Virginia. There was less than a fortnight until he left.

As a formality, Susan had been included in Aunt Dorothea's invitation. She had declined with equal formality, thanking her for her kind intentions and regretting her inability to accept. It was the kind of letter she would have written to decline an invitation to a house party. She had written so many of these letters that she was now numb to the feelings she professed. "You need to pack *clean* clothing. Anyway, since when do you pack two weeks early?" All through Eton, she had helped him pack the week he left.

"Since I'm a man."

Susan choked back a laugh. Isaac was scarcely eighteen and couldn't grow a beard to save his life.

"Besides," he continued, "you've already started packing."

"That medicine bag is more important than all your shirts combined. Some of those herbs are difficult to come by. Now, if you get seasick—"

He waved her off. "I'm determined not to be ill if I can help it. I'll bring your bag if there's still room in my trunk, but I don't need a lecture on the properties of feverfew and ginger." His brocade banyan swished as he turned on his bare heel, leaving her alone at the bottom of the stairs.

His dismissal stung.

Susan had only been fourteen when she had left school to take on Mama's responsibilities. She had bandaged Isaac's skinned knees and read him stories of faraway lands. As a boy of eight, he hadn't been embarrassed to need his sister. He had kissed her cheek and given her untidy bundles of flowers he had picked himself. He had loved her. Soon, he would leave for a year. He was so eager for his trip that he thought nothing of what he was leaving behind. After everything she had done, the least he could do was thank her for helping him pack.

"There you are, Susan." Papa leaned out his study door.

"Were you looking for me?" She followed him inside the room. His study was big enough to hold a village council. A modest fire was dwarfed by a fireplace large enough to roast a wild boar.

"Indeed, I was." He sat on the edge of the mahogany desk and gestured to one of a dozen claw-foot chairs lined up under the windows overlooking his wooded hunting grounds. "I have a business matter that involves you."

She took a seat. "I already spoke with Hill about putting a basket together for the Keats family. I'll deliver it this afternoon." She folded her hands on her organza apron.

"Good. Good. Will you be available to join me at ten? I'm interviewing a housekeeper."

"A housekeeper?" Her voice pitched upward. Papa only managed the manservants. He left the rest of the staff to Susan. They hadn't needed a housekeeper in five years. Not since the last one had run off with a footman and Susan had proved she could run Bailey Manor by herself. Her hands tightened. "We don't need a housekeeper." The last one had taken the credit for everything her young mistress had done. After she ran off, at least Papa had seen the work Susan did.

"Every country manor has a housekeeper," Papa said.

Bailey Manor had a music room with the latest instruments, a state bedchamber that Queen Anne had once slept in, a library, a chapel, several galleries, and the finest formal garden for miles. It was no less of a manor without a housekeeper than it was with one. "A bad housekeeper is more trouble than she's worth. The last one beat the scullery maid, drank a bottle of our best wine every morning, and spread the worst gossip. It's easier to manage the maids myself."

"Mrs. Weston comes highly recommended."

Susan frowned. As the acting lady of the house, she corresponded with every other gentlewoman in the surrounding country. They shared notes on their maids, who moved from one household to another. She had heard no recommendations or reputation of this Mrs. Weston. "If she's so good, why does she need a new position?"

"Her master, an old schoolfriend of mine, remarried, and his bride brought her housekeeper."

Muffled voices and footsteps echoed down the hall. "That must be Mrs. Langley. Excuse me, Papa. I'll meet you back here at ten."

She smoothed her petticoats as she walked. The familiar rustle of silk soothed her nerves. She was the lady of Bailey Manor. She didn't need help doing at four-and-twenty what she had accomplished at nineteen. She just wanted a little appreciation.

She froze on the threshold of the drawing room. Pacing in front of the fireplace and clutching a large bouquet of hothouse flowers was the reason she had left last night's assembly so early. She had met Lord Townsend in January when she had taken her mother to Bath. She had done nothing to encourage him. Nothing at all. But two months later, his lordship was staying in her village at a common inn. He had no other connections and no other business in Eversley.

She gestured for a footman to follow and stepped into the

room. "Lord Townsend. I didn't know you were such an early riser."

"When the incentive to rise is great enough." He handed her the bouquet. "You left the assembly so early. I had hoped to solicit another dance."

It wasn't her imagination. He had come to Eversley to court her. Her heart squeezed. She hated declining suitors. But it was no kindness to lead them on, either. "I never stay for a second dance."

"Never?"

She had rehearsed this in the mirror until her reflection had grown stoic, but she couldn't meet his eyes. Instead, she fixed her gaze on the unchanging portrait of great-uncle Horatio, the famed sea captain. Her heart hammered in her chest. "I hate to give a man the idea that I'm looking for a steady partner." There. It was done. She glanced at him.

"I see." His voice was distant and cold.

She squeezed the bouquet. A stem snapped. She forced a smile. "Your family must miss you. They're in London already?"

His gaze flickered from great-uncle Horatio's portrait to a Delft tulipiere to the hundred-year-old bust of Queen Mary. "They are. My sisters have great hopes for the season."

"If they are as courteous as their brother, they will do well." It was better to soften the refusal with a compliment. "And thank you for the flowers. They will look lovely in the drawing room."

He stared into the low fire. "I'm afraid I must take my leave. I'm hoping to reach my townhouse in London by suppertime. I have a long day ahead."

"Yes. Of course. Thank you for your visit." Every word was false. When the footman closed the door behind him, she sighed. There was no need to feel as horrible as she did. She had sworn not to marry—not before Isaac took a bride and Mama died. She wasn't free to consider offers for years, if ever. It wasn't her fault Lord Townsend was looking for a bride with a generous dowry to cover the setbacks from his father's gaming debts.

A maid began dusting the statuary. Susan thrust the bouquet

at her. "Put these in a vase." The broken stems had stained her hands green. She couldn't wipe them on her lace apron. She needed soap and water. She stalked off to her chamber. With a dowry as large as hers, she was popular with second sons, eager to avoid a life of toil. Being courted by the firstborn son of nobility was a novelty but not a compliment—not when he, too, was after her dowry. Suitors only cared about how they would benefit from her position and wealth. They never cared about her heart.

Two

THE BLOOD OF THE BAILEYS

A few minutes before ten, she entered Papa's study. He stood, arms crossed, looking up at the massive tapestry that hung over the fireplace. It had been commissioned in the prior century to illustrate the achievements of the great Baileys of yesteryear. Baileys fought alongside William the Conqueror, earning their claim to English soil. Richard Bailey, vice-chancellor of Oxford University, held a stack of books. There were Baileys in parliament. Baileys at court. Even the dissolute Henry Bailey, with a freshly killed stag draped over his shoulders. The enormous antlers still hung over Papa's desk. The family motto was worked into the grass under the Baileys' feet: *ubi bene ibi patria.* One's country is where one is well.

Papa turned on her. "You dismissed Lord Townsend already?"

She blinked. The footman must have reported her. "I did."

"He seemed pleasant enough."

"Always agreeable." She couldn't fault his manners.

"So what was it this time?" He said it as though she were in the habit of rejecting suitors every morning before breakfast.

She scoffed. "He lives fifty miles away. I cannot marry a man who will take me so far from my home."

"Is that your only complaint?"

It was enough. If an eligible man wasn't willing to move into the neighborhood, it didn't matter what other attributes he had. "There's no need to pity the man. He's on his way to London to shop for a wealthy bride. No love was lost between us."

"You didn't love him. You haven't loved any of them. What kind of man could you love?"

The question silenced her. No suitor had touched her heart. Courtship was nothing but a dance with choreographed words and gestures. Some men danced it more gracefully than others, but when she rebuffed them, there was always another partner to take her place. She couldn't love a man incapable of loyalty. She couldn't surrender her heart to a man who wouldn't treasure it more than he treasured her wealth. What she yearned for was deeper than a dance. She yearned for a man who meant every sweet word he said. She wanted a man of flesh and blood who would sacrifice his comfort for hers. She wanted—

The fire crackled, bringing her back to her senses. She was the lady of Bailey Manor. Whatever trials she had, she would bear with dignity. All romance was fiction to her. "Don't worry about me, Papa. One day, when Isaac is a man, he'll marry a woman who can share my responsibilities. Then I'll consider my suitors."

"When Isaac marries? That could be a decade—or more."

"Fortunately for me, I have quite the dowry, and the world keeps producing second and third-born gentlemen. If I wait until I'm five and forty, there will still be single young men in want of a large fortune."

Papa sighed. "Money might get you a second-rate husband, but it can't buy back time." At least Papa recognized her sacrifice.

"I know," she said softly. She had known for ten years. Her life belonged to her family. Time was no longer hers.

"As soon as we have a new housekeeper, I insist you take a holiday."

It would take time to train the new housekeeper in the ways and rhythms of Bailey Manor. It would be foolish to leave the moment she was hired. Besides, with whom would she go? Most of her school friends were married. Mama would refuse. Lucy would be enough company for dignified travel, but holidays were not in her nature. Susan would have to bring along the young daughter of some local gentleman and pretend it was an act of benevolence and not desperation. "I don't need a holiday."

"Everyone needs a holiday."

"I just got back from Bath."

"That was a holiday for your mother. Not you." Papa wouldn't accept her dignified excuses.

"I have nowhere to go and no one to go with."

"You could go anywhere. Everywhere." He ruffled through the papers littering the map table. "You could spend the season in London."

What would Lord Townsend say if he saw her at the famed marriage mart so soon after she had declared she didn't want a partner? Her face heated. "Not London." There was no need to return there until she chaperoned Anne's first season.

"Summer at the seaside?"

"Too much sand. Too much wind. Too much water." Before Papa could suggest another holiday, she added, "My heart is here. It always has been. What holiday could be better than the home I already have?"

Papa softened. "I appreciate everything you've done."

Susan warmed to his gratitude. "Mama needs me here. Anne needs me here. Isaac needs—"

"Isaac is leaving," Papa interrupted. "He doesn't need you here. Anne is fifteen. She can bear a little time without you." There was a sudden light in his eyes. "You could go with him."

"What?" She was stunned by the absurdity of his suggestion. "To America?"

"It's late notice, but you could do it. We'll have a housekeeper to manage the servants. You'll have a fortnight to train her." Papa grew more animated as he spoke. "I'll find a companion to keep your mother company. It's perfect."

She didn't travel more than ten miles without careful consideration. Papa was suggesting she leave for another continent within a fortnight. "I already declined Aunt Dorothea's invitation. I can't go."

"She's been inviting you for years. She'll be delighted."

"It's so far away. What if something happened? It would be weeks before I learned of it. Longer before I could get home."

"What if something happened to Isaac?" Papa countered. "I wouldn't know for weeks. But you would be right there. Don't you see?"

"I don't. I don't see why you're trying to get rid of me." She couldn't act as the lady of Bailey Manor from the wrong side of the Atlantic. Didn't he see how much she was needed here? How much she did for the family? Their home?

"Susan," Papa said in a placating tone.

A footman cleared his throat at the door. "Mrs. Weston to see you, sir."

Papa sighed. "Show her in."

Mrs. Weston's apron was blindingly white. The corners were starched to crisp perfection. She could manage a laundress. That much was obvious.

"Mrs. Weston, this is my daughter, Miss Bailey. She runs Bailey Manor."

Mrs. Weston curtsied to Susan. The movement made her starched apron crackle.

Papa began the interview, but he was inexperienced in running a home. Susan took over the questioning. She was impressed, despite herself, by Mrs. Weston's expertise. It wasn't every day such a highly qualified housekeeper looked for new employment. Would it be such a terrible thing to have some help? Then she saw Papa's face, full of hope. Hope was when you looked forward to something better. But Mrs. Weston wasn't better. She was good. Adequate, really. Nothing would improve under her direction. Susan had been managing just fine without her.

He brought the interview to a close. "Thank you so much for taking the time to meet with us." He was too warm. Too pleased.

Susan's nails dug into the palms of her hands.

He pressed on, unaware of her distress. "You can be—"

She caught his eye and shook her head vigorously. For a long moment, they fought silently.

Why not?

Just don't.

It's for your own good.

No. It isn't.

Papa returned his attention to Mrs. Weston. "I'll let you know by the end of the week."

Her brows raised. "Am I to stay at the inn that long?"

He brushed her concern away with a wave of his hand. "Have them send the bill to me. Thank you for your time, Mrs. Weston."

It was a relief when Mrs. Langley finally called. Susan led her upstairs to Mama's sitting room. Once Mama had become too ill to go downstairs, Susan had thought to turn a bedchamber near Mama's room into a cheery place to receive visitors. Papa had approved. That project had been her first time organizing the servants to get something done. She was still proud of it.

Mama lounged on a settee. What figure she had was lost under the shawls and sultana she wore, but she brightened at her friend's greeting. After catching them up on village gossip, Mrs. Langley asked, "Is Isaac ready for his trip?"

"Nearly," Susan said. "He wanted to pack his dirty laundry."

"Of course, you didn't let him. Whatever will he do without you?"

Guilt mingled with pride. That little boy with skinned knees had grown taller than her, but he still couldn't keep track of his shoes. This time, she wasn't preparing him for the civilized routines of Eton. Anything could happen to him in America, and she wouldn't know for weeks.

Mrs. Langley chattered away. "If I were the traveling sort, I would choose tamer waters. Paris is plenty foreign, and people don't die crossing the channel." She went on to detail everything she would do if she ever cared to visit Paris.

People did die crossing the Atlantic. People died in the colonies. Isaac would throw the medicine bag in his trunk and forget it until he was too ill to use it. She had nursed him through measles, mumps, and every other childhood malady. But this time, she wouldn't be there to save him.

After Mrs. Langley left, Susan spent an hour in the music room trying to master a complicated piece by Bach on the harpsichord. Her fingers stumbled through the chords. She had tried to talk him out of the trip. He had threatened to tour the continent instead. Papa had intervened in favor of Virginia. As going with him was unthinkable, there was nothing left to be done. The notes clashed like bayonets until she wanted to pound her fist on the keyboard.

"Susan?" Anne had come into the music room as quietly as a mouse. "Is now a good time for our walk?" She wore her cloak, mitts, and muff. The birds sang of spring, but there was ice in the wind.

"Indeed, yes," Susan said. She put away her music. "I was just waiting for you." In a few minutes, they were outside, Hill's basket in hand. Clusters of daffodils were beginning to bloom, as yellow as the petticoat Mama refused to wear. Their errand for the Keats family drew them away from their usual walks. Susan's worry about Isaac drew her away from her usual conversation. This was the time of day she asked Anne about her dreams for the future. Together, they had planned Anne's coming-out ball, her eventual wedding, fashions for her trousseau, and names for her babies. Today, Susan was preoccupied with memories of a lonely little boy who had desperately needed a mother.

Anne, for once, broke the silence. "Are you unwell?"

"Yes, I'm quite well," Susan said brightly. "Come, there's a lovely view on that rise."

Anne didn't ask again.

They delivered the basket to the Keats. It was filled with

freshly-baked bread, preserves, little cakes, and a leg of mutton. The family's profusions of gratitude failed to lift her spirits. She returned home even more distressed than when she had left. After dinner, Anne read aloud, and Isaac played chess with Papa. Susan rearranged the contents of Isaac's medicine bag on the table. Who needed her more: Anne, a conscientious fifteen-year-old whose elderly governess had been with her for six years, or Isaac, an adventurous eighteen-year-old who wanted to see the world but always mislaid his shoes?

It was easy to favor Anne, who was willing to be guided to a bright future that Susan wasn't free to dream of. Isaac no longer respected his sister, who was six years older, six inches shorter, and six inches wider than him. But she had mothered him from the time he was eight. What mother allowed her child to face the dangers of the world alone?

Anne's voice faded away. Her eyes moved down the page. She was reading ahead again.

Isaac slid his rook sideways. "I packed my trunk today."

She could only imagine the chaos he had created. "Did you put the heavy things on the bottom like I told you to?"

He rolled his eyes. "It's fine."

"And your cravats and garters in a separate bag so they won't get lost or crumpled?"

Papa captured Isaac's knight with his bishop.

Isaac scowled. "If you care so much, come yourself." There was an insolence in his tone that made her snap.

"I will."

Her family stared at her. After the initial shock, Papa looked ready to commission a tapestry in honor of this momentous occasion.

Isaac shook his head. "I only reserved one stateroom." He still didn't want her.

The blood of the ancient Baileys flowed hot in her veins. William hadn't conquered by vacillating. He had held his ground. She would hold hers. "Then you'll need to reserve a second."

This wasn't a holiday. A holiday was spending time with friends. Two weeks at a manor was a delightful way to enjoy the companionship of others. Except that was only a holiday if someone else was hosting. Susan always hosted. No, this would be no holiday. But Isaac did need her a little longer. And if he needed her, he might appreciate her again. She looked around the room again. This was her home. Her family. Her life. She addressed Papa in a low voice. "Are you sure you'll manage without me for a whole year?"

"I'll send a note round to Mrs. Weston. We'll be fine."

That's what Susan was afraid of.

Three

THE MINERVA

APRIL 2, 1774, PORTSMOUTH, ENGLAND

Charles Johnson scowled at the *Minerva*. She was the shabbiest ship moored in the harbor. He could scarcely make out the faded name. The ship rocked in the gentle waves, straining the frayed ropes that secured her to the pier. The wood was patched with irregular stains. Only the mast was unsullied wood. His misgivings renewed. If the original mast had not stood the rigors of ocean travel, how much longer would the original vessel stay afloat?

If only there were more time. It would be better to find a ship recommended by someone he knew and trusted. The *Minerva* had nothing to recommend her beyond a coincidence of timing: he needed to get to Virginia. This ship was going there. Today.

Last night in the pub, a man claiming to be its supercargo had offered passage on it for a hefty fee. The man's hollow cheeks had made him look devilish by candlelight. Charles had refused to pay until he saw the ship. Here she was.

Men attired more like pirates than sailors swaggered down the gangplank. They hoisted a trunk between themselves and carried it onboard.

Pirates had no respect for order and law. These sailors might not, either. He clutched his portmanteau tightly in one hand and adjusted the strap of his haversack with his other. He would not board the vessel before his luggage did. Ignoring him, the unkempt sailors picked up another trunk and began carrying it onto the ship. The brightness of the untarnished lock and clasps proved that this was the trunk's maiden voyage. Several trunks of similar newness rested on the docks. He wouldn't be the only gentleman on this journey.

When the untrustworthy sailors returned, Charles stepped aside so they could reach his trunk with their dirty hands. He followed the men up the gangplank, not taking his eyes from his luggage. They led him into the darkness below deck. The smell of mold and stagnant water accosted his senses first. He covered his nose with a handkerchief and looked about. Two shafts of light passed through open doors on his right. They landed on a haphazard arrangement of crates, trunks, and barrels. He blinked, and the details sharpened.

His barrels of biscuits and dried meat were clustered beside an ancient ship's stove. Food and meals were not provided, the super-cargo had said, but this stove was available for passengers. The sailors hefted Charles's trunk on top of the other gentleman's luggage between two more stacks of trunks. They brushed past Charles, grumbling about their work.

"And who would yeh be?"

Charles turned to see a weathered man leaning against the weathered wood between two doors.

"Mr. Johnson, sir. I was told there was a bed to rent."

"That there is. Are yeh the one as was speakin' ter our super-cargo, Mr. Sleeman, las' night?"

"That was me."

The man stepped forward and clasped Charles's hand so hard he pulled him forward. "Then welcome aboard. Name's Dave. The navigator."

"Just Dave?"

"Jus' Dave."

"Then I'm just Johnson. Can you show me my room?"

"I could. Or yeh could show yehrself. It's right there." Dave jerked a thumb over his shoulder at a Dutch door that opened directly off the galley.

Charles ducked under the lintel and stepped into his stateroom. Underneath a small window was a table lashed to the wall. The narrow bed to the right was already covered with a jumble of clothing and papers. The narrow bed to the left must be his own. An old hammock hung above the thin mattress. He would need to take it down. He lowered the handkerchief and was assaulted with the sour smell of seasickness. He gagged, took a gulp of galley air, and threw his haversack and portmanteau onto his bed. Then he stood in the narrow space between the beds and stretched his arms out. His fingertips brushed the opposing walls simultaneously. The stateroom was little bigger than a broom closet, and he was sharing it. He felt no better about his travel arrangements than he had last night when he had lain awake wondering what he had gotten himself into. Now he knew. Thus far, everything was worse than he had feared.

He returned to the galley and addressed Dave. "I see the other gentleman has been here. What can you tell me about him?"

"He's right young, that'un. From southwest o' London, I believe. He'll be having that bed, an' the ladies'll be one door down.

"Ladies? There are ladies onboard?" This decrepit vessel didn't appear to cater to the gentler sex.

"The gentleman is travelin' with his sister and the lady's maid. The gentlefolk are takin' dinner at a nearby inn." Dave frowned. "Tide's turnin' within the hour. They should be back by now."

"Hmm." He had problems of his own. "Where might I find Mr. Sleeman?"

"He keeps close by the captain, mos' times. Stay on deck and he'll likely find yeh."

Dave's advice proved prophetic. The supercargo approached

him within minutes, eager for payment. Charles made a show of emptying his pocketbook into Mr. Sleeman's hands. It would be best if the sailors believed he had no more money than what he had paid for the passage. After he paid the supercargo, Charles lingered on deck. Sailors still reeling drunk from their liberty ashore stumbled about their duties. These were the men he was entrusting with his life and safety for the coming weeks. He scanned the other ships in port. It might not be too late. He could demand a refund from the supercargo and wait in a seedy inn until a better opportunity arose.

"The tide's turning. Prepare to weigh anchor," the captain called.

It was too late. He would stay. At least he would have another gentleman for companionship. Except that the boy and his sister were nowhere to be seen. It was none of his business, really, but the possibility that the *Minerva* might sail without all its passengers made him anxious. It would be dreadful to have all your worldly possessions onboard and be left dockside. If Mr. Sleeman already had their money, honor was the only thing keeping them in port much longer—honor and the clumsiness of inebriated sailors.

"There they are!" The navigator's voice carried across the deck. One worry was relieved as his fellow passengers came into sight. Dave had been right. The other gentleman was young. It showed in his dark hair, his boyish face, and the swing of his arms as he sauntered up the gangplank. He had never doubted the ship would wait for him.

Foolish boy.

Behind him was a woman—the sister. If the boy had had an ounce of concern, he would have allowed her to go first. They barely stepped on deck before the sailors pulled in the gangplank. Charles forgot drunken sailors and foolish boys when she came fully into view.

Dark hair, lightly powdered, was pinned in sausage curls under a flat straw hat. She was a little shorter than her brother, but the differences didn't end there. Where the boy was built of awkward angles, she was soft and substantial. Charles had seen her somewhere before. The woman looked up. Dark eyes met his. Thousands of English women had dark hair and dark eyes. He looked away. Something about her tugged at an old memory. As a London barrister, several women had visited his office, seeking legal representation. That must be why she looked familiar. If only he could remember which case had been hers.

She tugged her brother in his direction. *Lord, help me.* He couldn't remember her name. The young man smiled. He had the lean look of a youth who had recently grown several inches. "Please pardon me for leading the introductions. I don't believe we have a mutual acquaintance. I am Mr. Isaac Bailey. This is my sister, Miss Susan Bailey. And you are—"

Relieved. They didn't expect him to remember them. "Mr. Johnson." There was no need to be tossing around his christening name as if they had a right to it. "This is your first time traveling?"

Young Mr. Bailey blinked. "How did you—"

"I saw the trunks loaded. Yours are new."

"Then you have the advantage. I am forced to ask in return, is this your first time traveling?"

"I will be crossing the Atlantic for the second time."

"Then you were not born in England. Are you American?"

"Virginian."

Miss Susan Bailey smiled at him. It was a smile that belonged in a pastoral painting, not on a ramshackle ship that could sink in a storm. A *painting*. That's where he had seen her before, or rather, something *like* her.

Seven years ago, he had begun studying law at Lincoln's Inn in London. A fellow student had toured the continent before settling into his studies. As a souvenir of his grand tour, he had filled a sketchbook with likenesses of the Renaissance beauties he had admired in Italian paintings. Madonnas and goddesses were all idealized as substantial women with serene smiles.

Charles had studied those sketches with pleasure. Miss Susan

Bailey looked like she had stepped out of that sketchbook and into contemporary traveling clothes.

And she was smiling at him. "So you're returning home. You must be happy to see your family again."

That was not her business. "What about your family? Are you leaving them all behind?"

A flicker of distress crossed her face like a small cloud skittering past the sun. It was gone in a heartbeat. "Our mother's sister moved to Virginia twenty years ago. She invited us to visit her."

Charles looked at the siblings in confusion. "You're crossing the Atlantic to visit family?" He had never done such a thing. There was so little time and so little money in the world. He addressed Mr. Bailey. "Aren't your parents anxious to see you begin your career? Can you afford to be gone for so long?"

Mr. Bailey shrugged. "I'm the eldest son. My father isn't worried about my career."

Charles was an only son. His father had been plenty worried about his career.

A bedraggled sailor eyed Miss Bailey as he walked by. Awareness of danger washed over him like an icy wave. This rough crew was starved for female companionship, and this comely woman was trapped among them for the duration of the voyage.

Bailey hadn't noticed the danger, but he was scarcely out of boyhood, hardly a fit age to be the sole protector of his older sister. At the advanced age of five and twenty, Charles felt a solemn duty to ensure the young man was aware of his responsibilities.

"Mr. Bailey, may I speak with you alone?"

"Of course." Isaac followed him to their stateroom.

Charles covered his nose with a handkerchief. The moment he was done speaking with young Bailey, he would air all the linens and scrub every surface. "Do you have any plans for this voyage?"

The boy shoved the jumble of belongings aside and dropped

onto his mattress. "I have a new deck of cards, some books and maps to look over, and I'm going to climb that rigging every day."

Charles sat near the foot of his bed so their knees wouldn't touch. "I am relieved to hear you have occupations for yourself; however, I was referring to your responsibilities, not your plans for amusement."

Bailey looked at him blankly. "I'm a passenger. A *gentleman* passenger. What responsibility do you think I have here?" He was too young to understand.

"You brought your sister on a ship full of unsavory men. What do you think your responsibility is?"

"Oh, that. She chose to come. I didn't bring her. And she has a maid. What does she need me for?"

"Didn't your father ever tell you that in his absence, it is your responsibility to protect your sister?" While Charles didn't have a sister of his own, he at least knew that much about them.

"He may have said something about that, but I'm not the one who keeps the ship afloat. That's the captain's responsibility."

The captain. In boarding this vessel, they had all put their trust in him. "If your sister's safety is the captain's responsibility, let's have a word with him."

Isaac rolled his eyes to the ceiling. Charles opened the door. Isaac sighed and followed him out.

Though the deck hadn't inspired trust, the stately wood furnishings in Captain Crawford's quarters gave a satisfying air of authority. The captain motioned for them to be seated. "What can I do for you gentlemen?" He was straightforward and pleasant, nothing like his supercargo.

"Mr. Bailey has a concern he wishes to discuss with you."

"What is it, boy?"

"Well, it's just a little thing." He glanced at Charles, who nodded encouragingly. "There are a lot of men on this ship. And then there's my sister." Isaac leaned back and folded his arms as if he had done them a favor by explaining everything.

The captain templed his fingers thoughtfully. "I think I see your point. She has the company of her maid, but sailors are, by nature, rough men." The captain was quick to understand the delicacy of the situation. "It would be in your sister's interests if the men knew another man, a gentleman, had a keen interest in her welfare."

This was just the lecture young Mr. Bailey needed to remind him of his brotherly responsibility.

"Mr. Johnson, will you assist Mr. Bailey in looking after his sister?" It was phrased as a question but spoken as a command.

Charles had no desire to tangle himself in his neighbor's affairs. But every good barrister respected the jurisdiction of the court. They were in Captain Crawford's jurisdiction now, and the captain had spoken. There was only one answer he could give. "Yes, sir."

Four

FELLOW STRANGERS

The wind mussed Susan's curls as England drifted out of sight. Papa and Anne had accompanied them to Portsmouth. Were they standing on the dock, watching the ship disappear into the horizon? Or were they already in their carriage, heading home?

Home. She blinked sea spray from her eyes. Until a fortnight ago, she had given her home, her family, and her neighbors her unfailing devotion. Her heart squeezed. Thanks to Isaac, she couldn't return for a year. So much could happen in that much time. Anne had promised to write everything. Everything that Susan couldn't be a part of.

Ubi bene ibi patria. One's country is where one is well.

What had she done?

A sailor brushed by her. "Beg pardon, ma'am." He continued on, not waiting for a response. In Eversley, every man bowed and waited and said, "If you please." No man brushed against her person like she was a misplaced fencepost. Her pride prickled. Either no one onboard understood who she was, or no one cared. They bustled about with their tasks. Everyone had something important to do. Everyone but her.

It was too late to turn back. It had been since the evening she had announced her decision to her family. But it was never too late for regrets. She shouldn't have left Eversley. She shouldn't have left her comfortable bed and her comfortable life, and the people who needed her. Isaac was speaking with the helmsman, delighted with the adventure. At least one of them was having a holiday. There was nothing for her here—no work to occupy her time and no pleasures to amuse herself with. There were no menus for her to approve, no neighbors to call on, no injured tenants to care for, and not even an out-of-tune instrument to play. But the sailors were people. And people always liked Susan.

By the time the light faded from the gray clouds, she knew every sailor's story.

Dave the navigator was a second son born and raised in Somerset. That explained his thick West Country accent. The captain was another second son. He had received a commission in the Royal Navy as a young man. After a few years, he had sold his commission and bought this ship. One young man had run away from school two years ago and joined the first ship that would take him. An older man had once been impressed into service— kidnapped off the streets. By the time the ship had ported back near his hometown, his family had moved. He never saw them again.

Behind their crude manners, the sailors were good people.

She glanced over at the shadowy figure of Mr. Johnson. His dark blond hair, like everything onboard, looked ashen in the cloudy twilight. He had been reluctant to speak much when they had first met. She scarcely knew a thing about him. They needed to improve their acquaintance. After all, he was the only other passenger onboard, outside of her small party. There was something melancholy about traveling alone. Surely he would appreciate being better acquainted. Several times that evening, she had moved in his direction. Whenever she did so, he moved farther away. If they'd known each other better, she would have suspected him of avoiding her.

While she had been coaxing others to talk, the sky had unceremoniously faded from gray to black. "I confess I'm disappointed in the sunset," she told Isaac.

He shrugged. "It's cloudy. Dave says we might be headed into a storm."

"Is that safe?" It seemed more prudent to sail away from a storm.

"I don't see why not." Isaac didn't believe in worrying.

"Well, there's no point in stargazing. It's time to test the mattresses. I don't suppose I'll sleep much."

"You go along. I'm going to learn how to calculate the speed we're traveling."

Susan had no interest in learning how to calculate anything. Mathematics had always been a slippery subject. Then she had left school at fourteen. It was fine. She knew everything she needed to know to run Bailey Manor. She didn't need her little brother crowing over her just because he understood calculus while she barely grasped the fundamentals of algebra.

Lucy was sitting, straight as an arrow, on the edge of her bed, hemming a petticoat by candlelight. She had refused to join them for dinner, insisting the cabin needed a good scrubbing before they could sail. She glanced up at Susan. "Good evening, miss. Are you ready for sleep?"

Susan sat on the edge of her bed. She hadn't expected a mahogany clothespress in her stateroom any more than she had expected perfumed toilette water. But was it too much to expect that her mattress be wider than her hips? "I don't think I'm tired enough to appreciate my bed."

"Let me know when you are." Lucy held the petticoat closer to her face.

"You've been working all day. Give your eyes a rest."

Lucy stiffened. "You're wearing this tomorrow. I can't wait for sunrise to finish it."

Mr. Johnson walked by their cabin carrying a bucket. His eyes met hers for the briefest of seconds before looking away. He didn't smile. Didn't nod. Didn't pause to talk. She still didn't know his story.

"Don't push yourself too hard," she told Lucy softly. "These sailors wouldn't know me from a farmer's daughter."

"*I* will know." There was no arguing with Lucy. Once she made up her mind on the principle of the matter, her body wouldn't rest until her conscience did.

Susan wasn't ready to sleep for other reasons. If Mr. Johnson would sit around the stove in the galley, they could talk until they were sufficiently fatigued to sleep in their unpromising accommodations. She stepped into the galley as his door closed. She hesitated. If he was undressing for bed, she didn't want to disturb him just because she was unable to sleep. Then the floor tilted under her feet, and the upper Dutch door swung wide open. Mr. Johnson was dressed. Mostly. His jacket and waistcoat were discarded on his bed. The man himself was on his hands and knees scrubbing the floor by lamplight with what looked like an old cravat.

She decided to disturb him. "That's probably easier to do by daylight."

He startled. There was a gasp and a gag, followed by coughing. Then he stared up at her in a rare combination of surprise and disgust.

"You left the door open," she said defensively. If he hadn't wanted his neighbor to see him scouring the floor in his shirt-sleeves, he should have latched the door properly. Besides, it was her little brother's room, too. She had a partial claim on it.

His eyes flicked to the upper half of the Dutch door. Too late now. She rested her arms on the lower door like they were old neighbors having a chat over the garden wall. "Where in England were you?"

For a moment, she thought he would close the door in her face. Instead, he plunged the rag in the bucket and rung it out. "London."

"How exciting. I've been there once myself. What did you do there?"

He wiped under the bed in big sweeping circles that displayed his shoulders to advantage. More gentlemen should forgo waistcoats for menial labor. "Work," he said, his eyes on the floor.

"There must be a lot of work to do in London, as there are so many people."

He grunted and rinsed his rag.

"What kind of work did you do?"

He glanced at her, his expression unreadable. "The kind I was paid for."

Was he always this difficult? This voyage was going to take even longer if the only gentleman passenger refused to answer neighborly questions. He continued scrubbing and rinsing as though she weren't there.

He didn't want to talk about himself. That was unusual. And irritating. After a long silence, she asked, "Is it wise to use water to clean the floors? The captain told us to be sparing with it."

He sat back on his haunches and looked at her with disbelief. "It's seawater."

"Oh. How clever," she faltered. "I hadn't thought of that." She watched him for a long minute, waiting for him to speak. When he didn't, she took her leave.

There was nothing else to do but go to bed. Lucy helped her out of her clothes. Susan wriggled into the scratchy bed linens. The thin mattress was too narrow for comfort. She turned on her side and watched Lucy hem her petticoat in the flickering light. Susan's back pressed against the wall. On the other side was a man determined to remain a stranger.

The sooner they reached Virginia, the sooner they could pretend they had never met.

GINGER TEA

Charles climbed the ancient stone steps of the tower. The menagerie was deafening. A jackal howled. Baboons screeched. A tiger roared. And above all that was the sound of waves crashing against stone. He looked out a window. Lions swam in the ocean below. A lioness saw him. She bared her teeth.

And then he fell.

Charles woke as he rolled off his bed. Heart racing, he flailed to catch himself. By luck, one hand struck the frame of Isaac's bed before the ship pitched in the opposite direction. He braced himself with one hand against the wall and the other on the table wedged between the beds. Muffled shouting assured him the captain was leading his crew through the storm.

In the near pitch dark, the ghostly hammock, strung above his bed, swayed back and forth in a rhythm that did not quite match the rocking of his narrow cabin. The storm tossed him from side to side while he watched the delayed sway of the hammock. Side to side. Back and forth. Side-back-side-forth. The pickled egg he had eaten for dinner sat uneasily in his middle. The dankness of the small cabin pressed in on him as he lay, confined under a heavy blanket, on his narrow bed. A sudden sweat broke across his arms and forehead. He threw back the covers and fumbled desperately in the dark for a bucket.

A minute later, he took a shuddering breath and wiped his mouth with the back of his sleeve. The cabin smelled better than when he had arrived, but not mild enough for his stomach in a storm.

He had waited all evening for Miss Bailey to retire to her cabin before cleaning his own. That had been a mistake. She wasn't the retiring sort. She was the sociable sort, wheedling confidences from unsuspecting men. It had been amusing to watch coarse sailors soften under her charm, speaking freely of home and family. Of old heartaches and new sweethearts.

The pleasant chatter had deepened his loneliness. He would never see his London acquaintances again. His friends in Virginia hadn't seen him in seven years. They had probably forgotten all about him. Any community he had once enjoyed was gone. He had almost wanted to speak with her himself. Then he had seen her moving in his direction and had thought better of the irrational impulse. He had never been a favorite with the ladies. If he bungled his words, there was no escape route. Not before they reached Virginia. There was no need to make a fool of himself on the first day of a long voyage on a confined ship.

He felt under his bed for the haversack. Somewhere deep inside was a precious apothecary bottle. His fingers brushed against the cool glass. He clutched it like salvation and added a prayer for good measure. "Dear Lord, please spare me this one misery." The saline drops fell on his tongue: one, two, three. He swallowed. For a few moments, all was silent, save the groaning of the ship beneath him. He was motionless, waiting for any sign of relief. Then he doubled over the bucket again. He fought back with controlled breaths, willing his stomach to calm. Nothing was worse than the all-consuming misery of seasickness. But he had done everything in his power.

He had even prayed for mercy, but God continued to howl

with the wind and rage with the sea, tossing the ship like a toy and thrusting Charles into an earthly hell. This was the God of judgment and action. The one who had taken his mother. Had his father been angry when she had passed? Had he missed her? Charles would never know. His final letter had arrived nearly a fortnight ago, sealed with black wax. The words haunted his sleepless nights.

I will be dead by the time you read this.

Charles had looked back at the date—two months ago. The funeral was long past.

In my will, I have left you all I have—the plantation and everything on it. I expect you to care for your grandmother. By law, she still possesses her widow's third, but her wits wander. She is no longer capable of managing her share. I've given her a companion who stays with her constantly. Aside from them, there is no one left for you to care for, and no one left to include in my will.

With your education and the estate, you will be in a good position to enter politics.

Until your return, Barton will manage the plantation. He charges ridiculous fees. Hasten home.

He wiped the sweat from his forehead. As always, he had obeyed his father. He had hastened to transfer his clients to other barristers and make his way to Portsmouth, where he had sailed straight into a storm. There was no telling how long a storm would continue. It could rage the entire passage, torturing him into starvation, death, and a burial at sea.

He amended his prayer. "If thou wilt not take away the storm or the sickness, then take me away." If he was going to die either way, the least God could do was shorten the misery of dying. "I have no one waiting for me to come home. No one who—" He was silenced by an image of Uncle Rob saying grace with his family, followed by another of Uncle Rob in his shop, carving a piece of wood.

He could almost smell the sweet pine shavings. He closed his eyes tightly, shutting out his noxious quarters. He pictured a workshop thousands of miles away. His breathing slowed. The waves receded to a gentle rocking. His grip on the bucket slackened, and his head grew heavy. He slumped against his bed.

He woke suddenly. His neck was stiff from leaning to one side. Gray light peeped through the boarded-up porthole. It was dawn. He stretched and was rewarded with a prickling sensation up and down his legs. Sailors changing watch spoke in muffled voices. The ship still rocked. His forehead pounded. The contents of the bucket—he gagged and looked away. It was too late. The smell pressed in on him.

Seized with a desire to be anywhere rather than his cabin, he yanked on his breeches and grabbed the bucket. He left the Dutch door swinging and scrambled up the ladder with bare feet. The cold rain drenched his linen shirt and showered his hair, but he gulped the sea air with the relief of a drowning man.

"Rough weather," Dave said cheerfully.

Charles slipped and slid his way across the rocking deck and emptied his bucket into the roiling sea. The waves greedily consumed the contents. The spray licked his face. He clutched the railing that kept him safe from the ravages of nature.

"Be glad yeh're not in the belly o' the ship. There'll be a right-foul stench abou' there."

Charles cast what remained of his accounts over the railing. His eyes watered, and his muscles trembled from the exertion.

"Blimey. If yeh feel like that, use the hammock. It don' rock as much."

He nodded. The wind blew hard enough to steal a man's hat. At least Charles had left that below. Rain dripped from his nose and ran in rivulets down his throat.

Dave continued talking. "'Course it'll be nice ter be clean, what with ladies on board. I dare say the maid looks as fine as her lady."

Charles was too tired to argue.

Lightning flashed across the sky. The thunder was a mere second behind. It rumbled through the belly of the ship and the marrow of his bones. There was no horizon to steady his stomach, but he had nothing left to lose. His hair was plastered to his head, his shirt was plastered to his body, and the bucket was half-full of rainwater. He emptied the bucket again and, shivering, went below deck.

The navigator was right. It smelled.

As he stepped off the ladder, he sloshed in a puddle of his own making.

"Mr. Johnson!" Miss Bailey cried, standing beside the stove. Her eyes lingered for a moment on his wet shirt before returning to his face. "What on earth are you doing out in that weather?"

He leaned against the wall and closed his eyes. If he hadn't humiliated himself with her last night, he'd done so just now.

"I would say you'll make yourself ill, but clearly you already are. Did you fall overboard, or is it raining that hard?"

"Rain." It came out as a hoarse whisper. "The air is better up there."

"Go change into dry clothes," she said in a voice of compassion and authority. A voice that knew nursing. "Nothing's better for a sour stomach than ginger tea. I'll bring some, by and by."

In Virginia, every housewife took pride in her hospitality, including offering drinks to travelers at their gate. He recognized the gesture, but it confused him. Who expected Virginian hospitality from an Englishwoman?

The question followed him to his stateroom, where Isaac slept like a baby. He squeezed his wet clothes over the bucket, then dressed in a dry linen shirt and a thin banyan. He propped the door open with a shoe and waited, sitting on the edge of his bed where he could watch Miss Bailey work. The old stove was lashed to the wall, but the kettle wasn't. Boiling water while the *Minerva* pitched looked dangerous, but she managed it with a deft hand and seemed pleased with the activity. After a few tense minutes, he decided to trust her. In his current state, he didn't have much alternative.

She swayed with the ship like an old sailor, never spilling a drop as she poured his cup. With some effort, Charles stood, shaking, and braced himself against the door frame. He would be useless as a protector today.

He accepted the cup and took a cautious sip. The ginger was there, peppery sweet, and just strong enough to wash the rancid taste that had lingered in his mouth. "Thank you." He took another sip.

"You're welcome. I packed it for Isaac, but he doesn't need it."

"He slept through the night."

"You didn't," she said pointedly.

He stared at her. How could she know?

She flushed. "I heard you...being ill."

"Oh." What was he supposed to say to that? "I'm sorry?" He turned his attention back to the tea. It had taken three years in London to settle into a circle of acquaintances. He never knew what to say to strangers.

"It's nothing." She waved a hand dismissively. "I hope we'll come out of this storm soon. I've heard such wonderful things about sunsets at sea, but it was cloudy last night." There was the faintest pout in her voice. Somewhere inside this matronly woman was a little girl who liked to have her way.

"Storms never last. You'll see your sunsets."

This close, her eyes were a soft brown, like the coat of a baby deer. Charles closed his own eyes to toss back the rest of his ginger tea.

"Would you like more?" Miss Bailey asked, beginning to raise her kettle.

"I don't dare." He handed her the cup, grateful to have kept down that much. "Thank you, Miss Bailey, for your kind nursing."

She smiled. It was that warm, pastoral smile that made her look like an Italian painting. The *Minerva* dipped between the waves, and his stomach went with it. That was enough ginger tea. He shivered.

Her smile turned to a frown. "You can thank me by keeping out of the rain. You'll take a chill if you're not careful."

"Yes, ma'am." It looked like they would be protecting each other.

Six

RIPPLES IN THE WATER

WEDNESDAY, APRIL 6, 1774

The sun came out on the third day. Innocent white clouds floated lazily against a blue sky. The gentle waves lapped musically against the hull. Susan turned away from the porthole. "I thought that storm would never end." Three days was a long time to be confined to these cramped quarters with scarcely any sunlight. She had exchanged pleasantries with the sailors, reminded Isaac of the dangers of remaining in wet clothing, added to her letter home, and alternated between making ginger tea and chicken broth for Mr. Johnson.

"It was a long one, miss." Lucy was arranging Susan's travel clothes on the coverlet of her bed. "I'm ready for you."

Susan stood. The beds on either side pressed against her legs. Getting dressed was usually the beginning of her day, an essential preparation for a series of important activities. Today, she had absolutely nothing to do. Not even Mr. Johnson would need her attention today. "Time passes so slowly at sea."

Lucy draped a linen kerchief around her neck and pinned it to her stays, overlapping the ends to protect the base of her throat from the sun. "If you say so, Miss Bailey." She tied a walking-length petticoat in front, and then Susan turned so she could tie the back. The petticoat had been hastily made over from a drab wool that had belonged to her great-aunt. Lucy had insisted the sea air would be detrimental to Susan's wardrobe, which was safely locked in trunks.

"Are you looking forward to reading the book your father gave you?"

Susan slipped her arm into the fitted jacket. "I could do that." She had read the first few pages the day they had left. Had her father meant something personal when he gave her a book about a boy who ran away from home and got shipwrecked? If anyone was running away from home, it was Isaac, not her.

Lucy finished lacing Susan's fitted jacket.

"I believe I will take a turn on deck. It will be nice to see the sun again."

"Let me get your hat."

Susan sat on her bed so Lucy could pin a straw shepherdess hat atop her hair.

"There you are, miss. Pretty as a picture." She offered the daily compliment in her usual stiff manner.

Susan choked back a laugh as she tucked the book in a pocket. There was no beauty in gray woolen petticoats or common straw hats. She opened the Dutch door and inhaled the aroma of coffee, so strong it overpowered the dankness of the galley. Mr. Johnson stood at the ship's stove, his dark blond hair pulled back in a tidy queue. He turned to reach something on one of the barrels. At near-profile, he hadn't turned far enough to notice Susan, but Susan noticed him.

Mr. Johnson wore no jacket. His waistcoat was fitted across his shoulders. He had shaved, revealing a firm jaw. When he wasn't languishing in a hammock, he stood so straight and tall he would have to mind the beams supporting the low ceiling. His color had returned, too. He no longer looked like a man on his deathbed but like a *man*. A man she would see every day until America. A man determined to remain a stranger.

A tiny sigh of irritation came from behind her. Lucy was waiting to carry off the wash water. It was time for Susan to face the source of her curiosity. She crossed the threshold, her shoes clacking decisively on the wooden floor. Mr. Johnson turned. "Good morning, Mr. Johnson. How is your health this morning?"

"Much better, Miss Bailey. And yours?"

"Fine, thank you. I'm delighted to see the weather has turned. I'm sure you must be, as well."

He grunted and turned to the stove, as friendly as a brick wall. With his back to her, he said, "Would you like some coffee?"

"Indeed, I would, thank you." She accepted a cup. "How gentlemanly of you." She glanced at his door, hoping Isaac was listening. "Not every man would have thought to—"

He cut off her gushing. "Don't make so much of it. I've spent the last few days consuming your stores. I'm simply paying my debt." With that cool set down, he gestured to the only chair in the room, then leaned against the wall, sipping his coffee.

Susan took the chair, suddenly cross. He had reduced her kindness to a calculation in an account book. If she was no more than a number to him then there was no need for them to speak further today. There was no need to bring him tea when he was sick. Let the man be an island.

Mr. Johnson dipped a biscuit in his coffee, undisturbed by her stormy resolutions.

She tasted hers. No sugar and no cream. It was bitter, just like him. The silence pressed in on her. She resorted to the weather. "It looks like a fine day."

"There are a few clouds, but it's mostly clear. There should be a good sunset tonight."

Her resentment softened to annoyance. He had, after all, remembered her whim. "I'm not going to wait all day to see the sky. I'm going to take a turn about the deck this morning."

"Not alone." Mr. Johnson said it so quickly that Susan raised her eyebrows.

"I won't get lost."

He pursed his lips. "I'm sure you won't. Let's tidy up from breakfast, and I'll go with you." He may have been an island, but she was at sea. An island was all she could hope for.

They took several turns about the deck. The morning light was as good as sea bathing without the sand. She said as much to Mr. Johnson. "I suppose," was his lukewarm reply. He couldn't have been more distant if he had already been in America. Since they had met, he had said nothing unless prompted to, and then as little as possible. By this point in their acquaintance, most single gentlemen were quoting sonnets and sending her roses. This man offered nothing and expected nothing. A balanced transaction in his books. There would be no sonnets from him. The idea of this reserved man quoting love poems was ridiculous. A laugh escaped her. He looked at her inquisitively.

"It's nothing." As difficult as he was, a lovesick suitor would be worse. On the *Minerva,* she couldn't reject him and be done with it. She would have to be in close company with him every day. Silence was better than sonnets.

They stopped at the rear of the ship—the stern, as the sailors called it. Mr. Johnson leaned forward, his arms on the railing. Light danced off the rippling surface of the ocean.

"I never realized the sea was so blue," Susan said.

"It's only gray and murky when you're close to land. This is the real ocean."

"You talk like a sailor."

He gave a dry laugh. "That is one thing I will never be." The silence that followed was softened by the waves lapping at the hull. It was the sort of silence that invited confidences.

"I almost went all the way to the Mediterranean. I was Isaac's age." She glanced at Mr. Johnson. His attention was on the sea, not her. Somehow, that made it easier to talk about herself. "An old school friend had invited me to be her companion on a grand tour of the continent. We were going to see Paris, Rome, Venice—

all the great cities." The old wistfulness tugged on her heart. "I wonder if it would have been like this."

"Wait." He turned to her, a furrow between his stormy gray eyes. "Your friend offered to bear the expenses of travel and provide companionship and a chaperone?"

"She did."

"And you wanted to go." He stated it as fact, though she hadn't said as much. "Why would you refuse such an offer?"

His question prodded the old bruise. She hastened to defend her decision. "Anne's governess had left without notice. She was only nine. Someone had to take care of her. And I'd already promised Isaac that he could bring friends home for the upcoming school holiday. If I had accepted, there would have been the awkwardness of rescinding all those invitations."

"Hmm." He looked at her like she was a riddle he was trying to solve. "That was kind of you."

She waved the compliment away. "It was essential. I've been mothering them since I was fourteen. Longer, really. I wasn't about to abandon them for a lark."

They fell into silence again, watching the ocean together. The calm waters stretched to the horizon, interrupted by a cluster of waves moving toward the ship. "What's that?" She pointed to the waves.

He followed her direction. "Dolphins, I think."

She had heard of dolphins before. They were like fish, only bigger. Fish were mindless, smelly creatures of no interest until properly cooked.

"Excuse me, miss." The navigator moved beside her. A shape crested the water and sank below it. Several other creatures echoed the performance. "Dolphins!" He cried. "We'll have good luck today."

The arcing waves moved closer. "I can't see—" Susan gasped as one of the dolphins leapt clear of the water, making a throaty noise that sounded like a chirruping laugh. She was momentarily speechless. "How charming!"

"Indeed," Dave said. "They're intelligent creatures, they are. Caught one in a net once, by accident. Blimey if it didn't look right at me an' open its mouth ter speak."

"It spoke?" Parrots could speak. But a dolphin?

"Not English, mind yeh. But its look was clear enough. 'Be a good chap and put me back in the water with me missus.'"

"Did you?"

"Certainly did. We lowered the net inter the ocean, and the clever creature swam free. Had a whole family waitin' for it, bleatin' happily when it escaped."

"That was kind of you to release it."

"It wasn't kindness. It was honor. Some creatures God made for the use of man. No harm keepin' sheep in a pen. But some creatures, God made special. Dolphins is one o' them. Meant ter be free."

They watched, entranced, as the dolphins drew alongside the ship. She could have watched them for hours, but Dave turned away and dropped a wedge of wood into the sea. It was tied to a line on a spool as big as a yule log. The log spun freely, letting out the line as the ship sailed away from the little wedge of wood.

"What are y—"

Mr. Johnson shushed her. She was so startled by the uncivil behavior that she was speechless. He didn't notice the shock on her face, as he was watching Dave, who was in deep concentration, muttering to himself as more and more of the line trailed behind the ship. "One...two..."

They were like a pair of schoolboys who had borrowed a rowboat and were fishing in a pond. She was left behind on the shore. She blinked. That was absurd. She was right here. The navigator was working, and she was watching him just as much as Mr. Johnson was. She studied the line herself, looking for a point of interest. There were knots evenly spaced along the line. It was like a ruler made from a yarn ball. That was not nearly as interesting as dolphins.

"Five," Dave announced, reeling the line back in.

"Five knots," Mr. Johnson repeated. "Is that good?"

"Good enough. So long as we're moving, we won't be becalmed. Five knots is more'un a hundred miles in a day. We'd move faster with another good tailwind. That storm pushed us right out inter open sea."

Mr. Johnson looked ill at the suggestion.

"Excuse me. I need ter check our speed against a map."

A hundred miles. Wind stung her eyes and filled the sails. Had she ever been a hundred miles from home before? She had been gone less than a week. A week was nothing compared to a year. The time stretched before her like an ocean without a horizon.

Was Papa reminding Anne to get out of her books? Was Mrs. Weston as capable as they had hoped? She couldn't even send a letter for weeks. Her spirits were quickly sinking. She tried to save them by looking ahead—but what was ahead? She had never taken her geography seriously. What she knew of America was a jumble of political cartoons and gossip, tempered by occasional letters from her aunt.

She turned to the man who had been born there. "Tell me about America."

He took a moment to consider her. "What do you wish to know?"

"Anything. Everything."

"The air is clean. Nothing like the London soot that blackens your clothes and stings your eyes. Whole forests of trees as tall as a ship's mast." His eyes were on the horizon, but he saw beyond it. "Taller, even. The heat of summer is heavy. The most genteel men and ladies wear only linen and cotton until it passes."

She had several gowns of Indian chintz mixed in with the silks in her trunk. If her aunt encouraged morning dress through July and August, she could readily comply. "What about the people?"

He looked at her now, his eyes resting on her face like it was another horizon. "Their manners are open and easy, though some forget the respect owed to rank and authority."

"And...they really do keep slaves?"

"Yes." He dragged the word out reluctantly and turned back to the ocean.

His manner resurrected every rumor she had discredited. She shivered in the sunlight. "What is it like?"

He exhaled wearily. For a long minute, he didn't answer. When he spoke, it was haltingly, as though pausing to consider each phrase carefully before speaking it. "What you'll see won't look much different from what you knew in England. There are liveried footmen, cooks and maids, tradesmen, and farmers. Except, instead of the poor class you keep in England, in Virginia, most of the help comes from indentured servants and slaves."

What she'd seen in England was Belle, who was a lady, not a servant. And those who were servants were free to seek other employment. "You don't think it's unchristian?"

"It's better not to think about it." This time his words were crisp and firm.

Susan didn't press the matter. Instead, she watched the dolphins leaping from ocean to sky, scattering droplets of water that shimmered like jewels in a crown. God had made them to be free.

Seven

BEYOND MERCY

Maps blanketed all of Isaac's bed save where he sat, studying them. For a young man who was planning to spend a year in Williamsburg, he took a lot of interest in the rest of the country. "What's the Cumberland Gap?"

Charles leaned over the maps. "One of the best passes to the far west. It cuts through the Appalachian Mountains." It sat near the border Virginia shared with North Carolina. "There are more roads to the north. The road through Ashby's Gap will lead a man all the way to Fort Necessity." Charles traced his finger across the paper. Fort Necessity was hundreds of miles northwest of Williamsburg.

"There must be a lot of wild game out west."

"Yes, and there's more the farther west you go." Charles sat on the edge of his bed. The hammock brushed against his neck.

"I wonder why the settlers are so intent on farming. Why be a farmer when you can be a hunter?"

"Why, indeed?" The sea was calm. He wouldn't need the hammock.

"You could make a fortune with just a canoe and a musket," Isaac said.

The knots were firm, pulled tight by human weight. "Muskets are useless for hunting. They load fast, but they're inaccurate. You only get one shot before the entire forest knows you're there, and the first shot often misses. Settlers have rifles. Muskets are no good outside a battle." He poked the tip of his penknife in the knot, rocking it up and down, coaxing the rope to relax its hold. "Of course, a fur trapper needs lots of traps, not just a gun." He felt the knot loosen and dropped the knife. His fingers pulled apart the knot. That end of the hammock slumped onto his bed. He glanced at Isaac. "You're not seriously considering moving to the frontier?"

Isaac shook his head. "I'm the oldest son. My home is in England."

A few minutes later, Charles untied the other end of the hammock. He wadded it victoriously and stuffed it under his bed. Footsteps echoed in the storage galley. Sailors passed through the galley day and night, but this was no sailor. There was a different timbre to this footfall—soft and deep. He had listened for it during those days he had been confined to a hammock—had waited for the relief it brought. It was Susan's. "Are you going to watch the sunset?"

"I might." Isaac unfolded another map.

"Your sister is."

"Susan can do as she likes."

Isaac was as naive as a schoolgirl if he didn't notice the desire in the sailor's sidelong glances, like hungry foxes watching a henhouse. There was nothing for Charles to do but go on deck himself. He owed her more than coffee for her kindness to him, even if the captain hadn't assigned him to this duty. And enduring her company wasn't as trying as he had first anticipated.

She could talk until the stars shone. Then he would sleep peacefully in his narrow bed.

～

Bang. Bang. Bang. It was Christmas Day, and merry explosions in the slave quarters echoed his father's gunshot.

Bang. Bang. Bang. Charles was seven years old. His nursemaid's wrists were coarsely bound to a peg above her head on the side of the barn. Charles had snuck out to play in the creek the Sunday they had expected the rector for dinner. When he stepped into the dining room, wet and muddy, his father was furious with the nurse. Helplessly, he watched his father raise the whip.

Bang. Bang. Bang. Charles woke in his narrow bed on board the *Minerva*. The banging continued.

"What is that?"

"I dunno." Isaac was already sitting up in bed. "It's been like that for a full minute."

"I don't like it." Charles shoved his nightshirt into his breeches and followed the sound.

The door leading down to the cargo was locked. It had been for the entire voyage. But the door shook—*bang! Bang! Bang!*

"Who goes there?"

"Thomas Finlay. With my wife. Please, have mercy on us!"

Stowaways. They would be punished severely. Charles rattled the lock and felt the hinges. Everything was solid.

"Please! She's dying!"

Fear shot through Charles. Behind him, Isaac gasped. His brocade banyan shimmered uselessly in the low light. The boy looked like he had spent a year's pocket money on a flashy garment he couldn't even wear in public. He couldn't be trusted in a crisis.

Every legal case involving stowaways rehearsed itself in Charles's mind as he cast his eyes about for something that might open the door. There. A hammer was lying in a tangle of ropes. For once, the chaos and disorder of the ship proved providential. But he looked at the solid door and hesitated to destroy an innocent captain's property. There would be no way of securing the cargo against a dissolute crew if it were damaged.

Isaac grabbed the hammer from Charles's hands. "Stand

back!" He began hammering into the door. Destruction of property was illegal and immoral. But if a woman was truly dying in the belly of their ship, what else could they do? Charles kicked the bottom of the door while Isaac smashed into the upper. Once a splintered hole formed, it was only a minute before the opening was big enough for a man.

A stench like a dead dog two days after a rainstorm came through the opening as Thomas Finlay carried a woman through. She was limp as seaweed and pale as death. She needed a nurse.

Charles was knocking on her door before he knew he'd moved. "Susan! Miss Bailey!" Had her Christian name just slipped from his lips? He scarcely knew her. It was beyond presumptuous, but he would apologize later. "There's a woman here. She needs your help."

She was still tying her bedgown as she opened the door. Her dark hair was barely contained in its nightcap. "Mr. Johnson. What? How?"

"A stowaway. Locked in the cargo hold. Her husband claims... she's dying."

Her eyes went wide. She picked up a bag and followed Charles.

"He was carrying her above."

"Good. The sea air is clean tonight."

Several sailors came above in the predawn light, useless observers drawn to a spectacle. Dave set a lantern beside the unconscious woman. "Hush. The captain's still asleep."

"The captain's alright," said Charles. "It's the supercargo I'm worried about." He had invited Charles and Isaac to join him for cards the previous evening. They had both left with lighter pocketbooks than they had anticipated.

"How did the captain sleep through all that racket?" Isaac asked.

Dave pantomimed tipping a bottle. "Those who are heavy drinkers become heavy sleepers."

The woman's thin body lay on the deck, a rounded stomach

the only relief to her thin and angular features. Finlay patted her cheek. "Marion. Marion." She didn't stir. This young husband, whatever his crimes against the *Minerva*, was being punished beyond justice in watching his wife die. Charles just stood there, as wide-eyed and useless as Isaac and all the sailors.

Miss Bailey knelt beside the wretched woman, laying her hand on her forehead. "She's burning up. How long has she had this fever?"

"It came on sudden-like, a few hours ago. She's been having trouble breathing."

"We need to get her fever down. And clean her." She opened her bag and pulled out an envelope. "Mr. Johnson, if you can make coffee, you can make tea. Add two pinches of this to two cups of boiling water. Isaac—soap and water. Lots of water. Mr. Dave, help with the water."

By caring for Charles when he was weak, she had his loyalty now that he was strong. He would have hauled a full barrel of water up the stairs if she had asked. As it was, he hastened to make tea.

Water had never taken so long to boil. He held his hand over the kettle. It was warm. He stoked the coals. Again. And waited. Miss Bailey might like having her way about sunsets and sailors, but she was kind to strangers and had sacrificed a dream for her family. It was good that she was on board.

He had once believed in a God of mercy, a God who would save his angel mother from illness and abuse. That faith had died with his mother. And yet, witnessing the agony of another man stirred something inside him. *Please, Lord. Let her save this woman.* The silent prayer slipped through the cracks in his heart, and the water finally boiled.

When he returned with the medicinal tea, Miss Bailey and Lucy were rubbing soapy water on the woman's arms. Miss Bailey spoke in a soothing voice to the fretful husband. "Was it a poor harvest?"

"It shouldn't have been. But our landlord wanted double the

rent, and we tried selling most of our harvest to pay him, and some of the furniture. It wasn't enough. He let us stay the winter, but he evicted us."

Miss Bailey looked up at Charles. "Good. The tea is here."

He had never had a woman look at him with such business-like satisfaction. He was warm despite the sea breeze tousling his hair.

She and Lucy rinsed the woman's arms and patted them dry. "Mr. Finlay, we need her sitting up so she can drink this. If you would sit behind her and pull her up—yes. Just so."

Mr. Finlay's arms wrapped around his young wife, just above her bulging waist. Her head fell back against his chest. Susan poured a few drops into her gaping mouth and stroked her throat until she swallowed.

Charles watched in awe as Miss Bailey nursed the woman. She was as competent in nursing as he was at navigating the law. How did a woman train for that? Did they teach nursing in girls' seminaries? Or was the sex that created life also divinely endowed with wisdom in preserving it? She held a person's life in her hands, and every man present submitted to her command. Miss Bailey inspired more trust in a bedgown and bare feet than a lady in a palace. All the accomplishments of fine ladies were nothing next to this.

Slowly, the teacup emptied. She felt the woman's forehead with the back of her hand. "It will take a little time before the fever goes down. Does she have anything clean to wear?"

"No. She only has two petticoats, and they're both soiled."

"Then we must see to it that you can do your laundry today."

The man looked relieved. "That would be a blessing. Most of the baby's linens are already soiled.

Baby. The soft word landed with the force of a cannonball. Isaac and the sailors looked at each other in bewilderment. Susan's mouth dropped open. Her eyes, full of horror, met Charles'. He had a sudden urge to fix this impossible situation; to break down any door she asked him to. Except what door would save a baby?

Her attention turned to Mr. Finlay. "When did she have the baby?"

"A couple of nights ago. We didn't think it was her time, but the storm made her so ill."

Hiding among the cargo on a dirty vessel could not be the safest way to bring a child into the world. Finlay should have told them sooner. Someone could have carried it up. Charles couldn't suppress the accusation in his voice. "You left your baby alone in the hold?"

"No. Of course not. I left him with my niece."

Charles put both hands to his head. The possibilities exploded in his mind like fireworks. "Your niece and the baby. Are they the only passengers still in the hold?"

Finlay gave a dry laugh. "Not even close. There's about fifty of us."

Charles raked his fingers through his hair. So many stowaways were impossible. "Fifty. I need to see this."

"Mr. Johnson?"

He stopped at Susan's voice. "Yes?"

"Tell the niece to bring the baby up here."

"Yes, Miss Bailey."

Charles covered his nose with a handkerchief as he descended into the ship. He had a fleeting image of himself being trapped down there and pocketed the hammer, just in case.

People weren't hiding behind the cargo. People *were* the cargo. It was the most wretched gathering of humanity Charles had ever seen. Signs of illness from the recent storm were scattered on blankets and in buckets. Susan should not come down here. Doubtless, Mr. Sleeman, as the supercargo, would sell their indentures when they reached Virginia. The laws governing indentured servants were less kind in Virginia than they were in the northern colonies. Few who came to Virginia came willingly.

All eyes were on him. The attention made him uncomfortable. "Mr. Finlay's niece?"

"Yes, sir?" A young woman of about fifteen was holding a bundle of dirty blankets.

"You've been asked to bring the baby on deck."

"Yes, sir." She stepped over a dirty blanket and looked back at Charles. "My aunt, how is she?"

"She's in good hands." Charles spoke from experience.

The young woman picked her way over the worst of the filth. Charles turned his attention to the dozens of people still below. "Why are you here?" he asked. "Are you emigrating?"

A middle-aged gentleman whose clothes did not need patching stood. "Ye might say tha'. Most o' these people here were farmers in Forfarshire, Scotland, on the same land where our families have lived for generations."

"Why did you leave?"

His face clouded. "Once, the landlords accepted rent 'in kind.' But they have begun demanding money. Money far in excess of wha' the land can produce. The first year, we sold everythin' we could ta meet the payment. The second year...there was nothing left ta sell."

"How did you come to this ship? Mr. Sleeman, the supercargo, did he make a bargain with you?"

"Aye, he did. We had no money for a passage. We were homeless. We sold ourselves for passage."

"How many years? How many years will you be indented to pay for this?"

"Five."

Charles had thought the price he had paid for passage was high. "Do any of you have trades? Beyond farming?"

"The young missus who just had the baby is a weaver."

"There is a small market for homespun cloth in Virginia. Most purchase imported cloth. Anything else?"

"Finlay was a farm manager."

"There are many farms. The rest of you are farmers?"

Several nodded glumly. He couldn't fix this, but he could offer hope. "After you complete your indentures, you could move out west. You would have to clear the land, but it would be yours."

"Are you from Virginia?"

It was a personal question, but they had told him where they were from. It was only fair to return the favor. Besides, they weren't asking for much. "I was born there."

"Tell us about it."

Charles rubbed his brow and tried to be reasonable. They weren't asking about him. They were asking about Virginia. That was something they had a right to know. He began with the basics. "It's the biggest colony. We'll port near Williamsburg. That's the capital."

Eight

HARBORING COMPASSION

Susan wrapped her arms around her waist and watched the Finlays sleep. Marion Finlay's cheek rested against her husband's chest. His arms cradled her. Their breathing was slow and steady. Susan's heart ached. To be loved like that—cherished even when she was ill and could do nothing to deserve it—was there anything greater in the world?

The navigator reclaimed his lamp. It was just light enough to see without it. A rosy glow separated the star-spangled sky from the depths of the shimmering sea, as radiant as the day of creation. The sunrise was nearly as beautiful as the sunset had been. The enigmatic Mr. Johnson had joined her last night at the railing, just out of reach. And then he had woken her before dawn, calling for her by name as if they were the closest of friends.

For a few minutes, they had been. He had pleaded for help. She had promptly given it. She had demanded assistance. He had hastened to give it. The friendly smile over their mutual patient had, for a moment, filled the empty chambers of her heart. Now the comfort ebbed, no more stable than the sea. A fickle friendship was a poor substitute for the steady love some women enjoyed every day.

Marion's cheeks were flushed with a fever that might take her life, might take her away from the man who loved her so ardently. Compassion subdued envy. That devotion wasn't hers to enjoy, but it deserved to live. Susan clasped her hands. "Lord, have mercy. Let me heal her. Let there be love on earth. Amen."

"Amen," the sailors echoed. She was surprised by their support. Sailors weren't known for their reverence. It might be that even the godless would turn pious in the face of death.

"A little help?"

The deck was rough against her bare feet. She had forgotten her slippers under her bed. Four days of travel, and she was as uncivilized as Isaac. A young woman of about fifteen stood at the base of the stairs, which were nigh as steep as a ladder. Susan knelt at the top, and the young woman passed a bundle of blankets up to her.

The blankets squirmed. Within them was the smallest baby she had ever seen. His eyes were scrunched shut. He turned his face toward Susan's body, his tiny mouth sucking on air as he rooted for the nourishment only a mother could give. He was so fragile. If Marion died, this child would die, too. She brushed a finger against his fist. He grasped onto it, five little fingers clutching one of hers. More than one life depended on her. "So strong," she murmured.

"I'll take him, miss. I just wasn't sure I could make it up another ladder without dropping him."

Susan passed the bundle to the niece, who took her place beside the Finlays. The bittersweet tableau begged her compassion, but there was nothing more she could do. A doctor would have bled Marion, but she didn't have the instruments or the nerves for that type of work. The sun was rising, liquid gold rippling over the horizon. The time for barefoot emergencies was past. It was time for this lady to be civilized.

She found Lucy tucking the bedding around her thin mattress with precise mitered corners. "I'm sorry, miss. Were you hoping to go back to bed?" Her voice was strained. She would allow Susan to muss the freshly made bed, but she wouldn't be happy about it.

"I couldn't sleep after all the excitement. I'd like to dress for the day."

"Just a moment, miss." Lucy ran a hand over the wool blanket, smoothing away one last wrinkle. "If you'll sit on my bed, we can start with your hair."

Lucy unbound her hair and brushed it in long, luxurious strokes. Susan closed her eyes and pictured Marion Finlay in her husband's arms. Marion wasn't beloved for her dowry. She couldn't have had much, if any. Her family was so poor that they were emigrating against their will. But she was a treasure to her husband. How did a woman earn a love like that—a love that was strongest when she was weakest? She had jested to Papa about second sons and dowries, but could a mercenary ever treasure her like that? And if not, who would?

"Your brother hasn't shaved since he set foot on the *Minerva*. He's becoming as sloppy as a sailor."

Susan bit back a smile. Unlike the sailors, Mr. Johnson had shaved after the storm, but not this morning. He was beyond unkempt. He was positively wild. Dark blond hair hung about his anxious face. Waistcoat and stockings were forgotten in the urgency of the hour. His shirt twisted about him before tucking into his breeches. No one had responded to Finlay's cries more quickly than he had.

The man might be an island, but that island hid a sheltered harbor.

After she was dressed, she set about making coffee. Susan usually left menial chores to the servants, but she hated being idle. Lucy had given her meticulous instructions on the proper way to brew coffee. It was a lot to remember, but in practice, no more difficult than the medicines she made herself. The coffee was nearly done when Mr. Johnson stepped into the galley and frowned at the sunlight shining through the stateroom windows.

"Mr. Johnson. Where have you been all this time?"

His head jerked in her direction. Had he not known she was there, or was he so unaccustomed to being addressed? If he was lonely, it was his fault for being so aloof. It wouldn't hurt him to smile now and then. She lined up three mugs on a barrel of salted pork. "The baby was brought up ages ago. I've had time to dress and start on breakfast. I was starting to think we'd lost you."

"No." He ran a smoothing hand over his shirt, then looked down in surprise at the twisted state it had been in since he had woken her. "I'm here."

She poured the coffee into the mugs. "Did you find out how many stowaways there are?"

"Fifty-three. Fifty-four, if we count the baby. But it turns out they aren't stowaways. They're all emigrating as indentured servants."

"Then how did we not know about them?" It was beyond comprehension that so many people could be hidden on a ship this small for even a few days.

"I've been thinking on that. This is the captain's ship, but the supercargo is responsible for buying and selling cargo. If he thought the captain might object..." He hesitated.

Susan understood what remained unsaid and couldn't resist saying it herself. "He'd want to keep it a secret until it was too late to turn back."

His eyes met hers. "Precisely."

For one long moment, she savored the satisfaction of her lucky guess. Those with more book learning might be immune to a pleasure they experienced so frequently, but Susan was no scholar. After she had left school, she had made herself ambitious reading lists that had delighted her father. A lady of her station should develop her mind through reading. But she found she couldn't live in books when the world around her was so much more colorful.

She handed Mr. Johnson his mug.

He took a sea biscuit from his barrel and dipped it in his

coffee. "Do you have everything you need for Mrs. Finlay's illness?"

"It's childbed fever." She shook her head. "I have enough Peruvian bark to last the week. It should be enough. Either she'll get better or…" She swallowed. She couldn't bring herself to say there would be a burial at sea.

Mr. Johnson raked his fingers through his hair. "I didn't realize it was so serious."

"It is. She should never have been down there when she gave birth. Women in that condition are especially susceptible to miasma. The air down there is noxious, isn't it?"

Charles grimaced and swallowed his coffee. "There's more than one way to be seasick," he stole a glance at her face as if expecting her to be shocked. She was. A little. He skipped past the details, simply saying, "And nothing has been cleaned since then."

"They need to be able to mop and do laundry. We could start a bucket brigade."

He set his mug on the barrel. "That's a good plan, but of course, we'll wait for the captain's permission."

Indignation flared. Susan didn't need anyone's permission to do what was right. And she had less respect for those who did need it. "Don't be ridiculous. Fifty-four lives depend on this."

"The only one who is ill is already on deck, breathing the good, clean sea air. I'm not asking her to give that up. We can afford to wait a little longer to do this right."

She put an unladylike fist on her pannier. "By waiting for the captain's permission?"

"Indeed. This is the captain's ship. We still have weeks of travel ahead of us. What good will it do to offend him so early in the voyage? He will be more compassionate in the coming weeks if we show him the respect he deserves now."

She exhaled slowly. There was some sense in what he said, but the sooner they got to work, the sooner people would feel better. "You'll ask him this morning?"

"As soon as I make myself presentable, I'll speak with the

supercargo and the captain." He turned to his cabin but stopped with his hand on the door. "Miss Bailey," his voice was tense, "I must apologize for using your Christian name earlier. Your brother uses it all the time. I forgot myself."

This morning, a great many informalities could be forgiven. Her name on his lips was no more scandalous than the state of his shirt, or that in his haste to assist the Finlays, he had neglected his stockings and shoes. Sailors went barefoot at sea, but even they maintained modesty with their long trousers. Mr. Johnson was a tall man. He couldn't help the expanse of bare leg his breeches didn't cover. She blushed and looked away. "There's no need to stand on formality." Not with a barefoot neighbor who had seen her in her bedgown. "With as much as we are going to be in each other's company the next few weeks, you're welcome to call me Susan." The man who had watched last night's sunset without speaking once to her wouldn't mistake a little familiarity for an invitation to courtship. She waited for him to reciprocate the invitation. She still didn't know his full name.

He was quiet for so long that he might not have known it either. Then he gave a tiny nod. "And you're welcome to use mine. It's Charles."

"Charles. It suits you."

Nine

APPEALING TO AUTHORITY

Charles closed the cabin door and slumped against it. What had just happened? He was supposed to be looking after her, not indulging in familiarities. He had tried to offer a simple apology. Miss Bailey should have given him a set-down for being presumptuous. He hadn't anticipated that she would encourage him to continue using her given name. Try as he might, he couldn't think of a way to reject her offer without giving offense. As a barrister, he couldn't afford to be too fine about feelings. But somehow...he didn't want to offend *her*.

Susan.

He yanked his portmanteau from under the bed and threw it atop the tangled blanket. The next order of business was to confront the captain and the supercargo. After shaving, he tore through his luggage, pulling out stockings, a shirt, a waistcoat, and breeches. He would not appear before the captain in the same state of disarray Miss Bailey had just witnessed.

He dressed with great deliberation. Stockings first, then breeches and shoes. He tucked his shirt in an orderly fashion. The waistcoat buttoned almost to the throat. He went without a cravat and jacket. The captain himself didn't bother with them, and he did not outrank the captain.

He had promised Miss Bailey—Miss Susan Bailey—that he would speak with him as soon as he was presentable. He put his portmanteau away and straightened the blanket. He was ready. A lady of quality might have argued the point, but there were none of those to impress on the *Minerva*. Susan was simply a lady. Following the captain's orders, Charles had spent hours discreetly observing her poise in conversation and her fine figure moving with grace. But she wasn't such a fine lady as to be difficult. Her apparel was unpretentious. She valued family duty over touring the continent. She knew the names of every sailor on the *Minerva*, down to the youngest cabin boy. Her greatest accomplishments were practical. She wouldn't fuss over a cravat and jacket any more than the captain.

Between here and Virginia, there was no higher court than this. It was his only chance to advocate for the Finlays. A shiver of anticipation ran through him. It was the same cold feeling he had before every trial, accompanied by the certainty that something was about to go wrong. An inaudible exclamation echoed through the ship. Charles hastened through the galley and up the stairs.

Mr. Sleeman was standing on the deck, looking at the Finlays like they were the contents of his chamber pot. "What are you doing up here?"

Thomas stood between his fragile family and the supercargo. His posture was brave, but there was fear in his eyes. The existence of his family was at the whim of an angry man. Charles caught his eye and held up a warning hand. He was the barrister. He would handle it. Except what could he say? Indentured servitude was not illegal. Nor was transporting human cargo. He addressed Mr. Sleeman. "Let's discuss this with the captain."

"Discuss what?" He spat the words like they were chewing tobacco.

Charles squared his shoulders. Briefs were not won with apologies. "This is his ship. He has a right to know what's going on."

Mr. Sleeman glared at Thomas, then led the way to the captain's quarters. Captain Crawford opened his door, a look of benign surprise on his face. "Come in, gentlemen. Come in." He invited them each to take a seat. "What seems to be the problem?"

"The problem," Charles began, "is that a woman almost died last night."

"Good heavens, are you certain?"

Mr. Sleeman scoffed, but Charles remembered the concern on Miss Susan's face. "I am, sir."

"Miss Bailey didn't strike me as the sickly sort. Was it her maid, the disapproving blonde?" His voice was oddly hopeful. She must have crossed him.

"It was not Miss Bailey or her maid." Charles took a deep breath. "I don't know if your supercargo was going to tell you that you are transporting indentured servants. He had them locked up in the cargo hold. The miasma down there is deadly. A woman had a baby last night in those conditions. She might die."

Mr. Sleeman's face reddened. "I've done nothing illegal."

The captain templed his fingers thoughtfully. "She could die? That won't do. Not at all, Sleeman. What were you thinking?"

"I was thinking our genteel passengers might not enjoy sharing the ship with dirty laborers. It was out of consideration for the gentlemen and ladies."

"But we can't have our cargo dying on us." The captain was a clever man, choosing the exact argument that would be most persuasive to the man who would sell off the indentures.

Charles took his opening. "With your permission, sir, they would like access to the deck so they can clean out the hold."

"Permission granted. We can't have people dying, can we?"

"Indeed, not." Charles rose to take his leave. By satisfying the demands of authority, he had protected the Finlays and honored Miss Susan's pleas for compassion.

"Just a moment," Mr. Sleeman said. "How did they get past the locked door?"

Blast. Confessions were dangerous things, but his conscience wouldn't allow a lie. "Mr. Bailey and I broke the door down." He looked at the captain. "I'm afraid you won't be able to salvage it."

"We won't be able to replace the door until we reach Virginia, and it will cost a fine penny when we do. I'll divide the bill between you and Mr. Bailey."

That wouldn't do. The Baileys needed enough money to get home once the year was done. "I'll cover it, sir," Charles said.

After speaking with the Finlays, he carried armfuls of wood to his cabin. Since he was paying for the door, he had a right to its remains. The bucket brigade would go more smoothly without scraps of lumber to trip on. On his last trip, he bumped into Isaac in the galley. "Pardon me."

"No harm done," Isaac said. He picked a long sliver off his shirtfront. "What's the wood for?"

"Nothing." Charles couldn't bear to see good wood go to waste. He piled the jagged boards between his haversack and his portmanteau. "Just something to keep my hands busy."

"Speaking of busy, would you like to soak your dinner with us?"

"I...what?"

"Dave said we should try soaking our salted beef in the ocean. I thought it was a capital idea. Susan and I are going to try it. There's plenty of rope. Would you like to join us?" Isaac had been pestering Charles for information about the colonies all week.

"What is it like on the frontier? How big are the mountains? I've heard they're not as big as the Alps."

Charles had never gone west and couldn't answer either question satisfactorily.

Isaac smoothed the map with his hand. "There is so much land beyond that. I heard talk about dividing it into another colony. Vandalia." He pronounced the name slowly, savoring the syllables. "Do they have many trees?"

But this was the first time Isaac had asked him for his company. Out of habit, Charles opened his mouth to decline, then closed it. Though their acquaintance hadn't been long, they had broken down a door together. Talking on the deck couldn't be any more difficult, no matter how many questions the boy asked about America. "I'll be up shortly."

There was one last thing to attend to. He couldn't in good conscience see the Finlays or Miss Bailey—Miss *Susan* Bailey—again until things were settled in the cargo hold. It didn't take long. Once Charles announced the captain had given them permission to clean up, it was only a moment before the middle-aged gentleman from before began organizing the process. He excused himself and found the Baileys waiting for him at the ship's stern.

"Johnson," Isaac nodded at him.

"Bailey. Miss...Susan." Her name caught in his throat. Isaac gave them a curious look.

"Don't look at me like that," she told Isaac. "The man shares a room with you, my brother. It's only natural to speak as though we're family." She turned her attention back to Charles. "Mr. Finlay said you spoke with the captain. How did it go?"

"Any minute you should be able to see for yourself. He's a good captain. The ship would be in much better shape if the sailors obeyed with more exactness. He reprimanded Mr. Sleeman and gave his permission for a proper cleanup."

"You handled that quite neatly." She smiled warmly.

It made him feel hot and cold, calm and flustered all at once. He looked down at the brisket of salted beef in his hand. "How do we do this?"

Isaac picked up a coil of rope. "Dave said we just tie it like a package and toss it in the water—hanging onto the other end of the rope, of course."

They wrapped the rope securely. It wouldn't do to lose their dinner to the fish. Isaac tossed his beef in his hands, his eyes twinkling. "Now we just throw it overboard like it's a chest of tea."

Charles rolled his eyes. "Just because I'm American doesn't mean I had anything to do with the tea incident in Boston."

Isaac swung the beef in circles over his head before letting it fly out over the water. It went so far that it tugged on the end of the rope before dropping into the ocean. It submerged briefly, then surfaced, bobbing in the water behind them. "I was only teasing. Didn't realize that was a sore topic."

"Not sore. Just serious." Charles imitated his throw. His beef landed a little past Isaac's.

The boy leaned against the railing, holding the rope loosely like it connected to a toy boat in a pond. There would be no recovering his dinner if the rope slipped through his fingers. "Do you think it was treason?"

Charles had listened to the House of Lords argue that point before leaving London. "Only if you believe a few crates of tea can overthrow the government."

Miss Susan laughed. "It *was* a waste of perfectly good tea."

"Indeed," Charles said. "Nearly £10,000 of perfectly good tea. That kind of property damage isn't a joke. It's criminal."

"But not treason?" Isaac asked.

"I think the small group of radicals would love their crime to be called treason. They would risk their necks for the absurd indignity of being called traitors. To let them go unpunished is to encourage them to create further mischief in the future. But to brand them as traitors will glorify them in certain circles."

"You've given this a lot of thought," Isaac said.

Charles shifted the rope to his other hand. "This isn't the first time someone has asked me about it." It was a regular question in his London office, as his clients noticed the Virginian accent. The more people talked about it, the more he was tired of the whole business. The sooner talk about the Boston incident died down, the better for everyone.

"If you ask me," Miss Susan said, "it seems like a whole lot of fuss over something so far away.

Ten

AN ANGEL OF MERCY

Susan shivered beside the fire. Early that morning, she had left her bed for the soft chair in Mama's bedchamber. Even the warmth of knowing her mother was near couldn't keep away the chill of early spring. Everything was cold—the crisp quilt wrapped around her bare arms and nightshift, the drafts that brushed her cheeks, her feet that kept peeking out from beneath the quilt.

A maid brought in the breakfast tray and helped Mama sit up. Home had been all confusion since the baby had come a fortnight ago. Mama hadn't gotten out of bed since then. The servants whispered that she might die.

"Susan, fetch me my shawl."

The shawl was across the room, inside the clothespress. Susan stumbled off the chair. Her bare feet recoiled against the cold stone floor. Her movements were slow and heavy.

"What's wrong with you?"

Anything. Everything. "My head hurts."

"Your head hurts?" Mama laughed dryly. "You have no idea what it's like to have your head hurt."

The maid handed Mama the shawl. Dejected, Susan returned to her room and climbed back into bed. She missed dinner, but no one came to see her. Her body ached and itched and was, in turns, too hot or too cold. Mama was too sick herself to be by her bedside, wiping her brow. She spent a restless night alone.

The next morning, a maid came to tend the fire. It was the maid who brought it to the housekeeper's attention that little Miss Susan had mumps. The doctor brought leeches, and the staff took turns checking on Susan once an hour.

Two weeks later, Isaac fell ill.

Susan had a bed made up on the floor of his room. She took charge of his care. She saw to it that the doctor's orders were followed through and that Isaac was made as comfortable as a sick person could be. She didn't leave him to be miserable alone.

He needed her. He appreciated her. He loved her.

It was a hard lesson, but Susan learned it well. The only way for her to be loved was to care for others.

SUNDAY, APRIL 10, 1774

Susan dipped a handkerchief in a bucket of water and laid it on Marion's forehead. "I thought the tea was helping?"

"It was. At first." Mr. Finlay rubbed his face with both hands. Between his wife and the baby, did he sleep at all? "But after a few hours, she's like this again."

How many days had she been so ill? Three days? Four? The days at sea ran together. Marion needed to take a turn for the better. There was only one thing Susan could offer. "I suppose she could take the tea more often."

Charles frowned at her. He had insisted on escorting her into the cargo hold and watching her work. "But then you'll run out early."

Blast the man. Half of nursing was offering hope and encouragement to the patient. Announcing the limited supply of medicine at their disposal was not encouraging. Marion tossed her head feverishly. Baby Timmy whimpered in his cousin's arms. Mr. Finlay looked more distressed than ever.

She glared at Charles for a moment, willing him to see what

he'd done. Then she turned back to Mr. Finlay and said, in her most soothing voice, "She would be more comfortable."

He shook his head. "Let's keep the usual schedule." He clutched his wife's hand as though he could hold her to earth a little longer.

Please, Lord. May my work be enough to save her. The only hope left to offer was kindness. "If you change your mind, don't hesitate to send for me, day or night."

"If you do that," Charles added, "be sure to wake me so she has an escort."

As they made their way up the steep stairs to the deck, Susan said, "Mr. Finlay would be a fine escort. There's no need for you to trouble yourself." It wasn't as if Charles had done anything useful by coming. If anything, he had added to Mr. Finlay's wealth of worries.

"The man is already beside himself with grief and worry. If he tore himself away from his wife's side to get you, it would be out of fear for her imminent death. Do you fancy he would leave her a second time just to walk you back to your cabin? I don't."

His brusque manner tightened her nerves. She fought back the tears that threatened her composure. Susan hadn't slept well in days. Marion might die under her care. The last thing she needed was a reminder that she wasn't worth two minutes of civil behavior. She snapped. "I'm doing everything I can. Besides, what would *you* know about caring for a wife?" Charles was distant and impersonal and had no understanding of proper feelings, especially not hers. He had no right to compare himself to such a devoted husband. He would be lucky if any woman allowed him the title.

A shadow crossed his face. "I know what I've seen." With no pretense at niceties, he strode as far from her as possible on the deck of the small ship, flicked open a penknife, and fiercely whittled chips off a block of wood.

She had half a mind to storm over and demand explanations and apologies, to lay siege to his fortress walls and draw out the man who sheltered within. Except...was she so hurt she couldn't recognize that he was, too? His forbidding scowl, the destructive energy focused on a benign piece of wood—was it possible his impenetrable walls sheltered a wounded soul?

She thought she was full of love, but what she had said was sharp and belittling. She was the reason those defenses were up. So she would take them down.

Softly.

Without meeting his eye, she came close enough to speak without raising her voice, but not so close that he edged away. "I'm sorry," she said, keeping her voice low and gentle. "You're right. I'm running out of medicine. I just didn't want to worry Mr. Finlay. But she looks worse today. So does the baby."

Charles turned the wood over. After a minute, the penknife moved again, this time with calm deliberation. Like her sister, he could listen without looking.

In the silence, she adjusted the burden that had kept her up half the night, alternating between worry and prayer. She was too exhausted to keep this burden to herself. "What if they die?" It was one thing to offer relief during seasickness. It was something else to have a woman's life depend on her. "It will be my fault." A hot tear ran down her cheek. She pulled a handkerchief from her pocket. No one liked a watering can. She should find some privacy until she could pull herself together.

The penknife stilled. "Don't cry." The words didn't surprise her, but the compassion in his voice did. "With the attentive care you've given, they could only die if it was the will of God. It can't be your fault. You've been an angel of mercy."

Susan stared. The praise was the more glorious for having been unexpected. Here was that hidden harbor. Here was the man within the fortress. He had been worth the wait.

"There you are." The supercargo interrupted her pleasant thoughts.

She disguised her annoyance with more warmth than the occasion demanded. "Good morning, Mr. Sleeman."

Charles scowled.

"The captain sent me looking for the gen'lemen. Apologies, miss." He nodded dismissively at Susan. "He was hoping for a friendly game of cards to pass the time."

"Before dinner?" Susan was scornful. If the men were going to maroon her, they could at least wait until a socially acceptable time to do so.

"Women don't understand these things," Mr. Sleeman told Charles, adding insult to the offense.

Susan bristled. She recognized a slight, no matter what quarter it came from.

Mr. Johnson's brow furrowed. His gaze met Susan's. "Your maid will stay with you?"

The men could break protocol, but expected her to behave with propriety. "Indeed." She spoke lightly but watched his face, daring him to see the hypocrisy. "We can do anything at sea except scandalize the neighbors."

Mr. Johnson opened his mouth to speak. Then closed it. "Just so, Miss Bailey."

She took a turn about the decks with Lucy, entertaining her with the little gossip she could collect on the *Minerva*. "He called me an 'angel of mercy.'" That afternoon she would add that delightful news to her ongoing letter home.

"I suspect he's taken a fancy to you, miss."

"No, thank heaven. Can you picture me settling in the wilds of Virginia? My loyalties are an ocean away, with family and civilization. No man can change that. We're just friends."

Before him, she hadn't known it was possible to be friends with a man. Attentions had always turned so quickly to courtship. Friendship never had a chance. But with Charles, she didn't have to inspect her words for false encouragement. She didn't have to play games and guess the meaning behind his actions. She didn't have to calculate heartbreaking hints. She could just *be*. With Charles, she was free of the botherment of courtship. It was refreshing to be with a man not determined to win her hand, heart, and dowry.

The navigator stopped as the pair crossed his path. He looked at Lucy like she was a dish of ice cream on a warm summer day. "The view this morning is exceptionally fine." It was at least the third time in a week he had shamelessly flirted with her.

Lucy turned her reddening face away. Dave could flirt all he wanted. Susan was in no danger of losing her old maid.

It wouldn't hurt to talk to him. He probably had a wealth of entertaining stories. "Speaking of views," Susan said, "where have you traveled to?"

"I've seen the Indies, East and West, sailed through winter gales in the North Sea an' battled pirates in the Mediterranean. I've seen all o' God's creations I care ter see 'cept for my own home and family. Gettin' on so's I wouldn' mind finding myself some work ashore. I just need a little anchor ter keep me there." He looked at Lucy again. She pursed her lips in a disapproving manner. If that was his idea of a proposal, he had been firmly rejected without a word spoken.

Susan felt sorry for him. "Are you quite certain you would enjoy land? You have spent most of your life at sea."

"I've enjoyed a few months out of every year at my sister's home. It's a picture of domestic felicity: home-baked bread twice a week, a garden, and a dozen or so children runnin' inside an' outside, always gettin' underfoot."

Lucy raised her brows. "I'm not sure I quite agree with your picture of happiness. I would prefer my children a little more docile."

"The docile ones are sweet enough. But the ones that get their exercise are always the healthiest."

"I always thought it was the cleanest children who were the healthiest," Lucy countered.

Susan took one step back, watching Lucy and Dave. They were too engaged in their conversation to notice her. They could all use a little cheer right now. And when had Lucy ever indulged in a harmless flirtation? There was more than one way to be an angel of mercy.

"Indeed. Yeh're probably right. But them that are clean and active will live the longest."

"And happiest," Lucy added.

Dave smiled. "And happiest."

Susan opened *Robinson Crusoe* and watched the drama unfold just beyond the pages of her book. Who was chaperoning whom, now?

Eleven

SUNLIGHT & SHADOW

TUESDAY, APRIL 12, 1774

Charles inhaled the sea air appreciatively. He would never acclimate to the stale air in his cabin. The seas were too calm to drive him back into the hammock, but he was always better on deck. He had insisted the cargo hold was Isaac's brotherly responsibility since he had a weak nose and a strong stomach. He and Miss Susan had gone to check on Mrs. Finlay not long ago.

The early morning sun sent long shadows alongside blinding rays of light. He sheltered his eyes on the dark side of the mast, facing west. He turned a piece of wood over. It was no bigger than the palm of his hand. The way the grain of the wood curved around a small knot reminded him of the lithe acrobatics of dolphins. Miss Susan had been delighted by them. He sharpened his penknife and chipped away at the splintered wood, freeing the dolphin within.

Dave was sweet-talking Miss Pryor again. She blushed and bantered, but there was a rare smile on her face. It annoyed Charles. He could never court a woman like that, showering her with flowery nonsense until she succumbed to his charms. When he went courting, he would be calm and collected. Personal comments would be grounded in facts. His future wife would feel safe knowing he was trustworthy and sensible.

At least, he hoped she would.

Children laughed and played on deck, ducking around bemused sailors and interrupting Dave's flirtations. Miss Susan had gone to the captain himself to advocate for them. She had won all the emigrants a rotating shift of fresh air and freedom. It would be amusing if he could see her try her charms in a real court of law.

There was a whoop overhead. He looked up just in time to see Isaac drop from the rigging. He landed in a crouch but was upright in a moment, chasing the children as they squealed with laughter. Charles had thought Isaac was with his sister. When had he come up? And, more importantly, where was Susan?

Her voice carried across the deck, light and happy. "Oh, Charles. I've been looking for you."

He turned to see her walking toward him. Joy radiated from her face.

"You—you have?"

"Yes. I have the most wonderful news." She stopped close enough to partner in a dance, her face tilted upward to meet his eyes. "Marion's fever broke. She's taken a turn for the better."

For the first time, he saw flecks of gold in her brown eyes. They scattered sunlight like ripples in the water. Like cut glass. Like a diamond brooch or a crystal chandelier. Too late, he realized he was staring. He dropped his eyes to his carving. She had just said something important. Something that filled her soul with light. What was it? Finlay's wife would live. Their baby would live. "You saved her."

She blushed. "I only did what I could." Her humility did her credit, but only she had known what to do. Only she had come prepared for this crisis. Only she had begged to be of use, no matter the hour. Because she was here, a woman lived. Because she was here, a family that would have been broken and grieving was instead rejoicing. Susan was a miracle. Not the kind that turned water into wine. The kind that made a man believe there was such a thing as heaven and that it wasn't so far away, after all.

She looked at him expectantly, but he couldn't say what he had been thinking aloud to a woman he had known for less than a fortnight. He cleared his throat. "What you did...was enough." There. There was nothing inappropriate in that. There was also no blush on her cheeks. No self-conscious glances. Just the tiniest pout of her lip, like a child offered bread and butter when she was hoping for cake.

She was so motherly, he couldn't help being amused by the childish reaction. She made a fine display of caring for others, but at the end of the day, she wanted someone to care for her, too.

"Why are you smiling? Susan asked.

Alarm wiped the expression from his face. "I'm not smiling."

"It wasn't much of a smile, but you don't smile often, and I wondered what sort of thing would make you smile."

The last answer he could give her was the truth: sometimes *she* made him smile. "It's nothing." He leaned against the mast and resumed whittling. This was safe. He would keep his eyes, hands, and mind focused on a block of wood. There was no need to lose his head over a woman who lived on the wrong side of the ocean. They were just acquaintances. As acquaintances, they would see each other only occasionally for a year, then she would vanish from his life forever.

She might not even write.

"What's that?"

The wood scrap now looked roughly like a crescent moon. "I was thinking I'd make a dolphin out of it."

"A dolphin?" Her face was full of hope. Hope led to disappointment. It was best to keep her expectations low.

"If we're lucky. You don't know how these things will turn out until they're done."

"You look like you know what you're doing."

He did. Uncle Rob had lived closer to the school than his

parents had, so he had enjoyed many weekends and holidays at the Gardiners' home. While his uncle built furniture, Charles had played with the scraps of wood left behind. "My uncle was a cabinetmaker. Is a cabinetmaker." It was difficult to think of his family and friends in the present. For years, their relationships had subsisted on occasional letters. At least Uncle Rob had replied. Quillan Morris had been like a brother to him until he'd gone to London. After that, he'd only received three letters in seven years. For all he knew, Quill could be married or buried by now.

"Did he teach you everything he knows? Can you build me a chair with lots of spindles and cabriole legs and carve a sunset in the back?" There was no need for her to be so enthusiastic. She was teasing him. It was the only sensible explanation.

"I had to go to school." He had once asked his father to let him be his uncle's apprentice. Father had struck him so hard he had toppled over the porch railing and into the shrubbery. Blessedly, it was his shoulder that bruised. He never had to burden his mother with an explanation of where that injury came from. "I just learned a little, here and there." He curled away the last piece of wood from the dolphin's dorsal fin. "My father had other plans for me."

"He wanted you to go to London?"

"Yes." His mother, ill with consumption, had pleaded to allow Charles to stay. In the end, it was kindest to placate his father by going. He thought it would protect her. Instead, news of her death was the first letter that had reached him.

"I'm sure your father must be proud of you."

Charles froze. "Miss Susan," he began, then stopped. This was personal, and his personal matters were not anyone's business.

"What is it?"

He felt for the security of the fortress wall between them, but it wasn't there, keeping him safe. She was. He couldn't remember why he needed to keep this a secret from her. It would be common knowledge once they reached Williamsburg, but it still felt personal. Certain he was out of his senses, he folded the penknife and pulled the letter from a waistcoat pocket. "This is why I'm going home." He clutched the folded paper tightly, lest she get any ideas about reading his mail. There were walls and then there were *Walls*.

She stared at the black sealing wax. "Your father?"

He nodded and returned the letter to his pocket.

"When?"

"More than two months ago. I left London as soon as I could get my affairs in order."

"I didn't know." The wistfulness in her voice made his own throat tight.

"You do now." The simple statement of fact masked the complicated feelings he was struggling to make sense of. She couldn't see the pressure building behind his eyes and nose. He opened the penknife and put all his attention on the dolphin's right-hand fin. There was nothing wistful or complicated about dolphins.

"Do you have any family left?"

Blast. If she could just stop asking questions in that tone of voice, he could pull himself together. "My uncle—I just told you about him—and his family." Facts were safer than feelings. "He married my father's younger sister. They have two little girls, Emmeline and Henrietta. They're my family." The Gardiners had always been his family. Boarding school had taken him away from Johnson Hall for much of the year. Then Uncle Rob had taken him as much as his father had allowed.

"My little sister is fifteen. How old are your cousins? They can't be that little if you knew them before you came to London."

In his mind, they were no older than the children Isaac was chasing. "When I left, Henrietta was barely out of leading strings, and Emmeline was only nine or ten." He frowned. "I suppose that would make her about as old as your sister." He had been gone far too long. Since smallpox had taken their brothers, the girls had been his responsibility. He didn't like to think that his little cousins had grown up without him.

"I'd like to meet her. I'd like to meet all of your family. I don't know anyone in Williamsburg, unless you count my aunt, and I think it's important to establish connections as quickly as possible."

Connections. His knife slipped and nicked his finger. The word reminded him of countless barbs his father had aimed at Uncle Rob. He was disappointed to hear it from Susan. He pressed his thumb against his finger to stop the flow of blood. His voice had an edge to it. "Most ladies don't expect a cabinetmaker's family to be a useful connection."

Her demeanor changed in an instant. One moment, she was warm and inviting. The next, her eyes flashed, her nostrils flared, and she threw her hands in the air. "Must you be so difficult? I want to meet my friend's family because they are my *friend's family.*" The relational words were spoken with a force to raise Lazarus. "If I see them at church or in a shop or on the street, I want to be able to speak with them because they are connected to you." She pursed her lips and surveyed him with disgust. "Just because you're cold and cynical doesn't mean I am."

Despite the calm waters, Charles lost his balance. She had just demanded an intimate friendship and then pushed him away. It would take him a sennight to sort out everything she had said, but he couldn't wait that long to put things right. "I—I'm sorry. I didn't mean it like that."

Her eyes narrowed, considering him.

He dropped his gaze to his finger. The bleeding had already stopped. It had been a small cut. Susan hadn't even noticed. "Your aunt, Mrs. Evans, dines with the most esteemed families in Virginia. She might hope for you to establish your reputation with them before you meet the Gardiners."

Her eyes widened. "You know my aunt? Why didn't you say so?"

"I don't know her well." She had been friends with his mother, but he had scarcely been eighteen when he left Williamsburg. What schoolboy paid attention to his parents' friends? And since his mother was gone, so was the friendship. "She used to powder her hair purple. I remember that."

Miss Susan shook her head in solemn wonder. "What else don't I know about you?" She had already coaxed more out of him than he ever revealed to a chance acquaintance. She was too easy to talk to.

He resumed whittling. "You know the essentials. The rest can wait." If they kept up at this rate, she would know everything about him within the year. There was no need for her or anyone else to know everything about him.

"I don't know your plans. Did your father leave you property to manage?"

What would it take to get her to talk about someone else? Begrudgingly, he answered, "Yes. Johnson Hall."

"Oh, that does have a nice sound to it. I hope, for your sake, that he left it in good repair."

"We'll see." It wasn't the house he was worried about. "He hired a man to oversee the crops until I could get home."

"Mr. Finlay knows everything about farming. You should talk to him."

He had. Finlay was a fountain of knowledge when it came to the latest in agricultural science. To fully modernize the plantation, he would need to purchase expensive machinery. Heaven knew when he would get his money back. "My father didn't want me to be a farmer. He wanted me to be a burgess."

"A burgess?"

"An elected member of the House of Burgesses. It's the parliament that runs Virginia. Half of it, anyway."

Her eyes lit with interest. "What a wonderful idea."

He stared at her. "Wonderful? What's so wonderful about it?" He hadn't thought she was the sort of woman to be chasing titles and prestige.

"Think of all the good you could do. You could create the laws. Laws about indentures and landlords, and slavery."

He might be cynical, but at least he wasn't naively optimistic.

He was unlikely to be elected and even less likely to be influential. The right-hand fin was complete. He turned the dolphin and started on the left one.

"It's a shame your father won't see you doing it. He would be so proud of you."

He brushed the praise aside like an ill-fitting waistcoat. "Actually, his death is what makes it possible."

Her face wrinkled in confusion. "I don't understand."

"Without property, I can't even vote, much less get elected. Virginia is ruled and run by men with property."

"I see." Her brown eyes softened. "Your father had to die before his dream for you was possible." She made dying of the flu sound like a grand gesture of paternal sacrifice.

He bristled. "I didn't say it was the only way."

"It isn't?"

"There are three ways to become a landowner. One is to inherit property, like me. The next is to purchase it. Even if a man is able to earn and save enough for acreage, the work isn't done there. He has to manage its development. It can be years of hard work and sacrifice to be successful, and success is essential for a political candidate."

"You said there were three options."

He rubbed a thumb over the fin, searching for imperfections in his carving. "There are. The third would be to marry a landowner."

"Is it common for women to own land in Virginia?"

"Common enough. Women inherit land all the time. A wife is entitled to her widow's third, and daughters can inherit a portion of their father's land. Until they marry, they manage the property *feme sole*—as a single woman."

"So my widowed aunt, Mrs. Evans, she's a *feme sole*?"

"Correct." He turned the dolphin over in his hand. It was done. But would Susan appreciate it? He stole a glance at her. She was watching the game of tag that Isaac was leading. That wasn't the only game in play. Dave slowly reached an arm around Miss

Pryor. It was a bold move, akin to seeking a verdict prematurely. The judge had only just begun hearing his appeals. The maid stood stock still for one long moment, then she twisted her shoulders out of the embrace and shoved him away with a scold. Overruled. Courting a woman was riskier than a court case.

One of the children wedged himself between Charles and the mast, panting. Isaac tagged him in a moment.

"No fair! I wasn't playing anymore." He burst into tears. It was a wretched sight, a thin boy in threadbare clothing who would soon be sold, with or without his family, sobbing as though he had already lost them.

"Here." Charles handed the dolphin to the boy. It was best to get rid of it before he did something foolish.

"I can't," the boy howled. "I have to go inside now."

"You can take this with you. It's yours. You should have something to play with when you have to sit still."

The boy wiped his sleeve across his face and grabbed the dolphin.

"Climb on my back," Isaac said. "Let's go show your mama what Mr. Johnson made for you." In the boy's hand, the dolphin leapt and spun over Isaac's back, then dove into the ship with them. It was for the best, but Charles couldn't help frowning.

Susan touched his sleeve. "That was so thoughtful of you."

He took half a step back, but his arm didn't follow, as if it now fell under her jurisdiction and not his own. "What else would I have done with a toy? I wasn't making it for myself."

Her hand dropped. "It meant a lot to him."

His arm reluctantly returned to his side. "I know. But it isn't fair for him to have a toy while the other children don't." The muscles in his hand cramped. He stretched his fingers and sighed. "I'll have to make more."

Her smile was warmer than sunshine. His heart, which should have been safe within its fortifications, melted. He smiled back.

Twelve

A FOOL'S FANCY

Susan basked in the brilliance of this beautiful morning. After days of work, worry, and prayer, the miracle had come. When she had gone to check on Marion, her patient was taking a turn about the cargo hold, bouncing and shushing Timmy while her husband slept. She had been most appreciative, thanking Susan for saving her and asking after her family in Eversley.

She and Charles had worried over the Finlays together. It would have been nice to rejoice together, but he was immune to joy, the way some people were immune to measles and smallpox. He must have come down with a serious case of disappointment in his youth. When had his mother passed away? That might have caused it. And now he had lost his father. No wonder he had a soft spot for children. He was an orphan.

He didn't look like an orphan. The word conveyed a waif-like child with unkempt hair and pleading eyes. Charles was tall and clean-shaven. His dark blond hair was combed and tied back. He never pleaded. But he was alone in the world. He needed someone to pull him out of his brooding. He needed a friend.

For the next few weeks, she would be that friend. She had

already coaxed one smile out of him this morning. "What animal will you carve next?"

"That depends on the wood. Sometimes I can see an animal in the knots or the grain."

"You can see it?" The whimsical expression was at odds with his stoic nature.

"That last piece, the way the grain curved about the eye, was similar to the shape of a dolphin leaping out of the water. So I carved a dolphin. It's easier to bring out what is already there than to carve the wood to your will."

That philosophy might serve carpenters well. It was different with people. What they needed was something that wasn't already there. She just tried to be God's hands on earth, helping people get what they lacked.

His eyes searched hers. There was no need. She didn't hide away her thoughts and feelings like he did. He blinked and stepped aside, putting more space between them. And more space. Without taking leave, he moved to a higher deck. She was trying to decide what to make of his apparent rudeness when he cried, "Susan! Come see."

Hoping for dolphins, she joined him at the stern. There were no dolphins. Charles pointed a dozen feet away. Squinting, she could see something round and green skimming along, just under the surface. "Is that a turtle?"

"It is."

"It's huge." She had only seen turtles around lakes and ponds. They were babies compared to this one.

"Don't let it get away," Isaac called from above. "We could have turtle soup."

She looked up. He stood on a small platform higher than a bird's nest. His hands loosely grasped ropes that passed him on either side. Then he tipped forward. He was falling. She was falling. Panicked, she clutched Charles's arm for balance. He looked at her, his mouth gaping in shock, then back up. Isaac grinned down at them, his body slung between a toe-hold and his grip on the ropes.

"Of all the childish pranks!" Her fright vented as anger. "Climb down now, before you break your neck." She released Charles's arm with a shaky laugh. If she'd had any presence of mind, she would have grabbed the railing. "This is why I couldn't stay home. Someone has to save Isaac from himself."

DAYS ON THE SHIP FELL INTO A COMFORTABLE RHYTHM. They ebbed and flowed about Susan like the tides followed the moon. Charles rose from bed and shaved each morning to hear her voice over breakfast. He escorted her anywhere she pleased to be and listened as young sailors solicited her advice and old ones wove yarns for her amusement. He carved animals for the children to play with, as much for her delight as theirs. Isaac vexed her with his words, his misplaced stockings, and his climbing tricks. She fussed and scolded him. Sensational sunsets were followed by starry nights. He fell asleep thinking of her. The chill of April faded into the warmth of May.

One evening, as the navigator pocketed his sextant, he said, "God willing, we'll reach Virginia within the week."

Charles was astonished by the announcement. "So soon?"

"Soon?" Dave laughed. "We should have been there already. Did yeh forget how long we were becalmed?"

Time passed so quickly at sea that he had scarcely noticed when there had been no wind to fill the sails. Everything would change when they made land. In a few days, he would be going over Barton's expenses, the state of Johnson Hall, and wondering how often he could call on the Baileys without making a fool of himself.

"A week?" Susan's face was eager. "I can hardly wait to see houses and trees again. I am filled with enthusiasm for every common thing." In a moment, her eagerness changed to worry.

"You're sure Williamsburg is still safe? Isaac keeps telling me about mobs."

"He should know as well as anyone that mobs are a Boston thing. The uncivilized ruckus that makes the London papers comes from the cities up north. Nothing could be more proper than Virginia's House of Burgesses." Charles thanked the Lord that what he said was true. He needed her to like Virginia. Scarcely a day passed without witnessing her wistfulness for her home in England. He was already at a disadvantage. He didn't need Isaac to make things harder. Not when he was foolish enough to dream of a future with a woman who couldn't wait to put an ocean between them.

Could he persuade her to give up her beloved family for life in the colonies? She would have to love him deeply to consider such a sacrifice. He didn't know if she loved him at all. Half the time he was with her, her attention was on other men. She was popular with the sailors, the emigrants, and especially the children. He was just one more person.

His family would be a poor substitute for hers. Both of his parents were dead. He had no siblings. Granny's wits wandered. He could only offer the Gardiners and hope she could love his cousins as she did her sister. In the meantime, his feelings were so big he had to fight to keep them tucked away—like a trunk packed so full, it can only be locked while sitting on it.

The sun melted into the ocean. Ribbons of clouds near the horizon glowed beautiful shades of rosy-orange, impossible for garment dyers to imitate. Miles of rippling water reflected the radiance. One evening star dared to compete with the riot of color at the sun's passing.

"I will miss these sunsets," Susan said.

"Sunsets are lovely, but they're gone so soon. I prefer the stars." Stars were steady and predictable. The same constellations he'd learned in his boyhood had followed him to England.

"They're beautiful."

Susan was beautiful. She was more beautiful in her woolen

petticoat than most women were in silks and ruffles. "Has anyone ever taken your likeness?" It was all the fashion for ladies to be painted as historical figures: Cleopatra, Joan of Arc—

"My friend painted me as the Madonna. She's an accomplished artist. It would have been a lovely painting if the baby we'd borrowed had held still for more than a minute."

Charles didn't need to see the painting. He had seen Susan cradling the Finlay's baby. She was a natural mother, at turns scolding and sweet, authoritative and compassionate. He could picture her beside the old cradle in the family nursery. She belonged to his home. He brushed the premature image aside. They had known each other for less than six weeks. It was too soon for such thoughts.

Within a sennight, they would be in Williamsburg, where any number of gentlemen could call on her whenever they pleased. She would be as warm and charming with them as she was with the sailors. He panicked. They didn't have enough time left together. "Susan?"

"Yes, Charles?" Her soft brown eyes sparkled in the starlight.

The longing hurt like homesickness, but fear choked his words. He couldn't confess his feelings to a woman he hadn't even heard of two months ago. And what were his feelings? He respected her, admired her, and couldn't stop thinking about her. Was this enduring love or fickle fancy? It was too soon to say with certainty. And she had given him no reason to believe she thought more of him than any other man. He couldn't ask to court her. If she didn't already return his affections, such a question might stop his suit before it began.

"Nothing." He looked up at the Pole Star, constant in the heavens. "I'm just glad I met you."

Thirteen

SEEKING HOME

WEDNESDAY, MAY 18, 1774, HAMPTON ROADS

Charles could smell land on the breeze. It was a combination of rich soil, spring leaves, and smoke. He could see it, too. Several ships were anchored in the nearest harbor. Old warehouses stood in the shadow of older woods. His muscles twitched to run down the gangplank and never set foot on a sailing ship again, but that would have to wait. Ever since they had passed the mouth of the Chesapeake, the ship had moved slower than ever.

Finlay solemnly studied their surroundings. "Is this Chesapeake Bay? Or are we in a river, now?"

"Neither." They wouldn't move up the James until the tide came in. "We're in Hampton Roads, the channel that connects the James, Elizabeth, and Nansemond Rivers with Chesapeake Bay." Charles didn't need a navigator to tell him where he was. These waters flowed through his veins. "Over there is the port town of Hampton."

"That's it, then? That's Virginia?"

"That's it. We're nearly home."

"Home?" Thomas scoffed. "For three hundred years, my

family has lived in the same house. We'll never see it again. We will be strangers in a strange land. My child won't even remember his true home. Poor Jenny should never have left it. We have no home. Soon, we won't even have each other."

Charles wanted to deny it, but he couldn't. The Finlays were in a precarious situation. There was no guarantee their indentures would be sold together. With his background in agriculture, Thomas was sure to be taken to a plantation. If Marion and Jenny were offered positions as housemaids, there was a small possibility that the women could stay together. It was unlikely. There wasn't much room for compassion when it came to business. Timmy would stay with his mother. That was the only mercy they could count on.

"You and your wife may never feel at home here. Mayhap your niece won't either. But it may be a blessing that Timmy won't remember another home. Children grow where they're planted. Virginia soil will be the first he ever walks on. And he'll be with his mother. That's what babies need most, isn't it? Your indentures should be up by the time he's breeched. Then you could go west, where the land is cheap, and start over together."

Thomas shook his head. "So much can happen in five years. So much. Back in sixty-nine, Jenny's father died, and I took her in. She was just a child of ten. Five more years and she'll be a woman. What if some worthless boy elopes with her the moment she's free? Or worse—"

Charles interrupted. "She's not that kind of girl."

"She doesn't have to be." He looked over at Mr. Sleeman, talking animatedly outside the captain's quarters. "Right now, we're nothing more than pawns in a rich man's game. Marion almost died, and for what? Not even Sleeman had anything to gain by it."

"They'll never be trapped in a cargo hold again. And Virginia air is cleaner than London's."

"We're not from London."

"I know." But Charles had never seen much of England

outside of the city. He couldn't imagine the region beyond Hadrian's Wall.

"You've done so much for us already. You and Miss Bailey. Forgive me for begging for one more favor. If we're separated, keep an eye on them for me."

It was too early for such promises. Charles didn't know who would be taken where. He didn't know how far they might be removed from Williamsburg. He didn't know how much time his father's plantation would demand of him. But he couldn't deny Thomas's plea. As solemn as a courtroom oath, Charles said, "With God as my witness, I will."

Thomas's shoulders relaxed. "Thank you. If there's ever anything I can do for you—"

Charles held up a hand. Thomas was indentured. He was in no position to offer him anything. "It's nothing."

"No. It's everything."

IT TOOK AN HOUR FOR CHARLES TO FIND A DRIVER WHO could take them and all the Baileys' trunks to Williamsburg. The vehicle was no fine carriage. It was so rustic that it was more of a wagon than a coach, with a flat roof made of wood planks and canvas curtains that could be let down in unpleasant weather. Charles was embarrassed that the first experience Susan would have with his home country was so coarse, but it could not be helped. What could she have meant by packing so much?

The sailors carried her luggage to the wagon while she walked slowly down the gangplank, taking in his home country for the first time.

He looked about, seeing it through her eyes, and was disappointed. This close to the port, all they could see were warehouses and rough roads. "Within half a mile is some of the loveliest scenery in the country." Thank heaven that was true. He needed her to like Virginia.

She brightened. "More beautiful than a sunset?"

"I like to think so. Sunsets are hard to see through all the trees."

"Tha's the last'n." The sailor wiped his hands on his trousers and held one out expectantly. Charles frowned. Unless times had changed, coins were hard to come by in the colonies. He reluctantly handed one to each sailor who had helped with the luggage. It would be wasted on liquor.

The wagon driver spat in the dirt. "The back bench is the most accommodating to the ladies."

Susan looked around, but there was no foothold, and the base of the wagon was waist-high. Charles knew his duty as a gentleman. He knelt on one knee in the dirt beside her and cupped his hands together. She placed a hand on his shoulder and her shoe in his hand. Helping ladies mount horses and carriages was the dirtiest work known to man, but as she clambered into the wagon, Charles had an excellent view of the elaborate clocks embroidered up her silk stockings. He looked away abruptly, brushing the dirt from his hand and knee.

"Where are you sitting?" Susan asked him.

"By the driver." He was eager to see familiar country again.

Rather than claim the seat "most accommodating to ladies," Susan sat on the bench behind him. Mayhap she wanted a better view, but he hoped it was because she enjoyed being near him. He flushed, his eyes forward. He shouldn't be thinking about the way her dainty ankles contrasted pleasantly with the curve of her plump leg. Such thoughts were for married men. He hadn't even made up his mind to court her. He shook his head and slapped his thigh. *Stop smiling!*

A breeze cooled his cheeks as they moved away from the warehouses and into the woods. It was May, and Virginia was as beautiful as he remembered it. Oak and pine trees grew straight in their native soil. At their feet, wildflowers bloomed. Columbine and butterfly weed. Lupine and sundrops. A breeze carried the sweet scent of magnolia blossoms mingled with traces of wood smoke.

The thrum of cicadas and the call of birds brought with them a thousand memories.

He turned to see how Susan was appreciating their ride. Her eyes darted from one side of the road to the other. She was as tense as a child facing a rattlesnake.

"Don't tell me your strong stomach can't handle a few ruts in the road."

"I'm fine."

He was unconvinced. "Let's rest the horses a minute."

The coachman eased to a stop. Charles jumped down.

"Where are you going?" Susan asked anxiously.

"I'll just be a minute." He spied a cluster of columbine nearby. They had been his mother's favorite. He cut a handful of stems with one swipe of his penknife. The blossoms bobbed as he walked back to the carriage. "You should be home in time for supper." He handed Susan the bouquet. When had he last given a woman flowers?

"We're making good time," the driver agreed as Charles returned to his seat. He flicked the reins, and the wagon lurched forward.

If being road sick was anything like being seasick, she had his pity. Charles looked back at her. She was quietly stroking the delicate red petals of the columbine. The sooner they arrived at her destination, the better. He had instructed the driver to take them to the Blue House first. Only after the Baileys were safely settled with their aunt would he continue to Johnson Hall.

Isaac was in high spirits and had questions about everything, from agricultural science to native animals. Charles found himself explaining the habits of polecats. "If you see one raise its tail, back away slowly and quietly, or you'll be counting yourself lucky to eat in the barn for the next two weeks."

"On account of the smell?"

"On account of the cows smelling better than you."

"Really? Have you smelled it before?"

"Smelled it?" He laughed. "I couldn't smell anything else for weeks. Luckily, it was summer. I wasn't allowed in the house for a fortnight."

Isaac launched into the tale of how he got a huge splinter in his foot the spring he was fourteen. As he rambled on, Charles only half-listened. He wondered which families still lived at the end of dirt trails that branched off the main road, which buildings still stood, and how much land had been cleared.

There was another cluster of sundrops up ahead. They brought the cheer of sunshine into the dappled shade of their path. Susan was unusually quiet. Would she be happiest if they got to her destination promptly, or would she appreciate more wildflowers? The sundrops were suddenly shadowed by a gentleman and a lady riding horseback. In his surprise, Charles forgot all about flowers. "Quill!"

The man pulled his horse to a stop and turned to the lady behind him. "As I live and breathe 'tis Charles Johnson!" They turned their horses about and kept pace alongside the wagon. "I havena seen ye in ages. Finally tired of London life, did ye?" If Charles hadn't recognized the freckled face of Quillan Morris, he would have known his speech. The entire clan spoke with the highland brogue of their immigrant parents.

"My father was deathly ill this past winter. He urged me to come home."

"Deathly ill, ye say? I remember hearing he was quite ill. And ye had no way of knowing. Well, let me assure ye that yer father, though not as active as he once was, has returned ta tolerably good health for a man of his age."

"You're sure?"

"I'm no' saying they didna have a scare last winter, but I saw him in town no' two weeks ago."

"You're *sure*?" He had left London with uncustomary haste, quitting his lodgings and passing off his briefs. Had it all been in vain?

"Och. What do ye take me for? Ye think I wouldna recognize yer father?"

"I didn't mean—of course, you knew. But this is so sudden. He seemed so sure when he wrote the letter..."

"He's out of all danger now. So sorry ye should have been worrying about him all this time." Quill looked over his shoulder. "And who's this ye're traveling with? Ye didna get married in England, did ye?" He laughed. "And with yer father so eager ta match ye himself."

Charles went hot. Couldn't Quill have the delicacy not to tease him in front of Susan? "No, no. Not at all. I would like you to meet Mr. Bailey. And this is his sister, Miss Bailey, with her maid, Miss Pryor." The maid looked as sour as a lime. "We became acquainted on the ship over. They will be staying with their aunt in Williamsburg."

"Pleased ta meet you, Mr. Bailey." He twisted in his saddle to nod at Susan. "Miss Bailey. Miss Pryor. I look forward ta calling on ye once I'm in town again." He always had been a favorite of the ladies, but there was no need for Quill to be calling on Susan. He gestured to the lady behind him. "And this is my sister, Miss Morris."

Charles frowned. There was a whole bevy of females who could be called Miss Morris. "Miss Polly Morris?"

She smiled widely. "Aye. That's me."

He shook his head. "I didn't think you'd ever mature."

Her smile turned to a scowl. "I did. Unlike present company."

Behind him, Susan laughed, but Charles was in no mood to be teased. It was a grave thing to learn a relation buried in your mind was alive and breathing. "I'm surprised to see you riding about in the middle of the day. I thought you had become a man of business."

As a boy, Quill had always been better suited to pleasure than work. "On such a fine day? Nay. I canna stay cooped inside. I have a gouty client who willna come into my office ta discuss his case, so I thought ta visit his estate so we could go o'er the details in person. What are yer plans now that ye're home?"

Home. Without his mother, Johnson Hall wasn't home.

Home was where people were loyal to you, even when you failed. It was where your socks were darned before you noticed they needed it. Home was a quiet fireside and a hot meal. His stomach rumbled. They had missed dinner today. Charles had a sudden longing for Aunt Charity's home cooking. He hadn't enjoyed a proper meal since he'd left London.

But what would he do with himself? He'd had two months to acclimate himself to the idea of his father's death. Finding him alive was unsettling. Had his father even been ill? Or was this all a trick to force him home? When his mother died, he had sworn never to live under his father's roof again. He had half a mind to take the first ship back to England. He should be happy that his father was alive. Instead, he was angry. "I won't be needed at Johnson Hall."

"Yer father has that well in hand."

He would. There was no need, no duty, no desire for Charles there. He had no training as anything but a barrister. "I passed the bar in London. I don't know any of the Virginia laws." It could be months before he achieved sufficient familiarity with the local laws to handle briefs. The prospect was as daunting as managing Johnson Hall had been.

"Ye'll learn fast," Quill said pleasantly. "If ye can handle London courtrooms, ye can handle Williamsburg."

"There's so much I'll need to learn. And the expense of a new library and an office, when I don't know when I'll be taking on briefs—" He had enough money saved for it. But if he wasn't inheriting Johnson Hall and wasn't sharing his father's roof, he would need that money to purchase a house.

"Dinna worry yerself. I have a legal library and an office. There'll be no expense until ye have some business." Quill was generous to a fault.

"You'd share your office?"

"The office, aye, but no' the furnishings. I canna share a desk."

"That's more than generous. I could help with clerk duties until I get steady business."

"My housekeeper would like that. She's been doing all the clerk duties since the last boy ran off." He winked over his shoulder at his sister, who was too busy talking with Susan to notice.

"It's a deal." Charles would have shaken hands, but Quill was too far away. "I'll start as soon as you're back in town."

"No need ta wait." Quill pulled a key out of his pocket. He smirked. "I'm sure ye're eager ta be studying."

Charles caught the heavy key. They had only exchanged three letters in seven years, but Quill still trusted him like a brother.

He told him the direction for the office until Charles was sure he would remember, then turned his horse about numbly and returned to the direction he had been traveling. Polly waved gaily. Charles twisted about in the coachman's front seat in time to see Quill tip his hat to Susan. She smiled warmly at him. Jealousy twisted inside him. His old friend had no right to be friendly with Susan.

Fourteen

THE BLUE HOUSE

A wild hope filled Susan. Charles had come to Virginia to manage his inheritance. With his father alive, he was free to return to England. Not right away. After coming this far, he would desire at least a few months with his father. Perhaps he would return home when she and Isaac did. They could keep each other company on the voyage. She might persuade him to set up an office in Eversley.

The wagon lurched over another stump. Susan gripped her seat. He was the oldest son. Isaac was free to see the world, but as heir, his home would always be Bailey Manor. Charles had taken his time in England, but now that he was here, he would keenly feel the duties to his father.

Ancient trees taller than a ship's mast crowded the road. Ten minutes ago, she had been scanning the upper branches for lions. Now she eyed the deep shadows and shrubbery for the dreaded pole cat. She could not meet her aunt smelling worse than a cow. She would die of shame. "I didn't expect Virginia to be so wild this close to the capital."

Isaac sighed contentedly. "Isn't it wonderful? Just imagine. You go for a stroll and have to fight off an alligator."

Susan bit her lip and looked about for water. That's where

alligators lived, wasn't it? She had to keep Isaac safely inside the wagon when he wanted to chase danger. It would be easiest if she spied peril before he did.

Charles turned sideways on his bench and leaned toward her. In a low voice with only a hint of amusement, he said, "There are no alligators in Virginia."

"Truly?" She held his gray-blue eyes and silently prayed for a merciful truth.

"Truly."

She took a deep breath. That was one fear allayed, but many remained. "Don't people own this land?" She gestured around them. "Surely such good timber is valuable for shipbuilding, and removing it would clear land for farming." And remove dangerous animals.

Charles chuckled. "You can't judge how many acres have been cleared from the road. Many plantations keep a wilderness. Gentlemen take pride in their hunting grounds."

"What do they hunt here?" She had to intercept any lion-hunting invitations Isaac might receive.

"Fox hunts are popular."

She relaxed. Foxes were small, fluffy, and shy of people. Her own father participated in the occasional fox hunt.

"But bigger game makes for good sport, too. One year my neighbor shot a bear."

"Her eyes went wide. "A bear?" She had hoped alligators weren't the only ferocious animals Isaac was wrong about.

"How big?" Isaac asked eagerly.

"Seven feet tall and as wide as two men. It made a fine rug. But we don't see many bears this close to the capital."

Susan didn't want to see any bears. She didn't want to see tree-climbing lions or noxious cats. She especially didn't want Isaac chasing after them. She looked down at the wildflowers Charles had given her. The blood-red columbine nodded their dainty heads as the wagon bumped along. As uncomfortable as she was, there was a light in his eyes this afternoon that she had rarely seen.

He belonged here, in the woods and fields of Virginia, pulling beauty out of a wilderness.

The trees gave way to pastures and small houses visible from the road. The whitewashed buildings grew closer together as they continued. The wagon dipped into smaller ruts.

"Welcome to Williamsburg," Charles said proudly.

There was no cobblestone. Instead, sand covered the dirt road to protect wheels from sinking into mud on rainy days. They rode past a large brick church, a tavern, a brick courthouse, and clapboard shops and houses. People bustled about, gossiping in the streets and shopping. She strained to see what was beyond the shop windows. A cat slept in a patch of sunlight on a cellar door.

Williamsburg was nothing to Bath or London, but neither was Eversley. Susan longed to explore the shops and hear the gossip. They had been too long at sea. The most commonplace sights were thrilling.

The wagon turned down one road, then another, lined with clapboard buildings. The steps to each front door came right to the street. "There's yer Blue House," the driver called. It was the first blue building they had seen. The door was perfectly centered with two windows to the left, two windows to the right, and four windows upstairs. It was small, compared to Bailey Manor, but symmetry and fresh paint gave a stateliness to it. After their long journey, it looked like a mansion.

How many guest rooms did it have? She had firmly declined her aunt's invitation and never notified her of the change in plans. The rudeness of her sudden appearance heated her cheeks. Her aunt's first impression would be of a dusty, frumpy young woman with no respect for social conventions. She clutched the columbine in one hand and shook dust from her petticoats with the other. *Lord, may she want me.* She exhaled slowly, picturing herself as the most helpful and delightful guest her aunt had ever had. Next summer, she would be begging her to stay.

"Wait here," Charles said. He lighted from the carriage and rapped smartly on the door. A footman answered. The sun reflected off an abundance of silver buttons. His long jacket was a brilliant blue. The ascot wrapped around his throat was as white as snow, which contrasted with his dark complexion.

Susan's stomach did a double flip. It hadn't occurred to her that her aunt might keep slaves. Was it one man or the entire staff? At least she had brought her maid. She wouldn't need to borrow her aunt's.

She ran a smoothing hand along her hair. Lucy was capable of doing so much with it. What she wouldn't give to freshen up first and have introductions second. That was impossible, but her aunt wouldn't see her arriving in this rustic wagon. "Isaac, help me down."

They met Mrs. Evans in the foyer. Susan knew her at once from Charles' scant description. Her hair, worn short with a row of tight curls framing her face, was powdered a delightful lavender. Though her hairstyle had gone out of fashion a decade past, she wore it regally. Her gown shimmered silver in the afternoon sun. The sleeves ended in a waterfall of sumptuous white lace that perfectly matched the lace kerchief about her throat.

Susan looked down at her petticoat and shortgown. It was unpressed, dusty, and as weary from the journey as she was. She should have found a way to wash up first. It was too late, now. She raised her chin. Baileys did not cower.

Surprisingly, her aunt's eyes settled on Charles first. "Vina's boy," she said softly. "It has been a long time. She has been sorely missed." The families were better connected than Charles had admitted if her aunt still called his mother by her Christian name.

It was good that they were already acquainted. She expected him to be a regular caller. He was, after all, her only friend in the colony. "Thank you, Mrs. Evans," he said with a slight bow.

"I understand you've made quite a name for yourself in London."

He was flustered by the praise. "I wouldn't say that."

"At any rate, you've made your father proud." She looked inquisitively at Susan and Isaac. "Are you going to introduce me?"

"Yes, ma'am. May I present Mr. Isaac Bailey—"

There was a gasp.

"And his sister, Miss Susan Bailey."

Their aunt's surprise equaled her delight. She grasped both of Susan's hands. "Let me look at you! You have your father's eyes. And your mother's smile. I'm so glad you've come." She turned to the liveried footman. "Graves, tell the housekeeper to prepare a room for Miss Bailey."

"Yes, ma'am." He slipped away.

"Come into the parlor and sit down. You must be exhausted." Mrs. Evans took one step in the direction of her clean parlor and its upholstered seating. "And you must tell me all about how you became acquainted. I had no idea. Have you known each other all this time?"

"No, Mrs. Evans," Susan said. "We booked passage on the same ship and became acquainted on the journey."

"How extraordinary. And Susan? Do call me Aunt Dorothea. It will make me feel immensely more comfortable. You, too, Isaac." She turned back to Charles. "Well, young Mr. Johnson, you must make yourself a regular visitor now that you're here. How is your father? He must have been delighted to see you."

"I have not yet been home, ma'am."

"How kind of you to escort my niece and nephew. Had you hoped to make it home tonight?"

"My driver is waiting. I just wanted to see the Baileys to the end of their journey."

"I hope you'll call soon."

"Yes, ma'am." He glanced at Susan. "I will."

After he took his leave, Aunt Dorothea asked, "Where did you find columbine?"

"The flowers? That was Charles. They were growing through the woods we passed through."

Their aunt looked thoughtful, but all she said was, "I'll get a vase for them."

The moment their aunt left, Isaac walked to the settee.

"Don't, Isaac," Susan whispered fiercely. "We need to clean up first."

"It's fine," Isaac said, settling his dusty body onto the furniture.

Her father had sent her to keep Isaac out of trouble. She couldn't even keep him out of the parlor. Their aunt returned with a Delft vase. Susan tucked the fistful of slender stems inside, then rearranged the blooms by height. They were too thin for a proper bouquet, but the red contrasted beautifully with the blue and white vase.

A dark-skinned maid brought refreshments to the parlor. She left as silently as she'd come, but Susan stared. She was in a foreign country with customs she didn't understand.

Mrs. Evans placed a dainty ginger cake and a slice of meat pie on a china plate. "I hope you remained in good health during your voyage." She handed the plate to Susan.

"Hmm?" She was too delighted by the appearance of civilized food to be interested in pleasantries. " Yes. Isaac and I didn't experience any seasickness." She took a bite of pie. The flaky crust and tender meat melted in her mouth.

"And Mr. Johnson?"

Isaac spoke around a mouthful of cake, "Sick with every storm." He swallowed. "Susan devoted herself to nursing him."

Aunt Dorothea raised her brows in interest.

Susan dabbed her lips with a napkin. "I would have done the same for you if you'd been sick."

"But I wasn't. Told you I wouldn't be."

"Just so." Their aunt ended the discussion. "Your rooms are ready. It's time to unpack." She put her teacup down. "I hope you brought all the latest fashions. All anyone can talk about nowadays is how elegant and stylish the Dunmores are. I hope my niece will outshine them all."

They followed her up the central staircase. "Isaac, you'll have the green room." She gestured to the room over the parlor.

"Susan, you'll have the blue room." She led the way into a neighboring chamber.

The walls were painted a soothing blue, which perfectly matched the shade of the toile curtains around the bed and windows. Besides the tester bed, it was handsomely furnished with a clothespress, a desk and chair by the window, and a little wash table with a blue-and-white Delft pitcher and bowl.

After her stateroom accommodations, it was breathtaking. She set the vase on the desk and leaned out the open window. A robin regarded her from the oak tree, then swooped down, perching on a rose bush. Robins and roses. She hadn't known that either lived in Virginia. Isaac certainly didn't talk about them. Her nerves had been tight all afternoon, watching for strange and wild beasts. But this room almost felt like home.

"Do you like it?" Aunt Dorothea pressed.

"Like it? It's positively charming."

Lucy was already unpacking the trunks. "Everything will need to be aired." She sorted the clothing and set it in piles on the coverlet: jackets and petticoats; robes à la française and robes à la polonaise; a riding habit; feathers and fichus; buckles and ribbons.

Aunt Dorothea ran her fingertips over the beading and embroidery and exclaimed over the abundance of bows. It was more thrilling than getting her gowns back after the mantua-maker had altered them to the latest styles. Susan had forgotten how much she loved color. Pink and red, yellow and purple mingled merrily on the blue coverlet.

Lucy lifted a pink silk gown from a trunk. A cascade of fine lace fell from the elbows. Susan and her aunt compared the effect of different stomachers against it. "You, my dear, will take everyone's breath away."

Her aunt said everyone, but her imagination chose Charles. He had never seen her wear anything half as grand. Rendering him speechless would be a fine little victory after all the difficulties he had given her. They settled on the stomacher embellished with Roman pearls.

"I'm glad you've brought ball gowns."

Susan waved toward the trunks. "I brought everything."

"Perfect. The burgesses are throwing a ball next week to celebrate Lady Dunmore's arrival."

Talk of society and engagements brought the usual bittersweet pull to Susan's heart. She longed to participate, to be in the swirl of people, but she needed to be responsible. That's what Mama needed. Except...Mama wasn't here. If her aunt delighted in a social calendar and wanted Susan to be her companion, it would be rude to refuse. Her heart tingled with hope. "Haven't the invitations already been sent? I wouldn't have been on their list."

"I was. Consider it a household invitation."

"I don't know..." A host liked to know who was coming in advance. Surprise guests were an unwelcome addition. She might need to wait until she had been introduced before joining her aunt's social events.

"Once everyone hears you've arrived, they'll be dying to meet you. It would be unforgivably rude to leave you home while I went to a ball."

"I'll be fine." She had years of practice in self-denial.

"Not rude to you, my dear. I was thinking of all those poor men who couldn't dance with you."

The ball was being thrown by the House of Burgesses. Charles needed to mingle with them if he hoped to be one of them someday. Her fingers brushed the ruffles down the front of her pink gown. She got the most compliments when she was wearing that. It might inspire Charles into one of his rare bursts of praise. "Are you certain they would expect us?"

"I am. But if it makes you feel better, I'll speak with Mrs. Randolph tomorrow and see if we can't get you a proper invitation."

"Please do." She had a sudden interest in Charles's career.

Fifteen

CLINGING TO CONSTANCY

Charles directed the driver south of town. The houses grew further apart, nearly swallowed up in the fields and forest. Miles before they would have reached Johnson Hall, they stopped in front of a white-washed house. A picket fence ran along the street, connecting the house to a workshop and enclosing a tidy side garden. He and the driver carried the trunk through the garden gates and rested it on the wide back porch.

He paid the driver and looked about. The leaves of the old apple trees fluttered in the spring breeze. Smoke rose lazily from the kitchen house. An old mare grazed in the pasture. Chickens scratched outside their coop. This was Virginia.

What would Susan think of it?

It was humble compared to the Blue House, but all the comforts of home were right here. She was a lady, but not too fine to be practical. If anyone could appreciate the industry of his dearest relations, it was her. She had, after all, insisted on an introduction to his oldest cousin, even knowing her father was a tradesman.

It would give him an excuse to call on her in a day or two. He needed to be the first man to do so before Quill or any other gentleman paid their respects. She was too handsome not to attract attention. And her aunt had all the best connections. He scowled. He couldn't compete with even a common sweet-talking suitor. He especially couldn't compete with ones that came from the finest families in the colony.

He just wanted to hear her voice every morning, to bring her flowers every spring, and to confide all his secrets in her alone. His impulsive heart pulled him along recklessly like a half-broke colt pulling a cart too fast. It was dangerous racing corners without knowing what was around them. What if she wilted in the summer climate? What if she didn't return his affection? What if his judgment was misplaced? He would call on her, but he wouldn't court her.

Not yet.

She deserved to know he was competent and established in his career. She needed to see the house she would manage. She needed to know she could live as comfortably in Virginia as she could in England. She needed time to make friends in the colony. She deserved to know she was more than a passing fancy for him. He deserved to know that, too.

He rested a hand on the rough trunk of an old apple tree. Small fruits clung to the branches, as green as the leaves around them. It would be months before they ripened. When they did, Aunt Charity would make her famous cider. He swallowed against the dust scratching his throat. All good things took time. He wouldn't bruise a relationship by trying to hasten it.

A pair of shoes was abandoned at the foot of the tree, with stockings and garters neatly tucked inside. His gaze traveled upward. Bare feet dangled above him. A young woman sat on a branch, so engrossed in a book that she hadn't noticed him. Her lips moved silently. Wispy blonde curls escaped from her cap, framing her face.

"You still read in trees?"

Emmeline startled at his voice and snapped her book closed. She stared in disbelief, then asked, "When did you get here?"

"Just now."

She tucked her book into a pocket and climbed to the lowest branch, where she seated herself. "Hand me my shoes, please."

Charles held them up. "I'm surprised you're not helping your mother in the kitchen."

Emmeline slipped her arms through her pocket slits to secure her stockings without exposing her bare legs. "I finished my chores early. Henrietta is learning to make vegetable pies."

The Henrietta he remembered was barely out of leading strings, but a lot could change in seven years. "How old are you, now?"

"Seventeen." She buckled her shoes. "My birthday was last week." She pushed off from the lowest branch, landing in an unladylike crouch. Standing, she dusted her petticoats. Seventeen made her almost a woman, but she was no taller than Quill. She would never achieve Susan's elegant stature, though she might aspire to more elegant manners.

"I would have helped you down."

"Oh." She blinked as if the possibility had not occurred to her. "Would you like something to drink?"

He cleared his throat. "Very much." He hadn't had anything since they'd left the ship. Mrs. Evans would have offered, but the driver had been waiting.

"Mama." Emmeline stepped into the kitchen, a small clapboard building a short walk from the dining hall in the main house. "We have a guest."

"What sort of guest?" Aunt Charity was a model of Virginian hospitality. She would feed any traveler who came to her door.

"An old one."

Aunt Charity looked out the open door. "Charles?!" Her voice leapt an octave in a single syllable.

A girl leaned around her mother. "Who?" Henrietta was as big now as Emmeline had been when he had left.

"Our cousin who's been in London," Emmeline explained.

Henrietta wrinkled her nose. He must look like a tramp after all that traveling. He would wash up before supper and brush his suit before calling on Susan tomorrow.

Aunt Charity hurried down the steps and handed him a tin cup. "This is such a surprise. I had no idea you were coming."

Charles drank the entire cup of lemonade like a drowning man breathes air. The tart beverage washed away the road dust that had been irritating his throat. "Neither did I. My father sent a grim letter predicting his death, and I packed up that very week. There was no time to write."

Emmeline refilled his cup.

"My brother was quite ill over the winter—apoplexy and a fever—but he pulled through."

"I ran into Quill on the way into town. He gave me the news." He drank the second cup slower, breathing between swallows.

"You'll...stay?" Emmeline asked hesitantly.

Charles nodded. "London was never my home. I only stayed as long as I did because my father encouraged it." Demanded might have been a more suitable word. His father had great hopes for his career. And Charles was too stubborn to return to the man who had sent him away. "Where's my uncle?"

"Working," Henrietta said in a saucy tone as if it were obvious. Aunt Charity gave her a scolding look.

Charles handed his empty cup to Emmeline. "I need to speak with him."

He opened the back door of the workshop. The sweet smell of wood shavings was as comfortable as an old banyan after a long day's work.

A man with graying hair looked up from the lathe and stared at him. "Charles! I was starting to think you would never come home." Uncle Rob covered the distance in two strides and gave Charles a fierce hug, covering his London suit in sawdust.

It was the sawdust in his eyes that made Charles tear up as he whispered, "I'm home now."

Seven years were covered in five minutes. Their letters had

already conveyed the essentials. A summary of the past two months occupied half an hour. The events were fresh on Charles's mind, and Uncle Rob was an active listener. Then he offered the old guest room before Charles asked for it. They carried the heavy trunk inside and up the stairs to his old room, across the hall from where Emmeline and Henrietta still slept, and set it under the window.

"Thanks," Charles said, panting from the exertion. His library of law books was heavy. He looked about the old room. There was the drafty fireplace and the old desk, just the way he remembered them. On his best school holidays, he stayed here. Back then, the bed had been a rustic pine frame. Charles had carved animal faces into the posts without asking for permission. Uncle Rob should have whipped him for it. He never had. This bed was new. He ran his fingers over the smooth oak frame, expertly turned and beveled. "When did you find time to make this?"

"About a year ago, when your aunt insisted I make time for it."

Charles fell back on the feather mattress. The ropes underneath were strung tight. The canopy and curtains were a crisp new fabric, white with blue flowers. He stretched luxuriously. "I will never sleep in a hammock again."

"You stay here as long as you want. I'm just happy you're home."

It had been a long, long journey. His muscles relaxed into the mattress, but something kept his mind alert. There was one more thing he needed to do today. He reluctantly sat up. "Uncle Rob? Do you have some old copies of the *Gazette*? I haven't seen the news since London."

"Let me see." He crossed the hall to the girls' room and stooped before the clothespress. "I thought so." He pulled out a thick stack of broadsides and thumbed through them. "Emmeline's always rescuing old papers bound for the fire." He handed the stack to Charles. "That's about six months' worth of news. Will that do?"

"Thank you. That's more than enough." He set aside the broadsides published before the Boston incident in December. The breeze ruffled the pages. He unlocked his trunk and weighted the stack down with a book.

"I need to get back to work," his uncle said. "I'll see you at supper."

"That sounds nice." Breakfast on the *Minerva* had been ages ago.

Uncle Rob's footsteps faded down the stairs while Charles read the papers. By supper, he had five months of evidence in support of the argument he had been forming. His countrymen had written and talked about Boston over and over. The broadsides were full of rational Virginian analyses of rash New England actions. No local mobs were disrupting the peace. Nothing had changed in his absence. Williamsburg would never be like Boston.

What he had told Susan was true. They were safe.

Sixteen

UPROOTED

The fragrance of tea pulled her into consciousness. *That's nice,* she thought drowsily. Charles had made tea this morning. She had fallen asleep wanting to ask him something. What was it? She opened her eyes. A tester of blue toile stretched above a luxuriously wide bed. Sunlight streamed through large rectangular windows. A pewter breakfast tray was at the desk beside the Delft vase.

Charles hadn't made tea. He wasn't here, and the lovely columbine he had given her had shriveled overnight. Their beautiful vase full of water wasn't enough. They belonged in the woods where he had found them. *Ubi bene ibi patria.* One's country is where one is well.

"Good morning, Miss Bailey." Lucy opened the wardrobe.

Susan sat up and yawned. "Morning, Lucy." She moved to the desk. There would be no turn about the deck this morning. No breathtaking sunset this evening. No cozy conversations to look forward to. She should feel happy to be safely at her destination, not empty.

She spread butter across a slice of warm bread. She hadn't come to Virginia for a holiday. She had come to keep Isaac out of trouble. It didn't matter to her where Charles was or what he did, as long as he kept his promise to call on her from time to time. She set the knife down and tore a piece of bread. It was soft against her palm. There was no need to dip it in her tea to make it edible. Taking a slow bite, she closed her eyes. It was as airy as a cloud. She left no room for longing as she satiated herself.

"Are you ready to get dressed, miss?" Lucy had already made the bed and laid out her clothes.

"Yes." Now that the drab traveling clothes were banished, she couldn't wait to dress. "I can't believe I slept so late. What will my aunt think?" She raised her arms so Lucy could pull the stays over her head.

"She said to let you sleep." Lucy pulled the laces until the stays were comfortably snug. "She's busy with callers."

"I should join her." Three days of playing the lazy guest, and her aunt would already be wishing her gone. "Do you know who has called this morning? Mr. Morris promised he would come."

"So did Mr. Johnson." Lucy tied a ruffled petticoat over the panniers.

"Hmm? He did, didn't he? I nearly forgot." She glanced at the door. People were talking, things were happening, and she was trapped in her room, unable to do anything. And then Lucy peered out the curtains as though she had never seen a robin before and would watch one all morning. There would be time for that later. Susan bit back a scold and closed her eyes. *In her tongue is the law of kindness.* Some days her favorite proverb was easier to live than others, but her loyal maid had been just as inconvenienced by their voyage as she had been. She released the breath she had been holding. "You're free to go exploring this morning once I'm dressed."

Lucy grabbed the sprigged muslin jacket from the bed. "I'm so sorry, miss. I thought I saw something."

"I can't get enough of trees and flowers, and birds either. I don't know how sailors do it."

Lucy pinned the edges of the jacket over a rose pink stomacher. "Sailors can't always be getting more than they deserve."

The heated words were spoken loud enough to be heard beyond the bedchamber.

"Did something happen between you and our navigator?"

"In all the years I've been with you, have I ever given you a reason to doubt my virtue?"

"No." Dave was the first man she'd seen even coax a smile from her maid. "I didn't mean that as an accusation, Lucy."

Lucy styled her hair in severe silence. Susan left her tidying the room and followed more genial voices down the stairs and into the parlor.

Aunt Dorothea reigned from the parlor settee in a lilac gown that matched her hair. "Ah, Susan, I was just telling Mrs. Yates about you. Mrs. Yates, this is my niece, Miss Bailey."

Susan curtsied.

Mrs. Yates lifted her chin so high she could look down her nose at Susan. "She's certainly well-fed, isn't she?" If this was the American bluntness her neighbors had warned her about, it was going to be a long year.

Aunt Dorothea turned the conversation. "Any news on your daughter? It must be getting close to her time."

A phaeton stopped beyond the parlor window, driven by a man with grizzly hair. "Drat," Mrs. Yates said. "It's the colonel. I'll be on my way before the war stories begin." She abruptly took her leave and whisked out of the house.

"I'm sorry about that. Mrs. Yates is always saying something regrettable."

"It's nothing," Susan said, eager to end the discussion before it became awkward. "I wanted to apologize for sleeping so late. I promise I won't keep doing so."

"You've had a long journey," Aunt Dorothea said. "When I arrived in Virginia, I wanted nothing more than to sleep for a week." She stood as the next callers entered. "Colonel and Mrs. Hendriks. How nice to see you again. How is your health?"

"Same as always," the colonel said, leaning on his cane as he limped into the room. "I could complain, but I won't."

"May I present my niece, Miss Susan Bailey?"

Mrs. Hendriks dropped her mouth in delightful surprise. "Surely you told me it was the nephew you were expecting."

"I did. Isaac arrived last night with my beautiful niece." Aunt Dorothea squeezed her shoulder as though she had wanted her.

"How wonderful for you," Mrs. Hendriks said.

It *was* wonderful. Surprising and wonderful. Susan would make certain her aunt's faith in her wasn't misplaced. She would be her favorite niece. She took a seat, enjoying the cheerful prattle between her aunt and the callers, listening for hints to guide her in pleasing Aunt Dorothea. It was turning into a lovely morning until the stairs creaked with footsteps, and Isaac entered the parlor in his banyan and bare feet. Susan closed her eyes in mortification.

"And this must be the nephew," Mrs. Hendriks said, as though nothing was shocking about bare feet in the parlor.

"Oh, no. Don't stand, Colonel." Aunt Dorothea waved him back to his seat. "If Mr. Bailey isn't going to stand on ceremony, neither are we. Have you had your breakfast, Isaac?"

"Yes, ma'am. Thank you."

"What brings you to Virginia, Mr. Bailey?" Mrs. Hendriks asked.

Isaac opened his mouth, but the colonel spoke first. "What brings any young man to Virginia? A healthy sense of adventure." He tapped his cane for emphasis. "Am I right, lad?"

"Indeed. I wanted to see the world, and Aunt Dorothea graciously invited me to see it from here."

"No better place. No better food. Now, Mrs. Evans, when we next come over for dinner, that apple custard tart—"

"You know perfectly well that's out of season. And you're always happy with anything Maurice cooks."

"Aren't we all?" Mrs. Hendriks said. "You say he's from France, but I say he's heaven-sent."

"Your cook isn't...African?" Susan ventured.

"Oh, no. I was very particular with Mr. Evans that I wanted a

French cook. They have such a way with eggs. It took us a few years to find him, but he was worth the wait."

Susan glanced toward the hall. No doubt, Graves was hovering near the door, waiting for the next callers. "Do you have other French servants?"

"Just Maurice. Most of my servants are Black, though I'm not opposed to a good indented one."

Aunt Dorothea had servants, not slaves. Susan felt a wave of relief. "Are you looking for any? We met a charming family on the *Minerva* who would love to be placed together."

"I'm sorry, dear. I don't have a need for anyone right now, much less a whole family."

If only Susan knew this community like she knew Eversley. She would have no trouble arranging a comfortable situation for the Finlays.

Isaac pulled out the harpsichord seat. "What kind of action have you seen, Colonel?"

The colonel slapped his right leg. "Went out to the frontier during the war with the French. Never been able to walk on it since, but we did get Quebec, so it's a fair trade."

Isaac snorted a laugh. Susan would read him a lecture on company manners.

After a leisurely chat and an impromptu tea, Mrs. Hendriks took their leave. "We have a few more calls to make. I expect your next few mornings will be busy, as everyone comes to look in on your niece and nephew."

When Colonel and Mrs. Hendriks left, Susan paced in front of the window. After weeks of travel, she had arrived at her destination, yet she was as restless as a bird.

"Are you waiting for someone?" Aunt Dorothea asked.

"No, of course not. Whom would I know here?"

"Charles," Isaac said. He was a provoking little brother.

"He said he'd call," Aunt Dorothea said comfortingly.

Susan didn't need comfort. "There's no hurry." She would be here all year.

"I don't know that he feels that way. He seemed quite attentive."

"Still following the captain's orders," Isaac said.

Susan stopped pacing. "What do you mean?"

"The captain told him to keep an eye on you. Wanted the sailors to know you had more than one protector."

Something sank deep inside her. She kept her words light. "When was this?"

"The day we left England."

Ever since they had met. Her reluctant friend had only ever seen her as a chore. "Oh." Some women were loved for who they were. She was loved for what she did. Except even then, she sometimes fell short. "Please excuse me. I've been cooped up for weeks and fancy a turn about the gardens just now." She wasn't going to wait in the parlor for him to call on her. She wasn't going to wait for him at all.

"There's no need to stand on formality. You're more than guests. You're my family. Enjoy the gardens whenever you please."

"Thank you, ma'am." Then she turned to her brother. "Isaac, do get dressed before you embarrass yourself further." Then she swept out of the parlor and to the back door, which opened off the dining hall. Susan's hand was on the knob when she heard loud voices through the open windows.

"I'd never know when you were telling the truth!" Lucy spoke in a tone of passionate desperation that surprised Susan.

"I didn' lie ter yeh." That was Dave, the navigator from the *Minerva*. What was he doing here?

She couldn't take a turn about the gardens without intruding on their intimate conversation, so she stood in the shadowed part of the dining hall and spied through the window. There was nothing to see. A robin flew from the rose garden. The kitchen, painted a deep blue to match the house, had the door propped open. But at the very back of the property was a wide pergola, covered with honeysuckle so thick it could easily hide two lovers... or two enemies.

Susan felt uneasy about eavesdropping, but she couldn't in good conscience allow her maid to be unchaperoned with a man... even if that maid was a decade older than she was. Besides, if they wanted to keep their conversation to themselves, they should have lowered their voices. Maurice, in the kitchen, couldn't help overhearing as well.

"You lied to me every day with every action and every sweet word that fell from your lips."

His reply was muffled. It was a good thing Susan had seen and heard them on the *Minerva*. Otherwise, she might think Lucy meant more than she surely did. She might think more of the muffled silence than she did. But no one was more precise and particular than Lucy. She wasn't one to compromise her morals. Especially with someone she was angry with.

As the silence stretched, it grew so loud she could only hear the truth—even Lucy could be loved for who she was. Why couldn't Susan? Why did she have to work so hard to earn what came easily to others? What was wrong with her?

Alone in the shadows, tears spilled from the brokenness she hid from the light.

Seventeen

ACCOMPLISHMENTS

A cool breeze teased Charles with bread, warm from the baker's oven. In his haste to get to the office before Quill, he had declined breakfast. With keys came responsibility. He turned the lock and pushed the door open.

The room was already furnished. There was a large desk, a tall bookcase weighted with law books, and a Windsor chair with a writing arm. Oil paintings brightened the walls. The office was complete. Had Quill even considered the available space before inviting him to share it? He meant well. He always did. But if the ancients had known his friend as he had, they would have included impulsiveness in their list of cardinal sins, alongside pride, greed, anger, and envy. It caused as much chaos as the other vices.

He adjusted the strap of his haversack. It was filled with supplies from his London office: an inkwell, a goodly supply of ink, and paper. It would be a relief to leave the heavy bag here. But there was no sense in leaving it in an office he couldn't share.

He had hoped to have his affairs in order by the time he called on Susan. She would be hesitant enough to leave her family. She deserved to know she could trust him to provide for all her needs. He would ask around, but it was unlikely he could find another office that morning. Certainly not on the easy terms Quill had promised. It would be a waste of his savings until he had paying briefs, and only a fool would hire a barrister with no understanding of the local laws. He would need to buy his own library.

The brief optimism he had enjoyed that morning sputtered out like a candle in the rain. He couldn't even go seeking a new place until he had returned the key. He cursed his friend's thoughtless generosity and pulled a book from the shelf. The least he could do was begin studying. After ten pages, he gave up. He did have other plans for his morning. Did Quill always begin work this late? When they had boarded together at William and Mary, he had dragged him out of bed countless times. He would repeat the favor now, except he hadn't thought to ask him about his lodging arrangements.

Charles opened the door and looked down the street. Mayhap Quill had expected to meet him elsewhere. For all he knew, his friend had ridden off to Johnson Hall and asked his father where to find him. He groaned. They really should have discussed this better. He had been so stunned by the news that he hadn't been in a sensible state of mind.

Above the town noise, a woman's voice cried, "Mr. Johnson!" Across the street, Miss Polly Morris waved from an upper window. "Wait for me." Then she disappeared. A minute later, she crossed the road. "Quill asked me ta keep an eye out for ye. I must ha' missed ye going in. What do ye think of our office?"

"It's quite—our?"

"Aye. Didna Quill tell ye? I'm his scribe."

"His scribe and his housekeeper? Is that what he meant?"

"Aye. Who else would he mean? Catriona is married. She couldna do it. And the other girls are home."

Every scribe he had ever met was a young boy whose parents hoped he would make the law his career. He had never heard of the position being filled by a woman, but was it any more peculiar than the sisters and daughters who worked the anvil in the smithy? If a woman wasn't born to privilege, she was born to work. "I suppose Quill is still too boyish to manage a child himself."

Polly had the dangerous look of a female who had just been insulted. "What is that supposed ta mean?"

"It means he offered to share an office that has no room for me."

She snorted and pushed past him. "Men have no imagination. We just need to rearrange things." She pointed to a wall. "If we move Quill's desk there, then the bookcase can fit where his desk is, and my chair can go beside it. That leaves nearly half the room for ye."

"But then the bookcase will block your view of—" he waved a hand toward the landscape. "Of whatever that is."

"The beach near Applecross. *Máthair* painted it. And don't be ridiculous. We can hang it somewhere else. Here, grab the desk." She grasped one end and looked expectantly at him.

He had his doubts about her plan for rearranging the office, but was too much a gentleman to stand by and watch while a lady moved furniture, so he obeyed. Once the desk was situated to her satisfaction, she moved Quill's chair so he moved hers—the Windsor with a writing arm. They were unloading the tall book-case when Quill wandered in.

"That's different," he said, looking about with benign curios-ity. "What are ye movin' things about for?"

Charles hefted another stack of leather-bound books from the shelf to the floor. "You invited me to share your office. Or did you forget?"

"I didna forget." He opened the windows. "Are we making space for yer desk?"

"Aye," Polly said. "Once we put the bookcase where your desk was, then his desk will fit over there."

"That's a clever arrangement."

Charles wiped the sweat from his brow. "Where have you been all morning?"

"I had some business at the coffee shop. I told Polly ta watch for ye. Here, let me help with that." He pulled another stack of books from the shelves.

Charles shook his head. Staying cross with Quill once he entered a room was like shooting lightning on a sunny day. It was against the laws of nature laid down during the creation: the separation of night and day, clouds and sea, Quill and anger. God spoke, and it was so. "Do you know where I might hire a desk?"

"There's a cabinetmaker a few blocks down who often has a few things for hire. I would try him."

After they had moved the bookcase and reshelved the books, Charles followed Quill's directions. He nearly thanked the Lord when the cabinetmaker showed him a slant-front desk returned to him the day before. The wood was worn around the corners, but everything else about it was perfect. The hinges that let the desktop down were as sturdy as the Old Dominion. Every drawer had a lock, and when it was closed, the desk would lock as well. It came with the most comfortable wood chair he had ever sat upon. The only problem was the fee. In a few short months, he would pay enough to buy one at auction. Rather than hire it, he negotiated a purchase price. He signed a contract to pay in full by the next day, and then supervised its delivery.

It fit beautifully in the space Polly had dictated. She had moved the beach painting to fill the void from the bookcase. With the pride of ownership, he emptied his haversack and arranged his paper and inkwell. This was his. "I have some more business to attend to today, but I'll be here for a full day's studying first thing tomorrow. Or do you usually start work this late?"

"I didna start late. I told ye, I had work at the coffee shop. But if I'm not here when ye arrive in the morning, come bang on my door and I'll lend ye the key."

His final errand before calling on Susan was at the printer's. The *Gazette* had advertised several properties in recent weeks. Charles inquired of Mrs. Rind after the prices and terms. Following some mental calculations, he realized it would take a year or two of well-paid briefs before he could afford a house in town. His frustration led to a lengthy conversation about the depreciating value of tobacco notes and the ongoing shortage of British coin. It would take even longer to save the money if half his clients paid in old notes and bartered goods.

By the time he was home, brushing his brown jacket, it was later than he had planned. He discarded the notion of asking Emmeline to change into her Sunday best. Today was for laying the foundation of trust. He had made preparations for business, had looked into purchasing a home, and would keep his promise to introduce one of his relations. If his cousin had a streak of vanity, asking her to change might delay him too much to call today. That was unthinkable. He had never gone this long without seeing Susan. Not since the day they had met.

He pulled on the jacket and studied his reflection, wondering what she would think. It would have to do. He opened the door. Emmeline was sitting on the floor of her bedchamber, tying a string around a bouquet.

"Is that for Su—Miss Bailey?" Now that they were in civilization, he would remember to speak of her more formally.

"I think so." She looked quizzically at the bouquet. "Does she like flowers?"

It hadn't occurred to him that any woman wouldn't. "I believe so." The doubt in her voice worried him. What if Susan hadn't liked the columbine? He should find out before the next time he gave her something. Did she like flowers? Townhouses? Williamsburg? Him in brown? Him at all? His sudden anxiety was making him seasick. "Get your hat. It's getting late for callers."

She stood and tugged at her shortgown. "Shouldn't I change?"

"Don't worry about your appearance. Miss Bailey is a pragmatic woman. She won't judge you by your clothing."

It was a two-mile walk to the Blue House. After being cramped on the *Minerva* for so long, it was wonderful to stretch his legs with Emmeline on his arm. She swung the bouquet, content with silence until a flash of red flew across their path. "I always imagine Ariel as a cardinal."

Charles was silently rehearsing everything he needed to do to gain Susan's trust. He was bewildered by Emmeline's abrupt comment. "Who?"

"The spirit trapped in a pine tree," she said dreamily. "In *The Tempest*."

"Shakespeare?"

"Mmhmm."

The works of Shakespeare belonged in classrooms or on stage, not walking down the streets of Williamsburg. "Do you read a lot of Shakespeare?"

"Not a lot. We only have five of his plays."

If she talked about them like this, five was more than enough. "Ariel is a spirit. Not a bird. More importantly, he isn't real. People don't talk about things that aren't real. They just read about them for amusement."

"Oh." The bouquet dropped to her side. Her head ducked, hiding her face under her straw hat.

He nearly regretted his words, but someone had to tell her. If her brothers had lived, they would have told her as much long ago. Such imaginings were childish. She needed to know what was real. He cleared his throat. "Mr. and Miss Bailey are visiting their aunt. This is their first time in Virginia, so they don't know anyone. She especially wanted to meet you."

There was a long silence. Then she said, "Did you know them in London?"

"No. They lived in the country. We were on the same ship back to Virginia."

"Is that how you became acquainted?"

"It was. I roomed with her brother. On such a small ship, we couldn't help being thrown into each other's company." For once, luck had been on his side. "She has pretty manners, but her education was more substantial than book learning and useless accomplishments. She saved a woman's life." Susan would be an improving acquaintance. Her influence might help Emmeline learn the poise and practical skills that a notable housewife should have. She couldn't continue to live on the froth of imagination.

The town streets were crowded with wagons and carriages, stray dogs and stray children. A man looked up as they approached, his eyes lingering on Emmeline so long, Charles scowled until he returned to his business. The girl beside him was still, at heart, the innocent child he had left behind, oblivious to the stares of every bounder in Williamsburg. It was bad enough that a woman like Susan needed protection. It was worse that a youth like Emmeline attracted the same dangers.

He pulled her closer to himself. "You don't ever come into town alone, do you?"

"Hardly ever. I take Henrietta."

Charles could well imagine how much help her little sister would be at discouraging the wrong sort of attention. As much as he admired his uncle, Charles couldn't admire this. There were many luxuries the Gardiner family had to do without, but ensuring the security of their daughters wasn't a luxury. It was a necessity.

"Now that I'm home, there's no need to use Henrietta as an escort. Give me your errands or let me walk you into town."

Emmeline smiled in amusement, not appreciation. "As you wish."

Should he tell her? No. Let her be amused. He wouldn't spoil what was left of her girlhood with tales of briefs he had failed to win. She had several years before she needed to be thinking about men. The way she looked at the world, like she was in a dream, was proof she wasn't a woman yet.

"Where did you say your office was?"

"At the north end of town. I was afraid it wouldn't work out. Quill—Mr. Morris—he often doesn't think things through. When he offered to share an office, he didn't think about whether there was enough space. We had to move everything around so my desk would fit."

They rounded a corner. "There's the Blue House." He was pleased that Susan had an affectionate aunt so creditably established in town. It would ease the pain of separation from her family in England.

"It's awfully nice." Emmeline's steps slowed.

It was nice. Not as grand as Johnson Hall, but fine enough to persuade any Englishwoman of the beauty of Virginia. Harpsichord music drifted through an open window. Susan might be listening in the parlor. He lengthened his stride and rapped on the door.

Graves answered. It was three steps from there to the parlor. Still in the foyer, he could see the performance. A fine lady in pearls and an extravagant silk gown was playing the harpsichord masterfully. Charles had seen enough of society through his colleagues at Lincoln's Inn to recognize high class when he saw it. Young ladies of quality would barely speak with a provincial lawyer, much less his cousins in the trades. If this woman was a frequent visitor to the Blue House, Charles hoped she would at least be kind to Susan.

Her song finished. Mrs. Evans clapped, and the young lady's brown eyes met Charles'. She smiled without warmth or familiarity. It was a society smile: polite and distant. A brick dropped through his stomach. He was unable to smile back. "That was beautifully done, Miss Bailey. I had no idea you were so accomplished."

Eighteen

PATRONIZING

When she had given up hope of seeing him today, he had come. When she had made up her mind never to look for him again, he had come. She had left her tears in the shadows, where all tears belonged. In the sunlight, she was obliged to greet him with a smile. He didn't return the favor. Instead, he regarded her with chilling solemnity.

She wasn't asking him to be in love. She was simply hoping for a little return on the kindness she had invested. If he couldn't manage admiration, she would settle for old-fashioned friendliness, but he was as warm as a stone bench on a winter day. She asked, a little too brightly, "Who is this with you?"

He startled and looked about, surprised to see someone on his arm. "Oh, this is my cousin, Miss Gardiner. Emmeline, this is Mrs. Evans, Miss Bailey, and Mr. Bailey."

It was impossible for a lady as fluent in fashion as Susan was not to notice Miss Gardiner's unfortunate appearance. Her shortgown was painfully small. The waist was too high, and the fabric strained at the bust, where a single pin valiantly held the gown together. What may have fit her well at fourteen was unsuitable for the woman she was becoming. It was past time to set the garment aside for her younger sister.

If she had been her relation, Susan would have escorted her to the nearest mantua-maker and commissioned something cut to her figure. Surely Charles's mother would have assisted her if she were still living. It was too much to expect of his father. Men didn't understand the importance of these details.

Miss Gardiner handed her a small bouquet. "How do you do?" Her voice was whisper-soft. Then she stared as though she had never seen a silk gown before.

The poor dear.

"I'm well, thank you for the flowers. The Virginia climate is lovely, though I hear summer can be a trial. What about you? Are you in good health?"

"Yes, ma'am." The answer was correct, but it was spoken with the tone of a young maid nervous about her position. She might be a tradesman's daughter, but she was also Charles's cousin. A little deference was charming. Too much, and she would be mistaken for a serving girl.

"Come," she took her arm and led her to the settee. "I've hardly spoken to another woman in months. You must tell me all about yourself." Susan's vast petticoat, gathered à la polonaise, spilled over the cushions.

Miss Gardiner sat primly against the other end, taking as little space as possible, as though painfully aware she did not belong here. "I don't know what to say." She would have to be coaxed into conversation.

"Have you lived in Virginia your whole life?"

"Yes, Miss Bailey. I was born here and have never traveled much."

"Already, we are so much alike. My mother's health is poor, and she dislikes travel exceedingly. She could not understand why I was coming to Virginia."

Miss Gardiner nodded hesitantly.

"You never went to London or Bath?" Charles interrupted their quiet conversation.

"Rarely. I went to London for a season when I was twenty, and we've been to Bath a few times when my mother felt it would improve her health. It is a pity we didn't meet the season I was in London."

He frowned. "It seems we did not move in the same circles." He was as cold as the week they had met. She didn't know what had undone their weeks of easy companionship.

Miss Gardiner's gaze had wandered to the bookcase.

"Have you read any of those?" The words were out of her mouth before she realized how unlikely it was. A young woman of such humble circumstances would have been just educated enough to read the Bible and her prayer book.

Miss Gardiner crossed the room and crouched beside the books. "*Hamlet, The Tempest, Macbeth.* I've read those. Not *Antony and Cleopatra* or *The Taming of the Shrew.* Yes, *Pilgrim's Progress* and *The Governess.*" Her fingers brushed the spines reverently. "Some of these I've never heard of."

"You like to read?" She could have just led with that when Susan had asked her about herself.

"Whenever I can."

"So does my sister. She's about your age. Her governess is constantly getting her away from her books so she doesn't strain her eyes."

"She has a governess?" Miss Gardiner asked with an awe that proved she had never been subjected to one. "What does she learn?"

"To take long walks and not spend all her time reading. She also plays several instruments."

"Does she play the harpsichord?"

"Yes, with more diligent practice, she will become truly accomplished."

"Like you."

Susan was surprised by the quiet admiration of this young woman. "Do you enjoy music?"

"I do."

"Do you sing?" She wouldn't have been trained, but Susan was prepared to flatter anything but the most dismal performance.

"Only for myself, but I do play guitar."

"You learned an instrument?" She continued to surprise her. Her education was far superior to what her clothing and manners had led Susan to believe. She just needed a woman's guiding hand. She needed a patroness, and Susan needed a sister. "We must have a concert. You bring your guitar and I'll play the harpsichord, and the gentlemen will have to compose flattering things to say about our accomplishments." She tossed a smile to Charles.

He shook his head, his brow lined. Something was wrong with Charles, and this time, Susan didn't know the cure.

"It has been far too long since I heard a guitar," Isaac said, smiling warmly at Miss Gardiner. She dropped her eyes and pressed back into the settee.

Yes, she needed training in the social graces, but they needed to win her trust first. She couldn't lend any of her aunt's books, but she had one of her own to spare. "Have you read *Robinson Crusoe*?"

"No, miss, but I've heard of it."

"Who hasn't? It's one of the greatest works of this century." Susan spoke warmly of a book that had failed to hold her attention. "I would like to lend you my copy."

Miss Gardiner's eyes grew round. They were a lovely color, a little more blue than Charles's. "Oh. I—" She shook her head decisively. "No, thank you."

"No?"

"I couldn't."

Susan read people better than she read books. She was either too frightened to borrow something so valuable, or she was too proud to accept charity.

"That's a pity," Susan said with affected remorse. "I was so looking forward to discussing it with someone."

The light returned to her eyes. She was wavering.

"But I would hate to force a book on anyone. I wouldn't dare. I believe outside of school, books should be read only for pleasure, don't you?"

"I enjoy reading," Emmeline said. "It wouldn't be any trouble."

"Are you certain? Because it would mean a lot to me."

"I'd be happy to."

"Wait here. It's in my room."

It took her a minute to find where Lucy had put it away. It was hiding in the desk drawer. As she returned to the parlor, she heard Charles's voice. "That's quite a large estate."

"The biggest in thirty miles," Isaac said.

Good heavens. She hadn't been gone long enough for her brother to babble about her dowry, had she? The last thing she needed was for every backwoods Virginian to come courting her. Since she wouldn't marry any of them, her dowry was none of their business. Not even Charles's. The conviction bandaged her pride, still wounded from Isaac's revelation that morning.

He prattled on. "Much of it is wide open countryside. I have a ginger gelding I ride on fine days."

"Fine days in England?" Charles asked. "So, about twice a year?"

Mrs. Evans laughed appreciatively. "There's nothing lovelier than a May day in an open carriage. My husband and I would take the phaeton out every day. Mr. Johnson, you should borrow it and show my niece about town."

Susan's cheeks burned with humiliation, but she kept her chin high as she said to Charles, "There's no need to trouble yourself."

"It's too late for that." His gray-blue eyes were solemn. "Is Saturday agreeable for you?"

She squeezed the book tightly with both hands. How could she accept when he had just admitted she was trouble to him? On the other hand, how could she refuse without an excuse? And she was so newly arrived she couldn't even pretend to have other plans. "Yes." Then she handed the book to his cousin and ignored him until, at last, he took his leave.

Nineteen

JOHNSON HALL

The picture Charles had created of a modest family, teetering on the brink of middling society, shattered. The property Isaac would inherit was the largest within thirty miles of their home. Susan's father had hired masters to teach her music and art. He didn't dare ask, but doubtless, she had a sizable dowry waiting for her marriage to an eligible man.

With her poise, her grace, her accomplishments, and wealthy connections, she deserved to marry a baron or at least a knight. A woman so desirable must have had dozens of marriage offers by her age. What were those men like, the ones she had rejected already? How many barristers and clergymen had been dismissed?

Or had he been the first one foolish enough to try?

Kindness wasn't love any more than coincidences were miracles. There was nothing personal or preferential in the way she had treated him. He had simply been the closest thing to a gentleman on the *Minerva*. An acquaintance, welcome only when there was no one else around. What a fool he had been. He had mistaken a rhinestone for a ruby.

He opened the garden gate and waited for Emmeline to pass. She looked at him with concern. "Are you feeling well?"

"I'm fine," he said firmly. The hurt was too intermingled with embarrassment to share. "Just tired. The beds on land don't rock you to sleep." His stomach growled. "And I'm hungry."

"Me too. I hope dinner is ready when we get home."

Sitting through a meal would give his uncle too many opportunities to ask about his luckless visit in front of the whole family. It had been a mistake, telling his uncle as much as he had. And there was one more thing he needed to do today.

He stood outside the open workshop door. "Uncle Rob, may I borrow the horse? I still need to visit my father."

Uncle Rob nodded. "The bay is in the pasture. Will we see you at supper?"

"I don't know." He followed his nose to the kitchen. A dozen vegetable pies were steaming on the kitchen table. They were the kind sealed in a tough pastry coffin that would preserve them for a fortnight on the pantry shelf until some traveler begged hospitality. Aunt Charity was nowhere in sight. Charles snatched one and ate it behind the stable, tossing the tough pastry in the pig's trough when he was done. His stomach satisfied, he saddled the bay and headed south to Johnson Hall, his mind full of Susan.

He had thought their time together was enough to understand her character. He had asked about her family, her childhood, and her life. He had neglected to ask about her rank. Her wealth. Her power and privilege. And she was too fine to mention such things when she hadn't been asked.

Two days ago, he had been questioning the prudence of his attachment. He had doubted his ability to woo a woman so in love with a home so far away. He didn't have flowery words or fine gifts to offer. All he could give was a lifetime of work and the promise that she would never fall into poverty. To a woman who had never known want, it was a cheap trinket, easily discarded for something finer.

After an hour of tortured thoughts, he spied the remains of his grandmother's split-rail fence, collapsed and overgrown with bushes. He turned down a dirt road, wide enough for one carriage. The bay's hooves clopped noisily on the bridge as they crossed a small ravine. Johnson Hall, freshly whitewashed, sat at the top of a rise. A handsome portico now framed the entry. There was no hint of neglect or disrepair. His father managed fine without him. But there would be no impressing Susan. Her home was grander by far. Isaac had told him all he needed to know.

He stood on the porch a full minute, inspecting the new columns and listening, like a child still vulnerable to his father's moods. But no voices charged through the open windows. He quietly opened the door and crept into the foyer, a stranger in his childhood home.

A thin old woman with thin old hair sat by the parlor window. Granny was more frail than he remembered. He pulled a chair beside her and sat down. She turned piercing blue eyes on him and pointed out the window with a shaking finger. "That dog has been chasing its tail all morning."

"So it has," Charles said, who hadn't noticed the dog before now.

"And who are you?"

He felt a sinking in his midsection. "Who am I? I'm your favorite grandson, Charles." It was an easy claim. He was her only grandson still living.

"Oh, you are, are you?" She didn't know, didn't care, that he had finally returned. In his absence, he had lost more than a mother.

"Of course I am."

"I think that dog is hungry. It keeps chasing the chickens."

He sighed, releasing his last hope for Johnson Hall in one long breath. "Yes, ma'am."

A fly buzzed about his head, then landed on the wall, above a young girl with skin as brown as Susan's eyes. She was dressed for housework, with a simple petticoat and shortgown. She watched the fly creep across the family portrait, frowning in concentration as her tongue wriggled in the gap where a front tooth used to be.

"Master Charles?" A dark man in gray livery stepped into the room. "Is that you?"

"Yes, Gideon." He stood, eye-to-eye with the footman who had hidden childish scrapes from his father's notice. "It's good to see a familiar face."

"It's been a long time. You're all grown up."

"I came as soon as I received the letter. My father, how is he?"

Gideon glanced down the hallway. "He was quite ill when he wrote. He almost didn't make it through. We had begun to hope —" Gideon clamped his mouth shut and looked at the floor.

The sheen of polish over the old scratches and scuffs gave the floor a refinement it did not deserve. His breath suspended, smothered by unutterable hopes until he blurted, "Begun to hope what?" The words echoed in his ears.

"Hope that he would recover, sir. Kitty, stop fidgeting."

The girl's tongue disappeared, and her head dropped. "Yes, sir."

Gideon glanced at Charles. "My granddaughter, sir. The daughter of your old nurse."

Charles raised his eyebrows. "I had no idea. Is she still around?"

Gideon frowned. "There have not been children at Johnson Hall since you grew. She was sold when Kitty was two. Excuse me, sir. Mr. Johnson will be displeased if I do not announce you promptly."

"Of course." He studied the quiet girl, trying to see a resemblance to his old nurse. It was there in the breadth of her nose and her sparkling, dark eyes. Perhaps she would resemble her mother more when she was grown.

Uneven footsteps echoed down the hall. His father smiled crookedly into the parlor. "Charles! Our London man. What took you so long?" The words slurred as if his tongue were as crooked as his smile.

Charles didn't meet his eyes. "I came as soon as I heard." He should have seen his father before setting up his office or settling in with the Gardiners. Wasn't his father the reason he had come home?

"The doctor thought they were going to lose me over the winter. That's when I wrote you. But I weathered through. Sit down, boy. Let's talk about your future."

Charles sank into a hard chair. "I have an office in town, and I'll start reading up on the local laws tomorrow."

"Excellent, boy. Excellent start. Now, George Wythe is clerk for the House of Burgesses. You need to make his acquaintance. I've already dropped a word in his ear about you a couple of times."

"I can't be a burgess."

"Not yet, you can't, and you'll never be if you don't make the right connections."

Charles wrestled with filial duty. It wasn't right, proper, or comfortable to introduce himself to his betters. But his father was telling him to. "Yes, sir."

"You're London-educated. You'll have opportunities I could only dream of, boy. You'll make our family proud and respected."

Charles grimaced. He had seen enough of the world to know that a little more education in one place or another would not change the class he had been born into. "I've done nothing you would be ashamed of."

"Good. You're about old enough to be thinking of marrying. Didn't leave a sweetheart behind in England, did you?"

"No. I wasn't courting anyone." And he wouldn't be courting anyone now. He needed to forget his fancy for the elegant and unattainable Susan Bailey.

"Good. Well, I've been looking about, seeing who might be suitable. Made a list, I did. Where is that?"

Charles watched helplessly as his father pulled a sheet of paper from the sideboard.

"Here we go. Miss Priscilla Ray. Lives up in New Kent. Just inherited twenty acres when her father passed away last year. Miss Verity Lyndon. Down in Norfolk. They say her grandfather wrote a generous will. Won't be a sure thing 'till he passes, but he's mighty sickly. Could be any time."

As his father rattled off the list, slurring the name of every *feme sole*, Charles wondered how he had acquired all this personal information. Had there been any discretion in his pursuit of knowledge, or had he developed a reputation as a mercenary?

"Miss Faith Ingram—"

"Ingram?" Charles interrupted. "That must be Nathaniel's sister."

"Who?"

"No one. Just a boy I went to school with."

"Never dismiss a good connection, boy. An old acquaintance can offer a valuable introduction."

"Yes, sir." It was easier to agree than to argue.

His father peered down at the list again. "Mrs. Underwood. Going on thirty. Widowed with two children. If you're going to—"

"Thank you, Father. But I'm barely back. I need some time to focus on my work." Any day but today, and he would have heard him out. Any day but the next several hundred. He couldn't court one woman while there was still the danger of his seeing one he esteemed higher. There would be no courting for him until Miss Bailey was safely out of Virginia. Once she was out of sight, mayhap he could put her out of his mind.

"There's no saying these young ladies will be available when you're ready for them."

"I understand that. I just.... I don't want to marry a woman who thinks she's above me."

"Above you? A wife can't think herself above her husband."

"Not when they're married, but I don't want to drag a gentle-woman down to my level." He spoke as if every woman on his father's list was Susan.

"You're thinking too much."

"That dog is chasing the chickens. Might be hungry."

Mr. Johnson, Senior, raised his voice. "Nobody cares about the dog. Kitty, take her to her room."

Charles winced. In her time, his grandmother had been a

respected member of the community. She still owned her widow's third of Johnson Hall, though his father had long since assumed the management of it. Granny's wits might be wandering, but it pained Charles to see her treated so callously.

"Yes, sir." Kitty put Granny's arm around her shoulders and helped her stand. They shuffled out of the room together.

"I trust you're staying for supper."

"I would like to return to Uncle Rob before dark."

"Robert? What does he have to do with anything?"

"He offered me a room. I took it."

His father's eyebrows drew together. "With all your privileges, you would choose to be associated with him at this time? Most unwise. It was a prudent arrangement while you were a boy, but it will not suit now that you are grown. It is unfortunate that my sister chose to marry without any advantage. I do not want you to suffer the consequences of it. I could pay for you to take a room in town—"

"I have enough for my needs, Father. If I wish to rent a room in town, I am prepared to do so." He did not wish to do so. After living in bachelor quarters for the last seven years, he had been looking forward to living in a family home. "As I told you before, I'm not ready to be courting anyone just now. I'm not preparing for any sort of union. And my uncle, though not of the class you would wish him, is a man of good character and fine company."

"Fine company, indeed! When was the last assembly he attended? Which families does he dine with? How will he promote your welfare, boy?"

Charles exhaled through his teeth. "I mean no disrespect to everything you've done for me, but I mean to stay with the Gardiners."

"Just don't let them trap you into marrying that bird-witted female."

"Who?"

"Your cousin."

"Emmeline? She's just a child."

"For now. But be on your guard. It would be just like the Gardiners to promote themselves while ruining you. Charity had her chance. Our grandfather may have come to the Americas indented, but my father made a name for himself. Charity had opportunities to marry to the family's advantage. Instead, she disgraced us by marrying a man in the trades. No self-respecting gentleman is going to marry a tradesman's daughter, especially one who doesn't have her wits about her."

"Perhaps she reads too much, but Emmeline is a lovely person." Susan had drawn out the best in her.

"Oh. That." He waved a hand dismissively. "She's not entirely without looks. I'm not saying men wouldn't fool around with her, but a gentleman won't demean himself by marrying a scrub."

His father was wrong about Emmeline's attractions. She was intelligent and sweet-tempered. If she could outgrow her flights of fancy, one day she would do well with a sensible, patient man. But was his father right about how other men would view her? Emmeline was in the most delicate stage of girlhood. She was still a child, but if men looked at her like she was a woman—

He slapped his thigh so hard it stung. More than one man had looked at her like that earlier today. While she could never be a danger to Charles, his father was right about the danger of other men to her.

"There is one matter of business I wish to discuss with you."

"Yes?"

"This seems like a prudent time to take on someone to manage the farm. I know just the man—"

His father waved a dismissive hand. "I already have someone. I have no need for another."

Charles pressed on. "Finlay was educated in England—well, southern Scotland, but that's close. And he knows all the latest in agricultural science. I've had extensive conversations with him."

"I've made all the improvements I intend to this year. I've no need to take on a Scot."

Charles rose abruptly. "Please excuse me. I'd like to take a look at those improvements."

Broad tobacco leaves blanketed the fields. Barefoot children wearing old shifts walked the rows, peering under the leaves for tobacco worms. Grown men and women hoed the weeds. If his talents weren't recognized, Thomas might soon be doing the same work. He walked the property line with the fierceness of an incoming storm. The hope of the morning sharpened the hurt of the afternoon. He never would have pinned his hopes on Susan if he had understood the truth about her position in society.

There was a natural order to the world. Staying within that order sheltered men from the dangers of life. Civilians obeyed their governor. Such obedience promoted commerce and secured individual property. Sons obeyed their fathers. The men who had walked the world a generation before had wisdom to impart. Sailors obeyed their captains. It was how they could make it through a storm.

And men didn't court women outside their rank.

He found shade at the top of the tree-lined ravine, where the land sloped a dozen feet down to a creek. As a child, he would escape here and play with the slave boys. They would collect sweet gum burrs and pine cones as ammunition, then play at war across the creek. The fun ended when the boys' fathers or mothers caught them, invoking the image of an enraged plantation master to frighten their children back to work.

He gathered a handful of pebbles and then threw them into the water, one by one. The world was full of cruelty and injustice. He had seen it, over and over. He had learned the importance of order and obedience in his youth. Laws and civilization had built protective walls for all to shelter behind.

But sometimes those walls were as unforgiving as the inside of a prison.

Twenty

THE LION & THE UNICORN

SATURDAY, MAY 21, 1774

Susan paced the parlor like a caged animal planning its escape. She had coaxed a lonely man to talk about his childhood, but she had never begged for friendship. She resented his begrudging compassion. She was no beggar. Beggars didn't wear the latest fashions for a phaeton ride. Beggars didn't receive all the callers and invitations she had in only two mornings. If Charles didn't care for their relationship, then pride demanded she show him that others would.

Crisp footsteps crossed the foyer. "Mr. Johnson to see you, miss. The phaeton is ready." Graves withdrew, leaving her to face Charles.

His eyes solemnly went up to the ostrich feather in her cap and down to her rhinestone buckles. Finally, he met her eyes. "Good morning, Miss Bailey. I hope you are in good health."

"I am quite well, thank you, Mr. Johnson. I was beginning to think you wouldn't come."

"Am I late? I'm sorry if I kept you waiting."

"Waiting?" Her voice brightened. "I've been busy all morning. There were ever so many callers. I had just accepted an invitation from someone else to go riding on Monday when I remembered you had invited me to go today."

He paled under his tan. "I see. Are you ready?"

She had been ready for an hour, pacing the parlor and startling at small sounds. "I am if you are."

After a long moment, he offered his arm. She waited an equally long moment before taking it. Once in the phaeton, she gathered her wide petticoats close while he settled in beside her. Releasing her petticoats, they draped against him. The arrangement was almost cozy.

Almost.

Charles shook the reins, and the horses lurched forward. The sprung seat bounced merrily, but his jaw clenched. At least on the *Minerva*, he had pretended to enjoy being with her. If this was how he felt, he should have declined the ride when she had given him the chance. They rode a full block in strained silence.

Strained silence didn't suit Susan. "Do you have much experience driving?"

"Enough." He steered around a wagon.

"Where are we going?"

He glanced at her. "I thought we would start with the palace."

"The palace." It was an enchanting word. The word did not lose charm even though it was used for a mere governor's dwelling. "I've heard so much about it."

Charles smiled, though it didn't reach his eyes. "It's the pride of Williamsburg."

"Then I can hardly wait to see it." They passed several shops in silence. She tried again. "Is your father in good health? I trust you've seen him."

"He's as well as can be expected." It was a hedged answer.

She pounced on it. "As well as can be expected? You mean he hasn't fully recovered from his illness. What did he have?"

He sighed. "Shortly before he became ill, he suffered an apoplectic stroke." That explained his somber mood. He wasn't displeased with her—at least, no more than he always was. He was concerned about his father.

Her shoulders relaxed. "I see. Can he walk? Can he feed himself?"

"He has a small limp. There's some lingering weakness, but nothing that will prevent him from continuing to manage Johnson Hall."

"I suppose that is both good and bad news." It could have been worse, but he remembered when things were better.

"Indeed. Whoa!" He pulled the reins as a boy chased a hoop across the street. He caught it and jogged along, guiding it with a little stick. Charles shook his head, but she couldn't suppress a smile. Children played the same games in Virginia that they did in England. She felt a little more at home. Which reminded her—

"Isaac said you're staying with the Gardiners?" It perplexed her that he wasn't staying with his father.

"As I said, my father is managing fine without me. Besides, I'm working in town, and the Gardiners live much closer."

"Thank you for introducing Emmeline to me. I was just beginning to think what a dreary stay this would be if I didn't have any acquaintances."

"You don't—I mean to say—" He turned in his seat. "I don't suppose you have. . . *connections* like that in England."

"We discussed this before. I wanted to make your family's acquaintance because they are your family."

"Yes. I remember. But that was before—" He clamped his mouth and shook his head. "Never mind."

She did mind. "What was that before?"

He sighed again. "Why didn't you tell me about Bailey Manor before?"

"I did tell you about it."

"No. You told me about your family—that your mom is ill and your sister reads too much."

"Don't you know? Baileys are what made it Bailey Manor. They still are. Family makes a home." A breeze stirred the ruffles on her petticoat and brushed his hat with her feather. He didn't notice. Didn't care. Didn't reply. She prickled in irritation as he focused much too hard on turning right.

"There," he said.

She looked about for what "there" was. The road ran alongside a green. At the end of it was a stately brick building. "Is that the palace?"

"That's the palace. Lord Dunmore has been serving as the royal governor for nigh three years."

"So long? His wife and children just arrived this year. I can't imagine being apart from my family for so long."

"Nor I." He spoke with quiet conviction. Charles wouldn't be leaving Virginia again. "If only the common man was more mindful of the sacrifices made for his security. The burgesses shouldn't give him such a hard time."

Susan studied the building thoughtfully as they rode along the green. The palace was smaller than Bailey Manor, but an octagonal steeple lent an air of importance to the brick edifice. "Don't forget his wife. She has been raising a family and managing an estate without her husband for three years. It is only because she braved the Atlantic crossing with all their children that she is here with him. I wonder what she thinks of the little palace she calls home."

Charles looked hurt. Susan hadn't meant to insult his homeland. "It's lovely," she amended. "So stately and symmetrical. This is my first time out of England. I should have known buildings would be smaller in an area so young."

"The kitchen is a separate building. And the ballroom is a huge wing that you can't see from the front. So it's larger than it looks."

"Of course it is." She would have agreed to the bricks being purple if it would have soothed Charles. "My aunt mentioned a ball to welcome Lady Dunmore and her children. It won't be in the palace, will it?"

"It's being given by the House of Burgesses. I believe they're holding it in the capitol building."

If he wanted to spend time with her now that they were on land, he would request a dance. She silently counted to ten before continuing, "Mr. Randolph—the young one, not his father—has already requested the first dance from me." He and his sisters had been among her first callers.

Charles glanced sharply at her and flicked the reins. The horses increased their speed, and the seat bounced on its springs. They came to a stop at the end of the green. An iron gate was mounted to two brick pillars. Susan tipped her head back to see the statues atop them. On the left pillar, a snarling lion reared. On the right, a unicorn in chains looked on. She gave a surprised laugh. "The lion and the unicorn. I didn't expect to see them here."

"You forget that British America is *British*. We fly the same flag, speak the same language, and use the same coat of arms."

"I never doubted you were British, Charles." She looked back at the statues. "Why is the unicorn always in chains?"

"I...don't know. Why is it a unicorn to begin with? There aren't any unicorns in Scotland."

"There aren't lions in England, either," Susan countered, "unless you include menageries."

Charles turned the phaeton down the other side of the green. "At times like this, all we can do is trust in the wisdom of good kings past."

"I suppose so," Susan said, "though that still doesn't answer my question."

A BREEZE TOYED WITH THE OSTENTATIOUS OSTRICH feather in Susan's impractical cap, teasing Charles with what had once seemed within his reach. He had been hoping to purchase a modest home in town after another year or two. He couldn't hope for one even as grand as her aunt's, and she had criticized the size of the governor's palace.

The world waited for Susan back in England, with a luxurious manor home, unlimited pin money, and titled suitors. Why did she allow connections with a tradesman's daughter and nephew when she could be dining with the Dunmores? Why was she here at all? People glanced her way with admiration. They paid no more attention to Charles than if he were a footman taking a fine lady for a drive. The disparity between their stations was obvious even to a casual observer.

"Have you seen your friend again?" Susan asked.

"Who?"

"The one you introduced me to. Mr. Morris."

"I see him every day. We work in the same office."

"Oh. Right."

"That's the church." He gestured to the right. "I suppose I'll see you there on the morrow." He sounded sullen even to his own ears. She had already attracted the attention of one of Virginia's leading families. How many esteemed connections would she make tomorrow? How many would request the honor of a dance with her? He couldn't. He hadn't been invited to the ball.

He turned onto Duke of Gloucester Street and nodded to an octagonal brick tower, almost as wide as it was tall. "That's the magazine, where we keep an extra reserve of arms and powder."

"What for?"

"The colony must be ready to defend itself on short notice." He found solace in impersonal facts. "Of course, every man is expected to keep his own musket, but in an emergency, you don't want to lose a battle because you ran out of gunpowder before the enemy."

"Every man?"

"Yes. It's part of the Militia Act. Every free man between eighteen and sixty must be enrolled in the militia and will be fined if he misses a training assembly or fails to keep a suitable firelock." Charles shifted in his seat. "That's something I still need to do.

With the trouble on the frontier, there's been extra talk of defense. I need to buy a musket."

"Surely you won't be called into active service." The anxious sincerity in her voice surprised him.

"I doubt it. There isn't a war going on. Just some skirmishes on the frontier." There was no need to share his worries with her. In truth, the skirmishes caused Charles a great deal of discomfort. It had been just over ten years since the last war had ended. What had begun as a "frontier skirmish" between the French, Indians, and British had escalated into a global war spreading across the North American and European continents. He had been too young to fight, but old enough to watch the injured veterans returning home. "The frontier counties will have their own militias. There might be a call for some volunteers to assist them, but it won't be every able-bodied man."

Away from the palace green, the streets were crowded. Aproned matrons carried bundles. Men gathered by a wagon, talking. Slaves and apprentices shuffled about, prolonging their errands. A wagon sat in the road. Charles carefully wove around it.

Susan was watching the people on the streets thoughtfully. "Of course, I read about the slave trade," she said softly, "but I didn't realize it was half the population."

Charles shifted uncomfortably. "The town has many free Blacks..."

"Does it? That is a relief to hear. Of course, I was worried when I first saw my aunt's staff that she was a slave owner too, but I distinctly heard my aunt proudly call Graves her manservant, which set my mind at ease."

Susan's comfort was Charles's discomfort. He was certain she'd misunderstood her aunt's meaning. Should he tell her?

"I was afraid there would be many slaves."

Charles wished she would stop using that word in public. She was drawing attention. "People don't use the word slave so much here."

Her brow furrowed under that ridiculous ostrich feather. "What do you mean?"

"Servant is the polite word."

"I don't see why you need a polite word for something crude."

What did she know about it? Nothing. And he would rather leave it that way. But something about her condemnation felt personal. He fought back like any self-respecting barrister would: with words. "There are laws to promote the welfare of servants and slaves."

"What kind of welfare?"

"Well, for example, masters are responsible to provide adequate clothing to their slaves."

"Adequate clothing? That man has no pants!"

Charles turned in the direction she pointed. A full-grown man walked down the street wearing only a shirt that went to his mid-thigh. "It is a warm day," he said weakly.

Fire sparked behind the warmth in her eyes. "Christian decency demands feeding the hungry and clothing the naked. I would be horrified to learn my neighbors didn't provide adequate food and clothing for their *servants*. Why aren't you?"

A man might jump into an icy river and cry out from the shock, while those who made it in long ago talked and laughed. Susan had just jumped into the river. His feelings were already numb. But her heated objections put him in danger of a painful thaw. It was childish to get emotional over something impossible to change. He had spent years distancing himself from the pain he had been a helpless witness to. He was a grown man, but she made him feel like a vulnerable little boy again.

He turned the phaeton toward the Blue House. It was time to establish a safe distance. He handed the reins to Graves and escorted Susan into the house. Isaac was sprawled on the settee, reading the *Gazette*.

"Any news?" Charles asked, holding his hat.

"There is an advertisement that sounds familiar. 'Just arrived in York river, the Brilliant Captain Crawford, from London, with choice healthy indented servants, the sale of which will begin at Williamsburg on Saturday the twenty-eighth of May.' It goes on to list the occupations and concludes, 'I will sell them very cheap, for ready money or tobacco.'"

"I'm surprised he didn't say whiskey," Charles said. He turned to Susan. This was goodbye. He wouldn't call on her again. They didn't move in the same circles. Sundays were the only times they might see each other. If he slipped into the back of the chapel as the sermon began, he could be gone before she could reach the aisle. Her life would soon be full of friends and activities more suited to her station. He would fade from her life. She would fade from his heart.

He bowed. "Miss Bailey. Mr. Bailey. If you'll excuse me, I need to purchase that musket."

Isaac looked up in surprise. "What musket?"

"The one I need for the militia." Charles returned his tricorn to his head.

"Wait!" Isaac tossed the *Gazette* aside. "I'll go with you."

Twenty-One

THE WELCOME BALL

FRIDAY, MAY 27, 1774

Charles smothered his hoecakes in butter and drowned them in honey.

"How are you enjoying work?" Uncle Rob asked.

"So far, there isn't any." Charles cut his hoecakes as he talked. "I'll just spend the day studying Virginia laws. Then if I ever get a brief, I might be ready to handle it." He stacked the hoecakes on his fork and took a big bite. He had missed homegrown Virginia foods in London.

"I'm sure you'll have important briefs soon," Aunt Charity said. "People will be impressed by your London education."

Charles swallowed. "My family thinks I'm worth so much more because I've lived abroad. In London, I was the pig-headed provincial."

Henrietta snorted a laugh and choked on her breakfast. She coughed until her eyes watered.

"Are you well?" Aunt Charity asked.

Henrietta wiped her eyes and nodded.

"Good. Tomorrow you can eat your breakfast in the kitchen after everyone else is done."

149

Henrietta opened her mouth to protest, then closed it with a snap. Talking back would only make things worse.

Uncle Rob spread honey with his fork. "Have you seen the Baileys again?"

"Not since Saturday."

"Miss Bailey is so elegant," Emmeline said dreamily. "All she needs is a gold crown shimmering with diamonds, and she would be just how I imagine Queen Charlotte."

"With or without diamonds," Charles said sternly, "she's a lady of quality."

Emmeline didn't recognize the significance of that barrier. "What if you make a sweetheart out of her?" Her naive hope pierced his wounded dreams.

He avoided his uncle's inquiring gaze. "Emma. Really." There was no comfort in hope now. Only pain. He pushed his plate back. "I need to get to work."

He was out the door before anyone could question him. He pushed aside thoughts of Susan. As he walked, he turned over in his mind yesterday's tumultuous news. The House of Burgesses had declared the first of June to be a day of fasting, prayer, and humiliation for the people of Boston. Lord Dunmore had responded by dissolving the sitting house. They would be powerless to act until the next election. The royal governor had responded with the power and authority granted him by the king. He was right to use that power to preserve peace and order.

But was it ever wrong to pray?

Despite leaving home early, Charles was not the first man to the office. Standing under the Sign of the Eagle, Quill was in deep conversation with Colonel Hendriks.

"It's outrageous," the colonel said, tapping his cane for emphasis. "Nothing in their resolve reflected on either his majesty or Parliament. It isn't as if it's illegal to pray."

"It was a cheap political trick," Charles said. "Boston dug its own grave. There's no reason for us to be buried with them."

"Come now," Quill's highland brogue was as soothing as a

lullaby. "They're just praying that we avoid the evils of a civil war. Everyone should want ta avoid that."

"Parliament is preparing for war," the colonel said. "I heard General Gage arrived in Boston with eight regiments. Eight!"

Charles shifted uneasily. The news made him uncomfortable, so he argued against it. "Parliament hasn't declared war on Boston. They're not foolish."

The colonel was not placated. "Then you suggest parliament keeps standing armies in peacetime?" Such an act would oppose the century-old Bill of Rights, signed by King William and Queen Mary.

Charles opened his mouth, then closed it. The decision to send General Gage had been announced shortly after he had left London. His Majesty's ships sailed faster than the *Minerva*, so the regiments had docked in Massachusetts before Charles had arrived in Virginia. He had only recently heard about it. He needed more time to think, to organize a proper defense of Parliament's decision.

"It's unconstitutional," Colonel Hendriks said passionately, "punishing the whole of Boston for the actions of a few unknown men! There was no trial, no jury of peers, no respect for the rights of British citizens."

"As unfortunate as that is for Boston," Charles said, "look what we've done to ourselves. Because the House of Burgesses is using a day of prayer to question Parliament's judgment, our legislature cannot legislate until after the next election."

"They're no sitting ducks." The colonel chuckled. "Did you read what our former burgesses published next?"

"I have it here." Quill shook the paper. "'An attack, made on one of our sister colonies, ta compel submission ta arbitrary taxes, is an attack made on all British America, and threatens ta ruin the rights of all.' Then they go on ta recommend that each of the colonies send delegates annually ta a congress that can discuss the matters of British America."

"A congress?" Charles repeated. "Whatever for?

"Think about it," Quill said. "Parliament can punish a city, but it canna punish all the colonies at once. That's why we have ta work together."

Charles spied one silver lining in the gathering storm. "What about that ball the burgesses were throwing for Lady Dunmore?"

"What about it?"

"I'll bet that's off now."

"Why should it be? The people love her. Mark my words, the former House of Burgesses will host a charming ball in honor of Lady Dunmore and her children. And if none of them get roaring drunk afore three in the morning, I say nothing but good will come of it."

Nothing but good? Every eligible young man in and around Williamsburg would see Susan in all her finery. There was nothing good that could come of that.

THE CARRIAGE LUMBERED FORWARD, HORSE HOOVES muffled in the sand. After a week of preparations, Aunt Dorothea still wasn't done talking about the ball. "I'll introduce you to the Randolphs, the Jeffersons, and the Carters. The rest of the Randolphs, I mean. The young ones did call last week, didn't they?" Without waiting for a reply, she turned to Isaac and said, "You'll dance with the Dunmores' eldest daughter, though she is scarcely out. And Susan, those rosebuds look lovely with your gown."

"I'm sorry about that. I hope you'll have roses on your table soon. Lucy can be quite zealous about my appearance."

"Don't apologize, dear. I am quite looking forward to the scene you will make. Not that I begrudge Lady Dunmore anything. I quite respect her. There's a woman who can govern the governor! When she arrived in Virginia, Lord Dunmore was using a room upstairs in the palace as his office. She wasted no time claiming it as her dressing room. Now the governor conducts all his royal business from the dining room."

Susan smoothed her silk petticoats. There was no need to feel jittery. It was just a ball. She had been to countless of those. Why should this one be any different? Because she had never danced with Charles before. Susan twisted her hands. She didn't want to live in the colonies, and she didn't want Charles to want her, because she would have to disappoint him. She just wanted him to think she was beautiful, just for one night.

The interior of the capitol building glittered with silks and candlelight. Aunt Dorothea escorted them to the front of the room. "Lady Dunmore, may I present my niece, Miss Susan Bailey, and nephew, Mr. Isaac Bailey, newly arrived from England." Lady Dunmore wore traditional court dress. The hoops made her petticoat wider than a carriage wheel.

Susan curtsied deeply, her pink petticoats pooling on the floor.

"I hope you will enjoy your time in Virginia."

"Thank you, my lady."

Her aunt then introduced them to her acquaintances. Susan's head swam with names and faces. It was irritating how many people at this ball were not Charles Johnson. The press of people made the room warm, despite the open windows. She fanned herself.

"Miss Bailey?" It was Charles' red-haired friend. She was surprised to find he was several inches shorter than her when he wasn't on horseback.

"Mr. Morris." Susan curtsied with her first real smile of the evening. "Is Mr. Johnson with you?"

"I regret ta inform ye he is not."

"Oh." He hadn't told her he wasn't coming. "Is he unwell?"

"Aye, and greatly ta be pitied."

Susan's fan stilled.

"He's studying law when he should be dancing."

Susan exhaled. "So he isn't ill?"

"Nothin' that will prevent him from breakin' my nose when he finds out I danced with his favorite lady. May I?"

She couldn't help smiling at the absurd picture he sketched. "Yes."

He led her to the floor, where they formed a set with three other couples. While waiting for the music to begin, Susan asked, "Does it not occur to Mr. Johnson that meeting with other influential people will benefit his career as much as studying?"

The violins drew their first notes. Every dancer turned to Lord and Lady Dunmore and bowed. Taking Susan's hand, Mr. Morris said, "He is too modest ta believe his hard work and carefully formed opinions will meet the approval of others."

"That I can easily believe. He is not one to speak openly of himself." She pursed her lips, fighting a self-conscious smile. "Surely he never said I was his favorite lady."

Mr. Morris grinned. "Not in so many words. Rather, he was determined ta say nothin' about ye at all."

Susan shook her head. "How did you turn that into a compliment to myself?"

"'Tis what he doesna say that speaks the loudest. When I tell him tomorrow that we talked and danced and laughed together, he'll be a regular thundercloud. That's how we'll know."

Though she knew he was wrong, it lightened her mood considerably. She meant to have a word with his sister, but he had scarcely returned her to her aunt before she was claimed for another dance. The next two hours passed in a whirl of embroidered silk. Despite the constant movement, she learned the names of half the burgesses.

It was a relief when she was finally allowed to rest for a set. Aunt Dorothea introduced her to Mayor Dixon, who was content to talk while the others danced. "You're so new to Virginia yourself, have you had opportunities to become acquainted with anyone before tonight?"

"A little. We made the acquaintance of one Mr. Johnson. He's a barrister, newly arrived—I should say returned—from

London." Charles should have been there tonight, meeting men like this who could promote his interests. He needed introductions as much as she did. More, even.

"London, eh? Did he pass the bar there?"

"Yes. He studied at Lincoln's Inn."

"So he knows nothing of Virginia law?"

"On the contrary, sir, he's done nothing but study law books since he's arrived."

"I suppose he would have a fair understanding of common law."

Susan knew nothing about common law, but it sounded like the sort of thing a barrister would learn in his first year of studies. "Precisely, sir. And before he left England, he sat in on Parliament and heard them debating America's interests himself. He has a keen mind when it comes to the law." She spoke with more enthusiasm for her subject than actual understanding.

"Did he, now? I've been reading all the broadsides, but it would be fine to discuss it with a man who's been there himself. With all due respect for his majesty," he turned and offered a slight bow to a large painting, "Parliament seems to have forgotten that English colonists are Englishmen. I'm composing a letter to Lord North. Perhaps I'll speak with this Mr. Johnson before I post it. Where did you say his office was?"

She had no answer. The only time she had heard the direction was before she had even seen the town. She didn't remember any of the details.

A voice at her elbow said, "Under the Sign of the Eagle."

Susan turned, and Mr. Morris handed her a drink.

"The Sign of the Eagle," the mayor repeated. "Do you know him, as well, Mr. Morris?"

"Quite well, sir. He is conscientious and hardworking. We'll have ta forgive him for havin' been in England so recently."

The gentleman excused himself, and Mr. Morris looked at her with amusement. "Miss Bailey, may I ask how many visitors my office will have this week?"

"Your office?"

"The one I share with Mr. Johnson. The one ye've been inviting every man of influence ta visit."

"He was the third." She touched the punch to her lips. "No, the fourth."

"I suspect ye've done more for Johnson's interests than he would have done if he'd come himself."

"If he had come, he would have sulked in the corner all evening." She had paid her debt for Charles' reluctant attentions. A lady owed nothing.

Twenty-Two

MORE THAN SILVER & GOLD

SATURDAY, MAY 28, 1774

Charles rubbed his temples. He had lain awake half the night. His fevered mind had presented him with a thousand possibilities for how Susan was enjoying the ball— most involving wealthy, charismatic gentlemen with words on their lips as flowery as a rose garden in June. Men who could charm her into staying.

Lord help me—

He slapped a hand on his desk. He was too old to believe in miracles. Such faith was the foolishness of children. If God were going to help him, he would have done so long ago. The office door opened, shaking him from his thoughts. Instinctively, he came to his feet.

It was only Quill and Polly, arriving for work.

"What took you so long?" Charles asked. He had stopped by for the key two hours ago.

"I fell back asleep," Quill said. "Dinna look at me like that. 'Twas a late night." He pocketed the key Charles had left on his desk.

"I trust you had a good time." The words were polite, but the tone was tainted with resentment.

Quill exchanged an amused glance with Polly. It seemed to say, *I told you so.* He unlocked a drawer and pulled out a stack of papers. "Miss Bailey seems nice." He thumbed through a brief. "Good dancer, too."

Charles exhaled slowly, pushing the air between his teeth.

"Oh, aye," Polly chimed in. "She and Quill made a lovely couple."

It couldn't be true. Quill was as homely as they came. But there was no logic in love. She wouldn't be the first woman irrationally charmed by his cheery disposition. Charles glared at his desk.

"Would ye like ta ken what she talks about when ye are no' around?"

He would trade every book he owned to know that, but he didn't trust the laughter in Quill's eyes. "I'm sure it can't concern me."

"Oh, but it does." Quill leaned back against his desk. "The lady has taken yer interests ta heart. When do we get ta congratulate ye?"

He was itching to ask what she had said or done last night, but he couldn't allow his friend to fancy himself a matchmaker. Not for such an impossible match. "You won't."

"And why not? 'Tis plain as day ye fancy her. Why else would ye be moping about the office?"

Charles glanced at Polly. She had the delicacy to be engrossed in the accounting book. He sighed. Wild ideas, like fires, were best smothered before they had a chance to grow. "Mayhap you didn't know, Morris. Her father owns Bailey Manor."

Quill raised his hands. "And yers owns Johnson Hall. She's a lady. Ye're a gentleman."

He was oversimplifying things. A middling Virginia plantation was nothing like a sprawling English estate. "She's a lady of a much higher class. A gentleman doesn't drag a lady down to his level."

"A chivalrous sentiment." Quill nodded sagely. "But if the lady can pull the gentleman up ta her level, what then?"

That wasn't how marriage worked. "She deserves an idle lord with a house in town and an estate in the country, not a mongrel American who works for a living."

Polly smothered a laugh that proved she had been listening. "What did ye call yerself?"

"Nothing I didn't hear in London first. The English don't look kindly on Americans. Mongrel breed wasn't the worst insult I heard."

Quill dropped the papers on his desk, suddenly serious. "Miss Bailey wasn't calling ye names of any sort. She was hoping ta see ye. And ye should have seen her. I nigh didna recognize who 'twas. She was turned out as fine as Lady Dunmore. I had ta elbow my way past the old gentry just ta talk ta her. And all she wanted was ta ask why ye were no' with me."

"I wasn't invited." He slammed his desk closed and locked it as if it could hide his feelings as easily as his paperwork. "I have to be somewhere." Thank heaven that was true. He wouldn't get anything done with Quill interrogating him.

"What? Where?"

"Business. By the courthouse." He had a promise to keep.

The walk should have cleared his head. May in Virginia was the closest thing he knew to paradise. But everywhere he looked, he was reminded of the phaeton ride with Susan a week ago. She hadn't seen a paradise. She had seen a humble town lacking in Christian decency.

The *Minerva* immigrants were lined up on the broad stone porch of the courthouse. Off to the side, Captain Crawford sat behind a mahogany table. A stack of papers was weighted against the wind with an inverted Delft bowl. A white portico floated heavily over the scene with no columns to support it.

Potential buyers crowded the steps. They interrogated and

examined their potential purchases like they were horses, comparing the strength of their biceps and the state of their teeth. Captain Crawford smiled broadly, answering questions and gesturing magnanimously toward the lot of immigrants. Thomas wrapped his arms protectively around his small family. Marion clutched the baby. Jenny huddled against her.

Charles pushed his way up the side steps. "Finlay."

Hope lit Thomas's face. "Mr. Johnson."

Charles stood there stupidly. He had no hope to offer, no assurances. Only a weak explanation. "I tried to persuade my father that he needed certain skills. I-I tried."

Thomas nodded, understanding Charles' fumbled apology. "Have you found a place for yourself?"

"I'm sharing an office with a friend."

"How is Miss Bailey?" Mrs. Finlay asked.

He swallowed. "Her aunt is delighted with her. She and her brother should find much to enjoy during their stay here."

"I'm glad. Give her our regard."

He nodded, unwilling to voice his refusal. He had no intention of speaking another word to their mutual acquaintance. The less he saw of Susan, the sooner he could forget her. It seemed more honest to just nod. "Is the baby in good health?"

Marion pulled back the blanket. The babe was sleeping, oblivious to the commotion around him. His whole life had been surrounded by turmoil. It was a blessing that he was too young to understand. Charles waited near the family as the first five indentures were sold from the steps of the courthouse.

Then, Sleeman broke apart the family. He pulled Mrs. Finlay to the front, clutching her baby. "Twenty-two years old," he shouted to the crowd, "in good health. Has already had smallpox. Skilled as a weaver, as well as in needlework. Because she comes with a baby, we'll put an extra two years of labor in the contract. Who will give me twenty pounds for this fine worker?"

A fashionably dressed woman waved her fan high in the air.

"Sold!"

Sleeman grabbed Jenny's wrist and pulled her forward. At fifteen, she was barely more than a child. She was no older than that sister Miss Bailey worried about. She had been brave enough to immigrate when she could have stayed with friends in Scotland. Now, her eyes were wide in her pale face. She was terrified.

If only she could be placed with her aunt. She was so young. *Please, Lord...*

"Speaks English well." The supercargo shouted over the crowd. He gripped her chin. "With this pretty face, she would be a valuable parlor maid."

A lone man raised his hand. He didn't stand apart from the crowd so much as the crowd stood apart from him. His buckskin shirt marked him as a frontiersman, come into town for business. His face was hidden behind a shrubbery of whiskers. Whatever his business had been, it had not included a barber. The captain waved him over for payment and paperwork.

It would be impossible to keep his promise to Thomas to look out for her if she lived fifty miles upstate. And what did such a rugged man want a delicate girl for? A shack in the woods didn't need a parlor maid. Sleeman pushed her toward the captain to complete the sale. Thomas darted forward but was instantly restrained by three men—sailors from the *Minerva*. He pulled against them. His resistance was both noble and foolish. Fighting against authority only brought losses. There was only one way to change her fate, and that was by playing the game.

Charles threw his hand in the air and shouted, "I'll take her!" There was no room for charity in business, but there was in friendship. Thomas would have done the same thing for him.

There was a greedy glint in Sleeman's eye. He gestured to the frontiersman. "This fine gentleman has already placed a bid for twenty pounds."

"I'll pay twenty-one." It had taken months of painful frugality to save that much money.

"Twenty-two," the frontiersman countered.

"Twenty-three."

"Twenty-four." The higher the man bid, the less Charles trusted him. A man like that should have been looking for a sturdy field hand. He could have gotten one for a mere twenty pounds, payable in tobacco notes. Thomas looked on anxiously, but he was just another pawn in the game. He had no power to play.

Charles did. "I will pay twenty-two pounds in English coin." The stunned silence told him he had won. Tobacco notes were a gamble. Their value often fell. English coins were worth their weight in precious metal. "Silver and gold."

"Done," Sleeman said.

"Thank you," Thomas said.

Charles looked the captain in the eye. "Keep the girl safe, and I'll have the money here within the hour." He kept a few small coins in his pocketbook, enough for a tavern dinner, but most of his money was kept safe in his lockbox. He ran more than a mile home and up the stairs. He latched his bedroom door, unlocked the trunk, and removed the books. The key trembled in the final lock. This decision would cost him months of savings. He wavered. If he had been a poor choice for Miss Bailey before this, he would be unthinkable now. He threw open the lid. He was already unthinkable.

Silver crowns and gold guineas were stacked with precision and divided by strips of blue paper. He was careful to abide by every other law, but when it was time to come home, avarice had overcome fear. It wasn't legal to bring these coins into the colonies. But he had worked so hard for them, and Virginia wasn't authorized to create coins. None of the colonies were. His countrymen wouldn't turn him in for something they needed so badly.

He slipped three gold guineas engraved with the face of King George III into his pocketbook, then counted out enough silver crowns to equal twenty-two pounds. By the time he was done, there were visible cavities in his savings. The sight hurt like a doctor's lance. He hastily locked it and hid it away.

The coins jangled as he jogged back. There was no guarantee

the captain would hold Jenny if he got another offer. There was no guarantee until he had the contract, and there would be no contract until he paid in full. His lungs burned from the exertion, but he pushed past the pain like a warrior in battle. On the courthouse steps, Sleeman was hawking another immigrant. Jenny stood behind the captain, her thin arms wrapped around herself. Charles slapped his pocketbook onto the table but kept it covered with his hand. "Where's her contract?"

The captain frowned. "I don't see the money."

"It's right here. I want to see the contract."

Captain Crawford pulled out a contract with Jenny's name on it. "You sign first. I'll sign as soon as I see the money."

That was reasonably fair. Charles signed, then counted out the coins, loud enough for witnesses. The captain took his time, weighing each one before completing the contract.

"There you are." He sprinkled blotting powder on his signature and offered the contract to Charles.

"Thank you." He flipped open his commonplace book. "Would you be so good as to tell me where Mr. and Mrs. Finlay were placed?"

The captain rifled through his papers. Mrs. Finlay's indentures had been purchased by a mantua-maker in town. Thomas was on his way to a plantation more than ten miles to the southeast.

Charles noted their direction in his book. One didn't break down a door for a man without a lingering feeling of responsibility. "Come along, Jenny. We've a bit of a walk ahead of us."

Once they were a safe distance from the courthouse, she asked, "Where am I going?"

"Since I have no need for a maid of any sort, I thought I would place you with my relations, Mr. and Mrs. Gardiner. You'll be safe there. They come into town every Sunday for church. You'll be able to see your aunt and cousin weekly."

Jenny's smile was as bright as a newly minted penny.

Given time, he might be able to forget how much that smile

had cost him. If only he could tell Susan about today. Though he was even less worthy to court her than before, she might be pleased with his actions. Her approval was more valuable than gold. But he had promised himself he would avoid her from now on.

And he kept his promises.

Twenty-Three

FASTING & FRIENDSHIP

WEDNESDAY, JUNE 1, 1774

The courthouse was so full that the crowd burst out the double doors and onto the steps and street below. Every inhabitant of Williamsburg was crushed shoulder to shoulder for a day of fasting, humiliation, and prayer for those in Boston. Everyone except Lord Dunmore's family.

Susan's stomach grumbled. There had been no breakfast, and dinner would be late, after the prayer meeting. She should be grateful that there would be dinner at all. Some Virginians wouldn't break their fast until sundown. But the breeze through the courthouse windows betrayed simmering stews and roasting meat.

The orator's voice swelled over the restless crowd. "The early settlers faced the dangers and deprivation of the wilderness. Our grandfathers carved civilization out of the trees. They crafted it with their very sweat and blood. Whether your family has lived here for one generation or has been here since the founding of Jamestown, this is your inheritance. Though this be American soil, we have the rights of Englishmen because we are Englishmen."

Her attention drifted to Charles. He was riveted on the speaker. There was a light in his eyes that she had only seen the day they had docked. It was the light of love for his native land. This was his country. It was where he was well.

It was also where he ignored her. She had paid her debts like a lady, but it had brought no reward. Not only had he not called on her, but now he wouldn't even glance in her direction.

She flushed beneath her rouge and looked away, her head high above the gray ribbon around her throat. It was the only ornament she and Lucy had agreed upon. To approach the day with suitable humiliation, some were wearing Virginia homespun. Susan settled for drab colors and a lack of ornamentation. That was humbling enough for her.

A hush in the room attracted her attention. Had she missed the conclusion? But then the orator thundered, "An attack on our sister colony is an attack on us all. Even now, General Gage is in Boston with his troops. The invasion has begun. Boston's ports are now closed by military force. And for what? Has the city itself committed any crime? Nay. But rather than punish the men responsible for the tea incident, parliament has passed an act to starve a free people into submission. If Boston succumbs to such tyranny, every colony is in danger of losing its charter as well as the rights held sacred by all Englishmen. We must unite with our sister colony in her time of need."

It was better to be Williamsburg, sharing her bounty, than Boston, desperate for aid. She was still the lady of Bailey Manor. Virginians hadn't lost their rights. She hadn't lost her dignity. She had never been desperate for a man's attention. Men had always come to her.

The light had gone out of Charles's eyes. He stood with his feet apart and arms crossed, as impenetrable as a fortress. It was the posture of a man who didn't need anyone. And yet, he had shadowed her all over the *Minerva*. Was it only duty, as Isaac claimed, or had he needed a friend?

Hope stirred in her heart. It was ridiculous to discount everything she had learned about Charles just because Isaac thought he knew better. Isaac was a mere boy. He never knew better. Mr. Morris, though prone to exaggeration, believed Charles thought well of her.

If that was true, then why wouldn't he speak with her anymore? They had become such easy friends on the *Minerva*. Why had their friendship withered on landing? Ever since they had parted to their respective homes, he had resumed being as aloof as he had been the first few days of their acquaintanceship.

He had his family and one close friend. That wasn't enough for anyone. He still needed the Baileys. She measured the distance between them with her eyes. With a few strategic steps on her part, they would exit the courthouse together. If he still needed her, there was nothing desperate or undignified in approaching him.

Once the speaker dismissed them, she made her way at a subtle angle toward the door.

"Miss Bailey." A soft voice interrupted her plans. Civility demanded she acknowledge the greeting.

"Miss Gardiner. I hope your family is in good health."

"They are." She ducked her head. All Susan could see was her round-eared cap as Emmeline spoke to the ground, hugging herself. "I've been meaning to return your book."

"You've read it already?" She had only had it a fortnight.

Emmeline unfolded her arms. *Robinson Crusoe* had been clutched to her chest. "And I took the liberty of copying down some of my favorite passages."

Susan accepted the book and pocketed it. "There's nothing wrong with that." The sun blinded her as they exited the courthouse. She blinked and looked down the steps. Charles stood at the bottom, looking up. Their eyes met. In that unguarded moment, she saw a man who had whittled toys for captive children and was the first to hear a stranger's predawn cry for help. He had consoled her when she was exhausted to tears and had stopped a wagon to gather wildflowers. None of that had been out of duty.

He turned sharply and moved ahead with the crowd. She took Emmeline's arm. Together, they walked to the church. Once they were inside, her protégée pulled back. Susan placed a hand over hers. "Please sit with me."

For the first time that day, Emmeline looked directly at her with startling blue eyes. "Yes, miss." She shuffled sideways down the pew. The chapel was so crowded that when they sat, Susan could feel the frame of her panniers pressing into her hips. There were more people in attendance today than she had yet seen on a Sabbath.

The room quieted as the reverend Mr. Price approached the pulpit. Susan bowed her head as he read a prayer. "God save our sister colony and protect her from this hostile invasion. God stay the hand of General Gage and endow him with a spirit of mercy for the citizens of Boston. God bless his majesty, King George, and his excellency Lord North. God bless the delegates to the Continental Congress. May they be blessed with wisdom and long-suffering that we may be spared the evils of a civil war. May peace return to all of Great Britain, and may the constitutional rights of all British citizens be upheld. Amen."

"Amen," Susan whispered. She didn't care much about politics, but she could agree with peace.

Mr. Price preached a powerful sermon. "'The Lord hath prepared His seat in Heaven, and His kingdom ruleth over all.' Psalm one-hundred-three, verse nineteen. We are all of us, from mighty King George to the smallest child, subjects of the King of Kings. We turn our faith to God's providence to guide our great nation. We will make our supplication to him for justice.

"In Genesis eighteen, we read, 'If there are ten righteous, God will not destroy it.' Look about you. We have far more than ten times ten gathered here, in this house of God, to pray for our sister colony. God will hear our prayers today. Boston will not be destroyed."

An hour later, they spilled out of the church. She kept Emmeline beside her, not allowing the crowd to separate them. If Charles came to collect his cousin, he would be forced to greet her. "What was your favorite part of the book?"

Emmeline looked down. She prodded a dandelion with the tip of her shoe. "I don't know that I could choose a favorite."

"You liked it enough to read it three times."

She looked up and clasped her hands together, as if preparing for a recitation. "If I read a book only once, I would admit it to the vast circle of my acquaintance but deny it the opportunity to become a particular friend."

Charles' cousin was odd. She would be shunned by society if she persisted in saying such peculiar things. She dropped her eyes again.

The poor dear. She really did need a patroness. And that plain cap needed a ribbon. She could hardly go about commissioning gowns for a young woman of no relation, but surely she could give her a ribbon. Blue would match her eyes.

"You remind me of my little sister. Have I told you that?"

Emmeline darted a look at her face. "Yes, ma'am."

"You will come and call on me, won't you?"

She took half a step back and studied her warily. Caution was the defining trait of Charles's family. "I don't go into town much."

"What if I sent my aunt's carriage?"

"Oh." Her eyes went wide. "I couldn't." Caution and stubborn self-reliance. This was like coaxing a mule to breakfast.

"Emmeline," Charles's voice interrupted, "your mother wants you."

Susan turned on him.

"Oh. Miss Bailey. I didn't—" He broke off, leaving the lie unspoken.

She glared at him, all generous thoughts forgotten. He *had* seen her. Why pretend otherwise? Why avoid her?

"Excuse me, Miss Bailey." Emmeline curtsied hastily and darted away.

Susan narrowed her eyes at Charles. She hadn't eaten since yesterday and was in no mood to be trifled with.

He ran a finger along the inside of his collar. "It's rather warm today, isn't it?"

"I suppose."

"What were you and Emmeline discussing so intently?"

"I invited her to visit." Susan flicked open her fan. "But she's as stubborn as you are."

Charles's brows creased up to his tricorn hat. "Stubborn?"

"I offered to send the carriage round and everything."

"I'm sure she was just too shy."

"Do you think so?" Now that he was conversing with her, she didn't feel as irritable.

"Indeed, yes. When we're alone, she speaks quite warmly of you."

The fan stilled. Charles had just admitted to having private conversations about her.

He broke eye contact. "What did you think of the sermon?"

"It was...not like any sermon I've heard in England."

"Nor I."

She was reminded of how long he had lived in her home country. She struggled to be away from hers for one year. He had managed seven. "How far away is Boston?"

"Far enough. Most people here have only read about it in the *Gazette*."

"Then Virginians have a lot of compassion for people they have never met."

"If they truly wish to help Boston, they should work with Lord Dunmore to find a way that shows less disrespect for our government."

Susan didn't read political broadsides, but she thought she had understood everything spoken. "What was disrespectful?"

"Having the House of Burgesses declare a day of fasting and

prayer in support of Boston is going to make it look like Virginians are criticizing Parliament's decisions about it. The last thing we want is for our government to be in opposition to a higher governing body."

"Is it ever wrong to pray?"

"I suppose not." Charles frowned at the crowds of people slowly exiting the church. "At least if it's sincere. Did the burgesses want God to hear them, or were they trying to provoke the politicians?"

"I don't know. Mr. Price sounded sincere." Politics bored her. "I was sorry not to see you at the ball."

Charles grimaced. "I'm sorry to have disappointed you."

"I should have known you'd spend the whole evening with your nose in a law book."

A shadow crossed his face. "Or perhaps we don't run in the same circles, even in Williamsburg." His tone was cold and aloof. After everything they had been through, he still put up those ridiculous walls.

"Then we make our own circle," she replied with fierce warmth.

Charles stared at her in disbelief. "Make our own?"

"Make. Our. Own." If there had been a table nearby, she would have pounded it for emphasis. "We crossed an entire ocean together. Don't you dare pretend we aren't friends."

His lips twitched as he regarded her. "Friends." The ghost of a smile appeared. "Who else is in our circle?"

"Mr. and Miss Morris. I expect the three of you for dinner next Wednesday." She flicked her fan closed. "Don't be late."

Twenty-Four

THE ROSES OF PROMETHEUS

THURSDAY, JUNE 2, 1774

Friend. There was no worse word in the English language. He couldn't avoid her, trying to forget. But he could never be anything more. Friendship was a boulder she had chained him to. He anticipated dinner with Susan like Prometheus anticipated having his liver eaten.

His breakfast had gone cold. The egg quivered as he moved it onto day-old bread.

Aunt Charity rattled off the day's chores. "Henrietta, remember to feed the chickens and weed the garden while Emmeline and Jenny tidy up from breakfast. I have a letter to write."

"Yes, Mother."

Jenny had adapted quickly to her new home. She wore one of Emmeline's old shortgowns and spent each day working alongside her. On Sunday, she and her aunt had enjoyed the service outside the open church windows. Thomas would be pleased. She was safe.

"And Charles," Aunt Charity continued, "I gathered some herbs for that lady."

He quickly asked, "Who?"

Aunt Charity was bemused. "The only woman you've mentioned even once in a fortnight."

That had been a mistake. He should never have mentioned the Baileys to his aunt and uncle before seeing how they settled in. His face warmed. "You mean Mr. Bailey's sister?" There. Put as much distance between them as possible. Put her brother between them.

"Miss Bailey, yes. You said she nursed you when you were seasick. A lady won't expect payment for her services, but she will need fresh supplies." She put several small paper packages on the table, each not much thicker than a letter.

He collected the packages. "I'll see her in a few days. She invited the Morrises and me to dinner." Her circle. One of many. He tucked the papers in a pocket and took his leave of the Gardiners.

As he walked to the office, the sun on his shoulders was warm, but his mind was heavy as gathering rain. What did a friendship with a woman look like? Did she expect him to discuss the fickleness of fashion? Would she tease him and slug his shoulder?

Absurd.

The papers crinkled as he walked. They would have to wait until Wednesday. That was only six days away. They crinkled again. Within the envelopes, the brittle herbs were crumbling as he walked. Six more days and he would be delivering nothing but powder.

Charles squared his shoulders. Prometheus had his liver eaten every day. It was best to get this over with. He was soon at the Blue House, asking the footman if Miss Bailey was available for callers.

"She's in the gardens," Graves said. "I'll inform her of your presence."

"There's no need to disrupt her morning. I'll meet her there." He let himself through the side gate. Maurice's voice carried through the open kitchen door, singing some inarticulate song. French, most likely. It was enough. They wouldn't be any more alone than on the *Minerva*. Windows were open. At any moment, anyone could see them. There was nothing clandestine about meeting in a sunlit garden.

Susan was turned away from him. The pink ribbon on her straw hat fluttered in the breeze. Sausage curls rested against her neck. A basket hung from the crook of her arm. Her other hand cupped a rose against her nose. He could almost believe this woman would be content living off the earnings of a middling barrister.

He opened the gate to the rose garden. His shoe crunched the shell path. She turned and straightened. Her cotton morning gown was beautiful in its simplicity. For a moment, he could forget she was a fine lady. This was the Susan he knew. The Susan of the *Minerva*. The practical, compassionate woman who had saved Mrs. Finlay's life. The Susan he would trust with his own.

"Charles. I wasn't expecting you today."

The gate closed behind him. "What kind of friend would I be if I only came by appointment?"

A smile lit her face. That smile would keep him chained to a rock in any tide. "Are you well?"

"Quite well. I won't keep you long. I may have mentioned to my aunt, Mrs. Gardiner, how you cared for me when I was seasick." The sun was too hot this morning. Sweat beaded on the back of his neck. He reached past his old pocketbook for the packages. "She wanted to repay you with herbs from her garden." He frowned. "I don't know if they're what you're used to."

"I'm sure they're wonderful." She held her hands out like a child expecting a present. He pressed them into her hands. She sorted through the envelopes with pleasure, reading the elegant penmanship label on each one. "Please express my gratitude to Mrs. Gardiner."

"I will." He glanced away. Her basket was empty. "Are you collecting herbs this morning?"

"Just flowers. Except I seem to have forgotten a knife."

"Allow me. I always carry a penknife." He removed his knee-length jacket and draped it on a bench. There was no need to sully it on the ground for a bouquet. He pulled a penknife from his waistcoat and crouched on the path, seizing the stem of a white rose. "Is this one good?"

"It's already in full bloom and would wilt too soon. The buds will be best, like this one." Her finger brushed a rose petal.

Charles cut the stems, dropping them in her basket. The more he disturbed the shrubbery, the more the world smelled of roses.

"That's four. It's a quintal vase, so one more."

He pinched a final stem between his left forefinger and thumb. A sudden pain caught him by surprise. He stifled a curse by inhaling sharply.

"You're hurt!" Her concern pierced the air.

He sucked the pad of his thumb. "It's just a prick."

"Let me see."

If she had told him to cut every flower in the garden, he would have done it. As it was, he obediently held out his thumb. A single drop of blood sat on it. It would heal in no time.

"Hold still." She pulled a handkerchief out of her pocket. In a flurry of movement, she wrapped his thumb, her fingers brushing his hand. "Just for a minute until the bleeding stops."

He stared at his thumb. Dainty flowers had been stitched all over the fine handkerchief. They would be ruined by a single drop of blood. Susan—Miss Bailey—had a funny idea of what friendship looked like. He shook his head and cut the final stem. "Can I help you with anything else?"

"I won't keep you. Thank you for your help."

"Anytime." He pulled his jacket back on. It was time for work.

"Here, let me."

Before he knew what she meant, she was adjusting his cravat and tucking it properly into his waistcoat. He stiffened. Adjusting cravats was an intimate service reserved for sisters and wives. But he couldn't step away. He had wanted this. Wanted her in the intimate details of his life. Wanted a lifetime of providing for a woman who fussed over him.

She stepped back and met his eyes. "I-I'm sorry," she faltered. "I wasn't thinking. I'm sure you prefer to do that yourself."

"Not at all." He ran a finger along the edge of the neckerchief she wore untucked over her shoulders. His heart raced. *Danger.* "Mayhap some time I'll return the favor."

Wide brown eyes met his in a look as soft as rose petals. Maurice's singing faded. It was miles away. They were alone, together. He came a step closer. The fragrance of dozens of roses was dizzying. Every muscle tensed, leaning toward her, aching to kiss her, alert for the slightest sign that she, too, had been waiting for this. He was breathless in anticipation.

A small wrinkle creased her brow.

He blinked and stepped back. *Idiot.* She had told him only yesterday that they were just friends. Had warned him not to imagine anything else. Friends didn't court. Didn't kiss. Didn't forget their place. She was a lady of quality. He was a middling barrister. He should be grateful she condescended to friendship. "I have to get back to work." His voice cracked like a boy's.

"As do I." She picked up the basket of rosebuds. "Until Wednesday." She was smooth and unflustered. How many men had made fools of themselves over her before? He wasn't the first.

Charles looked at the trees, the shells, the honeysuckle, the fence. Anywhere but her. "Wednesday?" he asked the basket of roses.

"For dinner. You did inform Mr. and Miss Morris, did you not?"

"I did." His words had been brisk and efficient. Quill had raised his brows anyway. "They'll be there." He cleared his throat. "We'll be here." He unlatched the gate and backed through it.

"Good. I forgot to include Miss Gardiner in my invitation. We could send a carriage round for her."

He paused, one hand holding the gate open. "Emmeline isn't out yet."

"I thought she was the oldest?" Susan came through the gate, her petticoats brushing his leg as she passed.

"She is, but she's not old enough." The gate swung closed. He fell in step beside her.

"Seventeen?" Susan laughed. "When I was her age, I presided over my family's table when guests came to dinner."

The table at Bailey Manor must have been quite fine. What kind of guests had she entertained? How many titled men? "Your family expects great things of you."

"I hope they're doing well. I haven't heard from them yet. I'm so anxious about my mother."

"I'm sure they've written. The Atlantic is a long passage." A lot had happened since he and the Baileys had left England.

She stopped, just shy of the back door. "I'm glad we had you."

We. She and Isaac. He made a fist, wrapping his fingers around that blasted handkerchief. *Lord, save me. I still want her, and it hurts.* At least this time, he wouldn't misunderstand her meaning. This is where he took his leave. He touched the brim of his tricorn. "Farewell." He turned sharply and walked away without a backward glance, exiting through the side garden. He would see her again soon. He might even smile while she pierced his vital organs, so she didn't know it hurt.

That's what friends did.

Twenty-Five

THE LAW OF KINDNESS

Susan slid a single white rose into the first finger of the quintal vase. For one breathless moment, she had thought Charles the Dutiful and Disinterested had been interested. Only a moment, thank heaven. In went the second rose. She was here to keep Isaac out of trouble, not plunge herself into it. The third rose was the tallest, like Charles. When he stood that close to her, she had to tip her head back to meet his gaze. It was attractive if one liked that sort of thing.

The fourth rose. Almost done. She was here for Isaac. Aside from the occasional social *faux pas*, keeping an eye on him had been almost too easy. He attended all the social gatherings their aunt arranged, read the *Gazette*, and went to bed when their hostess did. She had advised Aunt Dorothea to keep his introductions rooted in town. There was safety in the civilization of a picket fence.

Especially for a young man with an unhealthy interest in ferocious animals.

The final rose slid into the last finger. She turned the arrangement around, checking for symmetry. It was perfect. She carried it to the parlor and set it on a drop-leaf table against the wall. This morning was too quiet. The week following the ball had brought scores of young ladies eager to see the latest fashion plates, but it had been two days since she had last had a caller.

Earlier that morning, she had offered to assist Aunt Dorothea with her housekeeping. She had been rejected. Her aunt preferred to work "without interference." In desperation, she had sent a note round to Polly, inviting her to call. The note had scarcely left the house when she regretted it. The Morrises would think she had to beg for callers. She had tried to soothe her anxiety in the garden, replenishing the parlor bouquet.

Then Charles had arrived.

She brushed him from her thoughts like an errant cobweb. That was enough of that. She needed a worthy cause to occupy her time. And her thoughts. She cast her eyes about the room, settling on the large embroidered screen occupying the cold fireplace. It had been ages since she had indulged in needlework. Not since her father had delicately told her that none of the other chairs in the house were in need of a new cover.

Colorful woolen threads didn't bring the easy praise and appreciation that music did. She frowned at the harpsichord. One of last week's callers had asked her to play a new song he had brought music for. It turned out to be an exceptionally complicated piece. She had fumbled through with nearly a dozen mistakes. A few hours of practice would spare her future embarrassment.

Her fingers were flying over the keys when the front door opened. "Miss Morris to see you," Graves announced, then retreated to the foyer.

Susan rose and curtsied. "Good morning, Miss Morris."

"Please, call me Polly. I'll feel less of a scandal mendin' Quill's shirt during our visit. I have far too much ta do this week and must economize my time."

"Then Polly, it is, but only if you call me Susan." She turned toward the foyer, trusting the footman was just out of sight. "Graves, tell Lucy to bring down my embroidery kit. And my commonplace book." She would need to sketch out her design before beginning.

"Yes, ma'am."

The ladies seated themselves. Polly opened a huswif across her lap and pulled a wrinkled linen shirt from her pocket. "What are you working on?"

She could make a better fireplace screen than the one her aunt had, but the rejection this morning still stung. "I thought I might try my hand at a..." What could she do besides a screen? Not another seat cover. "A pocketbook." This had nothing to do with Charles. It was completely unrelated to his visit this morning. It was a coincidence that she had glimpsed his and was now thinking of it. Who kept a threadbare pocketbook, anyway? They were easy enough to replace.

"Ye're a kinder sister than I." Polly threaded her needle. "If Quill wants anything he can find at a store, I just have him buy it."

It was unlikely Isaac would appreciate a fine pocketbook, but as she didn't know who else to give one to, she didn't correct her. "Is his name really Quill?"

"That's what we call him. 'Tis short for Quillan. He's named after a relation. And it proves I was destined ta be a quill-pusher." After an awkward silence, she sighed. "Only businessmen understand that one. A quill-pusher is a nickname for a barrister's clerk."

"Ah." Susan offered a belated laugh. "How did you get to be a clerk?"

Polly anchored a button to the shirt cuff. "I ran away from home."

"You—what?" She wasn't sure she had heard right.

"My great-aunt came ta live with us. She and I had strong feelings about Na—well, about some things. When I couldna take it anymore, I packed my things and told a carriage driver ta take me ta the Sign of the Eagle, here in Williamsburg. He carried my trunk right inta the office. I dinna believe Quill was ever so bewildered in all his life. I proposed staying on as housekeeper, only he didna have his own quarters, only a room, so we walked all over Williamsburg that first day looking for an apartment. It was gettin' late, and we were discussing whether I should beg hospitality for the night when a man comes up, saying he heard we were looking, and would we like ta see the apartment he was renting? It had a front room and two bedchambers. The joke was on us, because after all that looking, what we needed was right in front of our faces—which is ta say, right across the street from the office."

"And you've been together ever since."

"Ever since," Polly repeated. "Which makes about two months."

"That's as long as I've known Charles." Speaking of him so informally might give Polly the wrong idea. "Mr. Johnson, I mean."

At that moment, Lucy entered the room. "Your things, miss."

"Thank you." She took the work basket and set it on the ground. "Since you're here, please take the fashion plates and those herbs up to my room."

"Yes, ma'am.

She turned the first few pages of her commonplace book. Near the front was a sketch she had made for decorating a small fire screen, the kind a lady held to protect her complexion in the winter. The proportions were wrong for a pocketbook, but the border of vines was very good.

"I must be going." Polly knotted off her thread and slipped the needle into her huswif.

"So soon?"

"I have work ta do, but thank ye for the pleasure of yer company. I dinna often meet adventurous ladies."

"Adventurous or adventuress?" No one had ever called her either.

"Adventurous. I ken ye're a lady. But crossing the Atlantic with naught but yer young brother as a guardian? 'Tis a bold, independent thing to do."

"It didn't feel like an adventure. I mean, the sunsets were beautiful. We did see dolphins a few times. There were a couple of storms, and someone had a baby. But most days were rather dull. I don't know what we would have done without—" She stopped herself before saying Mr. Johnson's company. "Without so many people to talk to."

"Ye'll tell me all about it next time I call. Or ye can call on me if ye dinna mind mismatched furniture, but no' this week."

"You said you were busy?"

"Aye. Collecting subscriptions for Boston."

"Subscriptions," Susan repeated. "You mean to donate food and clothing?"

"Aye. We're going to every door in Williamsburg, asking people what they will pledge."

"Let me come." She couldn't spend an entire year as a burden to the community. She needed to become active in it. This was her chance.

Polly hesitated.

"I can do it. I used to help the vicar's wife all the time, taking baskets to the poor and that sort of thing. Let me help."

"If ye're that determined, get yer hat."

They quickly fell into a rhythm. When a door opened, Polly would begin with the introductions. "Good morning, Mrs. Smith. How are ye doing? May I introduce Miss Bailey? Aye, she's Mrs. Evan's niece, from England."

After going through the niceties, Susan would introduce the purpose of their visit. "I believe I saw you yesterday at the church, fasting for the poor people in Boston. We're taking subscriptions for them—anything you can pledge. It will be picked up at a later date."

Then Polly would record the subscription, and they would excuse themselves to continue their work. They made it around one city block and halfway around the next before arriving at a house that, from the outside, looked exactly like Aunt Dorothea's, save that it was painted white. A footman led them into the parlor. Something cold trickled through her when she saw who was frowning at them.

Polly began the introductions again. "Good morning, Mrs. Yates. This is Miss Bailey—"

The woman interrupted. "We're acquainted."

That bit of rudeness flustered Polly. "Oh. Good. Well, we're seeking subscriptions for the people of Boston. As ye know—"

Mrs. Yates shook a knobby finger at Susan. "Newly arrived, and already turning your back on the king. Young people!"

She flushed but raised her chin. Baileys did not back down. "I've done nothing I'd be ashamed to admit to His Majesty."

"Said like you take tea with him every Wednesday."

"I haven't met him myself, but my cousin's aunt, by law, met him a year ago April. She declared him to be an upstanding Christian, and what is more Christian than feeding the poor and clothing the naked? The Boston Port Act is just a law. But our good king has made no law against charity. I assure you, my conscience is fully capable of honoring our king and feeding the hungry. As you know, once Boston's port closes, the people will have difficulty getting food and clothing. Charity is our duty. What can I put you down for?"

The woman blinked, then nodded. "Five chickens, three sheep, and a hundred pounds of flour." This time, she shook her finger at Polly. "Don't let it be said that the Yates family wasn't generous."

"Very generous!"

They made a dozen more calls before dinner. The Blue House was within sight when Polly suddenly said, "What do ye think of Charles?"

"What do I think of him? Why, Miss Polly, I certainly hope you aren't playing matchmaker. If I had wanted to get married, I would have done it in England."

"Ye're—what? Twenty-four?"

"Indeed."

"Only a year older than myself. Are ye no' anxious ta make a match?"

"Why should I be? I've never been a burden to my family. And a lady of good breeding is never too old to marry. If she is no longer handsome herself, she only needs a handsome dowry."

"If ye feel that way, then I willna play matchmaker."

"If you can promise me that, I won't even tease you about a man."

Polly held out her hand. "I accept the terms of yer contract."

They shook on it before parting.

Susan bumped into Isaac in the foyer. He looked out the door behind her and asked, "Where have you been?"

"Making calls with a friend." The words warmed her heart because they were true. She and Polly were going to be good friends.

Twenty-Six

WHOLESOME DIVERSIONS

MONDAY, JUNE 6, 1774

Susan curtsied as the Hendriks took their leave. The door had scarcely closed behind them when it swung open again. For the third time that morning, it was Isaac. He went straight for the stairs but paused when Aunt Dorothea called to him from the parlor. "Aren't you going to tell us about your errands?"

"There's nothing worth telling." He then took the stairs two at a time, disappearing from view faster than he removed himself from hearing. A loud creaking over the parlor suggested he had flung himself onto his bed. Boys had no regard for the well-being of furniture.

Aunt Dorothea frowned at the ceiling. "Is he often this restless?"

"From time to time. It may be the fine weather—one doesn't know whether to be inside or outside." In truth, he hadn't acted like this in over a year. Not since that time he had taken a fancy to the blacksmith's illiterate daughter. Thank heaven that was over.

"Town life may be a trifle confining for a young man with so much energy. I could arrange a trip to the countryside."

The countryside was the last place he should go. "Don't trouble yourself. I'm sure there's still plenty to see and do in town. Might I have the carriage? I'll take him out before dinner." He was her responsibility. And if there was a woman in question, she needed to find out who it was and how to discourage her.

A minute later, she hesitated outside his room. It was becoming more and more difficult to interest him in anything about town. She pulled out her commonplace book, intending to find her list of upcoming engagements he should be looking forward to. Instead, her book fell open to another list she had entitled, "Genteel Improvements."

Blue ribbon on plain cap
Play guitar for company
Poise in conversation
Avoid eccentric comments
Charity work
Dining etiquette?

Without further polish, Miss Gardiner would end up a tradesman's wife, doomed to chores from dawn to dusk. She would thank Susan for her assistance when she married a gentleman with a generous library.

If Charles hadn't declined Miss Gardiner's dinner invitation, Susan would soon have a better idea of how much work was ahead of them. Dining manners were as essential to good company as musical skills or charitable endeavors. It was beyond hope that the young lady could assist her and Polly with the subscriptions for Boston. Such work required poise, confidence, and appropriate eye contact.

She turned the pages. Written sideways in a margin was scrawled *Bray School*. A caller had mentioned the charity by chance, and she had noted the direction, intending to look into it further. On the next page, she found what she had been looking for. This week, there was a supper party with the Randolphs, dinner with the Carters, and a concert at the Apollo. And, of course, Charles and the Morrises were coming to dinner on Wednesday. But surely Isaac didn't fancy the Miss Randolphs, Miss Carter, or Miss Morris anymore than he fancied Miss Gardiner.

She turned back a page. *Bray School.* It would be new to Isaac and might be a suitable charity for Miss Gardiner. The idea wasn't brilliant, but it would kill two birds with one stone—or at least temporarily stun them. She pocketed her book and pushed the door open. Isaac was lying on his bed, reading a pamphlet on muskets. He glanced at her.

"I'm calling on a charity school as soon as the carriage is ready."

"A charity school?"

"Indeed. You've been going so many places, it's making me feel restless."

He turned a page. "Enjoy yourself."

"What? No. I was hoping you would accompany me."

"And *I* was hoping to stay here and read my pamphlet. I don't see what your charity school has to do with me."

"You did attend Eton. I thought you might have some opinions about education."

"Oh, I have opinions. But having completed my education, I am entitled to avoid it for the rest of my life."

"As you wish. Miss Gardiner and I will have to make the best of it ourselves."

She could see him wavering, calculating. Though she wasn't out yet, Miss Gardiner was close enough to Isaac's age to merit his attention.

He set down the pamphlet. "When were you planning to go?"

The carriage moved south of town before stopping in front of a small clapboard house. There could be no more than two rooms down and two rooms up. This was not the comfortable home she had pictured Charles living in. To the side of the house, a white-washed picket fence ran along the road, connecting the house with a workshop. A painted wood sign above the shop had the image of a chair carved into it. Between the two buildings was a small ornamental garden. Isaac and Susan looked at each other.

"Smaller than I expected," he said.

Though it was the same thing she had been thinking, she resented hearing it said aloud, like a slight on a friend. "But it's remarkably tidy."

"Do we knock at the front door or go through the garden?" Beyond the ornamental garden were the family outbuildings, including a kitchen house, a dairy, and a stable. The family could be anywhere.

"Let's try the front door first."

After a minute of waiting, they let themselves through the ornamental garden. Roses were blooming. A small tree offered pleasant shade. A second fence at the back of the garden protected it from animals. From here, they could see a one-story addition perpendicular to the main house, with a wide covered porch. A tabby cat, half-asleep, watched them from a windowsill. The house was no architectural triumph, but it was more spacious than it had first appeared from the road.

A girl of about fifteen was hoeing a vegetable garden. She glanced up, then recognition lit her features, and she smiled.

Susan couldn't have been more surprised if Charles took up stage acting. "Jenny? What are you doing here?"

Her smile faltered. "I thought you knew. Didn't Mr. Johnson tell you?"

She glanced at Isaac, who looked as perplexed as she was. "Mr. Johnson rarely tells anyone anything. Don't be distressed if he failed to mention something important. What happened?"

"He bought my indentures."

"He—what?"

"He didn't need to. But they were going to send me so far away, and he thought I might prefer it here. And I do."

Susan was temporarily stunned. Despite her placating words to Jenny, she was distressed that Charles had failed to tell her something so important. Had she not proved herself a woman to be confided in?

Her thoughts were in a tumble when Jenny absurdly added, "I always thought he was nicer than he looked. But where are my manners? You must be here for the Gardiners. I'll get them."

"Please do," Isaac said.

She leaned the hoe against the kitchen house, then went inside. There were muffled voices. A girl of about ten years peered out the door at them. Susan offered a warm smile, but she ducked out of sight. Miss Gardiner and a woman who must be her mother came out to meet them. Since Charles' cousin was the only one who knew them all, the introductions were her responsibility.

Susan gave her an expectant look, but it was wasted as she was looking down, wiping her hands on her pinner. Her mother elbowed her. She looked up. Everyone was staring at her. "Oh. Mr. and Miss Bailey, I would like to introduce my mother, Mrs. Gardiner."

Susan curtsied. "How do you do?"

"Well enough, thank you," Mrs. Gardiner said. "What brings you here today?"

"My brother and I are going to visit a charity school, and since Miss Gardiner reads so much, we hoped she would accompany us."

Emmeline's eyes shifted from the Baileys to her mother, uncertain.

"She may. Emma, take off that dirty pinner and wash your face and hands." Her tone was brisk, like a master correcting his apprentice.

Emmeline darted a glance at Susan and flushed. "Yes, ma'am." She stepped back into the kitchen house.

Isaac broke the sticky silence. "Are those apple trees?"

"Yes." Mrs. Gardiner followed his gaze. "The orchard is a

whole acre. We make the best cider in all of Williamsburg. Mr. Price himself says so."

Susan hadn't known the rector was an authority on cider. "You must be proud."

"I wouldn't say proud. It's a lot of long days to get that much cider put up before the apples spoil. But the neighbors say it's worth it. They come and help, and we let them keep a few jugs for their families."

"It must be quite good," Isaac said.

Emmeline quietly returned and stood off to the side, her eyes wide and her hands tightly clasped together.

"We must be going," Susan said. "We'll return your daughter when we're done."

Isaac held out a hand to help Emmeline into the carriage. She stared at it a moment too long and held it a moment too short, tripping over her own petticoat. Then she plopped onto the seat and pressed herself into a corner of the carriage, like a fox cornered in a hunt.

This would never do. A lady shouldn't be cowed by something as simple as a carriage ride. It was one more thing to add to the list. "Miss Gardiner," Susan said, "a lady is never ashamed to take all the space God has given her." She demonstrated by gracefully seating herself, taking every inch of the generous space God had created her to occupy.

"Yes, ma'am," Emmeline whispered, easing herself a scant two inches from the corner. *Heavens.* Isaac must regret having come.

He took the bench across from them. "Miss Gardiner, do you dance?" He spoke lightly, as though he hadn't noticed the awkwardness.

"Yes. No. That is to say, I do know how, but I do not attend the assemblies. Or balls. Or...or anything."

That was unfortunate. Isaac's reluctance to partner with older ladies left him with limited options. Not that Susan had any confidence in her protégée's grace on the dance floor, after witnessing her awkwardness in the carriage.

"Do let me know if that changes."

"It won't. Not anytime soon."

He leaned back in his seat. "I'm here for a year. It doesn't have to be soon."

"Ah."

Susan took charge again. "We're going to the charity school sponsored by the Bray Associates. Have you heard of it?"

"You mean Bray School?"

"That's the one. I'll introduce us." Susan took the hardest part on herself. "I was thinking you could ask the teacher about the curriculum." Curricula used books. That would be the most suitable topic to begin her charitable endeavors with.

Miss Gardiner's eyes went wide with horror.

"You can do that," Susan said in a voice that could coax a babe to walk.

"Yes, ma'am," she replied in a whisper.

"Do you have a favorite firearm?" Isaac asked, abruptly turning the subject to reflect his current interest.

Emmeline stared at him for a long moment before replying, "I don't use one."

Susan raised her eyes heavenward. Isaac could use some social training as well.

"Charles has a couple," she continued. "He bought a pistol in London, but that's not what they use for militia training in Virginia." She made a small sound that was almost a giggle. "I'm not sure that they use it for militia training anywhere. He bought a musket and bayonet for that. That's what Papa has, too."

"I'm thinking about purchasing one, but I haven't decided what. Rifles for hunting, muskets for the militia, pistols for defense. It all depends on what I'll be doing once I have one."

"Does anyone know when they'll be needing to defend themselves?"

"I suppose not," Isaac said. "If you knew for certain, you wouldn't be in that situation, would you?"

Miss Gardiner smiled. This was the least self-conscious Susan had seen her, and she was discussing weapons she didn't even use. She didn't make sense.

The carriage stopped in front of an unassuming brick building. Isaac stepped down first. As he helped Emmeline out of the carriage, the door of the school opened. Dozens of Black children poured out the door. The youngest, a babe of four, held the hand of a child of ten. They were dressed simply. The girls wore shifts. The boys wore breeches and shirts. Some were shoeless. Most were stocking-less.

Here was Bray School.

Isaac adjusted his jacket, slipping seamlessly from a tiresome little brother into a man of consequence. For all his boyish ways, he was the heir to Bailey Manor. He knocked smartly and opened the door, holding it open for the ladies. At least Miss Gardiner could walk through a door without a fit of clumsiness. A dark-skinned girl looked up at them with wide eyes, her broom frozen mid-swing.

"Do not stare, Fanny." Beyond the rows of benches, a woman of sixty sat behind a desk. She was dressed modestly, yet neatly. A crisp, white pinner covered her gown.

The girl looked at the floor and bobbed a curtsy. "Yes, ma'am. Sorry, ma'am."

The teacher stood slowly. She had the weary look of a person who has recently been ill. She walked around her desk and looked directly into each of their eyes. "I am Mrs. Wager, schoolmistress and sole teacher at Bray School."

Susan had the uncomfortable feeling she was about to be tested on her lessons and found lacking, but she maintained her poise and performed the introductions. "Mrs. Wager, may I present Miss Gardiner and my brother, Mr. Bailey? I am Miss Bailey."

"What can I do for you?" That stern gaze was enough discipline for a child caught drawing when she should be doing her sums.

"I am visiting from England and was curious about your school."

"Are you acquainted with the Bray Philanthropists there?"

"No, ma'am."

Mrs. Wager looked at Fanny, who suddenly resumed sweeping. "Fanny, you may go home now."

"Thank you, ma'am." Fanny placed the broom in a corner and darted out the door, closing it a little too loudly behind her.

Mrs. Wager scowled at the door, then turned her attention back to Susan. "What would you like to know about our school?"

She nudged Miss Gardiner. This was her turn. Her eyes went wide, but she spoke. "What is your curriculum?"

"After they have learned the alphabet and syllabary, I teach them out of *Dixon's English Instructor*. We also read passages from the *Bible*, the *Book of Common Prayer*, and notable sermons. Etiquette is important for all children of every station. And the girls receive instruction in needlework and knitting."

During this explanation, Miss Gardiner paid the speaker no attention, as she looked over the towering stacks of books on the desk.

"Those are good books," Susan said. "Don't you agree, Miss Gardiner?"

"Hmm?" Her attention returned. "Yes, very...wholesome. Do your students read any Newbery books?"

"Newbery books?"

"Like *Mother Goose's Melody* or *Tommy Gingerbread*?"

Mrs. Wager lifted her chin. "We use the precise curriculum dictated by the philanthropist group in England. It is a robust program capable of giving a thorough education to any student who remains here for the full three years."

"Yes, ma'am," she said, now studying the floor.

Susan refused to be cowed. "Are all of your students enslaved?"

"No. I have a few each year who were born free."

"Why do they attend?"

"Education helps everyone to better fill the station they have been born into. Each student will be able to read the *Bible* and *Gazette*, track their own expenditures, and show respect for their betters. For the girls, skill in needlework will be useful to them their whole lives."

"Isaac, wasn't there something you wanted to ask?"

He raised his brows. They both knew there wasn't. After a long, condescending look that reminded her he was here against his will, Susan asked, "What do the students do after they complete their education?"

"Those who were born free? They either learn their parents' trade or become indentured to learn another trade."

That wasn't what Susan expected to hear. "You don't make freedom sound much better than slavery."

Mrs. Wager shook her head. "You're a lady, Miss Bailey. A lady from England with no understanding of these matters. You don't know what it's like for those who must earn their bread by the sweat of their brow."

She glanced meaningfully at Miss Gardiner. "Freedom means earning money for the clothes on your back and choosing which clothing to purchase with that money. Freedom is the opportunity to choose to grow your garden or purchase your food, but if you fail to do one of those, freedom is having no one to blame but yourself when you are hungry. There are few people so privileged in the world that they can play an instrument, read frivolous novels, and go to balls every week, yet still be allowed to plead a headache when they find their company tiresome. Be grateful for what you have, but do not act surprised when the common lot of man differs from your experience."

Susan bristled. She didn't waste time reading novels. She didn't attend balls every week, and people *wanted* her to play an instrument. "Thank you for your time, Mrs. Wager."

"You're welcome. Now, if you'll excuse me, I have lessons to prepare."

As the door closed behind them, Susan sighed.

"Don't complain to me," Isaac said, handing her into the carriage. "This was your idea. Tell me again why you wanted me to visit a dame school." He handed Miss Gardiner in.

"You wanted to see the world. Charity schools are part of the world."

Isaac rapped the ceiling. The carriage lurched into motion. "The Cumberland Gap is part of the world. The Potomac River is part of the world. Should I drag you along to see them?"

"If they're not within a day's drive of Williamsburg, neither of us should see them." Turning to Miss Gardiner, she said, "You did your part quite well. It was thoughtful of you to suggest other reading materials."

They dropped her off and were back at the Blue House in time for dinner. She had a headache coming on, but she smiled through the meal and carried her full share of the conversation.

Being a lady hadn't made her selfish.

Twenty-Seven

FAITH & FOLLY

WEDNESDAY, JUNE 8, 1774

He had been back in Virginia for less than a month, but already Charles had several briefs. Every one of them came from a gentleman who had first visited the office because of Susan. "Social intricacies," she had said. Nonsense. She could bewitch a sailor into giving up the sea.

It was as good an explanation as any. He couldn't straighten his cravat without being haunted by her fingertips. His heart beat faster at the sound of her voice. His mind rehearsed their conversations when he was bent over his work. If love was an affair of the heart, why couldn't he get her out of his head?

He rubbed his temples and groaned.

Quill's chair creaked. "Is that brief giving you trouble?"

"It's fine." He only needed to defend the legal distribution of the estate: one-third to the widow, with the remainder divided equally among the surviving children. Justice would be served with arithmetic so simple he could explain it to a bricklayer.

"Hmm." Quill narrowed his eyes.

Charles turned to the window. "Isn't it almost time for

dinner?" He couldn't concentrate on work while a meal at the Blue House loomed before him.

"It can't come soon enough. I've hardly gotten a thing done with you moaning and sighing like a lovesick bull calf."

Charles straightened his shoulders. "I have not—"

"Yes, ye have." Quill's eyes twinkled merrily as he stacked his papers. He delighted in provoking Charles.

And Charles was provoked. Suppressing his feelings about Susan was already too much. His aggravating friend couldn't expect the same courtesy. He stood abruptly, his chair scraping across the floor. "Let's see if you're as easy to pin as you used to be." It had been years since he had bested his friend in a wrestling match, but only because it had been years since he had last tried.

Quill looked at him in surprise. "In the office?"

"Why not? There's no one else here." Polly had left ages ago to dress for dinner.

"As ye like." Quill shrugged off his jacket while Charles unbuttoned his best waistcoat. After pushing the chairs away, he and Quill began circling each other like a pair of cocks sizing up their opponents. The scattered tension he had felt all day was focused on attacking his closest friend.

The door opened.

They both jumped back.

"Are ye ready?" It was Polly, dressed for dinner. Her eyes widened as she took in Quill's and Charles's state of undress. "It is no' that hot." She pulled the door almost closed behind her, then added, "Do get dressed before coming out, will ye? There are children in the street."

The door shut, and Charles grabbed his waistcoat. The need for distractions was past. It was time for dinner at the Blue House.

"Remember, she's above your class," he told Quill as they walked. "Don't get any ideas about her."

"So, ye willna even try ta court her, but ye also willna allow anyone else ta try?"

It sounded absurd when Quill said it. "Something like that. Remember, she only invited you because we're friends."

"I'm already her friend," Polly pointed out.

"Heaven knows how you managed that," he muttered dryly.

Graves answered the door as she swatted his shoulder. The footman's laugh quickly turned into a sober cough. He allowed them to enter. Susan was at the blasted harpsichord again, her fingers dancing over the keyboard. She left off playing abruptly, standing to greet them.

Quill bowed over her hand, as pretentious as a macaroni. "Charles failed ta tell us what a gifted musician ye are."

Charles glowered at him. The first time he had spoken in court wasn't as a barrister. He had been a William and Mary student called in as a witness, defending his impulsive friend's honor after a foolish flirtation. If Quill started sweet-talking Susan, he would lose more than a wrestling match.

She flushed. "Thank you. Is there anything you'd like to hear?"

His freckled face was alight with hope. "Could ye favor us with 'Maggie Lauder?'"

"If I can find the music."

"Allow me," Polly said, quickly navigating Mrs. Evans's generous stash. She placed the sheet on the harpsichord and hovered, ready to turn pages as Susan launched into the sprightly tune.

Quill winked at Charles and made himself at home on the settee. The rascal. He had the heart of a saint but would trade his soul for music. Sneaking out to concerts at the Apollo had nearly gotten both of them expelled as schoolboys, but no shame marred his face today. He tipped his head back, smiled, and closed his eyes, lost in the enjoyment of the music that surrounded them.

Charles couldn't close his eyes. Now that he was over the initial shock of seeing her in so much finery, he couldn't stop staring. Roses nestled in her hair as if they grew there. The silk gown shimmered as she moved with the music. She had forgone a kerchief for dinner, instead wearing a ribbon about her throat and a string of pearls that draped across her chest, almost as low as her neckline.

Polite applause woke him from his trance. He gave her a stiff smile and a nod, then strode over to the window before he could be accused of staring. Enough amusements. He had come for dinner and couldn't leave until they had eaten.

"Where's yer brother?" Quill asked as a phaeton rolled to a stop in front of the house.

"He went out a couple of hours ago." Her voice was tense. "He said he would be back for dinner. Clearly, he'll be late."

"He's here now," Charles said.

She moved beside him, carrying the perfume of the rose garden. Her silk petticoats rustled against his legs. He closed his eyes, surrendering himself to the pleasure of her presence. If only he could escort her back to the garden, nay, to the greater privacy of the pergola. This time, he would untie the ribbon about her throat, then follow the path of pearls across the softness of her skin. His lips parted. He would—

"That's the colonel and his wife," she corrected, unaffected by his nearness.

He would drown his blasted feelings in the middle of the James River at high tide.

A young man helped the colonel climb down from the phaeton. "Oh," she said. "And Isaac. You were right. I wonder what he was doing with them."

He was right. Just not when it mattered most. There was nothing more wrong than falling in love with a woman he could never have. Lost in thought, he scarcely noticed the warm greetings and trivial talk. He scarcely noticed anything but her nearness until the chatter drifted away as the others moved down the hall. Belatedly, he offered his arm to Susan. She took it, and his skin prickled under her touch, like a thousand sparks had escaped the hearth and singed him all at once.

She leaned close enough to speak softly, the roses inches from his face. "You've been quiet today."

"Oh. Just thinking."

"What's on your mind?"

"Work," he said at random. "I've been busy, thanks to you."

That pleased her—there was a light in her eyes and the sort of half smile that stays long after it starts. He helped her into a chair and took the seat beside her. He was no good at the sort of flowery words that ladies adored. But was it possible that this lady enjoyed her praise when it was as plain as bread with butter? He was staring. Again. He tugged his gaze away. Across the table, Isaac was beaming at no one in particular.

"Everything looks delicious," Quill said.

"Thank you," Mrs. Evans dished vegetable pie onto each plate as it came. "This is from our third patch of peas. And the first of the raspberries."

The plates continued around the table. Charles lifted a slice of ham onto each one before passing it on to Susan. She added a raspberry dumpling. Once the plates had completed their circuit, they waited for Mrs. Evans to take the first bite.

She had scarcely done so when Isaac said, "I have an announcement."

The colonel and his wife exchanged a knowing look.

Mrs. Evans put down her fork. "I am all curiosity. What is the news?"

"You've heard that Lord Dunmore is taking a group of men to the frontier?"

She narrowed her eyes. "Yes." Everyone knew that.

"I'm going with him." He announced his decision with the enthusiasm of a boy getting his first hunting hound.

Susan paled. "You're—what?"

"We're going to travel up to the Potomac River, then west through the mountains. There are going to be peace talks with Indian chiefs and mountain men."

Susan half rose in her seat, the image of motherly intimidation. "You're not going."

"Yes, I am." His voice rose.

"It's too dangerous!"

"I'm not a child. *I* booked the passage and wrote the letters, and crossed the Atlantic. I didn't ask for a nursemaid to follow me."

Susan, who had a command and a cure for everything, sank into her chair, stricken. After a minute, her brown eyes found Charles. Prometheus knew nothing of suffering. He had only had his liver eaten. Somehow, witnessing her pain pierced like a dagger through his own heart.

"Say something," she whispered. It was a plea for help. For mercy. If anyone deserved mercy, it was her, but he was powerless to provide it. The boy's father should have been there, guiding his decisions. Charles was nothing to the family—a mere chance acquaintance. They needed a man with the authority to arbitrate between them.

But she trusted him.

"Your concern does you credit," Charles began gently, "and if he were throwing his lot in with just anyone, I would be concerned as well. But he will be under the protection of the royal governor. No one is more committed to preventing war in Virginia than he. No one in the colonies is more respected. Isaac will be as safe as a healthy young man has any right to be."

"You think it's for the best?"

"Of course it is," Colonel Hendriks said, drawing her attention. "A boy his age is meant to be out in the world doing something. He doesn't need coddling."

"Our parents will be worried."

"Only if they know." Isaac dug into his dinner with no further concern for his family.

There was a refreshing murmur of conversation and clatter of dishes from everyone but Susan. She was as downcast as a kitten after a rain shower. It wasn't right that someone who was a living miracle should be subjected to misfortune of any kind. There was no justice in that. For Susan, he would pray every night until Isaac returned. "It will come out right," he told her. The logic supporting his assertion was as insubstantial as a ladder built of clouds. He reached for the bottom rung and found he had the faith to climb.

PEACE & PROTECTION

SATURDAY, JULY 16, 1774

Charles wiped the July heat from his brow, then shifted his bayonet from one shoulder to the other. He had left Williamsburg so soon after turning eighteen that he had never before attended militia training. The crowd of men pressed from the perimeter wall surrounding the Williamsburg Magazine, into the streets, and to the steps of the courthouse. A cacophony of men's voices, arrhythmic drumming, and a dozen fifes playing as many different tunes surrounded the courthouse. A few musicians were clustered together. Some young men darted about the crowds, waving hats and calling for friends.

"Dinna worry yerself," Quill said. "The lieutenant will take roll, tell us some old war stories, and then set us at liberty."

"Liberty to do what?"

"There'll be a market in the street. By dinner, half the men will be drunk on the courthouse steps."

"You're telling me all that stands between our families and a French invasion is an army of drunkards?"

Quill grimaced. "I wouldna be worried about the French if I were ye." If he was referring to trouble on the frontier, he was wrong. Lord Dunmore's party, including Isaac, had left about a fortnight ago. Their mission was to promote the welfare of Virginia and to keep the peace. They were all in good hands.

They pressed up against the brick wall surrounding the magazine. Though Isaac had purchased a rifle for his "adventure," he had borrowed other campaign supplies from the public stores. Colonel Hendriks had helped him pick out a good bedroll and tent for his adventure.

"There's the lieutenant." Quill gestured to a man on horseback. The crowd parted as he made his way to the courthouse.

After roll call, the men were arranged by company and rank. Every freeman in Williamsburg was there. Some, like Uncle Rob and the colonel, were veterans of the French and Indian War. Former schoolmates from his time at William and Mary carried virgin muskets that had seen no more action than a duck hunt.

Every officer, every soldier who carried a weapon, was white. The free Blacks in his company were assigned to play fife or drum. They weren't allowed to own a firearm unless they owned a home, and those weapons stayed at home.

"HANDLE YOUR CARTRIDGES." The lieutenant spoke in a carrying voice. Charles slapped his cartridge box to settle the powder inside.

"OPEN YOUR CARTRIDGES." They weren't wasting powder on a drill, so the men pantomimed opening a cartridge with their teeth and tucking it under their chins.

"PRIME."

A pantomime of priming muskets was interrupted by an unkempt young man. He spoke loudly and languidly. "We know how to shoot a gun." Every head turned.

The men were so quiet that every step of the lieutenant's horse echoed in the street, parting the orderly ranks. The lieutenant rode close enough that he could have kicked the offender. In a voice of sweet condescension, he looked down and said, "So, you can shoot a squirrel, can you?"

The man lifted his chin. "Shore can."

"A squirrel ain't gonna shoot back. It isn't enough to fire a musket." The lieutenant looked around at the men and raised his voice. "In the chaos of battle, you must all fire when your commanding officer says fire, advance when your commanding officer says advance, and charge your bayonet when the commanding officer says charge. Fight as one, or die alone."

An uneasy silence filled the street.

The young man filled it. "Do they give us bayonets if there is a battle?"

Charles groaned. Some people didn't know when to hold their tongue. According to the Militia Act, every soldier present needed to own a bayonet as well as a musket. This fool could be fined for admitting he didn't have one.

The lieutenant spoke slowly. "If you value your own life, you'll buy one yourself." He rode to the front of the companies. "Every battle ends with a bayonet charge. If you don't have one, you're as good as dead."

By midmorning, jackets and waistcoats were abandoned. Foreheads glistened under the summer sun. Charles had prudently left his pocketbook at home. Leaning against the empty stocks, he tipped his canteen, catching the last drops of lemonade. "What were you saying about drill?"

"That it isn't usually like this," Quill said. "I'll wager it's because of the tensions on the frontier. If Dunmore can't settle things peacefully, the settlers may need reinforcements."

Charles dismissed Quill's doubts. "The Iroquois nations have already allied themselves with Lord Dunmore, and the settlers are bound to be in his favor."

Nathaniel Ingram, an old schoolmate, sat beside them. "Why doesn't Pennsylvania do its part? I thought they were claiming some of the new territory."

Charles tossed his empty canteen onto his jacket. "Because they're a herd of Quaker pacifists. They won't even protect themselves." Not that the settlers needed protecting. They just needed a strong show of force, something the Pennsylvanians refused to do. He picked up his musket and polished it with an old hand-kerchief.

"That suits Dunmore fine," Quill said. "He wants all of that new territory to be part of Virginia, the greatest colony in Britain."

Ingram drained his canteen. "I never thought he had any great love for the provinces. Why is he doing this?"

"Dinna ye know?" Quill asked. "His lordship was part of the Forty-five Rebellion."

Charles nearly dropped his musket. "The Jacobite Rising? No!"

"Yes," Quill said. "Our royal governor was pulled from school ta serve as Page of Honor ta Bonnie Prince Charlie. His father barely escaped execution."

It was extraordinary news, but Charles didn't embarrass Quill with questions. His father had been entangled in the rebellion and had fled to the Americas when it had failed. "That was thirty years ago. What does that have to do with the territory disputes?"

"Dinna ye see? He's still trying ta prove his loyalty ta the crown."

The man couldn't be faulted for obeying his father, especially at such a young age. "He *has* proven his loyalty," Charles said. "Why else would he have been appointed the royal governor?"

"ATTENTION!"

Every man rushed back into their company and rank and stood, shoulder-to-shoulder, firearms ready.

Twenty-Nine

FINDING TRUST

MONDAY, JULY 18, 1774

Susan discussed Isaac's journey with all their callers. Most agreed he would have reached the Potomac River by now. Everyone had enthusiastic tales of the wilderness, though not all thought she should be concerned.

"A proper adventure is essential for turning boys into men," Colonel Hendriks had said. "In the end, what's a scar but a mark of courage and a tale to tell when he's back?"

Susan disagreed, but out of respect for the elderly and infirm, kept her thoughts to herself. Most boys became men without endangering their lives. Otherwise, there wouldn't be enough men to go around. And Isaac wasn't just any boy. He was her only brother. She had agreed to leave her beloved home to keep him safe, to guide him away from dangerous and imprudent situations. Instead, she was stuck at her aunt's house, playing the harpsichord for callers and wondering if she would ever see him again.

She hadn't told her family yet. It should have been Isaac's duty, but he had shirked that as merrily as a truant schoolboy. She had sent a last letter at the end of June, omitting his plans. She couldn't in good conscience send another letter without informing their family that he was no longer with her. That was unthinkable. It was tantamount to admitting failure. Her song ended on a sour chord. She shook out her hands and tried again.

"Susan," Aunt Dorothea interrupted, "would you change into your violet gown? The one with the sacque back?"

"For dinner?" That was still hours away, and the sticky July heat made her silk gown impractical.

"I'm going to my mantua-maker this morning. I would like her to alter my gray gown after that fashion."

Feeling the flattery of imitation, Susan went up to change. When she opened the door, Lucy was crouched on the floor by the clothespress.

"Did you drop something?"

Lucy straightened with more haste than grace. "No, miss." She didn't meet Susan's eye. "Did you need something, miss?"

"My aunt would like to make over one of her gowns like my violet sacque-back." The compliment warmed like sunshine.

"Does she?"

"Indeed, yes. She would like me to wear it to see her mantua-maker this morning."

"I'll get it out right away, Miss Bailey."

Within the hour, the mantua-maker turned Susan about like a doll, running her fingers over ruffles and seams. "Mmm. I see."

"Can you do it?" Aunt Dorothea asked.

"If we borrow some material from the upper back of the petticoat, I can patch it with cabbage from another gown—then we could alter this panel here, and still have material for a matching bow."

Aunt Dorothea and the mantua-maker continued discussing the alterations. Susan's attention strayed. Seamstresses sat silently in hard-backed chairs, bent over their work. A small whimper caught her ear. "Shh. Shh," one of the seamstresses whispered.

Susan's eyes went wide. "Mrs. Finlay?"

Marion darted a look at the mantua-maker, who had paused her conversation.

Susan didn't want to bring trouble. "Forgive us. Marion and I are old acquaintances. I wanted to see her baby."

Aunt Dorothea raised her brows. Susan didn't have old acquaintances in the colonies.

The mantua-maker looked uncertainly between her and Susan. Surely she discouraged her seamstresses from wasting time conversing with the customers. "Certainly, miss. Let me get you a chair."

Susan smiled. Shopkeepers never denied her anything when she was properly dressed as the eldest daughter of a wealthy landowner. Seated beside Marion, she could see the baby in a padded basket. He had grown a triple chin below cheeks as round as apples. One plump fist had wrestled free of the swaddling.

"He's doing well."

"Yes, thank you."

"How is your health? I was worried you weren't out of danger."

"I'm well. Thank you for your concern."

Susan untied the ribbon about her throat and dangled it above the baby. His eyes widened. He gurgled happily. Susan slowly moved the ribbon side-to-side as the baby followed it with his eyes. "Your husband, does he work nearby?" Surely he wasn't indented to a mantua-maker.

Marion shook her head. "Didn't you hear? He's on a plantation." Her voice was a whisper. "I haven't seen him."

"I'm sorry to hear that." The words were weak, a too-small plaster on a too-large wound. This problem was too big for Susan to fix. "Why would I have heard?"

"Mr. Johnson, of course."

The July heat warmed her face. Charles had neglected her again.

~

CHARLES STACKED THE PAPERS TOGETHER, TAPPING them upright on the desk before locking them away. His first brief was in order. He closed the books that littered his desk, returning them to their places on the bookshelf.

The office was quiet. Polly had demanded that Quill escort her for a little shopping. It was a lovely day to be out. Little wonder they hadn't returned. Charles ate an early dinner of bread and cheese that Aunt Charity had packed. It was no better than a common supper, but he felt satisfied as he brushed the crumbs from his desk and breeches.

The breeze from the open window was inviting. The next brief could wait. He wanted to clear his mind with a brisk walk. Tired of borrowing keys when the Morrises were late, Charles had paid for a duplicate for himself. He locked the empty office behind him.

After a few blocks, he realized he was walking toward the Blue House. *Blast.* The one place he should avoid. He had no business there. He turned onto the next street and began to make his way back to the office. A girl ran a hoop down the street. Men loaded heavy crates into a wagon. Mrs. Evans's carriage waited outside a shop.

Charles slowed. He could cross the street as if he hadn't noticed. No. It wasn't as if he was avoiding Miss Bailey. Mayhap the ladies would need help carrying their purchases. It would be ungentlemanly to pass by. Charles pushed the shop door open.

~

"ISN'T IT WRONG TO PURCHASE THINGS IMPORTED BY the East India Company?" Susan whispered.

"It was a recommendation," Mrs. Evans replied, "not a law. Besides, these goods would have been ordered before anyone heard about Boston's unfortunate fate. It would be cruel to punish our local merchants by withholding our business."

Susan hadn't thought of that. "Have you had less business of late?"

The shopkeeper looked appreciatively at her silk gown. "Yes, ma'am. Much less."

Susan was wondering how many shoe buckles she should relieve the good merchant of when a tall gentleman walked in. For a moment, the harsh sunlight behind him put his features in shadow, but she could recognize him by his silhouette, the way his jacket hung from his shoulders, his gait, or his mannerisms. She smiled. "Mr. Johnson. I hope you are well."

"Well enough. And yourself?"

"I find Julys in Virginia rather warmer than I like." She plied her fan. "But I am glad to see you." She tilted her head. "I ran into a mutual acquaintance this morning. You remember Marion Finlay?"

"Naturally."

"I met her at the mantua-maker's. I found it interesting that she thought I already knew she was there. So did Jenny."

"Oh." He swallowed. "Did they?"

She tapped his shoulder with her fan. "Have you known where they were this whole time?"

His eyes darted around, like an animal seeking its escape. "I made it a point to attend the auction. So, yes. I knew."

"You knew and didn't tell me. Why? Don't you trust me?"

His blue-gray eyes met hers. "I trust you."

For two heartbeats, she stared. She had expected an evasive monologue, not a blunt compliment. "Well, good. You should. But next time, tell me. I don't like secrets."

"The next time you save someone's life and she gets auctioned off, I'll tell you."

It was unlikely to happen again to a mutual acquaintance. She sighed. This wasn't the last time Charles would keep secrets, and she would be annoyed. "What brings you out of your office today?"

"The view." He dropped his gaze and picked up one of the buckles she had been considering. "Do you need new buckles?"

"Need? Oh, no. I was only planning to buy a blue ribbon. I hadn't planned on buckles today, but the shopkeeper has had so much less business of late."

"Miss Bailey," Charles said in a voice that was affectionate and firm. A voice that knew business. "You are not responsible for the town's economy."

He spoke so confidently that Susan was persuaded he must be right. It was a relief. If she was going to keep buying books for her little library, her pin money might not last the full year anyway. She returned the buckles to their basket. "Is Miss Gardiner enjoying *The Taming of the Shrew*?"

"She's already done. Miss Bailey, I cannot thank you enough for your exceeding kindness to Emmeline."

"You should expect me to be nothing but kind to your cousin."

"Thank you."

That night, Susan lay awake remembering the day. Aunt Dorothea had finally needed her for an errand. Mrs. Finlay and her baby were in good health. And Charles trusted her.

She trusted him, too.

A few months ago, she wouldn't have believed it possible that the difficult man she met on the *Minerva* would become a faithful friend. He was still quiet and sober. But he never depressed her spirits. Rather, he listened attentively to her concerns before speaking. She always felt better after talking with him.

It was such a comfortable friendship. It was a pity it couldn't last. Once she returned to England, they would never see each other again. A night breeze came through the open window. She shivered. It was best to ignore the clouds on the horizon. There would be time to run for shelter when they came.

She rolled over. The moonlight shone on the clothespress.

Lucy had been odd this morning. It was probably nothing, and yet...

Susan parted the mosquito netting and swung her feet to the floor. Kneeling beside the clothespress, she ran a hand underneath, searching.

Nothing was there.

Thirty

ARRANGING FLOWERS

TUESDAY, AUGUST 23, 1774

Hummingbirds flitted through the pergola, untroubled by the sticky August heat that followed Susan into the shade. Lucy had set aside her silk gowns and wool petticoats for the cooler weather Aunt Dorothea promised would return. Until then, she had been spending the worst of the afternoons in her bedchamber, dressed down to her shift, praying Isaac was safe wherever he was.

The pergola pulled in a gentle breeze. She lifted her cotton petticoats a few inches and shook them, stirring the air. She almost didn't hear the soft step approaching across the path of crushed shells. Emmeline had come as requested. She handed Susan a bouquet of deep yellow and brown and curtsied. "Miss Bailey. Are you well?"

Susan held the flowers in one hand and maneuvered the fan with the other. "As well as can be expected in this climate." By fanning off to the side, she relieved the sticky sensation on the back of her neck.

"Oh." Emmeline looked doubtfully at the bouquet.

"Thank you for the flowers. They're so cheery."

"You're welcome. Charles thought you should have them since they're black-eyed Susans."

"Charles? Is he at home this morning?"

"No, but he's said it before. Have you heard from your brother?"

"No, but Isaac never was a reliable correspondent." And now, Susan wasn't. She had covered the front and back of only three sheets since he had left a month ago, with no intention of posting it until his safe return. That was weeks away, at best.

Emmeline fingered tendrils of honeysuckle. "What did you want to see me about?"

Susan fanned her face desperately. "You remember the charity school we visited a couple of months ago?"

"Indeed."

"I thought the headmistress looked ill." She hadn't done anything to help her. "She died." A bee landed on her bouquet. "I heard they were planning to close Bray School."

"That's unfortunate," Emmeline said with the sweet simplicity of a girl who hasn't realized she has the power to change the unfortunate.

"I have the direction of the gentleman who oversaw the school. I thought we could call on him."

"To offer our condolences."

"N-yes. Yes, of course. But also to persuade him to keep the school open."

It was late morning when a footman escorted Susan and Emmeline into a stuffy parlor. The climate had no right to be so insufferable this early in the day. The windows were open, but the curtains were drawn, shutting out sunlight and fresh air. "Miss Bailey and Miss Gardiner to see you, sir."

Mr. Nicholas was a respected merchant, planter, treasurer for the colony of Virginia, and member of the House of Burgesses. Susan had gathered this much from her aunt, confirmed by gossiping callers. In person, he was a well-dressed gentleman approaching fifty.

He gestured to a pair of wing chairs by an empty hearth. "What can I do for you, ladies?" He sat on the edge of the settee as they took their seats.

"We heard about Mrs. Wager," Susan began.

"Unfortunate, that. Her health had been poor these past few years." His tone was as indolent as the climate.

"Our condolences."

He nodded politely.

"However, we were distressed to hear you were planning to close the school."

"Another unfortunate circumstance, but I assure you, a necessary one." He waved a dismissive hand.

She was irked by his dismissal. "Traditionally, when one headmistress dies, the school does not show its grief by closing. It honors her memory by hiring another."

He dusted his sleeve with his hand. "A fine sentiment, but how many women will teach a full class of thirty barefoot children when she could tutor one wealthy child for the same wage?"

Susan was aghast. "You paid her so little?"

"Her wages came from a combination of what the Bray Philanthropists sent from England and what the children's masters contributed. That is to say, her wage was entirely paid for by English philanthropists."

"Virginians have been so generous in caring for the poor of Boston. I'm sure if they understood the need for the school—"

Mr. Nicholas cut her off. "The Bray Associates expected the community to take on the financial weight of the school, but in fourteen years, it has not happened. I am weary of being caught between idealistic philanthropists and a disinterested population."

Susan looked to the only one on her side, but Emmeline was out of her depth.

He spoke firmly. "Mrs. Wager has died, God rest her soul, and the Williamsburg branch of Bray School has died with her."

The man was clearly beyond persuasion.

~

Despite small disappointments, the weeks passed quickly, and the heat of summer mellowed into the glory of autumn. One afternoon, Graves entered the parlor while she was practicing her instrument. "A letter for you, miss."

Susan abandoned her music to take the letter. It had been more than a month since she had heard from home.

"And one for Lucy," he continued. "Shall I give it directly to her?"

"Yes." She couldn't be bothered with trivialities when facing the immediate joy of news from home. She broke the family seal.

> *August 11, 1774*
>
> *Dearest Susan,*
>
> *We received your letter dated June 16th and were happy to see that you and Isaac were in good health at that time.*
>
> *I trust you are keeping him out of mischief and are a blessing to your aunt.*
>
> *Papa wants me to add that the housekeeper is doing an excellent job, so you don't need to worry about us.*

The letter continued with a brief description of the weather and agricultural concerns of the community. A neighbor had a baby. A cousin took ill and then recovered. It was signed Mama, but the penmanship was Anne's.

Susan set the letter down with a sigh.

Aside from brevity, there was nothing wrong with the letter. She could easily picture her family and neighbors going about their quiet lives. But there was nothing of herself in the picture.

Between her sister and the housekeeper, she had been replaced. Her own family didn't miss her.

They would, eventually, They would miss her when this housekeeper ran away or when Anne was out and preferred the attentions of young men to the burden of caring for their mother. Meanwhile, she would be glad they were doing so well without her.

That's what love did.

She watched the bustle of town beyond the parlor window and smiled until her cheeks hurt and she couldn't pretend any longer. She should have been happy to hear from her family, but that letter was a painful confirmation that she was being forgotten. At last, she saw familiar faces in the street—Polly and her brother, with Charles a step behind, carrying a redware jar full of flowers. They lacked all the elegance of a hothouse spray, yet her lonely heart yearned to know they were for her and her alone. If they were, then at least one person had thought of her even when she was absent.

Once they were announced, she could see the bouquet was full of black-eyed Susans—the flowers Emmeline had insisted reminded him of her—interspersed with dainty purple flowers with fluffy edges.

"Here." Charles thrust the bouquet at her as if there weren't adequate words in the English language to cover the embarrassment of bringing a lady some flowers. There was no reason to be shy about it. He had given her flowers before. But this time he had arranged them in a jar and then carried them over a mile to work. These had sat on his desk all morning, reminding him of her.

She buried her smile in the bouquet. "Thank you. These are lovely."

"They're from Emmeline. She picked them."

"Oh." Her smile wilted. "Give her my appreciation. Excuse me. Mrs. Gardiner will be wanting her jar back. I'll just move these into a vase."

Between the back of the parlor and the dining hall was a

narrow passage, typically used by servants. Cupboards above and below a counter were locked to secure the silverware and candles. It was a small space for one, and Charles followed her there. An empty vase had been left on the counter. She set the jar down with an unnecessary clank. The water inside sloshed. As she moved the flowers, one at a time, her elbow brushed his chest. He didn't step away, but he didn't step closer.

Polly began playing the harpsichord.

"I got another letter from home," she said. He stood so close that there was no need to raise her voice over the music.

"Is your family well?"

"I—yes. They're all well." Except perhaps Isaac.

"But you're worried."

Was it that obvious? She sighed. "I feel so guilty for not having posted my letters since Isaac left." He had left in late June. It was nearly October.

"Your family hasn't heard from you in months?" The concern in his voice cut through her defenses.

How much had she hurt them by not writing? "If I send a letter now, they'll worry about Isaac. I should wait for him to return."

"But now they're worried about you."

She shook her head. She was far too capable, too trustworthy. It was a source of pride and hurt. "No one worries about me."

"I do." The words were low and soft.

She looked up.

His blue-gray eyes held hers. "And I cannot believe your nearest relations don't worry either. You're precious to them. Some people aren't very good at showing their feelings, but that doesn't mean they don't have them."

Her eyes stung. She looked away so he wouldn't see. "Of course, my family loves me." That's what families did, even if their letters were short. Even if they didn't ask about her.

"If you love someone, you worry about her. Is she safe? Is she happy? I know they want to hear from you."

"Mayhap you're right." She turned the vase around, looking at the arrangement from every angle. "I have a whole bundle." It was a lovely bouquet. Even if Emmeline had arranged it, Charles had still carried it all this way. "I'll post them this week."

"Would you like me to? I could do it today."

She shook her head. "I need to add a postscript."

"I'll wait."

"That won't be until after dinner."

"I understand. I'll wait."

After dinner, Mr. Morris returned to work, leaving Polly to converse with Aunt Dorothea while Charles waited. Susan deliberated on a postscript. After several false starts, she wrote,

Virginia's royal governor, Lord Dunmore, has been out west in the new territory. Isaac has been in his company. Charles assures us he is in good hands and as safe as a boy of eighteen should be. We expect them in a few more weeks.

Sus. Bailey

"Ready?" Charles asked as she sealed the letters.

She handed him the packet. "I am."

He took it, and with it a weight she had been carrying alone. "I'll post this on my way to the office. Ready, Polly?"

She was, and they took their leave. Though she was left alone again, she wasn't lonely. She ignored the new music on the harpsichord she had promised to learn and carried her bouquet up to her chamber. The oak tree outside her window was turning a brilliant red. The whole world was full of color. She spilled dozens of thread cards on the desk, seeking matches for her flowers.

The afternoon flew by as she painted her bouquet with needle and thread. It might never bring joy to anyone but herself, but on this one golden afternoon, she was enough.

Thirty-One

THUNDER AT THE APOLLO

FRIDAY, OCTOBER 21, 1774

Charles could have walked faster than the carriage was moving. The streets were so thick with people that it would take an act of God to part them. The General Court and the reelected House of Burgesses were both in session. The wives and daughters of the prominent men had followed them, hosting a dizzying series of dinners, balls, and other activities. He had thus far avoided everything save the dinners—he had to eat, after all—but Susan had ordered him to attend at least one ball. And she had insisted Emmeline was more than old enough to attend.

Polly had lent her a silk gown for her coming out. The soft blue fabric spilled across their laps, taking up far too much space in the carriage. Emmeline reverently traced the embroidered vines and birds on the stomacher, finer than anything she would ever own.

At last, they arrived at the Blue House. Graves welcomed them in. "Ladies, if you'll follow me to Miss Susan's room. Gentlemen, you're to wait in the parlor."

Emmeline followed Polly and the blue silk gown up the stairs. Graves knocked on Susan's bedroom door.

Quill elbowed Charles. "The parlor is that way."

He hated the parlor. He hated how wonderfully expensive every piece of furniture in it was. He would have been happy to start a family in a home half the size of the Blue House. Susan came from a home more than ten times its size. The frivolous harpsichord was imported. A library of unread books occupied a shelf that was only touched when it was dusted. The blue and white vases were from China. The walnut legs of the settee and chairs had been turned and polished by a master carpenter—a carpenter who sat on a three-legged stool, trading his skill for food.

"Ye dinna have ta frighten the chair afore ye sit in it."

"Frighten it?"

"Ye were scowling at it something fierce."

Charles dropped into the chair. He wasn't a humble carpenter, but he also wasn't wealthy enough to convince Susan he could provide comfortably for her. "Tonight was a bad idea."

"Since when was a bit o' merrymaking a bad idea? I'm rather fond of it myself."

"You don't think it's a mistake, letting them dress up Emmeline like she's a doll?" Laughter echoed through the house, followed by a murmur of voices. "And how many of them will it take?"

"Ladies always flock together when ribbons are involved. Let them have their fun."

"And the devil will have his dues." Emmeline was no gentleman's daughter. She would never be more than a satellite to the glittering world she orbited. And he would never be more than a friend to Susan.

"Who needs the devil when ye're a thundercloud yerself? Can ye at least *pretend* ta be happy?"

"What's there to be happy about?"

"Dozens of things. Good health. Fine weather. Shoes on yer

feet. An evening out with the woman ye fancy. No leaks in the roof. How many briefs ye won before the General Court. Isaac should be home soon."

The *Gazette* had announced over a week ago that Dunmore's party was expected any day. They should have been here already. He had prayed every night for four months for his safe return. But he had also prayed for his mother, and she had died. "I worry about that."

Quill laughed. "Charles, I've known ye for years. I love ye like a brother. Ye're always worried."

At the sound of the women on the stairs, they rose to their feet. Susan stopped just before the threshold of the parlor. The light in her eyes shone brighter than the jewels about her throat. "Presenting Miss Gardiner."

She stepped aside, revealing a young lady. The transformation was so complete that it was a full second before he recognized his cousin. He glanced back at Susan, who was smiling victoriously. Thanks to her handiwork, Emmeline could pass as a gentlewoman from one of the first families of Virginia. The blue gown matched her eyes. It had been cleverly tucked and pinned to look like it was made for her. Sapphires swung from her earlobes and ringed her neck. Gone was the plain cap she always wore, revealing an abundance of blonde curls pinned high on her head. Paint and powder had been applied to her face with a delicate hand. And Susan looked expectantly at him, as though awaiting his approval.

He wasn't entirely sure he approved, but he was impressed. "Well done, Miss Bailey." At least for one night, Emmeline could be respected and admired, even if the devil had his dues on the morrow when she returned to her labors.

Quill played along, offering a dandified bow. "My dear Miss Gardiner, am I too late ta request the honor of the first dance? Or has another of your many admirers already claimed it?"

She clasped her hands tightly. "Oh, yes. I mean, no. That is to say—that would be nice."

With Susan and Mrs. Evans, the carriage was too full to admit gentlemen, so they rode alongside the driver, looking down on the bustling streets as they crept to the Apollo.

The room was much as he remembered it from his youth. The wainscoting below and dentil molding above were painted a deep bluish-green. High above the hearth was a gilt inscription: *hilaritas sapientiae et bonae vitae proles*—jollity, the offspring of wisdom and good living.

The musicians tuned their instruments while gentlemen with lace cuffs and cravats sought their first partners. Several eyes turned to their party. Charles wore a sober brown suit, but the ladies were turned out especially fine. He felt a flicker of jealousy at sharing Susan, but at least he had the first dance with her. That was the condition on which he had agreed to come.

She took Emmeline aside. "You look lovely. Please don't duck your head and wince every time you're introduced to someone. It spoils the effect."

She blushed through the rouge. "Yes, ma'am."

"Oh! The sets are forming. Are you ready for the first dance?"

"Yes, I—" She broke off as Quill offered his arm and led her to the floor, leaving Susan with Charles.

A smile threatened his composure. "I believe you are promised to me."

She took his arm with a smile of her own. "Then we must dance."

They took their place at the top of the set. Dancing might be a communal activity, but at least he was partnered with the woman he fancied. His movements were rusty, but he could still hear his old dance master's voice calling out the steps. *Ladies, round to the left. Gentlemen, round to the right. Chassé up and down.* He lost himself in the rhythm and movement of the familiar dance, catching Susan's hand, turning about, catching her eye. He couldn't remember the last time he had enjoyed himself so thoroughly and was sorry when it was over.

He danced next with Emmeline and then with Polly. Then he

sat out, watching Susan dance with another partner. She was just as graceful, but he flattered himself that her smile lacked the warmth they had shared.

"She is happy tonight," Mrs. Evans said. "I'm glad we came. If only she could be happy here always. I want her to stay."

Charles was surprised to hear her voice his very desires. "When she has so much in England?"

"It's a selfish wish. I never had children of my own. Susan is a great comfort to me. No grandmother could dote more on her children than I would."

It couldn't happen. Susan dearly missed her family; she despised the summer climate, and he could never provide for her in the manner she was accustomed to. He finally said, "She worries about her mother."

Mrs. Evans flicked her hand, as though shooing a fly. "She has been caring for her mother so long, she has forgotten that others can do so. She has a sister, or they could always hire a nurse or companion for her mother. No, she is free to set up her own home when she takes a fancy to it."

He pressed a hand to his temple. Was it possible that his other concerns were as ill-founded? He had been rehearsing, in the lonely courtroom of his mind, damning arguments for months. Now, an unlikely ally offered salvation with a rebuttal.

He danced with three other ladies before standing up with Susan again. It would be their second and last time this evening. There was no need to draw the attention of gossips. Neither of them was as light on their feet as they had been at the start of the evening. The room was overwarm with people, despite an open window. After the final bow, he said, "Let's sit the next one out. I'll get us some punch."

They found refuge in vacant corner chairs. Susan sipped her punch. "I think your cousin is doing well."

"I agree. I hope this doesn't turn her head."

"One evening of fun? I don't think that's possible."

"I hope you're right." He frowned. Quill was standing up with Emmeline for a second time.

Susan followed his look. "Don't glare at Mr. Morris. Like as not, Polly put him up to it." A little sigh escaped, almost too quiet to hear over the noise of the ball. "I had hoped Isaac would arrive this week. He would have evened out our numbers."

"Any day now. But I wish Miss Morris would keep her brother to herself. Dancing twice with the same partner isn't the thing. It may start rumors."

"I can settle any gossip that comes my way. But really, Charles, did you not think of that before dancing with me a second time?" Her eyes sparkled over her punch.

"It isn't the same thing. You're a respected member of the community. She isn't. You know what you want. She doesn't. And she has seen so little of the world. You've made her appear like a gentlewoman, but at heart, she's still a child. Her expectations, even her desires, are highly vulnerable. She's seventeen. A little fiction can do great harm, especially if it's a fiction about herself."

Her amusement softened to thoughtfulness. She opened her mouth to reply, but they were interrupted.

"Mr. Johnson?"

Charles rose. "Mr. Barton. How are you?"

"Quite well. I must congratulate you on your good harvest. I hear the barn has never been so full."

That was the first Charles had heard. With the General Court in session, he had been far too busy to visit the plantation. "I will pass the congratulations on to my father. The credit belongs to him." As long as the ban on imports didn't put a stop to the tobacco trade, the family home would be safe for another year.

"Who's this handsome woman?" Barton eyed Susan appreciatively.

If this were a militia drill, Charles would have pushed the man back with a bayonet point. Since it was a ball, he offered an introduction through clenched teeth. "Miss Bailey, may I present Mr. Barton?"

"How do you do?"

"Fine. Just fine. How well do you know Mr. Johnson, miss?"

"We're well acquainted."

"Good. Then you know the family has a tidy plantation south of town. Nothing grand, but since his father has no wife or other children, Johnson stands to inherit it all."

"I hope, for the family's sake, it will be a long time before that happens."

"As do I," Charles said.

"Only time will tell. We nearly lost him last winter. Lucky for Johnson here that he didn't. He can focus on a future in politics. Meanwhile, his father keeps expanding. Bought an additional ten acres last year. Thanks to a promising harvest, he was able to buy some extra hands last month. Five men and three women. He'll pay them off as soon as the tobacco sells."

Susan gaped, her eyes wide open.

"Enough, sir. I have no interest in discussing my father's business on an evening of leisure. And if you're looking for a dance partner, try the wallflowers over there. Miss Bailey needs to rest."

"No offense meant, Johnson. It would do you well to take more interest in the land you will inherit."

The punch glass in Charles's hand shook. "Enough."

Mr. Barton moved on to punish others with his conversation.

"Sorry about that, Miss Bailey."

"I didn't know." Her brown eyes were troubled.

He had told her he had grown up on a large property in the country. Had she not understood what that entailed?

She gave a weak laugh. "This would never have happened in England. How can you devote yourself to justice in the community and turn a blind eye to your home? How can you have so little care where your comforts come from?"

The jury was casting its verdict before the defense had spoken. His honor, and his country's honor, were at stake. "My comforts?

When you lived in your fine English mansion, did you ever stop to think where your sugar came from? Your silk and cotton? Your coal? Do you know where coal comes from?"

He leaned closer. "Colliers never see a ray of sunlight because they toil deep in the earth from early to late, breathing soot until their lungs turn black. Who defends their justice?"

She put a hand forward, stopping just shy of his chest. "You told me," her voice shook, "that I would only see what I had seen in England. That a slave was just a servant. But since then, I've witnessed families auctioned from the tavern steps, naked children torn from their mothers' arms. I have seen faces cut and swollen from beatings and wondered what scars were hidden from my view. I have seen children stealing food and wondered how they could be hungry when we are surrounded by orchards and fields of grain. I didn't arrive yesterday. And I have seen things here that I never saw in England."

Charles had hoped she would never be pained by the sight of what he had already seen. But it was too late now, and her accusation could not remain unchallenged. "Once, a wealthy farmer had a poor harvest. He would have to sell off most of his possessions to satisfy his creditors. He would have to sell his sons off as indentured servants. His daughters would lose their dowries. In desperation, he hired a thief. Every night, the thief would slip into a different neighbor's barn and steal bits of their harvest. After five days, the thief was caught. Who do you think was guilty? The thief, or the farmer who had hired the thief?"

Susan considered for a long moment. "Both," she said softly.

"Correct. They were both convicted. In 1772, our legislature attempted to abolish the importation of slaves. They were unsuccessful because the Board of Trade in London persuaded King George that to do so would be harmful to trade and commerce. England is every bit as guilty as the colonies. And there is no earthly court big enough to appeal this injustice to."

She broke his gaze, watching the dancers. After a minute, she spoke coolly. "I may not have attended university, but that doesn't make me ignorant. I'm not foolish enough to think I can right every wrong. But that's a poor excuse for neglecting your own home. Start there. Like my aunt. She can't free everyone in Virginia, but she does what's right under her roof."

"Susan, your aunt hasn't freed anyone."

"Of course she has. That's why her servants are so loyal."

"I'm not saying her heart isn't in the right place, but in Virginia, only the royal governor has the power to make someone free, and he never does. Slaves can be inherited, bought, or sold. They are not made free."

She took a step back. "You're wrong."

"Ask her then. You'll see."

Susan excused herself and spent the next two hours as far from him as possible. While she danced, he paced. He had said too much. She was hurt and angry, and it was because of him. But it wasn't fair to blame him for his father's actions. He was no more responsible for the slavery in his father's house than Susan was for the opinions of the Board of Trade.

"Johnson, it's a ball," Quill said. "Ye shouldna frown so much."

He couldn't smile with the weight of Susan's accusations upon him, and he couldn't leave the ball until the ladies were done. A lanky university boy returned Emmeline to Mrs. Evans. She hadn't lacked partners all evening, but the exhaustion showed on her face. She should sit the next one out. But sets were beginning to form, and Nathaniel, a latecomer to the ball, was moving toward her.

Quill followed his gaze. Without taking leave, he strode across the room, cut in front of Nathaniel, and escorted Emmeline across the floor with such haste that she struggled to keep up. His rash actions did not go unnoticed. Mrs. Evans stared. Ladies whispered behind fans. The gossip would spread through every parlor on the morrow. Quill flushed until his ears turned pink. It was the only sign he was conscious that half the room was staring at him.

As soon as the blasted song was done, they were leaving. He

addressed their hostess. "Emmeline is unaccustomed to these late hours. With your permission, she needs to go home soon."

Mrs. Evans watched Susan, a wrinkle on her brow. "I think we've all had enough merriment for one evening."

Charles paced by the door for the remainder of the dance. He didn't want to leave Susan like this. There had to be some way to apologize, except he couldn't retract what was true. He just wanted to go back to the way things were three hours ago, when he had begun to have reason to hope.

Once their party was in the cool of the street, he approached her. "Susan, I—"

"Excuse me, Mr. Johnson. I have a splitting headache." She side-stepped his hand and pulled herself into the darkness of the carriage. The other ladies promptly followed. There was no room for him.

He closed the door more forcefully than necessary and swung up beside Quill on the driver's bench. There was the one person he could always talk to. Charles punched him in the shoulder to get his attention. "You scoundrel. What were you thinking, hanging over my cousin?"

There was fire in Quill's eyes. "People dance at balls, Charles. That's why they go. What did ye expect?"

"Three times?" His voice thundered with indignation. He hadn't even danced with Susan three times. "You don't dance with a woman *three times*. Not before the banns are read." It was tantamount to an announcement, and there was nothing to announce. Would Emmeline be confused when nothing more happened? Hurt? Heartbroken? "She's too young for courting, and I won't have you playing her. Never dance with her again."

"I'm not courting anyone, least of all yer cousin." The contempt in Quill's usually amiable features frightened Charles more than his father in a drunken rage. This he hadn't predicted. "I know by name every man my sisters hold in contempt. Some of them were here tonight. If they wanted ta dance with yer cousin, I beat them ta it. If it was three times, it was three times. I thought we were friends. But ye would've trusted any one of those men more than me, would ye?"

"Nathaniel? I'd trust him with my life."

"Aye, with my life, but no' my sister's happiness. No' yer cousin's, either."

Charles scowled into the darkness. Susan had made it clear she would never trust him with her happiness.

Thirty-Two

GRAVES IN THE NIGHT

Susan rested her fingers against the cool glass of the carriage door. She had been miserable ever since her quarrel with Charles. His challenge throbbed through her head: *ask her. Ask her. Ask her.*

"Aunt Dorothea?"

"Yes, dear?" The gentle concern in her voice was at odds with Charles's cruel accusation. Aunt Dorothea would never have torn children from their families. She would never have beaten anyone under her roof. It was impossible.

"Nothing." She rested her head, heavy with thought. At Bailey Manor, she was constantly having to find new staff since many workers stayed only a few months. Her aunt had never mentioned hiring new servants. Mayhap Charles was right.

But wouldn't a mistreated slave have even more reason to leave than a servant? They must be servants. In a land of slavery, they stayed because they were treated so well, at least by comparison. If she could look through her aunt's account book, their wages would be recorded between payments to the laundress and the butcher.

After Lucy put her hair down and bid her goodnight, Susan couldn't sleep. Charles's accusations echoed in her mind. *Guilty.*

Every bit as guilty. At last, she threw the covers back. Her mind wouldn't rest until she had proved her aunt's innocence, and through it, her own.

She tied her bedgown with the fierceness of a soldier facing battle. If anyone asked why she was out of bed, she would say she needed paper. It might have been two in the morning, but it was never too late to write to family. She had sent several letters since Charles had posted the one with the news that Isaac had gone west. Any day now, and she would send one chronicling his safe return.

She lit a candle in the low fire. Armed with the single flame, she slowly opened her door. The windows were closed against October's chill, silencing the late carriages and creatures of the night. An eerie hush filled the hall. Surely she had tossed and turned until the entire house was sleeping soundly. The second step creaked under her weight. She froze. Why did they only do that at night? After each remaining step, she waited, listening, as guilty as a thief. Once her feet were firmly in the foyer, she released a long sigh. She was nearly there.

There was a small sideboard in the parlor. Setting her candle on top of it, Susan grasped a handle. The drawer slid forward like warm butter on hot toast. She pulled the account book from the shadows. Weak candlelight illuminated splotchy entries. On the fifth page, she found a payment to Maurice, the French chef. She checked the entries above and below, but they were unrelated. Hoping it was an aberration, she turned the pages. Maurice's name recurred monthly, but no other household names were listed. Not Graves. Not the maids.

A muffled sound startled her. She dropped the book into the drawer and closed it hastily. She had seen enough. Charles was right. She picked up the candle and turned to the stairs, only to see a man inches away. For a long moment, she stood there, too frightened to scream. Then she raised her candle to his face. "Graves! What are you doing up?"

"I heard a sound and came to stop an intruder." He spoke low and slow, neither guilty nor frightened.

Susan swallowed her guilt. "It's just me."

He studied her gravely—is that where his name had come from?

"I needed paper." Her voice was high. "For a letter." Blood rushed to her cheeks, heating her face. She opened another drawer and took out a leaf of paper. Had he seen her reading the account book? It was an insolent thing for a guest to do, even if she was family. When she closed it, he was still there. Waiting.

Suddenly, she wondered if the farmer's daughter in Charles's tale had known her father's plan to save her dowry. Gooseflesh ran up her arms. She hadn't agreed to this. She hadn't wanted it. But neither had Charles. She couldn't hold him responsible for his father's actions without holding herself responsible for her aunt's. "May I ask you a question?"

"You already have. But you may continue."

Her mind tripped in the darkness. She scarcely knew where to begin. "How long have you been at the Blue House?"

"Fifteen years, come February."

That was longer than her family had retained any of its servants. "And you...like living here?" After a long silence, she said pointedly, "You haven't left."

"Where do you think I could go?"

"I don't know, but you're not in chains. You move freely. There's nothing to keep you here if you don't like it. Is there?"

He looked over his shoulder, then lowered his voice. "I could leave any night, and no one could stop me. But there's nowhere to go. Some men run away to the frontier, but even in the wilderness, they can't claim land unless they can prove they're free. So they join roaming bands, stealing to survive, until they're hunted as outlaws. That isn't freedom. And if they run to the cities, they'll be thrown in jail and a notice will be placed in the papers. Then they're beaten and auctioned off. In the end, they have even less freedom than when they started. I stay because there is no place to go.

"In this life, freedom is a birthright. Either you're born free, or you spend your whole life serving those who are." Candlelight flickered across his face. "I don't suppose I'll see freedom 'til heaven when the Good Lord makes the first last and the last first."

A breeze whistled down the chimney. Susan went hot and cold in turns. Some things just shouldn't *be*. "I'm sorry," she whispered.

He gave a low chuckle and shook his head. "I'm sure you think you're sorry." He stepped back. "It's late. Everyone should be abed. And in the morning, I don't tell Mrs. Evans that you were snooping, and you don't tell her what we discussed. Agreed?"

"Agreed." She meant it. Betraying his trust could have serious consequences, and there was already enough guilt to go around.

Thirty-Three

WRESTLING WITH CONSCIENCE

SATURDAY, OCTOBER 22, 1774

Daylight bled through the curtains, and the Gardiners' voices echoed through the house. Charles pulled the pillow over his face and squeezed his eyes closed, willing himself to return to sleep. Heaven knew he needed it. He had lain awake long after the whispers in the girls' room had silenced, wrestling with his thoughts.

Susan's accusations weren't fair, but they weren't entirely false, either. Though he no longer profited from the business of Johnson Hall, as its heir, he inevitably would. It wasn't enough to distance himself from the plantation and pray his father outlived him. She demanded he return now and put everything right.

But he couldn't.

He couldn't correct the world any more than he could get back to sleep. He shoved the pillow aside and knelt on the bare wood floor, as he had every morning for four months. "Dear Lord, bless Isaac to get home safely." He paused, wanting to say amen and be done with it, but his conscience pushed back. Susan thought he could do more. But she was wrong. Two years back, the Lord Chief Justice of the King's Bench had ruled that Somerset, a slave who had been brought by his master to Britain, could not be forced back to the colonies. Debates had erupted in London and New England, with some arguing that it was time to put a complete end to slavery in those regions. They had not succeeded.

Virginians had pushed for a smaller change—attempting to abolish the importation of new slaves. Though willing to allow emancipation in England, the king had overruled Virginia's modest attempt at change. Further appeal was impossible. Charles was trapped in the artifices of a fallen world, stained with the blood of a parent's transgression.

"I'm trying to be a better man." The defense was spoken with all the vulnerability of a hungry child caught sneaking gingerbread. He had avoided and withdrawn. But what good had he done? Nothing. The affairs of Johnson Hall were no better or worse from his lack of involvement. "If there's something more I can do, open my eyes to the opportunity. Amen."

He dressed and went down. Henrietta was wiping breakfast crumbs from the table. She glanced up at him. "You slept late. Emma didn't. I saw her gown this morning. It's so pretty. I wish I had a gown like that. She said the other ladies were so pretty, too. Miss Bailey was wearing pink, and Miss Morris was wearing yellow. I don't know what Mr. Morris was wearing. She forgot to say. But she didn't have to tell me what you looked like. I saw you before you left. Why did you wear brown to a ball? It's the least pretty color there is."

"My best suit is brown," he said with dignity. "I had it made in London." He had hoped Susan would ask about it. She had not.

Henrietta was not impressed, either. "Did London not have other colors?"

"They did, but I'm a barrister. I chose a serious color so people would know I'm serious about my work." Then he had worn that serious color to a night of merriment.

She wrinkled her nose. "Did anyone dance with you?"

"Lots of ladies danced with me. Gentlemen don't need to wear bright colors to dance with a lady."

"When I go to balls, I hope everyone wears bright colors. I like them."

"Then it's a good thing you won't be old enough for a long time. You can't choose your dance partner based on the color of his jacket. And your mother wouldn't approve of you standing around and talking when she told you to clean the table." Prayer had not brought him patience. He had slept poorly, was still distressed from last night, and had missed breakfast. He didn't need Henrietta making him feel worse about everything.

She frowned at the table, but resumed her work, chasing the crumbs with a damp rag while he let himself out the back door. Aunt Charity was in the side garden, speaking with a neighbor, but the kitchen house was unlocked. Inside, Emmeline was chopping vegetables, her eyes dull from the late hours they had kept.

"Get your cousin his breakfast. I'll do that," Jenny said, taking the knife. She was more like family than a servant. Certainly, Aunt Charity kept her occupied, but it was work she did alongside the family. She was also kept well-fed and adequately clothed. She slept in the house and was rarely, if ever, disciplined.

If the "servants" in his father's house had been as well cared for, Susan's accusations wouldn't have stung like a nest of wasps. But she had stirred up too many painful memories. He had once known the names of every ill-clad child, every overworked man and woman on his father's plantation. They had pulled him out of the creek when he had fallen in, taught him to fish, bandaged his scrapes, and sung him lullabies. But his father was not a man of compassion or fair play. Small kindnesses were quickly forgotten. Small offenses were whipped and beaten.

Emmeline handed him a plate of cold chicken, toast, and greens. He leaned against the door frame and ate ravenously, dulling the ache within. He couldn't free anyone. Neither could his father, even if he wished to. Home was an old bruise that wouldn't heal. No good would come of another visit. He could suggest smaller changes, but they couldn't happen without his father's approval. Offense was more likely than approval. The most he could expect from his efforts was a black eye.

He chewed slowly, considering. Is that what he was afraid of? He'd had a black eye once or twice before. The world hadn't ended. Was he such a coward that he would allow fear of a fight to stand between himself and doing what was right? He shoveled the last of the greens into his mouth. His conscience, which was beginning to sound like Susan, wouldn't rest until he tried.

He saddled the bay mare. Since his return, he had avoided Johnson Hall as much as possible. He had satisfied familial duty by a monthly visit with his grandmother and a brief discussion with his father, but had made no attempt to acquaint himself with the family business. It would look odd when he turned up this morning. The bay walked down the country road. Flaming leaves waved overhead, October's warning that winter was coming. Now that the harvest was in, the plantation should be busy drying the tobacco as well as making preparations for the annual homespun suit of clothing given to each slave: a shift for a child, a shirt and pants for a man, a shift and petticoat for a woman, plus a wool petticoat for winter warmth. Last year's clothes would be worn to rags by daily use.

The mare's hooves clopped on the bridge, scattering his thoughts. He was almost there, and he still had no plan. Without a plan, he would bumble like a fool. Abah, his nursemaid, had more than once been whipped for his foolishness. His hands twitched, fighting the urge to turn the horse around. He should have gone to work. He should have visited the printer, or the butcher, or the cobbler. He should have run any fool errand save this one.

But Susan thought he could do more. Her faith propelled him forward. He stabled the mare, then stood under the white portico for a full minute, listening. At last, he wiped his clammy hands on his breeches, knocked on the door, and let himself in.

Gideon met him in the foyer. "Master Charles." He bowed,

his manners as formal as the livery he wore. "Is your father expecting you?"

"I'm afraid not."

"Wait here while I inform him."

Charles nodded. He was in no hurry. He still didn't know what he was doing here. Susan would have known what to do. She could have charmed his father into agreeing to her plans, too. He should have invited her along.

"Open wide," a child's voice said. He followed the sound and peered into the dining hall. Kitty was sitting at the table, feeding Granny. Though she was just a child, she had been issued a petticoat, stockings, cap, and shoes. She and Gideon wore finer clothes than the more numerous field hands. They worked in the house, where anyone might see them. They also had better access to food and warmer shelter when winter came.

Gideon returned and followed his gaze. "She does that every morning."

Something ached within Charles's chest. His grandmother had once been a respected woman. Johnson Hall had been known for its hospitality. Passing strangers had been welcomed like family, even if she and her husband had to give up their bed and sleep on the nursery floor to make room for them. Now she couldn't even feed herself. "If someone has to do it, I'm glad it's Abah's girl." Though he had been unable to prevent their family from being separated, at least he knew his nursemaid's daughter didn't spend her days in the fields and nights in a drafty one-room cabin.

Gideon made a sound deep in his throat, then cleared it. "Your father is waiting for you in his study."

Charles took a deep breath and released it so loudly that Kitty looked back at the doorway. Her deep brown eyes went wide when she saw she was being watched, as though anticipating a reprimand. While she stared, a lump of cornmeal mush fell from the spoon onto her lap. Charles waved her back to her work. Addressing Gideon, he said, "Well then, I best not keep him waiting." He strode to the study with a show of confidence he wished he felt.

The elder Mr. Johnson rose. "Charles, have a seat." He gestured to a wingback chair that matched his own, then seated himself. "What brings you here?" His curiosity was as benign as a summer morn, but Charles watched for lightning.

"I apologize for not being of any assistance during the harvest. I was tied up in court for weeks. I'm here to make up for it."

"Now that all the work is done?" Mr. Johnson's voice tightened. The weather was turning. "When I told you to focus on your career, I didn't tell you to neglect your family."

"I'm sorry. But the General Court was in session. As a barrister, I needed to be there. Octobers are as important for legal work as they are for tobacco."

His father smiled crookedly. "Harvest season for the courts as well, eh?"

"You might say that. I won my share of briefs. I even represented several prominent businessmen."

"Excellent." His father settled back into the cushion of the chair. "I worried you wouldn't be making connections, living as you are. But you are. You are." He nodded sagely. "Now you're here. How can I use you?"

"I hear the tobacco is already in. A great harvest, so I'm told."

"Our best. Last year's crop was poor. The old tobacco fields were about worn out, so we cleared more trees and hired some land down the road."

Charles had heard this explanation every Sunday visit and was weary of the details. "I'm glad you have that in hand," he said before his father could say more. "Barton also said you recently got some more help. Do they have everything they need? How are their clothes?"

His father grunted. "They didn't come naked. I'll give them new clothes next year when they've earned it."

The injustice itched like measles. Children were given clothing when they needed it, not when they earned it. The same philosophy should have applied to those in bondage. They hadn't asked to be bought or sold. He clenched his teeth, holding back his thoughts. Arguing with his father could do more harm than good. "What about everyone else? Will they be getting new clothes before winter?"

"Same as usual. The weaving's already begun. Clothes should be done sometime in November or December."

Charles still didn't have a plan, but he had a purpose. He wanted to see that everyone had sufficient clothing, blankets, and shelter for the winter. "I propose to do an inspection, sir. I'll see how the weaving is going. While I'm at it, I'll look over the cabins and see that everything is conducive to good health. We don't want to lose anyone over the winter, do we?"

For one long moment, he watched and waited, certain he had angered his father. The changing weather was first noted in the eyes, the movement of the hands, or tension in the shoulders. By watching for storm clouds, one could retreat to shelter before the worst of the storm. His father simply grunted. "It's about time you helped the family business. Barton was saying so just the other day. Now, where is that book?" He unlocked several drawers in his desk, then handed him an ink-smudged book, the record of all business at Johnson Hall.

Charles turned the pages until he found the list. A broad, masculine hand had recorded every slave by name, age, and trade. Since Abah had been sold years ago, he had assumed his father would have been quick to exchange others less closely tied to the household. To his surprise, he recognized most of the names. "I'll begin at once." He offered a curt bow and went out to the slave cabins.

Thirty-Four

HOMESPUN

Where there had once been three, there were now five one-room cabins in a row, the front of each building facing the back of the next. Between them were gardens used to supplement the cornmeal rations. In the center of each garden was a blackened pine torch, a silent reminder that these gardens were only tended after it was too dark to see the master's field.

He knocked on the door of the first cabin and opened it. The shutters were closed, but a ray of sunlight cut across the dark room, beginning at the roof where a shingle should have been. Smaller shards of light pierced the cracks between rough timber walls. He began his notes. Cabin number one needed to be chinked again, and the roof fixed. He counted a dozen wool blankets, one shy of the number of occupants who slept on this floor. It needed another.

He knocked on the door of the second cabin and opened it. The shutters were open, allowing light and a chill breeze into the room. A gray-haired woman looked up from her loom. "Mas'er Chawz, is tha' you?"

"Yes, it is, Auntie Sarah. Can you tell me what you're doing?"

"Have your eyes gone dim? I'm weavin' linen, same's I done

ev'ry fall since I were a chil'." Coarse seeds littered the fabric and would scratch a child's tender back as easily as a kitten's claw. Textiles were England's main export. Americans were careful not to compete with the mother country, in quantity or quality. Those who could afford to import fine wool and linens did. Despite the recent patriotic fervor, homespun was still for those who could afford no better.

At least until the ban on imports took effect in December. Then they would all suffer together.

Sarah resumed her weaving, shuttling the linen thread from side to side as she answered his questions. She anticipated a little more cloth than in previous years. It would be enough to complete the annual ration of clothing, possibly including the newcomers. He would need to return in a few weeks to be certain of the results. His hand was on the door when she asked him a question.

"Do you'ave a sweetheart?" She drawled the impertinence with the ease of an aging woman secure in her heavenly reward.

His face heated. "I—no."

"You're not married?" It was half statement, half question. More confidently, she added, "I woulda heard." That was true. Family gossip had a way of traveling from the parlor to the cabins. When Charles didn't answer, she pointed the shuttle at him. "Marry a guhl who makes you smile. You always was a nice boy, but you nevuh smile. Not then. Not now."

Charles forced the corners of his mouth up. "I'll do my best, Auntie Sarah." He touched his cocked hat in farewell. "I'll see you in a few weeks." He would return to see her finished work before it was distributed.

As he surveyed the third cabin, distant voices drove sentimental thoughts from his head—voices that sounded more like socializing than work. Though the fields were cleared, there was still work to be done. He hesitated to move on to the next cabin. He hadn't come to discipline, but to smile at idleness would be worse than not seeing it at all. So he stood just behind cabin four, straining his ears while wondering what to do.

Around the corner came Marcus. He swung his muscled arms as he walked, his face grim, but at the sight of Charles, he startled back. "Chawz." He drawled the name into one long syllable, as he always had. They were nearly the same age. In the old days, they had challenged each other in a never-ending series of athletic contests. "Master Chawz," he amended with a deference he had never offered as a child. "Can I help you?"

"Possibly." He looked beyond Marcus, but he could not see what the trouble in cabin four was. "I'm doing an inspection."

"An inspection? Now?" Fear flickered in Marcus' eyes. "We've been busy with the harvest."

They both turned at the sound of feminine shouting. Charles frowned. "That isn't what it sounds like." It sounded like several women were cheering on a game of chance. Winter was coming. What was the point of ensuring everyone had blankets and clothing if they were just going to gamble everything away?

"I know. It's just...my wife. She's—" Through the thin cabin walls came an audible splash, a smothered gurgle, then a lusty cry.

"It's a girl!" A young woman ran around the cabin. "Mark, it's a—" She stopped at the sight of Charles, as though he had the fearsome power to undo what only the Creator could accomplish.

"A baby?" Charles forced a laugh. "You might have told me." What had he ever done to make Marcus fear him?

"Yes, sir."

Attempting to lighten the moment, he said, "I hope she doesn't have your throwing arm." No one laughed. No one smiled. He sighed. "Go see your baby while I look into cabin five. I'll save yours for last."

Marcus swallowed. His Adam's apple bobbed. "Yes, sir. Thank you, sir."

It took hardly any time to see that the last cabin also needed chinking, patching, and another blanket. Charles waited out of sight while the distant voices spoke urgently. His very presence had turned a moment of joy into fear. But he was trying to help. Why couldn't they see that?

Thomas had welcomed assistance, had begged for it even, when his young family had faced life and death. Charles had pitied him, unable to provide even a chair to elevate his wife from the dirty floor. Marcus' wife had just had a baby in an unfurnished cabin, one they shared with several other families. Then the son of the man with the power to separate their family arrived on the scene when their happiness was most vulnerable. His spirits sank. It was no wonder his old playmate was alarmed to see him.

He read through his father's list again. There was no note of Marcus having a wife. His father might not have known. More likely, he hadn't cared. There was no legal requirement to honor family connections among the enslaved. Metaphorically, the master was father and husband to all. Society expected him to provide for those in his extended household. The law left all rights and responsibilities with him. It was a transient relationship, one easily bought and sold. And the loyalty demanded was one-sided.

After what felt like ages, he realized the voices had lost their urgency. He pocketed the book and went out.

Marcus was pacing in the garden. "Are you ready? Come in."

Cabin four had been swept until not one leaf marred the floor. Patched shirts hung from a row of nails. Pine needle baskets held the few personal items. One blanket draped across the new mother, half-sitting against a wall. The others were folded and arranged side-by-side. He tallied everything up. By his count, they had two more people than blankets. That was without the baby, who was sharing with her mother.

His father's list did not include this new child. Whether she was recorded now, by Charles, or in five years, by his father, didn't matter. In Virginia, a child's freedom was determined by the mother's status. This one had been born into bondage. "What's her name?" The least he could do was give them a chance to name their daughter.

"Ain't had time to think." Mark shook his head, dazed. "She's a guhl, just like her mama."

The last time Charles had seen a newborn was on the *Minerva*. Susan had fussed over the mother's medicine and the baby's linens. "Wait. Do you have linens for the baby?" A newborn's skin was too delicate for homespun.

Mark gestured to some folded rags in a pine needle basket. "A few. Old ones are best. They're softer."

His wife spoke up, her voice soft from exhaustion, "We'll have more once everyone gets their new clothes."

Worn linen was not enough to keep a babe warm through the winter. "I'll see that you get another wool blanket." They might lay it under them at night to keep the drafts away or use the material to make a pudding cap and a little jacket. If Susan were here, she would know exactly what kind of medicine a new mother needed. She didn't have childbed fever, but she did look rather peaked from her labors. "And a bottle of whiskey, for the mother."

Mark stared at Charles, then grinned and grasped his hand. "That'll be right fine."

"If your wife takes ill, send me word." He would see to it that she got the medicine she needed.

He brought his report back to his father. It was always easier to argue with facts in hand. "Every cabin needs repairs to the roofs, and the walls must be rechinked."

Mr. Johnson, Sr., crossed his arms and scowled. "I hired a roofer two years ago."

"Well, it's time to hire one again."

His father's jaw clenched.

Charles softened his demand. "Then again, how hard can it be to put up a few shingles? If you just order the supplies, the men who live under the roofs can be the ones to shingle and chink."

His father leaned back again. His scowl had softened to a pout. "MacAbery owes me for a plow."

"Then I'll visit him today and negotiate the details."

His father scoffed. "You?" His tone irked Charles. He had spent years studying and practicing law, and his father thought he still couldn't handle a simple barter.

"Who better to represent your interests? I'm your son and a barrister. People listen when barristers talk business. Now, which merchants do you have credit with? Every man needs his own blanket. We're a few short."

There was a long silence. His father studied him, as though seeing him for the first time. At last, he said, "If you insist on buying blankets, go through Yates. Anything else?"

This conversation had been more successful than Charles had dreamed possible, but there was one last thing he had promised. "Could I have the key to the cellar? I need a bottle of whiskey."

His father threw his head back and laughed. "You're as bad as Barton." He threw the keys. Charles fumbled to catch them. "Get me a bottle while you're down there."

"Yes, sir." As he selected two dust-covered bottles of whiskey from the cellar, he wondered at his father's behavior. It may have been the effect of the stroke or a repentant heart after his wife's death. Or mayhap Charles had finally gained his father's respect.

Thirty-Five

A STORMY WEATHER FRIEND

WEDNESDAY, NOVEMBER 9, 1774

The last few weeks had been the longest in Susan's life. Each day had dawned with the expectation of Isaac's arrival. His room was dusted, his bedding aired, and his favorite dishes prepared. Day after day, they had eaten without him and gone to bed disappointed.

She peered out the parlor window and sighed. "What could be taking them so long?"

"We won't know until they get here, dear." Aunt Dorothea removed her reading glasses and looked at her thoughtfully. "We have an hour until dinner. We've been too much at home. Let's take a walk. We can do some shopping. You said Lucy needed supplies for your cosmetics, and I need to stock the cupboards while I can."

Beginning December first, most imports from Britain would be banned. They had known that ever since Patrick Henry and Edmund Pendleton had returned from the Continental Congress in October. Her aunt had immediately inventoried every cupboard in the house and filled them until they would scarcely close. There was no need to go shopping again. It was a distraction, but Susan welcomed it. She didn't have delicate nerves, but spending all day, every day, home by the window waiting for a brother who never came, was enough to strain the most robust nerves. "I'll get my cloak."

The heavy wool she swung about her shoulders was as red as a cardinal. The autumn wind made it flutter like wings as they made their way down the street, exposing the cheery taffeta lining. "They can't ban imports forever," Susan said. "It's so drastic. Surely this won't last more than a couple of months." There was a long silence. She glanced curiously at her aunt.

There was a furrow between her brows. "You may be right," she said slowly. "It depends on whether this turns into a civil war. A few years, at most, I imagine."

Susan stared. It was a ridiculous thing to say. Civil wars didn't start like this, with normal people living normal lives, organizing their cupboards, and calling on their neighbors. Civil wars belonged to unusual people in faraway places. Except this *was* far away. Farther even than France and Spain. "You wouldn't stay here, not if there was a war." She would be welcomed home. Indeed, she should have returned three years ago when her husband had died.

"This is my home." Aunt Dorothea said it with the tone one would use to explain a simple truth to a child: gentle, yet firm.

"It hasn't always been. You're from England. I understand you needed to come here when your husband did, but that reason is gone." It may have been rude to speak so dismissively of the dead, but she wanted her aunt to be safe. They could return together.

"I may have been born in England, but I built a life here. I own a fine home. I planted that honeysuckle and have watched it grow until it covers the pergola. I see the birds return as the seasons change. I've watched my friends marry and have children. I've watched those children grow. I will belong to this community until the day I die. If I suffer for lack of salt or tea, I suffer with friends."

Susan couldn't find the words to argue back. She now had friends on both sides of the Atlantic, and she hated to think that, come summer, there were some she would never see again. They walked in silence past the printers. There was a cheery window display of books and pamphlets. She had bought a new book just last month, but Emmeline had already read it twice. They turned into Aunt Dorothea's favorite shop, Greenhow's General Store. There was a chilling sparseness about it today. Her aunt hadn't been the only one stocking up before the ban. There were no new shipments to see, either. After pretending to amuse herself for a few minutes, Susan said, "If you'll excuse me, I'm going to the printer's. Lucy, have the shopkeeper put everything on my account. I'll settle it later."

"If you'll just wait a few minutes—" Aunt Dorothea began.

"I won't be long. Don't trouble yourself." The printer's shop was just a few doors down. When she entered, she was surprised to see no one was manning the counter. Voices echoed from the back room. It must have been a printing day, which was odd. The *Gazette* didn't come out until Thursday. Even she knew they waited as long as possible so they could include same-day news.

"Hello," she called softly. It was unlikely they heard her, but she was too ladylike to call louder. Safe behind the counter, two bookshelves were laden with the written word. Folded broadsides from faraway cities like London and Boston were stacked on a low shelf. Pamphlets—small books featuring popular sermons and political speeches—were stacked on the next shelf. Above them were several rows of books. She squinted at the titles. It was a jumbled assortment of plays, novels, and academic works.

There was *Moll Flanders* by Daniel Defoe. The author's name was familiar. She'd seen or heard of him somewhere. She had also heard the novel criticized as "excessively bawdy." Certainly not the sort of book to lend to a child. Next were several volumes of Shakespeare's plays. They were also bawdy at times, but the Gardiners had accepted them on literary grounds.

Out of the back room came a boy of about thirteen or fourteen. He wiped his fingers ineffectively on an ink-stained apron. "Afternoon, miss. May I help you?"

"Good afternoon. I was considering purchasing a book, but I haven't decided which. May I look at them more closely?"

He gathered books from the shelves, cradling them in the crook of his arm.

She filled the silence with light conversation. "I thought you didn't run the presses until Thursday morning."

"Special edition. More pages."

"Oh," she said, confused by his cryptic answer. "What for?"

He turned and spilled the books on the counter. A few covers were now smudged with ink from his fingers. "Battle on the frontier. Just got the report."

"Not anything to do with Lord Dunmore, I hope?"

"The same."

"But it was a diplomatic expedition. They were just supposed to talk."

He grunted, arranging the books side by side, face up on the counter. "They must've run out of words."

"An actual battle?" It wasn't possible. "Surely there weren't casualties."

He snorted. "Fifty dead. 'Bout as many wounded."

A draft as cold as frost on a tombstone crept up her arms, making the hairs stand on end. She leaned over the counter until she was nearly nose-to-nose with the boy. "Tell me the names," she ordered. "Who died? Who was injured?"

He stepped back, eyes wide. "The report didn't give names. Just numbers."

Something cold curled inside her, but Isaac wasn't a number. He was a boy. Her brother. He couldn't be dead. He couldn't be injured. It couldn't be him. And yet—

"Hey, miss. Where're you going?"

She didn't answer as she strode out the door and down the street, stirring up dried leaves as she walked. She could never stand still in a tragedy. She had to be moving and doing. There was always something to be done. But Isaac wasn't here. Lord Dunmore and his men weren't here. There were no wounds to bandage, no fevered foreheads to cool, no one coming to her for comfort.

Isaac could be dead or dying, and there was nothing she could do. Nothing. The street swam before her eyes. Carriages and buildings blurred together until all she could see were memories of the little boy he had once been. The boy she had done everything for. And now, when he needed it most, she could do nothing.

"'Scuse me, miss, but are you alright?"

She blinked her vision clear. A roughly dressed man sat on a wagon, looking down on her with pity.

Pride pushed back her tears. "I'm fine." Everything that mattered to her was falling to pieces, but she was fine. She was well fed, well-dressed, and her heart was shattered. She turned her head and hastened from his pity. She longed for comfort, but he couldn't give it to her.

There was only one person she could go to like this, when she was falling to pieces. Charles. She needed Charles. They had done more than cross an ocean together. He had seen her in those ghastly traveling clothes, crushed with worry, and somehow their friendship ran deeper after all they had weathered together. He was as much a friend in rain and storm as he was by fair sky and radiant sunset. She needed his steadiness by her side. She needed someone who wouldn't think less of her for having moments when she wasn't enough.

She knew where to find him. She had walked by his office many times and spied him through the window, bent studiously over his work. Never before had she interrupted. Never before had she admitted to needing him.

It was a half-mile walk, but she was under the Sign of the Eagle before she knew it. She straightened her shoulders, smoothed the scarlet cloak, and opened the door. Mr. Morris was twirling a quill in his fingers and humming to himself while reading some papers. There was no one else in the room. The one time she needed help, Charles wasn't there. Tears pricked her eyes.

Morris glanced up and leapt to his feet. "Miss Bailey." He eyed her with concern. "Are you looking for Polly? She just went home, but I can walk you over."

The Morrises were pleasant company for pleasant times. Right now, she needed a friend for adversity. She needed Charles. She shook her head and sniffed.

"What happened? What do you need?"

"Charles." Her throat tightened around his name. "Where is he?"

"The coffeehouse." He plunged his arm into a desk drawer, pulling out a set of keys. "I'll take you."

The moment the door closed, she grabbed his arm. He pocketed his keys and moved with haste as they passed a dozen or so places of business, then turned onto another street. A stone's throw away hung a sign, painted with a coffee pot in the act of pouring. Beneath it, a tall man walked out the shop door, his head turned toward his companion. His dark blond queue was brilliant against a black cloak. The tightness in her throat eased. She had found him. She wouldn't have to carry this burden alone.

Morris waved an arm high above them. "Johnson!"

Charles turned. His tricorn was as black as his cloak and cast a sharp shadow across his somber face. He could masquerade as a storm cloud. When his eyes fell on her, they flashed like lightning.

Thirty-Six

LIKE LIGHTNING

Charles broke through a cluster of children playing ball in the street as he took the most direct path to Susan. The anguish in her unwavering gaze pierced his soul and pulled him toward her. Something was wrong. Her face was splotched red. She had been crying. Something or someone had hurt her. His hands tightened into fists. He had to fix it. He had to put a stop to whatever was wrong.

An angry voice interrupted him. "Watch where you're going!"

He pulled up short before being trampled by a horse whose rider had the audacity to obstruct his path to Susan. In the few seconds it took him to pass, a dozen questions ran through Charles's mind. Where was her aunt? Her maid? How had Quill found her? And what dreadful thing had happened? He calculated the distance to the nearest apothecary. If the hurt was of a physical nature, he would appeal to a professional.

The horse flicked its tail in his face as it passed. His eyes stung, but they could still see that Susan was standing without support. There were no visible broken bones, blood, or bruises. The splotches were the only thing marring her complexion. It was worst around her eyes and on her nose, almost like she had come down with a head cold. A cold wasn't life-threatening.

But it might not be a cold.

He stumbled over a rock. When they had first arrived, he had watched her carefully for signs of the seasoning all immigrants had to endure. But her health had been perfect. He had begun to hope she would never succumb to the illness that found new victims every spring and fall, the illness that claimed the lives of grown men the way measles and mumps took infants.

She waited for him, as still as a statue, until he was only a few yards away. Then she broke free of her pedestal and hastened to meet him, stopping so close she had to tilt her head up to keep her gaze on him.

"Susan. What is it? What happened?"

She opened her mouth to speak, but her chin quivered, and the gold flecks in her brown eyes shimmered under a pool of tears. She squeezed her eyes and mouth shut. She was fighting to keep the hurt inside, to keep it from showing. He had done so himself as a child many times. The practice had built a fortress wall around his heart, one rough stone at a time, until he no longer needed to close his eyes to keep his feelings inside.

He clenched and unclenched his fists. He was ready to fight any battle for her, but he couldn't bear to just stand there and watch her hurt. If only she would tell him what was wrong. Quill, who had lingered a few paces behind, raised his hands, palms up. He didn't know either. Charles looked about the street, half expecting a clue, but nothing seemed out of the ordinary. "Susan," he said again, this time more gently.

She opened her eyes but kept her lips pressed tightly together.

He cast his mind about for a question so mundane she would start talking. "Where's your aunt?"

"Oh!" She exclaimed, as suddenly as if she had been pricked by a needle. "Oh, no! I forgot to tell her. I was supposed to meet her back at the shop. At Greenhow's."

She wasn't the only one who had forgotten someone. In his haste to reach her, he had forgotten to take leave of the client he had met at the coffeehouse. He turned about, half expecting the man to have followed him. He was nowhere to be seen. It was just as well. Turning back to Susan, he said, "Don't worry. We can meet her there."

Quill waved them away. "Dinna worry yerselves about her aunt. I'll let her know ye're safe. Take yer time. She can meet the both of ye back at the Blue House when ye're ready." Then he marched off, whistling like a fife.

The wind knifed through Charles' cloak. If she was ill, this weather wasn't good for her health. He offered his arm. She took it, the tips of her fingers red from the cold.

He covered them with a gloved hand. "Winter is coming. You should start wearing mitts, or a muff, or something to keep your hands warm."

She didn't answer. She didn't tell him how to fix anything. She just clung to him, silently pleading for help. Where was the Susan he knew? What problem was so distressing that she couldn't voice it? He pulled her closer as they walked, conscious of her blood-red cloak brushing against his somber black one. She needed shelter first. Only then would he press for answers. His office was close, quiet, and out of the wind. They had no chaperone, but it was a place of business. From time to time, his clients were female. Not even the most determined gossip had made anything of it. This would be no different.

Their silent walk passed quickly. In less time than it took to cross the street, they were there. She bit her lip and glanced up at the sign as he took his key out. "Let's get you out of the wind," was all he said. He turned the key but didn't feel the familiar resistance as he turned it. Quill had forgotten to lock it. He sighed. His friend must have dropped everything to help Susan. And then he had gone off whistling without a care in the world. Someone could have robbed them. But he soon found everything was still in its place: his desk was locked, the books were shelved, and papers were scattered all over his partner's desk. Nothing had changed.

"Here." He offered her his chair—it was the most comfortable piece of furniture in the room—then drew up Quill's for himself. After a moment's hesitation, he tugged off his gloves and placed a hand on her forehead. Either it was a little warm, or his fingers were cold. But before he could pull back, she leaned into his hand. The pressure was so slight, he might have imagined it.

"I—I'm not sure if you have a fever." Feeling foolish, yet not wanting to end the touch, he placed his other hand on his forehead. It was about as warm as hers. "I think not, though it may be too soon to tell."

She pulled back, and he dropped both hands to his knees. They were large and clumsy and bare. He wiped his palms on his breeches and pulled his gloves back on. "Something happened," he said, adjusting them. "Are you hurt? Did someone hurt you?"

He glanced up, but she just shook her head. Relief and annoyance fought within him for dominance. He was relieved that no one had hurt her and annoyed that she didn't just tell him what was wrong. This was like that stupid parlor game where he had to guess what someone else was thinking. There was no real logic to it. Or was there? He had just ruled out physical harm. What else might distress her? "Your family, have you had news of them?"

The tip of her nose went red again. She nodded fiercely.

"Your mother, is she—"

Susan cut him off. "No. It's I-" Her chest shuddered. She tried again. "I-Isaac." Then her tears gushed like a rain shower.

He felt like she had thrown a pitcher of cold water at him. Like the world had tipped upside down. The boy was supposed to arrive in Williamsburg any day, eager to share tales of his adventure. Dazed, he pulled a handkerchief from his jacket and handed it to Susan. It was his fault Isaac had left. He had done nothing to stop him. And now he was—what? Injured? Dead?

He turned on Susan. "How do you know? Was there a letter?"

She shook her head. "It was the printers. They had a report."

He had half a mind to march down to the printers and demand to see that report with his own eyes. Surely there would be a copy of it in the *Gazette* tomorrow. But he needed to know everything now. "What happened? Was Dunmore's party ambushed?"

"There was a battle. People died."

"Was there a list? Did they have the names of the dead and wounded?"

"Fifty dead," she said in a hushed voice. "Fifty wounded. But no names."

He paced the room, turning over the facts she had offered. They didn't know how many had joined Dunmore on the frontier. It may have been hundreds. But even so, fifty was a substantial number, and any of the wounded might yet die before they reached home. It was maddening that there were no names. And Susan's sobs shook the room like thunder.

He threw his tricorn on the desk and raked his fingers through his hair. *Lord, how am I supposed to comfort her when—*

Hope flashed like lightning across his mind, illuminating something so obvious, it had to be true. He sat across from her. "You said there were no names—so there's nothing to worry about." He leaned forward. "Don't you see? Isaac was with Lord Dunmore. If Dunmore had died, surely even a hasty report would have included his name. It didn't. So Dunmore can't have died, which means Isaac didn't either."

She took a great shuddering breath and hiccuped. "Do you really think so?"

"I don't think so. I know so." He couldn't say where his sudden confidence had come from, but it was comforting both of them, so he leaned into it. "If I were a betting man, I'd wager twenty pounds that he was the royal governor's errand boy. Lord Dunmore himself probably wasn't even in the battle. I imagine he would have stayed in the fort during the fighting. And he would have kept Isaac close."

Susan's breath had steadied. "You must be right." She dabbed her face with his handkerchief. "Forgive me. I couldn't help imagining the worst."

He scooted his chair beside hers so they sat hip to hip. Just as he had known what to say, he knew what to do. He needed to put his arm around her shoulders, pull her close, and whisper something comforting. Even if she didn't fancy him, she needed to know someone cared. He was reaching behind her when a movement at the window caught his eye. It was Quill, grinning widely. His confidence faltered. Instead of the half-embrace that had seemed so right just a moment ago, he patted her shoulder, then stood, pushing back the chair that had moved too close. "Come, I'll walk you home."

She had come to him because she was worried about her family. As long as they were well, she didn't need him to care. But because he cared, he wouldn't do anything that might drag her into gossip.

Thirty-Seven

THE LIBERTY POLE

WEDNESDAY, NOVEMBER 16, 1774

Charles locked the office door. Then he and Quill set off for dinner at the tavern. The November sky was a cold, bright blue. Leaves blanketed the road, crackling with each footfall. It felt good to stretch his legs, which were cramped after a morning under a desk. But as they passed Susan's street, he slowed. He couldn't help looking at the Blue House anytime he came near, hoping to see her.

"Do ye know," Quill said, "when I first met Miss Bailey, I thought ye'd be engaged by the end of the summer. Mayhap 'twas my imagination, but I thought the reason ye kept going back ta Widow Evans's had more ta do with her fine company than her fine table."

Charles loosened his cravat. The day was too cold without a cloak and too warm with one. "I have a responsibility to watch over Miss Bailey while her brother is gone."

"Responsibility?" Quill scoffed. "The way ye look at her is no' responsible. Though I grant, ye certainly behave responsibly about her—a wee bit too responsibly. Alone in the office when she had come ta ye crying, and ye pat her like ye would a dog. Ye fancy her something fierce, Charles. Why deny it?"

"It doesn't matter who I fancy if she doesn't return my affection."

"Dinna be daft, Johnson. I asked her what she needed, and she said—" Quill paused dramatically, clutching his hands under his freckled chin and batting his muddy green eyes. In a syrupy voice, he sighed, "Charles." The facade dropped. "Why would she say that if she didna fancy ye?"

"I'm sure I don't know." A week ago, he had hoped she returned his affection. But then she had avoided him at church that Sunday and had scarcely met his eye yesterday when he had gone to the Blue House for dinner. So doubt had followed faith. Everything she had done that tearful day had been out of character. That included her behavior toward him. "What do you know about love, anyway? I don't see you courting anyone."

"Nay, but ye dinna see me moping about, either. I dinna truly fancy anyone just now. I'll feel a flicker here and there when I see a pretty smile or enjoy a dance, but the feeling passes afore I know 'tis there. But, God willing, one day I'll meet a lass who can light the love fire in my heart, the kind of flame that doesna go out. And when I do, I willna hide my feelings under a bushel." He smiled wryly. "I'll save my moping for after I've been spurned."

Quill made it sound so easy, as though love was nothing more than following the impulses of one's heart. But every time he thought he saw a flicker of "love fire" in Susan's eyes, it was quickly followed by a rejection. Whatever she felt toward him, he couldn't pretend it was the kind of flame that would endure a month, much less a lifetime. He wouldn't embarrass himself by courting a woman who had made it clear she only wished to be friends.

They walked on, silent save for the crunch of leaves underfoot, until Raleigh Tavern was in sight. A small crowd had gathered outside. "Perhaps we should try Chowning's instead," Charles said. The tavern food was all the same to him.

Quill frowned. "They're not here ta eat."

"Then why—"

"Huzzah!" A cry went up as men raised a pole. A bag hung where an ensign should have been. A man on a ladder pounded the pole into the ground. White feathers flurried out of the bag, then drifted, soft as snowflakes, onto a barrel smudged with tar.

"For liberty!" A man cried.

"Liberty!" The crowd roared louder than an incoming tide.

Charles's stomach turned. He had read of liberty poles in other colonies. They were crude instruments of intimidation. He had believed Virginians were too civil to erect one. But then, he had believed Virginians would never throw tea off a privately owned ship. That had happened just last week in Yorktown, even though the Continental Association's ban on imports wasn't supposed to take effect until December.

He turned to a man on the edge of the crowd. "What is this for?"

"Just a precaution, sir, for the merchants who won't sign."

Charles frowned. It was bad enough to punish merchants for violating the ban. But to tar and feather them for not signing a document swearing they would follow it? There was no law or order governing this ban or the committees that were springing up. The sooner Lord Dunmore returned, the better. The frontier could handle its problems. Virginia needed its royal governor at the capital ensuring peace.

"Excuse us." Quill pushed through the crowd like they were a cluster of gossiping matrons blocking the church aisle.

Charles jogged to catch up. "What are you doing?"

"Getting dinner."

"Here?"

"That's what we agreed. I dinna wish ta walk any farther for food."

Charles wanted to escape the patriotic fervor, not enter a building hemmed in by it, but he refused to leave his friend alone and at their mercy. All that stood in the way of this crowd dissolving into a mob was a keg of whiskey.

A tense waiter greeted them. "What can I get you, gentlemen?"

"What's the diet today?" Charles asked.

"Oyster stew."

"I'll have that, with bread and beer."

Quill sighed. "Same." He turned to Charles. "Do ye ever think about ordering something besides the cheapest meal in the house? Sometimes I think briefs don't pay us enough."

"I don't want to waste all my money on food. I might need it one day." It had taken him months to recuperate what he had spent on Jenny's indentures. He couldn't say what he was saving for now. It was foolish to hope a house in town was all he needed to make Susan happy, but he had fallen into the habit of inquiring at the printers for more information on every property they listed. It didn't hurt to ask any more than it hurt to eat on the cheap and live with the Gardiners while he squirreled away his funds.

They sat at a table with a clear view of the room, the door, and two windows, so he could see if anything escalated. He had read all the stories that came out of Boston. There was more than tea in the harbor. There had been fires. He wondered, if it came to it, how long it took to open one of those windows, compared with how fast fire could spread. "Even your unconstitutional congress said we had until the end of the month. Erecting a liberty pole in Williamsburg." He shook his head in disgust. "Parliament is going to notice."

"We *want* parliament ta notice. We want them ta see that they cannot force us into action if they will not listen ta our elected representatives."

"Will you cry liberty with the mob? Try it. I dare you. Parliament is going to bring a blockade on our heads, just like they did to Boston."

The waiter placed bread and steaming stoneware bowls in front of them. A cheer rumbling through the walls dulled his appetite. He poked at his stew. Quill had no such reservations, eating so quickly that Charles feared his tongue would scald. "Did Polly not feed you today?"

Quill spoke around a mouthful. "Mice got into the bread last night." He swallowed. "Do ye know anyone with kittens?"

Charles dipped a corner of his bread into the stew. "Ingram's cat just had a litter. He'd be glad to get them off his hands."

"Not Ingram."

Charles looked up, surprised by the cold resentment in Quill's voice. Not just anyone could provoke him. But at the ball, he hadn't allowed Nathaniel to dance with Emmeline, and now he wouldn't accept a kitten tainted by his association, though he needed one. "What happened?" They had once been schoolmates. They hadn't been the closest friends, but they had never fought. Not to his knowledge.

Quill stabbed his stew with a spoon. "Nothing." It was as plain as the freckles on his face that something had happened, but Charles knew the value of privacy. He wouldn't force a confidence from a friend.

They finished their meal in silence. While they had eaten, the crowd had separated into tight knots, gesturing at the liberty pole as they discussed which merchants had yet to sign the association. Once they were safely beyond earshot, Charles said, "When the governor returns, peace will come with him." It had to. No one wanted war less than Lord Dunmore.

"That seems awfully optimistic for a man of the law. When Dunmore marches back inta town and hears about the Committee of Safety and the ban on imported goods, I sure dinna wish ta be in the room. He was mad enough about the day of fasting and prayer for Boston." Quill glanced over his shoulder. "I'll wager the liberty pole will be pulled down first thing."

"Good." The pole could only deepen the divide between those who sided with the Continental Congress and those who didn't. "I don't want a civil war."

"Nobody wants war, Charles."

"Nobody wants it?" He gestured behind them. "That crowd is itching for a provocation."

"We've had enough of those."

"Not lately. The Continental Congress was reacting to how the events of last year in Boston were handled. Not something recent. Not something in Virginia. They want us to treat their decisions as law, but there is no constitutional basis for their existence."

"Ye wish ta argue for the constitution? Ye know as well as I that the men who threw the tea in that harbor were never arrested. There was no trial by a jury of peers and no due process of law. Instead, parliament sent a standing army in peacetime, punishing the innocent along with the guilty. Everything that has happened since the Boston tea incident has been a violation of the English Constitution." Quill dragged a piece of bread across the bottom of his bowl, mopping up the last of the stew.

"I know," Charles said hotly. He had lost count of the number of times they had been through this same conversation. In the end, Quill always blamed parliament. "But we aren't going to prove to London that the constitution is our primary concern unless we follow it ourselves, and there is nothing in the constitution that allows powerful committees to rule by the tyranny of tar and feathers."

Quill leaned back in his chair. "I dinna approve of the liberty pole anymore than ye. It may be a good thing when Dunmore returns."

At last, they had found something they could agree on.

CONSIDERING COURTSHIP

THURSDAY, NOVEMBER 17, 1774

Charles stared up through the darkness, his hands behind his head. Sleep had fled prematurely, leaving him alone with his thoughts. She had come to him when she was troubled—to him, when she might have preferred her female friends or relations. Quill had asked what she needed. It was him. She said she needed him.

That was why he couldn't sleep.

Had she meant it the way it had sounded? And if so, why had she been avoiding him ever since?

His uncle's footsteps echoed in the darkness. A door opened and closed. Weary of bed, Charles dressed in the predawn light. The number of people Charles could confide in could be counted on one hand with fingers to spare. Uncle Rob was among them. He carried his shoes down the stairs and sat on the porch step to put them on.

Uncle Rob was in his shop, fitting spindles into the seat of a chair by lantern light. As the door opened, he looked up.

"Couldn't sleep," Charles explained.

"That makes two of us." His uncle resumed working.

Charles crouched by the dust pile, turning over scraps of wood. Though he had never learned enough of the trade to assist his uncle, he could whittle animals. Emmeline would paint anything he made and place it in the front window to catch the eye of travelers with a coin to spare, who could fit the toy in a pocket or saddlebag. In a small way, it helped him repay the Gardiners for sharing their home. He picked up a thin, curling piece of pine. The shape reminded him of a single rose petal. He gathered the curls and sat at the workbench, cutting them into petals with a sharp blade.

They worked in companionable silence. It was one of the nice things about his uncle. He never pushed for confidences, but he always kept them. At last, Charles broached what had been on his mind all night. "Quill thinks Miss Bailey fancies me."

"You don't sound as happy as I would have expected."

A petal splintered under his knife. "He could be wrong."

"Or he could be right." His uncle picked up another spindle.

Charles looked up. "Do you think so? How can you be sure?"

Uncle Rob smiled and shook his head. "Only a fool waits for certainty before he begins courting. It's difficult enough to be certain of your own feelings. You can't expect a woman to declare hers when you've done nothing to earn it."

"I'm not that foolish. But Miss Bailey has declared plenty of other things, such as how much she is looking forward to seeing her family again. How she wants to go home to England."

"It is unfortunate that she has to choose between you and her family, but she wouldn't be the first one. You'll just have to work harder."

"Sir?"

"Charles, I never thought I had to explain this to you. Courting is your opportunity to persuade a young lady that you don't deserve that her best chance at happiness in this life is to marry a common young man who thinks the world of her."

"I never thought of it like that."

"It's time you did. Take my advice, Charles. Stop moping and start courting."

They fell back to working in silence. Charles wrestled with his uncle's challenge. The old fear of vulnerability and failure was strong, but his faith in his uncle was stronger. He cupped his hand and arranged the wooden petals in it. It was beginning to look like a rose. If he carved a stem with a wide cupping base, he could glue the petals in place. He found a brush and a bottle of red paint. Nothing said courtship like roses.

Susan pulled her needle until the lavender thread dimpled into the fabric, nearly disappearing. Using the tip of the needle, she nudged it back up until the thread relaxed, filling its place. It was the last stitch of the last feathery purple flower, part of a bouquet of black-eyed Susans. She picked up her prayer book, which fell open to reveal a delicate pressed flower. It was so tissue-thin that daylight shone through it like stained glass. She held it beside her canvas, comparing the original with her creation. A smile warmed her face, impossible to suppress. Charles had brought her that flower.

She turned over her hoop to cut the thread and was dismayed to see tangles and knots. The back of crewelwork was never a thing of beauty, but this looked like the work of a child. Her mind had not been on her work because her thoughts and feelings were just as tangled. She had been right about Charles—she had felt better about Isaac after speaking with him. But now she felt worse about their friendship. Despite her initial confidence, she did worry that he thought less of her for crying like an infant over a problem he was convinced didn't exist. And worse than that, she had needed him.

Susan didn't need people. It wasn't her way. She loved them, helped them, and hoped they loved her back. But she didn't need them. She tugged at the messy threads, but the knots only tightened. Every tricorn that passed on the street claimed her attention but when it was him, she couldn't meet his eye. Her ears strained for the timbre of his voice, yet she refused to approach him. She was proud and ashamed, longing for him and rejecting him. She was ridiculous without a cause.

This was nothing more than a friendship with a tall, handsome barrister. She wouldn't hurt herself—or him—by turning this into a passing flirtation when it could never be anything more. Charles was deeply rooted in Virginia soil. She wasn't. And, unlike her aunt, she could never be. This trip was an aberration in her carefully planned life—a life that revolved around her own home and family. Anne's coming-out ball had been postponed on her account. Preparing that would be the first thing she did as soon as she was home. They had been discussing the details for years. After that, she would chaperone her sister's season in London and arrange her a trousseau worthy of a titled lady.

It's what Mama would do if she were well.

There had been no one to do all that for Susan. Papa had arranged for her ball and declared it a success. She had bit her tongue, not wanting to hurt his feelings by pointing out the lack of some things she had considered important—details only a woman would think to plan. It would be different for Anne. She had long been determined of that.

She smoothed her needlework. The family motto should be stitched under her flowers: *ubi bene ibi patria.* Her country was where she was well. The reminder would serve her well.

But Charles.

How long would she wonder about him, once she had left the colony? Would he be safe? Would he be happy? Would he find a good wife, one who would support his career as well as she—

She shook her head to clear it. There was no sense in imagining things that could never be. He needed a good wife, a *feme sole* who could further his career. He had been uncertain about whether he could succeed in politics. He was wrong. Everything about him—his manner, his knowledge, his steadiness of character—commanded respect. There was no reason he couldn't be a burgess if he pleased to, provided he made a suitable match. Such a wife would need poise as much as property. The respect she commanded in the community would reflect on him.

She picked up her commonplace book, intending to write a list of attributes, when an idea struck her. She could do better than describe his ideal wife. She could find her for him. It couldn't be any harder than turning Miss Gardiner into a gentlewoman. She titled a page *feme soles* and began listing all the women she could think of who had property and were neither too old nor too young. She crossed out several names as soon as she had written them. He was much too fine to settle on a woman just because she was of suitable age and had property.

There had to be someone who would make him a good match. She left the book on her desk and went downstairs for assistance. Aunt Dorothea sat on the settee in a morning gown of deep purple, reading a letter. "Susan, do you need something?"

"I don't wish to disturb you. It's just..." As she spoke, it occurred to Susan just then how odd it might sound if she tried to explain her plan to her aunt. It was safer to talk around it. "Mr. Johnson, he's a barrister, you know. Well, he was talking about how women in Virginia often inherit property, sometimes even young women, and I was wondering if it was really all that common and how many ladies like that you knew."

"Myself, of course. We had no children, so I inherited everything. Then there was Mrs. Jenkins and her two daughters. The property was divided into thirds for them—"

"Are the Miss Jenkins married now?"

"Only the eldest." Aunt Dorothea peered at her over her reading glasses. "Why does that matter?"

She couldn't admit the truth without admitting the whole of her plan. "Well, if they were married, their property would be their husbands' now, wouldn't it?"

"In a legal sense, yes. Though in a practical sense, they would be wealthier, since they would also benefit from property their husbands had brought into the marriage."

"I suppose that's true, but since Mr. Johnson is a barrister, I'm interested in the legal ownership."

"I see. There's also Mrs. Underwood, a young widow who will be visiting a relation in town next month."

Susan seized the opportunity without giving herself a chance to hesitate. "Can we invite her to dinner? If she's young, she might enjoy meeting the Morrises and Mr. Johnson."

"I suppose." Her aunt frowned. "If that's what you want. But I'm not sure you'll—"

They were interrupted by a light tapping on the front door. Graves had yet to return from stabling the horses. "I'll get it," Susan said. She opened the door and her heart stopped. It was Charles. He wore his usual black cloak and plain tricorn hat. A good wife would find a tasteful way to embellish it. She fought back a smile. "Charles, do come in."

He shook his head as he stepped into the foyer, tracking leaves inside. "I need to get back to work. I can't stay."

The smile slipped from her face as she latched the door behind her. "Then why did you come?"

"It's nothing." His hand twitched. "It's just...you've been a little down lately, and I, well..." He shook his head and pulled something from inside his cloak. "Here." He held out a rose in full bloom—only it couldn't be, not in November. Her bare fingers brushed his gloved ones along the stem as she took it. The rose had been whittled from wood, with delicate ruffled petals and a curving stem complete with two blunted thorns.

"You made this," she said stupidly.

"Yes. It's too late in the year for flowers. And the leaves are losing their color. You like color."

There was no name for the feeling that swelled inside her, threatening to spill over as tears. She blinked fiercely. The thoughtfulness behind the gift meant more than a hothouse bouquet and a dozen compliments. This flower wouldn't need to be pressed or dried. It would never wilt. It would last forever in a vase, an everlasting reminder that someone had remembered her.

She looked up to thank him. She had sworn to meet his eye the next time she saw him, but now he wasn't cooperating. He was looking anywhere but her—the lintel of the door behind her, a framed still-life of fruits and flowers, the doorway to the parlor where Aunt Dorothea must still be on her settee, just out of sight. He was tall enough that he could avoid her gaze by looking straight ahead. They had known each other for more than six months. It was ridiculous to be shy now. That's what she had told herself all morning. She placed her hands on his shoulders and tugged, forcing him to face her. At least, that had been her intention. But she had anticipated resistance. He offered none. She had pulled too hard, and suddenly his head bent low beside hers. His stubbly jaw, still cold from the walk, scratched her cheek, and her breath warmed his collar.

Her traitorous lips parted, yearning to turn and whisper something sweet against his skin. *Friends,* she told herself fiercely. They were friends. They had to be. Soon, there would be a whole ocean between them. Her grip tightened on his cloak, the stem of the wooden rose pressing its blunted thorns against the flesh of her right hand. If Aunt Dorothea leaned forward on the settee and saw them like this, standing cheek-to-cheek with her hands on his shoulders, she might think—

"What is it?" Charles asked in a low voice, cutting through her thoughts.

She fumbled for something, anything, to say. "It's nothing. I —thank you." Then, with great self-control, she removed her hands from his shoulders and backed into the door, clutching the rose.

There was a peculiar expression on his face, half-masked as he tipped his hat. "I'll see you Sunday."

"Sunday?" A fog had filled her mind. She couldn't recall simple plans, like who they had dined with yesterday, and whether they were attending a concert or a lecture on Friday night. Had her aunt invited him, or did he intend to come calling in the cool of the evening?

"At church."

She blinked. "Indeed." Like they did every week. Not like a courting couple who spent every free hour together. "Until Sunday." She closed the door behind him but didn't return to face her aunt in the parlor. With leaden feet, she walked up the stairs. Still open on her desk was The List.

She slammed the book shut, hating every woman she had carefully considered less than an hour before. It was unfair. There was only one name that belonged on that list, and she could never add it. She had a duty to her family. He had a duty to his. And there would always be an ocean between them. Her heart fractured in two—one for each side of the Atlantic, and hot tears ran down her cheeks.

Sometime past noon, the ache in her chest dulled, and the tears ran dry. Only then did she pick up her quill and record the names her aunt had given her. She sanded the wet ink and left the page to dry, a wooden rose holding the book open.

His country was where he was well.

Thirty-Nine

DUNMORE'S WAR

SUNDAY, DECEMBER 4, 1774

Susan was three rows away, but unless Charles climbed over the pews like an errant schoolboy, it might as well have been three city blocks. A cluster of wizened gossips blocked the aisle, though it was hardly any warmer inside the church than outside. Of the many obstacles he had anticipated in courtship, this was not one of them.

"Did you hear?" The lady in the blue muff asked. "Lady Dunmore had her baby."

"Wonderful," the lady in white gloves gushed. "Boy or girl?"

"Girl," Blue Muff said, at the same time Fur Muff said "Boy." They eyed each other suspiciously.

Susan glanced back at him before following her aunt outside. Charles drummed his fingers loudly on the pew.

"I'm sure it was a girl." Blue Muff tipped her chin to look down her nose at Fur Muff. "Mother is doing well. You must have wondered not to see her at church today."

White Gloves spoke soothingly. "Well, it was close to her time."

"I'll say," Fur Muff replied. "She's a strong woman. Ten children and managing the palace by herself."

"No. Nine children," Blue Muff contradicted.

"Ten."

"She has a fine family," White Gloves said. "I do hope Lord Dunmore returns soon."

"Oh, didn't you hear?" Fur Muff asked. "He got home today. Becky told Jim, who told Matthew, who told me."

Charles gaped. Thoughts collided with each other: Dunmore. Isaac. Susan. He had to tell her, even if he had to climb over the pews to do so.

"Do come over to my place," White Gloves said. "I want to hear all about it."

The gossips finally moved up the aisle. He followed on their slothful heels until they reached the door and spilled out. A quarter of the congregation still lingered about, but Mrs. Evans's carriage was already on the far side of the Palace Green. Susan had to know.

In his haste, he almost didn't see his cousin. Doubling two steps back, he said, "Emma, I'm going to the Blue House now."

"*Now?*"

"Yes. Tell my uncle." He broke into a run, passing family after family walking home. The carriage was rolling away to the stables by the time he reached the door of the Blue House. His heart was pounding so loudly he could scarcely hear himself knock. Then, remembering the footman would be with the carriage, he boldly opened the front door himself. A stunned Susan stared into the parlor. He followed her gaze.

A young man rose from the settee. Dark hair hung, uncombed, about his tanned face. His breeches were patched with clumsy stitches, and one shoe, having lost its buckle, was tied on. He had forgone a waistcoat and cravat and looked rather wild in a fringed buckskin jacket. Black marks on the sleeves suggested he had gone too close to a fire on more than one occasion. Discarded on a chair was a lumpy felt hat that bore a remarkable resemblance to a drowned rat.

Susan, still radiant in her Sunday best, dropped her muff. She darted forward, straightened his stained collar, and laughed.

Charles walked into the room. "Welcome home, Isaac." He picked up the muff and stepped beside Susan, her wide petticoat brushing against his leg. She smiled up at him, as though his sudden appearance at this happy time was the most natural thing in the world. Her joy was contagious. He smiled back. Then they faced Isaac like an old married couple welcoming a wandering friend back into their home. In a casual tone that belied months of worry and prayer, he asked, "Still have all your fingers?"

Isaac held both hands up for inspection. "And my toes." He lifted a foot. The front of his shoe gaped widely where stitching had once held the sole to the upper. He wiggled his toes and grinned. It was so ridiculously pathetic that they all laughed.

Susan wiped her eyes. "We'll get you to a cobbler first thing on the morrow."

"He'll need the carriage," Charles said. "There's no way he can walk that far in those shoes."

Isaac looked back and forth between them, frowning slightly. "Did something happen while I was gone?"

"A great many things," Charles said. Thankfully, the liberty pole had been taken down before anyone was hurt, but there was still that ban and the committee enforcing it. "But first, we've been dying to hear about everything you've been up to."

"That'll take all day." It was Sunday. They had all day.

Mrs. Evans joined them in the parlor. "Mr. Johnson, how nice of you to join us. I was just speaking with Maurice about an early dinner."

"I don't wish to intrude." It was the polite thing to say, even after he had let himself into her home.

"Not at all, Mr. Johnson. You're like family."

"Yes," Susan said. "Please stay."

"How can I refuse an invitation when you put it like that?"

Isaac looked at them as if they had announced they would become traveling musicians. "You do remember that I actually am family, right?"

"Don't be ridiculous." Susan dusted at a stubborn scorch mark on his shoulder. "You're my brother. I wouldn't be here if it weren't for you." She frowned at the mark, which hadn't improved. "Though if anyone has a right to complain about neglect, it's us."

"I didn't make you come."

"No, but after I came here, you went hundreds of miles away and didn't write even once," Susan scolded. "We heard there was a battle and had no idea if you were wounded. And you're late. The *Gazette* told us to expect you weeks ago."

Isaac grimaced. "The *Gazette* was wrong. We were hundreds of miles away. And you've always known I'm a terrible correspondent. Suppose I had written you after the battle, insisting I was fine. Would you have believed me? I don't think so."

"I would have known you were alive." Her voice rose. "Fifty dead and fifty wounded."

"Who told you that?"

"It was in the paper."

"Again, the *Gazette* was wrong. Quite a few more dead. More than twice that wounded. And that's on our side. We don't know how many the enemy lost. They kept dragging them to the river."

A maid spoke to Mrs. Evans, "The table is ready."

"Very well." She looked at Isaac, "Let us continue this discussion after dinner."

Though the table had been hastily set, it had been done properly. Arranged symmetrically around the table were four settings, including four steaming mugs. Mrs. Evans must have heard him come in. Serving platters offered cold ham, dried apple tart, stewed carrots, and potato cake.

Isaac stared at it like a beggar eying a bakery window, then sank into a chair with a sigh. "It's good to be back."

"What have you been eating?" Charles asked as he helped Susan into her chair.

"Camp food, mostly. We took turns cooking it, even his lordship. We also had wild fruit when it was in season: pawpaws, sour gooseberries, currants. We ate what we found."

They bowed their heads while Mrs. Evans said grace. "Bless, O Father, Thy gifts to our use and us to Thy service; for Christ's sake. Amen."

"Amen," Charles repeated, though the brief recitation had failed to mention Isaac's safe return. He would have to thank God for that when he was alone. They passed the plates around and ate quietly, respecting Mrs. Evans' request that they eat before hearing Isaac's story.

But when Isaac sent his plate around for seconds, he broke the silence. "We first met with the leaders of the Delaware and Six Nations."

"*Six* Nations?" Susan asked.

"Honestly, Sue, don't you read?"

"Of course, I read."

"Then I shouldn't have to explain it to you." And he didn't.

Charles dished another piece of chicken onto his plate and returned it to him. "Did you sit on the councils?"

Isaac took a large bite of cake and nodded. "I wasn't allowed to speak, but I got to listen."

"Did everyone speak English?" Mrs. Evans asked.

"Not everyone did, but we had good interpreters who understood all the languages. Everyone kept talking about the 'chain of friendship,'" He shook his head. "'We must preserve the chain of friendship. We should keep our chain of friendship bright.' If I had a drink for every time someone said 'chain of friendship'—"

"Wait," Susan said. "I thought the conflict was between British Americans and the Indians. *They* wanted to preserve the chain of friendship?"

Isaac turned to Charles. "Hasn't this been all over the *Gazette*?"

"Some of it. There's been a lot more about the Continental Congress."

"Huh. I have a lot to catch up on."

"I've saved every paper since you left," Mrs. Evans said.

"Thank you. Where were we?"

"The chain of friendship," Charles said, anxious to hear the whole tale.

"Right. Well, there are lots of Indian nations. Some of them have treaties with us and fought on our side during the French and Indian War. Others didn't. Britain has been allied with the Six Nations and the Delaware for a long time. That's the 'chain of friendship.' We're allies." He returned his attention to the cake.

After a minute, Charles prompted him. "So, you met with the Six Nations and the Delaware. Did they agree to help?"

"Well, they said they were on our side, but they didn't want to go to war. In the end, it was Virginians who fought."

"They fought the Shawnee? Is that correct?" He didn't dare quote the *Gazette's* report to someone who had been there.

"They did."

"But why?" Susan asked. "Why would the Shawnee fight?"

Isaac rested his silverware on his plate. "Even though Britain bought the land from the Six Nations, the Shawnee insisted on using it as their hunting ground."

"Why would they do that?" Mrs. Evans asked. "Why not use their own hunting grounds?"

"Well..." Isaac dragged out the word hesitantly, "I'm not sure, but it might have been their hunting ground. That's what they said. I don't know who to believe, since the Six Nations insisted it had been theirs. That's what Lord Dunmore believed. But the Shawnee insisted they had never signed the treaty allowing the settlers to enter. And once his lordship decided the Shawnee were enemies to the Virginians, there was no more talk of friendship."

A chilling silence followed. Charles considered what Isaac had said. No one wanted peace more than Lord Dunmore. He would have studied the old treaties before leaving the palace. He had gone all the way to the frontier and held peace councils along the way. There must have been a reason for the battle at the end.

"Did you see the battle?" Susan asked.

Boyish levity was gone, replaced with the gravity of manhood. "I did." His solemn admission was followed by silence—silence filled with the phantom of war. He picked at a crumb on his plate. "During the battle, Lord Dunmore stayed in the fort. I was running back and forth carrying messages between him and the officers."

"Then you didn't fight," Susan said cheerfully, willing to forget the casualties as long as her brother wasn't among them.

"I didn't. But it was the longest day of my life. Running to the fort to report the movements and the deaths. Returning to the battle to witness Shawnees and Virginians all fighting and bleeding and dying with rifles and tomahawks. All wearing buckskin shirts and moccasins. They were so alike, they might have been brothers."

Charles decided never to ask Isaac how he came to have an old buckskin jacket. "I am glad you were at Lord Dunmore's side."

"So am I. He's a decisive man. I would hate to be his enemy."

Forty

MRS. UNDERWOOD

Charles strutted with the pride of a new father. Isaac was safely returned, and Lord Dunmore's mission had been a success. "He put himself in grave danger to secure Virginia's borders."

"Aye, Charles." Polly didn't look up from her writing. "Ye've told us that."

"I did, didn't I? Was there anything more selfless he could have done?"

"Nay," Quill said wearily. It served him right, all those months of doubting their royal governor and sympathizing with radicals.

Charles breathed deeply, his chest swelling with pride. His loyalties had been well-founded. "He labored solely for the welfare of Virginia. Even our commerce will benefit." Dunmore had pushed a treaty requiring the Shawnee to trade exclusively with Virginia. They would no longer be competing with Pennsylvania.

Lord Dunmore deserved a hero's welcome, and he was receiving one. Profusions of gratitude had been sent to the *Gazette.* The gentry were holding balls and feasts in his honor. The criticisms he had received in May when he had dissolved the sitting house were forgotten. Charles needed Susan to like Virginia. She deserved a country at peace. Dunmore had done that and more for the colony. For one glorious moment, all was well.

He was in a fine mood when they arrived at the Blue House for their weekly dinner. She had said it would be a special dinner in honor of Isaac's return and had insisted on sending the carriage around for Emmeline so they would have a full table. But when Graves announced them, there was another guest already in the parlor.

Susan made the introductions. The woman intruding on their cozy circle was a widow by the name of Mrs. Underwood. She wore a round-eared cap over her thin blonde hair. There were a few lines about her eyes. Her figure was harsh and angular. She looked poorly beside Susan, who was soft and plump from her dimpled hands to her rosy cheeks. If Susan was the plush settee in her aunt's parlor, Mrs. Underwood was an over-polished walnut chair in his father's study.

"Mrs. Underwood is visiting her late husband's family near Williamsburg."

Charles glanced instinctively for a mourning band. She wore none. The loss was not recent, but deserved civility. "I'm sorry for your loss."

"Thank you. It will have been two years in March." She clutched a handkerchief to her heart.

The awkward silence was broken by Susan. "She has two beautiful children."

Polly smiled bravely. "Boy or girl?"

"Both," the intruder replied. "That is to say, one of each. My son just turned six. He has his father's eyes. My daughter is three. She has her father's hair." Mrs. Underwood punctuated the melancholy facts by dabbing at her dry eyes.

"How lovely," Polly said. "Our sister had a baby girl a few weeks ago. We're looking forward ta meeting her when we visit for Christmastide, aren't we, Quill?"

"Aye, indeed. I've thought of little else."

Charles suppressed a laugh at the obvious falsehood. Just then, Graves announced dinner. In a moment, everyone else had paired off: Isaac with Emmeline, then Quill with Polly. They left Charles to escort both Susan and Mrs. Underwood.

"Shall we, ladies?" He forced a smile.

"The hall is too narrow," Susan said. "I'll walk behind."

Susan—and civility—demanded that Charles walk Mrs. Underwood to the dining room. It was such a short distance. He shouldn't begrudge it, but he did. How was he to prove he was courting Susan when he was forced to escort another woman in her presence?

Mrs. Evans was waiting for them in the dining hall, but Mrs. Underwood was more interested in the table than her hostess. "Oh! Are we having mince pie? How droll. My cousin told me once that I had the best hand at making those she had ever tasted. At least, that was when I was younger, before I had my own household. Naturally, I never set foot in the kitchen anymore."

Charles was impressed. Mrs. Underwood had insulted her hostess's food before it was even served. Under other circumstances, she might be an entertaining dinner companion. He helped the women into their chairs, then sat between them.

Susan spoke across him. "Miss Gardiner just finished reading *Gulliver's Travels*. I should say rereading, as she's read it several times before. Have you read that novel, Mrs. Underwood?"

"Oh, I don't read," she said dismissively. "It makes my head ache."

Emmeline stared at her, mouth agape. Susan tapped the bottom of her own chin, and she closed her mouth.

"Miss Gardiner does enough reading for all of us," Isaac said, smoothing over another awkward moment.

"Does she?" Quill carved a slice of ham and placed it on a passing plate. "Then I must thank her for relieving me of the burden of doing it myself." He winked at her.

Charles kicked him under the table. "Isaac, have you enjoyed being back in civilization?"

"I feel like I'm on holiday. I think we won't return to England until June or July, if that's alright with you, Sue."

"I would like—"

Charles looked up sharply. Such a delay in their return would give him another two or three months to persuade her never to leave. Unfortunately, Mrs. Underwood interrupted before he could find out what Susan thought of the idea.

"England! Oh, my brother visited there once. He was awfully fond of the food. I, for one, couldn't understand what he saw in it, as I think the food here is highly superior."

Mrs. Evans spooned potatoes onto a plate. "Have you been to England yourself, Mrs. Underwood?"

"No. And I could never. My neighbor's ship nearly capsized. I had been considering going to England at the time, but after that shocking tale, I couldn't sleep for a week. At last, I told my brother that it was simply unthinkable for us to be taking such risks, but he wouldn't listen to me, and until we got his first letter, I was certain he must be dead."

"Your poor nerves," Polly murmured.

"Thank you," she said, not noticing the subtle sarcasm. "They are quite delicate. In truth, my sister has told me that I have the most delicate nerves of any person she has ever met."

Quill served the last plate. "How taxing."

"Oh, it is. I assure you. I have often wished I had a more complacent temperament. But I bear it admirably."

She then launched into a lengthy description of her precocious children. It was impossible for anyone else at the table to turn the conversation, as she didn't pause to think. The words flowed from her mouth like a river flows to the ocean. He would have to wait until the woman left to find out if Susan would seize the opportunity to stay.

He had called on her every Sunday for three weeks in a row. He had carved and painted a rose when there were none in season.

He had complimented her music. He had spent a Saturday helping Mark and the others repair the cabins and, when it was clear there wasn't enough linen after all, he had purchased one of the last bolts of imported cotton and given it to Auntie Sarah, who had laughed and cried over the fine material. And he had told Susan everything. She had, after all, told him not to keep any more secrets from her.

The only thing he hadn't told her, not in words, was how he felt about her, or even that all this, in his mind, added up to courtship. He thought she knew. But she was even more reserved in courtship than he was. A lady often hid her feelings until a gentleman had declared his. But if she looked his way or smiled shyly when she told Isaac that she wanted to stay, it would be the encouragement he needed. The process of asking her father for permission would take months. He was anxious to send a carefully crafted letter as soon as possible, but what kind of fool would write when he didn't know how his lady received him?

Mrs. Underwood finally tired of her children and turned her attention to Mrs. Evans. "Sometimes being a widow is so taxing. You have no idea!"

Mrs. Evans blinked in surprise. "I don't?"

"I'm constantly pestering my brother to manage my estate. There are so many tasks that are better suited to men."

"You might be surprised how much a woman can do when she puts her mind to it."

"I have no head for numbers. I am determined to only do what is suitable for a lady of my station."

"Have you considered hiring an assistant?"

"That sounds so extravagant."

"With an estate the size of yours, I imagine the assistant would pay for himself."

"You mean he would work for free?"

Charles exchanged an incredulous look with Quill.

"No. I mean that a good one would help you to minimize

waste to such an extent that you would save more money than he charged."

"Do you have references for a good one?"

"I do not. I manage my property on my own."

Mrs. Underwood frowned as though struggling to diagram a difficult sentence. "Are you a widow?"

Isaac choked on his potatoes. Polly slapped his back until he waved her off.

Mrs. Evans returned her attention to Mrs. Underwood. "Of several years."

"Then you must understand how impossible the situation is."

"Indeed. No one understands impossible better than she who has accomplished it."

Susan said, "We met an immigrant who was highly suited to that line of work, didn't we, Mr. Johnson?"

Charles swallowed. "He managed a large farm in Scotland and knew everything about the latest in agricultural science."

"I don't trust immigrants," Mrs. Underwood said. "Immigration seems like an easy way for criminals to escape their local crimes. He might have been fleeing from the law."

Charles's knuckles went white. "Mr. Finlay is a good man. I can vouch for his character myself if you would like."

"No, thank you. My brother is perfectly capable of managing my estate. His is so much smaller, it hardly takes any time at all."

At last, the meal ended, and they said their goodbyes.

"Thank you for dinner, Mrs. Evans. It is so refreshing to have a change in society. Where I live, I find the society quite restrictive. I would be pleased to see you again." Mrs. Underwood clearly hoped for another invitation.

Susan looked at Charles questioningly. Why would she want his opinion on her new acquaintance? Couldn't she see the woman lacked delicacy and sense, and talked enough for any two people?

"I am sorry," Mrs. Evans said, "but we are engaged until— when did you say you were leaving?"

"Boxing Day."

"Ah, yes. Well, we are engaged through then. But that will allow you more opportunities to be with your dear family. Thank you for the pleasure of your company today. It will not be soon forgotten."

When the door closed behind Mrs. Underwood, the remaining company let out a collective sigh.

"Susan," Isaac said, "I don't know where you dug up an acquaintance like that, but next time, warn me before dinner. I'll need to be otherwise engaged."

Susan smiled. "Otherwise engaged? How?"

"Simple. I'll be having dinner at the tavern with Charles and Quill." They laughed.

"Don't leave me out!" Polly cried.

Susan pursed her lips thoughtfully. She looked straight at Charles and asked, "Was she really that dreadful?"

"That question requires a delicate answer."

"Then, yes. Yes, she was. Well, you needn't be afraid I'll invite her again for my own sake."

The Morrises took their leave. Charles hung behind as Isaac walked Emmeline out to the carriage.

When their nosy friends were out of the house, he asked, "What about Isaac's proposal?"

"What proposal?" Her soft brown eyes were curious.

His heart hammered in his chest. "The pro—" His voice caught on the word. "The proposal to stay longer. Here. In Virginia."

She busied herself with rearranging music on the harpsichord. "If that's what he wants."

"Oh."

The answer was flat and detached, neither warm nor shy. If she wanted to stay, she was doing a good job of hiding it. He couldn't write her father today.

Forty-One

THE TWELFTH NIGHT BALL

FRIDAY, JANUARY 6, 1775

Mrs. Evans' carriage rolled to a stop in front of Johnson Hall. It was a fraction the size of Bailey Manor but looked stately in the twilight, with a handsome portico. Susan had expected it to be much farther from town. Charles had never invited them before. She had always blamed the distance. Now she didn't know what to blame.

A footman took their wraps. Charles looked more handsome than ever, greeting guests with his father in the unfamiliar foyer. He wore a dark suit embellished with silver threads at the cuffs and lapel. A lace cravat was starched into a rippling waterfall against a lusciously embroidered waistcoat. Where nature had made him handsome, fashion had made him distinguished.

His father was sharing a parting laugh with Colonel Hendriks when Charles saw her. His lips parted. Then he jerked his gaze away. "Father, I'd like to introduce Mr. and Miss Bailey. They're friends of the Morrises." He said all this with a detached drawl she didn't recognize.

Susan blinked. Was Charles ashamed to claim friendship with her?

He continued the introduction without meeting her eye. "Mr. and Miss Bailey, this is my father, Mr. Johnson." He had gotten the introduction backward as if the Bailey family was of inferior consequence.

She curtsied, her face aflame.

Charles gestured down the hall. "The Morrises have already arrived. I'm sure you're eager to see them." Without waiting to see what she would do, Charles turned to greet the next guest.

Susan had never been so slighted in her life.

Isaac accompanied her deeper into the house. "A rather cool welcome, if you ask me."

Susan lifted her chin and her pride. "I'm sure he's anxious about helping his father host."

"If you say so." Isaac raised his hand in greeting. "Quill! How was the fox hunt?"

Polly took Susan's arm. "Are ye feeling well? Ye look a mite pale."

"I'm fine, I just—" Susan bit her lip. "Polly, you've known Charles's family for years?"

"Aye, since Quill went ta town for school."

"Is there any—" Her voice shook. She took a breath and started over. "Can you think of any reason why Charles wouldn't want to admit a connection with my brother or me to his father?"

Polly's mouth dropped open. "Of all the pig-headed things that man has done, this takes all. He didna introduce ye to his father?"

Susan pulled a fan from her pocket and twisted the silken cord. "He did. After a fashion." She looked up. "Oh, Polly, I've never felt so dismissed in my life."

"Take heart, Susan. This is Johnson we're talking about. Back in May, he wouldna speak of ye to me, either. Remember? I wouldna have known ye existed if I hadna met ye by chance."

She had forgotten about that. Charles had been difficult until she had demanded his friendship. Everything had gone fine since then. Why was he being difficult now?

Polly took her shoulders. "Come, I want ta show ye where all the mistletoe is hiding."

"What good will that do?"

"Ye do na wish to be caught under it with the wrong man, now do ye?"

In truth, she did want to be caught under it with the wrong man, because the wrong man had never seemed so right. But she had promises to keep—promises to her mother, her sister, and herself. Allowing herself a moment under the mistletoe with him would be flirting with disaster.

CHARLES TUGGED AT HIS CUFF. BEING SO DANDIFIED made him self-conscious, but his father had insisted on something fine for the ball they were hosting. The suit had been his when he was of courting age. A tailor had altered the fine fabric to suit current fashions. It wasn't a complete waste. Susan kept looking at him in a way that made him fancy a stroll under the greenery.

But he couldn't. Not yet. For now, he needed to turn his attention to the responsibilities of hosting. He had opened the ball by dancing with Miss Morris. He would have preferred Susan, but was afraid of what his father might say to her if she attracted his attention. Ideally, they would stay at opposite ends of the house.

There hadn't been so many people at Johnson Hall since before his mother took ill. As a child, he hadn't appreciated the burden of hosting. Now the heavy weight was on his mind. What if there wasn't enough food for supper? What if there wasn't enough room for everyone who wanted to dance? He had rearranged the musicians twice before the guests arrived, trying to expand the dance floor. Where was the cake? Why was Susan smiling at another man?

He paced the house, trying to keep track of everything. He had completed his third circuit when he saw Kitty sitting at the top of the stairs. Charles sighed. She would be in trouble tomorrow if his father caught her near the ball. She saw him frowning at her and fled toward Granny's rooms.

"Master Charles," Gideon said, "another guest has just arrived."

"With the cake, I hope." The woman who had found the pea last year was honor-bound to provide the traditional cake this year. It should have arrived hours ago. It wouldn't be Twelfth Night without it.

In the foyer, an angular blonde peered into the parlor, a cluster of mistletoe above her head. He stopped ten feet away. "Mrs. Underwood?" She was the last woman he wanted to entertain tonight, much less kiss. What was she even doing here? Charles knew every guest on the list, and this one had never been invited.

She startled at her name, moving away from the parlor like a child caught sneaking candy. "Mr. Johnson." She minced across the foyer like a common chicken attempting the airs of a peacock. Her artificial elegance was cheap and tawdry compared to Susan's beauty and manners. Unaware of his disgust, Widow Underwood batted her blonde lashes and tapped his shoulder with her fan. "You didn't tell me what a fine home you have."

He stepped back. "It's my father's. I don't live here."

"The family home, then."

"Yes."

"My family home was every bit as grand as this one." She looked appraisingly at the molding. "I don't live there now. I have so much to keep me busy at my late husband's home. I scarcely have time for neighborly calls."

"What brings you here? I thought you returned on Boxing Day." He hoped the coldness in his voice would turn her away. He could do nothing more. It would be an unforgivable breach of hospitality to be more direct. His mother and grandmother would never have done so.

"I did. Or, I was going to, but a dear friend pleaded with me to stay, and I couldn't refuse. Then she was so kind as to invite me to your ball."

Charles scowled. She was determined to stay. "I hope you enjoy yourself." He gave a curt nod and walked off before she could open her mouth again. He couldn't afford to be cornered by the monologue of an uninvited guest when he had so much else to attend to.

He scanned the ballroom for Susan. She was dancing again. Even if the parlor was vacated—even if he had the nerves for it—he couldn't take her there.

Mr. Johnson, Sr., stood opposite the musicians, speaking with a bald man. His broad, unsteady gestures suggested he had begun drinking early. That didn't bode well for the evening's success. Reining in his father's loose tongue would be more difficult than arranging the musicians had been.

"Small family." Charles could hear him halfway across the crowded room. "Wife only had one child. Lucky it was a boy. Sent him to London to pass the bar. Destined for big things. Hmm? Come from a small family myself. Just a sister. She got most the money, but I got Johnson Hall. It's been here for generations."

What his father said was only partially untrue. The plantation had been in the family for generations—his grandmother's family. His father's father had come to America indented. He had worked in the trades until he was forty. Then he had married the young heiress of the plantation and changed its name to Johnson Hall. None of those facts would give his father the air of gentility he craved.

"No. No sons there. Just a bird-witted chit of a girl."

Charles pushed through the crowd, suddenly alarmed. Emmeline didn't deserve to have her night ruined by drunken insults.

"Pretty to look at. I mean, not for me. I'm her uncle." He laughed loudly. "I should introduce you."

Charles cut into the conversation. "Excuse us, sir. There's a matter that needs my father's attention."

His father looked at him in surprise. "Charles? Where've you been?"

"Meeting guests," he said at random. "Come, there's someone you need to meet."

He led his father away from the bald man and out of the over-warm room. He had to put him somewhere quiet. His study had been converted to a card room. That would at least get him away from the Baileys and his cousin. He plunged into the room and bumped into a woman.

"My apologies," he began. Then he saw who it was. Here was an opportunity to kill two birds with one stone. "Father, allow me to present Mrs. Underwood, a widow from Portsmouth. She was interested in Johnson Hall. It reminds her of the home she grew up in. Mayhap you could give her a tour."

His father bowed. "I would be honored, Mrs. Underwood. Whereabouts did you grow up?"

Charles left them comparing the grandness of their homes. Another dance had just ended. "Quill, have you seen Emmeline?"

"She's talking ta Miss Bailey."

Susan was easy to find, even in a crowd. It wasn't just the height of her hair or the width of her figure. Charles knew the grace of her movements, the lilt of her voice. Even when he wasn't looking for Susan, he found her. They still hadn't danced, but now he had a duty to his cousin.

"Is something wrong?" Quill asked.

"My father was talking about her." Charles clenched and unclenched his fists. "He's her *uncle*."

"I'm afraid ta ask. What did he say?"

What had he said? That she was pretty to look at, and an offer to introduce her. The simple words didn't match the intensity of his reaction. "It was more *how* he said it."

"Is she safe? Should we leave early?"

She was smiling. The man in question was nowhere near. "Just help me keep an eye on her."

Quill crossed his arms and scowled. "Mayhap ye should ask someone ye trust."

"I trust you."

"'Never dance with her again, ye scoundrel.' Those were yer exact words."

Was he still sore about that? That had been more than two months ago. He had forgotten it had happened. "I didn't mean *never*." He had been upset because Susan had been upset, and Quill had provoked him by dancing with Emmeline a third time in the same evening. "I may have spoken in haste. I'm sorry."

Quill nodded. "Do ye still forbid me from dancing with her?"

"No. You may dance with her, but only when necessary. I don't want her getting ideas."

"Ideas? What sort of ideas are ye frightened of? That Christmastide is for merrymaking? That dancing is a wholesome amusement? Or that bounders and rakes aren't the only fellas ta notice a pretty girl?"

"Forget it." It sounded ridiculous when Quill went on like that.

"Fine. Whom do we suspect of ungentlemanly conduct this evening?"

"The bald one." Candlelight glistened across his bare scalp.

"They have wigs for that," Quill said in disgust. "All right, she has the protection of Clan Morris. That man willna have a chance to get near her."

"Master Charles," Gideon interrupted. "The cake has arrived."

At that moment, another man escorted Susan to the dance floor. Charles bit back a curse. He was doomed to spend the night providing for everyone's happiness save his own. "Quill, you go speak with your clan. I need to see to the cake."

It took longer than he expected to work out the supper arrangements with Graves. The musicians were lowering their bows again when he finally returned to the ball. He found Susan by the punch bowl. "Miss Bailey, might I have this dance?"

She raised a brow as though he had done something amiss.

He tried again. "If you are not otherwise engaged, would you do me the honor of standing up with me?"

"I thought you would never ask." She took his arm, and he wondered at the meaning behind her words. She had been expecting him to ask her sooner. That much he was confident of. Did she mean to hint at a preference for him? He remained uncertain. She might have said the same thing to other men tonight. He could hardly write to her father with no better encouragement than that she had expected him to be one of a dozen men to dance with her at a ball.

He led her to the top of the set. Though he had been looking forward to this moment for hours, he could not enjoy it. The bald man had disappeared, but so had Emmeline. Quill had promised to protect her. There he was, five feet away, bowing foppishly over the hand of a young lady surrounded by a bevy of females. "Miss Gardiner," he said, "would you do me the honor of partnering me in the next dance?"

Charles groaned. He had asked Quill to shield his cousin from undesirable advances, not to play the besotted suitor.

Susan laughed. "If you won't trust her with your dearest friend, who will you trust her with? It's Christmastide. Let her have her fun. We'll have ours." Her smile was as warm as summer.

He would set his worries aside, long enough to enjoy a few minutes with the woman he loved. Charles bent and kissed her hand. "As you wish, my lady."

THE QUEEN OF TWELFTH NIGHT

When Susan had set sail, she had anticipated a lonely Christmastide in Williamsburg. She had not expected to find herself surrounded by friends. Aside from Charles's cool introduction, the evening had been one of felicitous greetings, joyous laughter, and invitations to dance. Thanks to Polly, she also knew exactly which corners of the house to avoid. Her resolve this evening had strengthened. There was no sense in flirting with disaster.

She sat across from Charles during supper. His eyes darted around the table as drinks were refilled. He was anxious for the success of his father's ball. Susan had not missed the slight droop to one side of his father's face and his uneven step. Naturally, Charles felt responsible for helping him succeed.

"Charles," she said softly. His eyes found her. "You've done well."

"Do you think so?" He spoke in earnest, as though her good opinion was all he needed.

She smiled and gestured around the room. "This is the merriest I've seen people all Christmastide."

He followed her direction. A little of the tension eased from him, then his attention was arrested by two men carrying a large cake to the table, decorated with marzipan and royal icing. Slices were passed around to all the guests. The room quieted as people ate. A Twelfth Night cake had to be eaten cautiously. Susan had heard of coins and chess pieces baked into it, but the Johnsons weren't making this easy for their guests. A pea and a bean could easily be overlooked around the chewy currants. She broke her cake into the daintiest bites and ate with great concentration until her teeth came down on something hard. She removed it with her handkerchief. She had found the pea.

She shouldn't have. The woman who found the pea was honor-bound to supply the massive Twelfth Night cake at next year's ball, just as the man who found the bean would be hosting it. But she wouldn't be here, making merry with her Virginian friends and family. They would celebrate the holidays without her. Her eyes stung, and she stared at that ridiculous pea she should never have found, wondering what to do.

"You got it?" Charles asked. He knew she wouldn't be here to fulfill the duties, but he loudly announced, "We have our queen."

Susan tucked her handkerchief in her pocket. A day of reckoning would come, but she wouldn't sully today's merry-making with tomorrow's troubles. She finished her cake in a few bites.

There was a shout. Quill raised his hand high, pinching a bean. She nearly laughed. No one was less suited to host a ball. Polly could scarcely handle callers in their little apartment. He would have to beg or borrow a space. The Apollo might do if he reserved it early.

He didn't dwell on worry as he came to stand beside Susan.

Mr. Johnson, Charles's father, announced, "All hail the King of the Bean and the Queen of the Pea." The cheer was accompanied by exaggerated bows and salutes. Susan waved her hand magnanimously over her mock-subjects.

"A toast!" Quill cried, extending his glass. "To His Majesty, the King."

"His Majesty, King George III," the room chorused, then sipped their punch.

Susan raised her glass. "To the health of the Queen and her family."

People were still drinking to the queen's health when Quill raised his glass again. "To American liberty!"

Virginians drank to liberty with the same enthusiasm they toasted their monarch. Susan took a polite sip, then raised hers again. "To the people of Boston. May they have food to eat and clothes to wear."

"And to the year 1775!" Quill said. "May we see the peaceful union of Britain and her colonies."

People resumed their conversations, and Susan turned to Quill. "Mr. Morris, what did you mean by toasting American liberty?"

"The liberty of Boston from its military blockade, as ye said. And the liberties in our Bill of Rights. May Parliament remember that the rights of Englishmen and the rights of British Americans are the same."

"I understand. You want more clemency from Parliament." She pressed her hand against her heart. "For a moment, I thought you were toasting the idea of liberating America *from* Britain."

Mr. Morris raised his brows. "Surely ye dinna suspect me of treason."

"Not at all, Mr. Morris. Not at all."

IT WAS NIGH TWO IN THE MORNING WHEN CHARLES danced a second cotillion with Susan. The figures of the dance were a dizzying sea of moving color, but Charles only had eyes for Susan. She passed under his arm, her full petticoats brushing against his legs. Her face was flushed with exertion, her brown eyes sparkling. Her hand was in his. His feet were heavy, but his head was light. When the dance closed, she placed her hand on his arm.

"Are you tired?" he asked.

"A little," she admitted.

"Let's sit down somewhere quiet." This was the opportunity he had been waiting for all evening—a chance to see whether the preference he suspected she had for him was true. He prayed the parlor was unoccupied. As they crossed the foyer, he kept his eyes on the greenery suspended from the lintel of the parlor doorway. Five feet, four feet, three feet, two. He swallowed and, on the last step, began to turn toward her. But she stepped briskly across the threshold and into the parlor, dragging him along.

His heart sank. Was she determined to avoid the mistletoe, or had she not noticed it?

There was one more sprig hung over the window, bedecked with holly. It had more privacy than the foyer. Was that all she needed? Or had she meant to reject him? In his moment of hesitation, she released his arm and seated herself on the settee. His eyes measured the distance from her to the mistletoe. A few feet, or a few miles. Both were hopeless. Charles could more easily have navigated the Cumberland Gap.

He clapped his hands together and smiled bravely. "Would you like a drink? There's punch and chocolate."

"Chocolate sounds nice."

He crossed the foyer to the dining hall and caught a flash of movement. He crouched low and lifted the tablecloth. Kitty sat under the table. She should have been in bed hours ago. Her eyes were wide, pleading. Reminding. When he was a boy, every ball and dinner party had been a trial. He would slip down the stairs to spy on the adults, sneaking food until his nursemaid caught him. That had been Kitty's mother, Abah. She wasn't here to help her child.

"Come here, Kitty."

She shuffled obediently out and stood before Charles, her

body tense and her eyes squeezed shut. He picked up a pewter pot and lifted the lid. It was half-full of tepid chocolate. She opened one eye.

"Kitty?"

She bobbed a curtsy. "Yes, Master Charles?" That was what her mother had called him, what her grandfather still called him.

"See to it that the chocolate is reheated, then bring it and three mugs into the parlor."

"Yes, sir." She grabbed the pot and darted away before he could change his mind.

Charles piled a plate with an assortment of cold meats and cakes left out since supper to feed the guests who would dance until daybreak. It gave his hands something to do. Susan might be hungry, but even if she wasn't, he wanted to see that Kitty got a chance to try everything without hiding under the table. As a boy, his father had spanked him for being out of bed during a party.

Was it foolish to reward misbehavior with treats? Or was it cruel to punish children for wanting what adults claimed a right to have? Twelfth Night was a backward kind of day. He was more concerned about the happiness of a child than his duty toward his father. But she wasn't just any child. She was the daughter of his nursemaid. She was the child who cared for his grandmother. He crowded every delicacy on the plate and returned to the parlor.

"Hungry?" Susan asked.

"Me? No. But I thought you and Kitty might like some."

Susan's eyes narrowed. "Who's Kitty?" There was a hint of jealousy in her voice that soothed the sting of rejection.

"She's the little girl who takes care of my grandmother. Her mother was my nursemaid until I went to grammar school. She really should be upstairs in bed."

"It must be difficult for anyone to sleep with a dance going on."

"Especially for a child." Charles knew that from experience. How odd that a little slave girl reminded him of his boyhood.

She entered carrying a tray too large for her. Charles rescued the wobbling tray and arranged it on a table. Kitty gaped at Susan. She was young, but didn't she have any company manners? With the wrong audience, she could find herself in a lot of trouble. He would have a word with Gideon in the morning.

"Master Charles. Sir?"

"What is it?"

"Is she a queen?"

Charles looked back at Susan, the Queen of Twelfth Night, regal in silk and jewels.

"She is tonight. Here. You can eat anything on this plate."

Kitty's eyes went wide with joy. She quietly sampled the meats and cakes while Susan poured the steaming chocolate into three mugs. She gave Charles a quizzical look as she handed Kitty a mug. He had promised not to keep secrets anymore, but this time there was nothing to tell. He shrugged. "Children like food. That's all."

The smile Susan gave him was warmer than chocolate. For one long minute, he smiled foolishly back at her. Then they passed the time, talking over the distant music in a drowsy sort of way until Kitty yawned for the third time.

"That's enough," he said. "It's late. You sleep in Granny's room?"

She nodded.

He needed to get her to the stairs without his father noticing. He hated to think of something happening to the girl after the company left in the morning. "I'll walk you to the stairs. Don't come down again until daytime. I don't want you to get in trouble." He saw her safely to the stairs and watched her hurry up them.

When he returned to the parlor, his regal queen was asleep. Her dark lashes fanned across her petal-soft skin. Hair ribbons fluttered in a draft. Embroidered silk petticoats pooled across the cushions. She was as beautiful as the sketches he had once admired of Renaissance women, but she was more than a pretty picture. She was practical and kind and confident. She was one of the few people he could confide in. He loved her enough to marry her. She didn't love him enough for a kiss—not even a little one. There was no need to write to her father. He wouldn't offer for a woman who didn't want him. Charles stood alone under the parlor mistletoe until the ball demanded his attention.

Forty-Three

BOUND BY HONOR

TUESDAY, JANUARY 10, 1775

Susan slept the better part of a day and a night, recovering from the ball. When she finally came to herself, the festivities were over, leaving her to manage the doldrums of January. That Tuesday, Polly brought mending and gossip to the Blue House. The gentlemen would come closer to dinner. Isaac had asked if Miss Gardiner was coming, too, but Susan had been unable to persuade Charles that she should become part of their weekly dinners. This week's excuse was that her mother couldn't spare her so soon after the ball.

She pulled out her embroidery. Around the bouquet, she was adding honeybees, a robin, and a cardinal. The crewel thread was as red as a woodland wildflower. She smiled over her needlework.

Polly pinched a button against Mr. Morris's shirt. "What did you think of Johnson Hall?"

"It was fine." Actually, it was confusing. If Charles had such a respected family home an hour's ride outside of town, why was he living with his uncle? And if he was callous to the slavery around him, why was he kind to Kitty?

Polly smirked over her mending. "You should have heard our

dear friend Mrs. Underwood. She admitted the parlor was grander than hers. She seemed to think being mistress of Johnson Hall was a desirable thing."

Susan clipped her thread.

"Unfortunately for her, Charles made himself scarce. After he stood up with you the second time, you both disappeared. I hope you were showing him the mistletoe."

Susan's cheeks flamed. "Mistletoe is for lovers."

"And ye're not?"

"We can't be. Nothing would come of it."

Polly's brow creased in confusion. "Why are ye so set against the man ye fancy?"

Despite the fortifying lectures she'd given herself on the subject, there weren't words to persuade another of their validity. "It's difficult to explain."

"Ye *want* him. I can see it when ye look his way."

Longing pressed against her bruised heart like a spring flood against a dam. "What I want doesn't matter." The desperate words escaped her with childlike pathos. "I promised my mother I would care for her 'til her dying day. I'm not even supposed to be here." Her voice broke. "I'm not supposed to be making new friends and enjoying myself and falling in love." Tears welled in her eyes. "It doesn't matter how much I want him, because I'm not free to stay."

The truth had escaped her, not in neatly packaged words, but in shards, like a broken vessel incapable of holding water. She bowed her head under Polly's stare and dried her eyes, careful of her rouge, determined to preserve what dignity she had left.

Polly shook her head solemnly. "You poor dear. There must be a way around this."

"Please don't." She couldn't bear the disappointment that would follow hope.

"As ye wish." They stitched wordlessly for several minutes.

Susan broke the silence softly. "I almost wish he *had* kissed me. But he didn't."

Polly threw her mending to the ground like a gauntlet. "Sometimes ye have to stand under the mistletoe if ye want to be kissed."

Susan scoffed. She had already written the next potential bride, inviting her to call the hour she came to town. "It's too late, now. Christmastide is over."

"So ye say. But I see not all the greenery is down."

The kissing ball still hung from the door frame. Her aunt had forgotten to have it taken down. Charles would pass under it soon. She shivered. Mayhap Polly was right—they did deserve one kiss before their fated separation. This would be her last chance.

She stuffed the pocketbook into her sewing basket and strode across the room.

"What are ye doing?"

"Everyone is going to pass through here. Help me move it to the window frame."

Polly grinned. "Good thinking."

The bough of ivy and mistletoe hung innocently in the window. "Don't you dare tell the gentlemen that we moved it."

"Lady's promise." Polly was a true friend. "I'll be at the harpsichord when they come in."

"Perfect." She frowned at the window. "I don't want to be *too* obvious."

"No lady does." Polly took her by the shoulders and walked her beside the window. Then she stepped back and studied her, like a painter considering his subject. "That will do. Ye'll want to step forward to greet them. If ye stay close to the wall, that will bring ye to the target in the most natural-looking way."

"What target?" Isaac asked.

Susan was startled by his sudden appearance. "Mending," she said at random. "Nothing that would interest men."

He accepted the comment and settled onto the settee. Polly shook with silent laughter, holding her sides as though she might burst her stays. After one shuddering breath, she sat at the harpsichord, wiping the laughter from her eyes.

He would be here any minute. The reality of what she was about to do hit her like a wall. She couldn't kiss Charles in front of everyone. Her palms were clammy inside her mitts. She couldn't kiss Charles at all. The greenery hung motionless and innocent. It would be gone soon. She had worked so hard to keep him from getting too close to her. Now she was the one inviting him to close the distance. This was insanity.

The front door opened. Her heart pounded like a drumbeat. Charles's eyes sought hers as civilities were made. He drifted to her side. She barely heard Polly directing her brother to join Isaac on the settee before returning to the harpsichord. Polly winked at her, then faced forward with a poker face, pretending she needed to see the music for "God Save the King" when she was playing "Greensleeves" by heart. Her maneuverings were painfully obvious to Susan.

"I trust you're doing well," Charles said. Was he ignoring the mistletoe, or just oblivious?

"I am," she said breathlessly. "Thank you. And yourself?"

"I've heard of several people being ill due to the chill in the air, but blessedly, I am not."

She was standing under the mistletoe, speaking civilly of health and weather. "How is business?" She glanced up.

He didn't. "There's plenty of it. I took two days off for Twelfth Night and have a lot to catch up on."

"That's nice," she said, then realized it wasn't. "I mean, I hope you're able to catch up soon."

Polly gave her a pained look.

"I have plenty of time before the courts are in session."

Why had she allowed Polly to push her into this? It would be awkward to kiss with spectators and mortifying not to be kissed at all. Charles rambled on. All she wanted was to wake up from this nightmare she had created.

Aunt Dorothea cleared her throat from the doorway. "Should I have been chaperoning?" Her eyes were pointedly fixed on the greenery.

Charles looked around in confusion until he followed Quill's direction. "Oh," he mouthed.

Her aunt knew very well the kissing bough hadn't been there an hour ago. Mortified, Susan stepped back. Charles caught her fingers. Such a gentle touch couldn't have restrained a kitten, but she stilled, her bare fingers curling around his leather glove. Isaac made a sound of disgust before burying himself and Quill behind the *Gazette*. Their aunt stepped over to the harpsichord, intently turning sheets of music that had no relation to what Polly was playing.

Charles slowly interlaced their fingers and tugged, pulling her back under the mistletoe. In a voice so low it resonated through her, he said, "We're bound by honor." He was too noble to deny a lady's advances.

With her free hand, Susan fingered his cravat shyly. She had missed her opportunity in the rose garden. She had missed her opportunity by starlight, and sunset, and arranging flowers. She needed to deny herself many things to bring happiness to others, but this one time, she would not deny herself this.

When she looked up into his eyes, they were a blur of blues and grays, like the sea after a storm. Then they shuttered closed, and his lips were soft against hers. For a few beautiful seconds, she embraced what she desired. It wasn't an ocean away. What she wanted was living and breathing, right here, right now. She squeezed his hand as her lips explored his, just this once. Only she didn't want it to be just once. She wanted—

Papers rustled. "Enough," Isaac said with disgust. "She's my sister."

Charles released her so quickly that she grabbed the windowsill for balance. Her brother's disgust she'd expected, but her cheeks flamed under the Morrises' smiles, and she couldn't meet her aunt's eye. She should have kissed him in privacy on Twelfth Night—should have kissed him in the garden or the hall. She should have kissed him anywhere but in a room full of people. She shrank back into the curtains, willing them to look at something else, to say anything to break the heavy silence. Kissing under the mistletoe wasn't an announcement. It wasn't a commitment. It wasn't...anything.

Charles cleared his throat. "Is dinner ready?"

❧

THAT EVENING, CHARLES WROTE IN THE PRIVACY OF his bedchamber. He had shied away from this duty while he remained uncertain of Susan's reception of him. He ran a rough finger over his mouth. She had received him just fine.

Several discarded sheets of paper littered the floor. He got to the bottom of a page and sanded the wet ink. Then he reread his painfully crafted letter.

January 10, 1775
Dear Mr. Bailey,
You may have heard of me through your daughter's diligent correspondence.
If not, I must make my own introduction. I was educated at Lincoln's Inn and now work as a barrister. I have enclosed a list of men with whom I conducted business in England. You may apply to them for my character.
Mrs. Evans can also attest to my character. She is an old friend of my late mother and has frequently invited me to her home and table, where I have been in the company of young Mr. and Miss Bailey.
I have an esteem for Miss Bailey that is the result of a lengthy acquaintance. Out of deference to

you, sir, I have not yet spoken to her of my affection, but she gives me hope that mine is reciprocated.

I am the heir to Johnson Hall. While my father lives, I intend to purchase a comfortable yet modest home in town. Enclosed are some details of my financial matters. I believe I will be able to provide a life of comfort for Miss Bailey, though not as grand as I am persuaded she deserves.

As a parent, you must be concerned by the idea of her settling so far from your home. I must assure you that Mrs. Evans loves her like a daughter and has spoken to me of her wish for Susan to begin a family here in Virginia. Mrs. Evans hopes to be like a grandmother to her children.

I anxiously await your reply.
Your humble servant,
Chas. Johnson

Charles wiped a handkerchief across his forehead. There was so much at risk with every word. A year of planning could unravel in a single sentence.

Looking at his neat rows of figures to enclose, Charles felt his misgivings rise. What gentleman would support the marriage of his daughter to a stranger with such inferior financial footing? He might cast the carefully crafted letter into the fire and write directly to forbid Mrs. Evans from allowing him to see her. He hoped Susan had written a flattering description of himself. If she pleaded his cause, he felt sure to win. How could a father deny his daughter's most ardent wishes? How could any man deny Susan anything?

Forty-Four

A WANDERING HEART

Lucy wished her goodnight and pulled the bed curtains closed. The print on the curtains matched the coverlet and the tester. Susan was surrounded by the repeating image of a happy pastoral couple. Their benign felicity mocked her restless mind.

She had kissed Charles. The indulgence hadn't quenched her desire or satisfied her longing. It had crippled her resolve. Returning to her mother was the right thing to do. Her mind was firm, but her heart wandered. She wanted a future with Charles. Her old life was stagnant and oppressive. Life with him was growth and possibilities. She could craft a place of her own in the community, be mistress of her own home, and, God willing, have children of her own. And Charles. More than anything, she wanted to be with Charles.

Like a prisoner desperate for escape, she explored every possibility. If only he were a second son, free to follow her to Bailey Manor. If only she were a second daughter, free to stay. If only she were not the one responsible for her mother's care. If only an ocean didn't separate their homes. These four walls were solid. She couldn't break them, even for Charles. Perchance *she* would get a letter with black sealing wax. Her mother had been ill for years. It was possible.

Hope was like a moonbeam, piercing her bed curtains. She sat up, brushing them aside, expecting dawn. All was dark save the moon. She dropped her head against her pillow. It was wicked to think such things about her mother. It was worse to feel hopeful about it.

Yet, it was the only way she could see a life with Charles.

Ten years of her life she had sacrificed for her mother. She had taken pride in her service. Pride was her comfort when her duties isolated her from her friends. She had been lonely. She would be again. Why was so much asked of her? Hot tears moistened her pillow.

I've tried so hard, Lord. Is this so wrong?

Other women fell in love and got married. It was unfair that she couldn't. She rolled to her side and yanked the coverlet so hard her feet were uncovered. She was angry at England. At Virginia. At the vast ocean that separated them. She was angry at Isaac for bringing her here. She tossed to her other side. The ropes under the mattress groaned in protest. She would have been happier if she had never come. If she had never met Charles. She resented her father for sending her where she couldn't stay, and her mother for needing her to return. She was angry at herself. She shouldn't have allowed herself to be in this impossible situation.

She twisted in the coverlet. It was already a hopeless mess. Lucy would comment in the morning, and Susan would dismiss her concern. She had shared her distress with Polly, and now things were worse. No mortal could help her, and God had turned his back. Tears flowed onto her pillow with the constancy of a river. If God could part the Red Sea, surely he could have opened a way for Susan to be happy. Didn't she deserve a miracle as much as anyone?

At last, the moonlight passed, her tears ran dry, and she slept.

~

Susan maintained a quiet dignity through breakfast. Her bed was put in order. She dismissed Lucy's concerns. She was dressed. It was time to arrange her thoughts for the day. There were many things about her relationship with Charles that were outside of her control. The sooner she put that misguided kiss behind her, the better. She would focus on what she could control and accomplish.

She sat down at her writing desk and opened her commonplace book. Mrs. Underwood was the first *feme sole* on the page. Charles had been firmly disinterested. Susan smiled. It would have been disappointing if he had settled so easily. She decisively dragged her quill across the name. One woman down. She felt better already.

She glanced down the list. Polly had mentioned Miss Priscilla Ray by chance. Susan had learned she was a young heiress who had never been married and was a friendly acquaintance of the Morrises. As she was the most promising woman on the list, there was no harm in letting the others wait until Susan met her. It wasn't Susan's fault that Priscilla was unlikely to visit the capital until spring.

Proud of her businesslike handling of a delicate situation, she turned the pages back until she came to one titled "Genteel Improvements."

Blue ribbon on plain cap. Susan placed a neat check beside the item.

Dining etiquette. If only Emmeline could attend dinners more regularly. She wrote "ongoing" beside the improvement.

Play guitar for company. If she was as shy with her music as she was with her speech, it would be best to initiate her with the smallest possible audience. Some Sunday, she should come with Charles and bring her guitar.

Charitable endeavor. Susan's quill hovered above the word. Their attempt to support Bray School had ended in failure. They must find a new cause.

Sprightly harpsichord music flowed through the open door

and interrupted her thoughts. She hadn't heard the first callers arrive. Susan put away her writing supplies. The time had been well used. She was now composed enough for company.

It was not a caller, but her aunt who sat at the instrument, playing and singing. "The heavy hours are almost past that part my love and me. My longing eyes may hope at last their only wish to see."

Susan took a slow breath. Many songs were about love. It was best not to mind the lyrics. The last verse completed, her aunt turned to her.

"I wondered who was playing," Susan said. "I thought we had callers already."

Aunt Dorothea smiled. "I do play, you know. That's why my Julius bought this instrument." She caressed the harpsichord.

Susan had never before heard her aunt play a note, much less an entire song. "You play very well."

"Yes, well, I haven't had the heart to do it much since he passed. It always reminds me of him."

"Why did you stay? After you lost him?" Though she had asked before, Susan still didn't understand.

Her aunt raised her brows. "Do you think so little of my home?"

"I love your home." Susan gushed to smooth over the offense she had not intended. "It's beautiful, tasteful, and your very own. I love Williamsburg, too. The people are charming. I can easily understand your following my uncle here. I followed Isaac, and he's only my brother."

"Actually, moving here was my idea. You might say Julius was the one who followed me."

Susan blinked. "I didn't realize you were so adventurous."

"Adventurous? I suppose you could call it that. He was a fourth son, and I was determined to have a place of our own. In England, everything good is inherited. Here, we had an opportunity to create our own life. I miss him dearly, but that kind of ache can only be healed in heaven. Returning to England now wouldn't fix anything."

If only Charles were a fourth son. Susan shook her head. That line of thinking led to nothing but tears. She turned the subject. "Are we staying in for callers or going out?"

"Going. Mrs. Hendriks has a new companion she would like me to meet. A widow by the name of Mrs. Kemp."

Companions were often young ladies with limited family or resources. Susan thought she had exhausted the local supply of young widows. "She's not a woman of property?"

"Yes. She has her widow's third of an old plantation."

Susan's heart sank. "Another *feme sole*?" She had expected another week or two to pass before needing to brace herself for this.

Aunt Dorothea frowned. "I thought you'd given that up." Somehow, her aunt suspected what she had been up to.

Susan lifted her chin bravely. "Not at all."

Her aunt studied her for an uncomfortable moment. "You have a big heart. Don't waste it."

An hour later, Susan stared out the carriage window without seeing the people on the street. She tried to imagine the joy on Charles' face when he would meet the wonderful bride she had found for him, but her imagination refused to be bridled. He was watching her from a hammock in a storm. He had stopped a carriage to pick wildflowers for her. She was worried about Isaac. His hand was on hers as he held her gaze. They were under the mistletoe, standing so close his eyes were a blur.

"Here we are," Aunt Dorothea said.

Susan forced a smile. The greater the good, the greater the sacrifice, she reminded herself. She had left the tears behind in the moonlight, but her broken heart hadn't healed in the sunlight.

The colonel struggled to his feet as they entered, leaning heavily on his cane.

"Good morning," Mrs. Hendriks said. "Mrs. Kemp, I would

like to introduce you to Mrs. Evans and her darling niece, Miss Susan Bailey."

"How d'you do?" Mrs. Kemp's country accent was crippled by a missing front tooth. Wrinkles fanned out from her friendly eyes. Her wrinkles had wrinkles. She was old, far too old for Charles.

Susan loved her. "Mrs. Kemp. I'm delighted to meet you."

Forty-Five

FINLAY'S PLEA

MONDAY, FEBRUARY 6, 1775

Charles turned in front of the wood stove, his cloak still on.

"Still cold?" Quill asked.

Charles had been chilled to the bone that morning during the militia drill. They were released so early that he and Quill had agreed to come to the office, but not even a hot drink at Chowning's had warmed him. "It's absurd to drill outside campaign season," he grumbled.

"Ye got something in the post," Polly said. "'Twas written so poorly, I nigh refused it."

She handed Charles the letter. His name and direction were barely legible over smudges and scribbles. It had been sealed by white candle wax, imprinted with a button. Charles winced, imagining four small burns where the wax would have pushed up through the button. One trial as a child taught him the folly of using buttons for a makeshift seal.

There was no way this letter was from a client capable of paying for legal services. Yet he would have to pay the Morrises back at the end of the month for the expense of getting his mail, since Polly had chosen to accept it. She would have made a note in the account book already.

The candle wax seal crumbled as he opened the letter. A grocery list had once been written on this paper. The sender had written his message crosswise to the list. Charles had to read slowly to separate words like behalf from bread.

> *Mr. Johnson,*
> *I trust you remember me from the Minerva. I write on behalf of another man who works with me. He suffered a serious injury at the hands of our master. He is beaten daily for his inability to work, but he can barely stand. I believe his leg is broken. Is there anything in the law that would protect him?*
> *Your humble servant,*
> *Thomas Finlay*

This wasn't the first time Thomas had pleaded for his help. But it wasn't Charles who had saved his wife. That had been Susan's doing.

"Well," Polly looked at him expectantly, "what is it?"

"An indented servant, injured by his master."

Quill gave a low whistle. "That's rough. The law will do little for him."

"I know," Charles said. In 1705 and again in 1723, the Virginia legislature had codified merciless laws against indented servants and slaves. Those who knew better and had a choice immigrated to the other colonies. There had been an increase in the number of people brought to Virginia against their will to make up for the decrease in willing labor. Thomas was as good-hearted a man as he had ever met. He had been separated from his family and asked for no personal comforts. Charles tapped the letter thoughtfully on his desk. There wasn't much he could do in this case, and yet...

"I'm going."

"What?" Polly asked.

Loyalty pulled on his heart like magnetic north pulled on a compass. He put his tricorn back on. "I'll be out of the office for the rest of the day."

"*Where* are ye going?" Quill asked.

"A plantation this side of Cliveden."

"But that's halfway ta Hampton."

Charles opened the door. "Then I should make haste." Haste should have meant going straight to the stables to hire a horse. Instead, he braved the cold a little longer to call on Susan.

"Charles!" She exclaimed as he removed his hat. "Did the drill finish early? I hoped it would. No one should be out in that weather."

"It did." He pulled out a handkerchief. The cold made his nose run.

"You look like you could use something hot. Can I get you anything?"

Charles had drunk two mugs of coffee at Chowning's. He didn't want more coffee and wasn't about to deplete Susan's tea stores. "No, but thank you. I came with news of our mutual acquaintance, Mr. Finlay."

Susan's eyes went wide. "How is he? I heard he was put on a plantation outside of town."

"You heard correctly. He—" Something caught in Charles's throat. He coughed to clear it. "He had nothing to complain of. But a friend of his has been injured. He was vague on the nature of the injury, but I fear a broken leg bone."

Susan rose from her chair. "It should be set—by a doctor, of course. I have no skill in setting bones." She shuddered. "But he'll need comfrey for healing, of course, and laudanum for pain. That *might* be what he needs, but without knowing more, I can't be sure. I'll bring my whole bag, just in case."

She brushed past Charles. He turned and caught her shoulders. "I appreciate your advice, Susan, but I'm going alone." Her lip turned down in a pout. It took all his self-control not to kiss it, but there was no mistletoe this time, and he was still awaiting her father's blessing. "I wanted your advice, but more than that, I want to know you're safe." What more could he say without worrying her? *It's a legal matter. I'm a barrister. I love you.*

She raised her chin. "I'm never not safe." That might be true, but with her stubborn refusal to believe anyone would hurt her, she wouldn't know otherwise.

"Let's not change that." He kissed her cheek, as surprised by his boldness as she was. Her wide eyes were inches from his face. He slowly lifted his hands from her shoulders. How long had they been there? His feet had grown roots. For two heartbeats, he couldn't move, couldn't breathe. Then his senses returned. He stepped back.

She blinked. "I'll get the medicine."

While she was gone, Charles prodded the fire. Had he *needed* to speak with Susan before going? No, but he'd been wanting to see her all day. Any excuse would have brought him. And mayhap the medicine she gave him would be what was needed. Sparks flew from the logs, floating lazily before winking out. Charles had not grown up in a physically affectionate household—his uncle's house barely more than his father's—but even he knew a kiss on the cheek was a common gesture for many families and friends. Not his family. Not his friends.

But she had kissed him before—had kissed him fearlessly in front of her family and friends. From a lady like her, that could only mean one thing. He stabbed the log. As soon as he heard back from her father, he could formally ask for her hand. The log smoldered brightly.

Today's brief wouldn't pay. It would do nothing for his savings. He would pay for the post and hire a nag, and expect nothing in return. Christian decency pushed off the home that he would purchase by another day. That was why he had needed to see Susan. This errand wasn't bringing him close to her in any other way. She respected his decision to respond, and she deserved any news he had of the Finlay family.

She returned and handed him a small bag. "That's for you. Fortunately, we made a fresh batch yesterday."

He cradled the lumpy bag in his palm. "What for?"

"You have a cold."

"Oh." That would explain the pressure behind his nose. It was such a wifely thing to notice and care for. He tucked the bag into a jacket pocket.

Then she handed him a small bottle and an envelope. "And this is for Mr. Finlay's friend. Now tell me: why isn't this safe?"

"Besides the weather?" Charles shivered, measuring his words carefully—what was needed, and what would alarm. "I'm hoping to come and go without his master noticing I'm there."

"So you're putting yourself in danger."

"Not much. I'll be careful. But it's easier to be cautious as one than as a party of two." He wanted to kiss her goodbye, to see if her affection could warm him when fire and coffee had failed. The ungentlemanly urge alarmed him. They couldn't be engaged until he had her father's permission. And what woman wanted to be wooed by a man with a cold? He shoved his hat decisively on his head. He was leaving before he forgot himself.

He was almost to the door when Susan spoke. "Marion Finlay was in good health last I saw her, a week ago. Timmy has grown so much. He can say, 'mama' and can stand without help."

He nodded. "Thomas will be pleased to hear it. I'll see you at dinner tomorrow." They would have chaperones again, to prevent him from making a fool of himself.

"May you bring good news," Susan said.

The afternoon was colder than the morning. It was miserable weather for riding horseback. His nose ran more, and he began to cough in earnest. He took a pastille from the bag Susan had given him and slipped it into his mouth. The sweet licorice and anise coated his throat and soothed his cough, at least for a few minutes. After a couple of hours, he asked for directions. He turned down a narrower road and watched warily for the great house. The master would not be pleased to know a barrister was meeting covertly with the indented, even if there was nothing the law could do against him. The bare branches of shrubs and trees did little to screen him from view.

Smoke rose from the great house and the kitchen. Further into the property, he could discern another column of smoke. Where there was smoke, there were people. With any mercy, the man he was looking for would be there. He slipped off the hired nag and led it along the edge of the property. He bowed his head, using his hat and the horse's body to shelter him from the windows of the house. The smoke led him to a cluster of shacks. One forlorn woman stirred a pot over the fire as rain drizzled on her. She looked at him warily.

"I'm looking for Mr. Finlay."

She pointed to one of the shacks but offered no explanations. He was not welcome here. After tying the horse, he stood outside the shack and clapped his hands loudly. The door opened. The room was dark. The only windows, which held no glass, were shuttered against the winter wind. A dozen men, black and white, were crowded in the single room.

"Mr. Finlay?"

A man stepped over the sprawl of humanity and grasped his hand. "Mr. Johnson. You got my letter?" The hope in his tone made Charles despair of the answer he brought.

"I did. The good news is your wife and babe are in good health. And Jenny. She has been under my uncle's roof this whole time."

Thomas bowed his head. "Thank the Lord." The poor man. He hadn't had news of his family since May.

"The bad news—"

Thomas's head whipped up.

Charles persevered. "The bad news is that the law offers little protection for the situation you described." He felt the eyes of every man in the room. Did they blame him? The law had been written long before he was born. Slaves and indented servants were at the mercy of their masters. They could die at their master's hands with no guarantee of protection from the law. There had been a few cases won, but the attempt was more likely to bring further harm on the heads of those seeking protection.

"May I see the man in question?"

Mr. Finlay led him to a man lying on a pallet against the drafty wall. "Mr. Johnson, this is Bob."

"You don't look yer best," Charles said.

"I can't stand. It's my leg. I can't put weight on it."

"Let me see." He gingerly pulled back the blanket. There was no stocking on his leg to cover the swollen bruise. "It's broken?"

"I believe so."

"When?

"'Bout a week ago."

Charles wished Susan were there. He would trust her with his life. But this man depended on Charles for his life. What would Susan do? "Thomas, help him sit up. He needs to take his medicine."

"Ye brought some?" The relief on Thomas's face restored Charles's confidence. There was something useful he could do.

"Thanks to Miss Bailey. She keeps a whole apothecary in a bag."

Bob panted with pain as he was moved into a sitting position.

"Good," Charles said in what he hoped was a soothing tone. He pulled out the glass bottle. "Let's start with laudanum. That's for the pain."

Bob drank the bitter medicine eagerly.

Charles pulled the bottle back. "You'll be wanting more later." He corked it and handed it to Thomas for safekeeping. "Next, the comfrey. It helps with healing."

Bob swallowed quickly. This part of nursing was surprisingly easy. Charles's eyes had adjusted to the dim interior. He studied the bruising on Bob's leg. His shin bent in the middle. It would need to be set.

"Where else is he injured?"

"His back."

"Let's see."

Bob swore while Thomas undressed him like a baby. Lacerations criss-crossed the man's back, red and swollen. Charles had suspected as much, though he had deliberately not said so to Susan. Instead, he had raided Johnson Hall's wine cellar on the way.

"That needs to be cleaned. Bob, we need you to roll onto your stomach and lie still."

Bob cursed freely as Charles slowly poured wine over the wounds. If it hurt this much, had he not administered enough laudanum? Or did it need more time to take effect?

Finally, he corked the wine bottle. It was still half full. The other servants leaned closer. Wine was a valuable commodity. Charles spoke with authority. "Thomas will guard this until the doctor comes."

Thomas accepted the bottle uncertainly. "Our master won't send for a doctor."

"He needs a doctor to set the bone."

"But our master won't pay him."

"He might, if he thinks he's in violation of a law."

"But I thought ye said—"

Charles winked solemnly. "And if he still won't, I'll pay."

"Thank ye, Mr. Johnson," Thomas said. "If there's ever anything I can do…" He looked around himself, seeming to just now remember he was not free to serve anyone but his cruel master. He sighed. "Give Miss Bailey our thanks. And, if it isn't too much trouble, please tell Marion and Jenny that I'm fine. Just fine."

The ride home was colder still, especially as the light faded. It had been worth it to help Finlay, but it wasn't enough. He deserved to be where he could watch over his family, with a lenient master who wouldn't penalize them if his wife had another baby.

Forty-Six

MUSTARD PASTE

The wind blew icy rivulets down his collar and into his shoes. It was dark when he returned the nag to its stable. By the time he had walked home, he was numb from the cold. He hung his clothes to dry by the fire, then pulled on his old banyan and lay shivering in bed.

There was a knock on the door. "Charles?" Emmeline said.

"Come in." He sat up shakily as she entered, carrying a tray. Steam rose from a mug and bowl.

"You looked so miserable, Mama said you could take supper in your room tonight." She pushed aside a book on his desk, set the tray there, then handed him the earthenware bowl.

The tasteless soup scalded his throat, warming him from the inside. The room pulled the heat from his body, and not long after he finished the soup and hot cider, he lay shivering again. His lungs were heavy as he coughed. It was nearly morning when he was able to sleep soundly.

He slept late. Only the promise that he would see Susan at dinner pulled him from a bed that was finally warm. He dressed in his warmest clothes and stumbled downstairs. Emmeline and Jenny sat in the front room, the mending basket between them.

Emmeline looked up. "I heard you coughing during the night. Will you stay home?"

Too much depended on the work he did. Especially if he was paying for another man's doctor bill. "I didn't work yesterday. I need to go in." He wouldn't miss two days in a row. And if he was well enough to go to work, he was well enough to visit Susan.

The walk to the office was exhausting. Charles leaned against the side of a shop to catch his breath. By the time he got to work, the day was half gone.

"We were just speaking of ye," Quill said.

Polly waved the ledger. "Taking wagers on what was keeping ye. I said ye were dead by the side of the road."

A violent cough prevented Charles from answering.

"Quill was more optimistic."

"He thought I was alive?"

Polly smirked. "No, he wagered ye had finally eloped."

"Then you're both wrong."

"Pity," Quill said.

Charles couldn't have agreed more.

MISS PRISCILLA RAY WAS COURTEOUS, ACCOMPLISHED, beautiful, and a recent heiress of twenty acres. She would be perfect for Charles. Susan despised her.

Thank heaven Aunt Dorothea was here, asking all that was decent and polite. Susan did not feel polite. Right now, she was anxious to see Charles alone. Had yesterday been as dangerous as he had expected? Had he been injured? What was his news of Mr. Finlay? Had he really almost kissed her?

That mattered least of all. Her whole family expected Susan to spend the rest of her life overseeing the care of their invalid mother. Her future was fixed. Susan couldn't encourage Charles' attentions. So she sat primly on the settee, hating Priscilla, who could.

"How was the Queen's Ball?" Priscilla asked.

"It was lovely," her aunt said. "Lady Dunmore was in good health. She has such an elegant figure, and so soon after her most recent baby. Did you hear what they christened her?"

"No. What?"

"Virginia."

"Oh, that is sweet."

The carriage arrived. Susan braced herself for the introductions. Watching Charles enjoy speaking with the pleasant Priscilla over dinner was going to be torture. Graves announced their usual three visitors. Emmeline, Polly, and Quill looked pleased to be there. Charles looked like he could barely stand on his own.

Aunt Dorothea introduced Priscilla. Susan barely heard her. She didn't care. Let the others talk to the perfect Priscilla. She needed to speak with Charles. She stepped closer. Someone needed to catch him if he collapsed. "What happened, Charles? I've been so worried."

"Nothing happened. I'm fine." His voice had dropped an octave below its natural state. His nose was red. His eyes were half closed, even as he stood there.

"We both know that's a lie." She spoke firmly, earning an amused look from the Morrises.

"It's just a little cold."

"You were outside far too much yesterday. You should have hired a carriage. I was afraid this would happen." She hesitantly placed a hand on his back. "Breathe deeply."

CHARLES INHALED. IT WAS LIKE CATCHING HIS BREATH underwater. Gravel churned somewhere deep in his lungs.

A worry line appeared on her forehead. "That doesn't feel good."

On the contrary, her hand on his back felt very good.

"Have you been to the apothecary?"

"No," he said huskily.

"Stubborn man," she said affectionately. "Wait here and I'll make a poultice for you."

She walked through the house, past a maid setting the dining table for dinner, and out the back door. Charles followed. He caught the kitchen door as she was closing it.

She looked at him with exasperation. "You should stay inside as much as possible until your cough improves."

"I'll go back when you do."

Susan shook her head and let him in. "Maurice, where's the mustard seed?" She took a mortar and pestle from a shelf. Maurice murmured something in French and handed her a jar. She tipped the contents into the mortar and pounded until the air was fragrant with mustard seed. She scraped the paste into a small jar and handed it to Charles.

"Apply this every night."

"Apply it...where?"

"It's for your lungs. Right here." Susan placed the flat of her hand across his chest.

He stopped breathing. He could feel the warmth of her hand through his waistcoat. "Every night," he repeated softly. The warmth in his chest spread across to his shoulders and down his arms, banishing the cold. A minute ago, he had felt like death. Now his heartbeat under her fingertips, very much alive. He would gladly submit to this every night.

She looked up at him curiously. Her brown eyes were the most intoxicating sight in the world. The longer he looked into them, the less aware he was of his surroundings. Not even the sound of muskets firing could have disturbed this moment. Susan's eyes fell to her hand on his chest. She pulled back as suddenly as if she had been burned.

He stepped forward as she stepped back. He paused, confused. She had kissed him once. Since then, he had ached for her to kiss him again, but was determined to wait until they had her father's blessing. The wait was agonizing. Weakened by the fever, he had surrendered to her touch. But now her eyes were as wide as a frightened child's. He didn't understand.

"Susan—"

"Be careful not to leave it on for too long. It can cause burns." Then she turned and fled back to the house, leaving him clutching a jar of mustard paste. Maurice muttered something in French, making almost as little sense as Susan.

Forty-Seven

A LADY'S ENDEAVORS

MONDAY, APRIL 3, 1775

Spring had come softly. Freed from the woolen weight of her cloak, Susan's muslin petticoats bounced as she walked down the street with Polly. Soon, there would be flowers again and leaves on the trees. This morning, she had watched a pair of robins building a nest in the oak outside her window. The bitterness of winter was forgotten. The worries of summer were months away. Spring was the season of hope and new beginnings.

This morning, she had abandoned an ambitious song on the harpsichord when Polly had stopped by. Susan had been away from home for so long that she had begun to take certain freedoms for granted—like accepting invitations to balls and concerts or leaving the house on a whim to spend the morning with a friend.

"Do ye mind if we stop by Greenhow's?" Polly asked.

"Not at all," Susan said, hoping the general store had received a new shipment. There hadn't been much to see the last time she had stopped by. Still, they were better off than Boston, whose harbors were entirely closed. Rumor had it that people were escaping from the city to the countryside, desperate for food. At least Virginians weren't hungry.

Her steps slowed as they passed the milliner's. In the window was a new display: an elegant pair of shoes, a delicate fan, and a lacy cap, all in the purest white. With the awe and longing reserved for sleeping babes or sunsets with Charles, she gazed at the bridal millinery. If she could have every shop in London at her disposal, she couldn't have found something so perfect. It was exactly what she had once dreamed of wearing at her wedding. If she were going to be a bride, she would wear it with her pink taffeta gown. Lucy would weave rosebuds and ribbons in her hair.

"See somethin' ye fancy?" Polly asked with a teasing lilt.

Susan squeezed her eyes shut and turned away, dragging her friend down the street. They left the bridal millinery where anyone might see it and buy it. "It's nothing," she said. "Just a new window display. There are so few of them lately."

The door to Greenhow's General Store opened as they neared. A gentleman dressed in the uniform of a lieutenant in the Royal Navy stepped out. She knew that uniform well. Several officers had attempted to court her in years past. It was one of the few careers available to younger sons. Many died before seeing success. Seeing them approach, the lieutenant held the door and offered a playful salute as they passed inside. The door had scarcely closed behind them when another customer complained about him to the shopkeeper. "He could ha' bought that in England. We're short enough on goods as it is."

The shopkeeper wrapped something in blue paper. "Who do you think keeps the pirates away so we get our goods?"

The woman snorted. "What goods? Hardly anything has gotten through in months." She gestured at the barren shelves.

The shopkeeper's jaw tightened. He handed the woman her package and bid her a good day. Then his weary eyes went to his next customers.

Polly stepped forward. "Good morning."

"Good morning, miss. How can I be of service today?"

"I need a packet of pins and a bit of salt."

"Salt, I have. Unfortunately, we ran out of pins two days ago."

Susan cast her eyes around the shop as though a packet of pins might have been forgotten on an empty shelf. "That can't be."

"I'm afraid it is," he said, measuring the salt onto a scale. "Is that enough?"

"Aye," Polly said. "Thank ye." She took a small coin pouch from her pocket while the shopkeeper packaged the salt.

Susan was too shocked to mind the trivialities. Pins weren't a luxury, like feathers and beads. They were an essential part of daily living, at least for women. A gown couldn't stay together by itself. Silk stomachers needed pins, but so did the shortgowns worn by dairy maids and lowly laundresses. It wasn't possible for a woman to be dressed without them. Running out of pins shocked her more than the possibility of running out of tea.

As they emerged from the shop, the sun glared in her eyes. Disappearing down a side street, she thought she saw Lucy on the arm of a swarthy man. She blinked, and they were gone. It couldn't have been Lucy. She was in her bedchamber, mending a small rip in one of her gowns. And, save for her brief flirtation on the *Minerva*, she had never allowed a man to be close to her. Susan peered down the side street as they passed, but Lucy wasn't there.

"What is it?" Polly asked.

"Nothing. I thought I saw someone, but it seems the sun was playing tricks on my eyes."

Polly led her up a narrow stair and fumbled with a key. The door opened into a space that attempted to be both a parlor and a dining room. It failed at both. A dented table with three chairs made up the dining room. One of the table legs was shorter than the others and was supported by a block of wood. A threadbare settee was against one wall, almost touching the table. Polly tucked her petticoats close as she walked sideways past the hearth to the cupboard that hung above the table on one wall. She unlocked it and put the salt away.

Susan pulled up a chair. It wobbled uneasily as she sat on it. Her fancy had taken flight with the songbirds. She needed to ground it. She ought to be more serious about the *feme soles*, but she had tried. The problem was that the more women she met, the more she was convinced that she would never be able to picture another woman with Charles.

What would he think if he knew she had seen a white fan and immediately started daydreaming about a wedding? There had been moments in the passing months when he had looked at her in a way that made time stand still. Moments, she almost believed he was in love—that he had wanted to kiss her as much as she had wanted to kiss him. That he still did. But what she had thought was courtship had continued in the same friendly way for months. He hadn't spoken or hinted at any intentions.

He just came. Came and looked. Then left again.

After he left, she would lecture her wandering heart to be still. The stillness hurt, but so did the wandering. Either way, thoughts of Charles were increasingly unable to ground her fancy. "He still won't allow his cousin to come to another dinner," she complained aloud.

Polly blinked at the abrupt statement. "You mean Mr. Johnson?" She sat across from her. "I'll wager it's your brother he's worried about."

"Isaac? He's harmless."

"Aye, he's harmless. There's no harm in what he does."

"What do you mean?"

"Ye canna tell me ye havena noticed. He is always in the right place ta hand her into a carriage or escort her ta dinner. Every Sunday, he finds her in the churchyard and smiles and talks 'til she has ta leave. Take her ta a ball and he'll stand up with her afore anyone else knows she's there. Bring her ta dinner and all his smiles will be for her."

"It's just a passing fancy," Susan said. "Miss Gardiner is a darling girl, but she would be so...so unsuitable for Isaac. And he knows that. I've told him so." The wife of Isaac Bailey, heir to

Bailey Manor, must be poised and practical. She must be capable of managing Bailey Manor and of being a leader in the community. A daydreamy daughter of a tradesman would be miserable in such a position. "I hope one day she marries a gentleman wealthy enough to have a handsome library, but not so prosperous that their neighbors will depend on them. Right now, what she needs is a charitable endeavor."

Polly raised her brows. "The Gardiners are known for their charity." The family took pride in their hospitality.

"What they do is good," Susan admitted, "but I want her to have a noble cause that sets her apart from the other tradesmen's daughters—something that will help her forge connections with genteel society, so she might be seen by the right sort of man."

Polly sighed. "She works so hard. When will she ever find the time for that sort of thing?"

"She has to," Susan said fiercely. "Can you picture her working her fingers to the bone, married to an ungrateful tradesman who can't afford meat for their ten children?"

Polly's eyes widened. Then she laughed. "Ten children? Is that what ye're hoping ta have yerself?"

"What? No." She would be lucky to have one. "That was just a number to illustrate my point. It would be better for her to find the time now than not to have the time later."

"She's seventeen," Polly said. "She doesna need ta think about marriage afore she's nineteen or twenty."

"I won't be here when she's nineteen or twenty." A familiar ache strained her heart. "But I am here, now."

There was a long silence, and then Polly nodded. "What did ye have in mind?"

～

THAT AFTERNOON, AS EMMELINE CLIMBED IN THE carriage, Susan asked, "Do you remember Mr. Nicholas? He oversaw Bray School before it closed down."

Emmeline seated herself gracefully in the carriage. "I remember."

"Good. I wanted to meet with him today."

"Whatever for?"

What had seemed like an excellent idea when she had discussed it with Polly was fraying under closer inspection. "To inquire after the library. I want to know what happened to all those school books. "

"Oh." Emmeline twisted her hands in her lap. "What do you want me to say?"

Susan herself wasn't sure. "I'll leave that at your discretion."

Soon, they were ushered into a fine parlor, considerably less stuffy than the last time they had visited.

"Mr. Nicholas," Susan said. "A pleasure to meet you again."

"You as well, Miss Bailey, and—" he cleared his throat.

"Miss Gardiner," she prompted.

"Yes, Miss Gardiner. Please, have a seat."

Susan could feel Emmeline watching her as she settled into a soft wingchair. She copied the movement with the chair opposite the fireplace.

Mr. Nicholas sat on the settee. He leaned forward, resting his forearms on his knees. "What brings you here?"

Emmeline leaned forward. "It's the Bray School, sir."

He frowned. "When we never found a suitable teacher, the associates agreed to close the school. We cannot accept students or even donations any longer."

"We understand that," Susan said.

His brow furrowed. "Then why are you here?"

"We were wondering what became of the books."

"The schoolbooks? Boxed up and collecting dust."

"That's a shame," Susan said. "Books like that should be used for teaching."

"I told you before. Bray School will not reopen."

"We hear you," Susan said. "But I know a lady who could use a set, for charitable purposes."

He straightened. "They're not exactly mine to give."

Susan seized the moment of hesitation. "They're not exactly anybody's at the moment, are they?"

Mr. Nicholas looked thoughtful. "The Bray Associates haven't asked for them back. I suppose I could give you one of each."

"Thank you. If you could deliver them to Mrs. Evans at the Blue House, we'll make sure the lady in question receives them."

Once they were safely in the carriage again, Emmeline asked, "Who is the lady you're giving them to?"

"You, of course."

"What? I can't. There's no reason. I—" Emmeline broke off in confusion.

"There's no need to use them right away. But this way you'll have them at your fingertips when the time is right." Hopefully, by the time they sailed in July, Susan could help her settle into her charitable endeavor. If not, at least she had given Emmeline the power to seize an opportunity, once it came her way. "And I need a word with your father."

"Whatever for?" Emmeline asked in wide-eyed bewilderment.

"It's high time you joined us for dinner." Even Charles wouldn't dare retract the permission of Emmeline's father.

# Forty-Eight

WHISPERS OF TREASON

THURSDAY, APRIL 6, 1775

Charles straightened his desk again, hoping the visitors would take a hint and let him get back to work. Men had been stopping by all morning, talking treason. This wasn't a seedy tavern. It was a respectable place of business.

"People are leaving Boston," the man said. "The New England Restraining Bill is going to leave them starving in the streets if they don't. Nothing gets into their harbor anymore. Nothing."

The hypocrisy was ridiculous. "Nothing gets into our harbor anymore, either," Charles countered, "but that's thanks to the Continental Congress and your Committee of Safety. You can't blame everything on Parliament."

Quill made a warning gesture with his hand. Mayhap he was right. It was better not to argue with idiots.

"Be careful how you speak," the man said. "People might doubt your loyalties." The door slammed behind him.

Quill let out a long breath. "Ye need to watch yer tongue, Charles. 'Tis no'safe to speak so bluntly."

Charles gave a mirthless laugh. "Unless one is speaking bluntly in favor of the Committee of Safety or your Continental Congress.

"Aye, 'tis no' fair, but that's how it is. Ye dinna wish ta bring the wrong kind of attention ta yer uncle's family."

It was a sobering thought. The Sons of Liberty down in Charleston and up in Boston were doing more than making noise. He wouldn't forgive himself if the Gardiners were harmed because of something he had said. "No one need doubt my loyalties. They don't waver with public opinion."

"Aye. I respect ye, but I dinna wish ta see ye in trouble."

"I'll be more careful."

The office door swung open. "Carriage is here," Polly said.

It was only a few blocks from the office to the Blue House, but since Emmeline would be dining with them, Mrs. Evans had insisted on sending the carriage round to everyone. This time, Susan hadn't given him a chance to object to her invitation. She had gone straight to Uncle Rob. Charles wouldn't even have known Emmeline was coming if Aunt Charity hadn't said something over supper last night.

They climbed into the handsome carriage. Emmeline tucked a book in her pocket and returned their greetings. Then she looked out the window. He rapped on the ceiling and they lurched into motion. There was no Committee of Safety in here to offend, and he hadn't finished his argument with Quill. "His Majesty's protection during the French and Indian War was costly. If we want his continued protection, we are as responsible for paying taxes as anyone in England." It was simple logic.

Polly raised her brows. "And those troops are in Boston for their *protection*?"

"This isn't about Boston. If we want our constitutional rights, we need to honor our duties."

"Ye talk like a Tory," Polly said.

"I am a Tory."

Emmeline turned her blue eyes on him. "If His Majesty needs taxes, he should write to the House of Burgesses. They're our elected officials, and they can decide how we should be taxed. Then the king would get the money he needs without violating the constitution."

Quill looked at her in surprise. "That's the most sense I've heard all day, Miss Gardiner."

She blushed and looked out the window. Charles shook his head. He had been trying to make sense to him all day. Instead, his cousin and his closest friends were joining against him. That was one of the dangers of the radical patriots—that they persuaded moderate, sensible people to their extreme views.

For Susan's sake, Charles stopped discussing politics when they arrived at the Blue House. Over dinner, he found himself calculating how long it had been since he had written to her father. It had been three months. He should have heard back by now. Had Mr. Bailey not even bothered to reply? His carefully written letter may have been tossed in the fire, his hopes reduced to cinders. He would give him a few more weeks. There was no saying what kind of weather the ships had been fighting against. If he didn't hear anything by the end of April, he would speak with Susan anyway. As they took their leave, he held Susan's gaze until Quill grabbed his arm and pulled him out the door.

Once they were beyond earshot, Quill said, "If the rector could see the way ye look at each other, he'd publish the banns this Sunday."

"Hush," Charles said. He lowered his voice so Isaac, helping the ladies into the carriage, couldn't hear. "I'm waiting for her father."

"Oh?"

"I wrote him in January, asking his permission."

There was a pause long enough for Quill to consider how much time had passed. His eyes widened. He clapped a hand on Charles's shoulder. "I'll be praying for ye."

"Thank you. I need it." He turned to the carriage. "Excuse us, Bailey."

Isaac stepped aside, closed the door after them, and told the footman to drive on. Charles didn't have the heart to continue his argument from earlier. Instead, he was the one looking out the window. They passed children playing and a man unloading a wagon. They passed a man in a blue jacket and white waistcoat, the elegant uniform of a naval lieutenant. One of His Majesty's schooners was moored only a few miles from the capital in the James River. With so much fuss over regiments in Boston, he was surprised not to have heard more complaints over the situation.

But then, the Boston complaint was against standing armies in peacetime, a contradiction to the British Bill of Rights. Everyone understood the need for constant vigilance against pirates. Not that that mattered for them, with so many imports and exports at a standstill.

When the carriage stopped, Charles stared at the man waiting for them under the Sign of the Eagle.

"Looks like ye have a client," Polly said, moving to cross the street to the Morrises' apartment. She pushed her brother's arm away. "Dinna fuss over me, Quill. I have a key. Go see what the mayor needs."

"Yes, ma'am," he said with mock formality, then turned on his heel to join Charles. "Mayor Dixon." Quill gave a slight bow. "How can we be of service?"

The mayor glanced down the street. "If we could discuss this in private?"

"Yes, sir." Charles unlocked the door and gestured for the mayor to enter.

When the door was firmly latched, the mayor spoke. "I trust you've heard the rumors."

Charles frowned. There were dozens of rumors at any given time.

"About the magazine?" Quill guessed.

"Yes."

"They're not true," Charles half-stated, half-queried. He hadn't put any faith in those rumors. They were too far-fetched.

"The difficulty is that we cannot prove or disprove any rumors about what has happened inside the magazine. Mr. Miller, the Keeper of the Williamsburg Magazine, was ordered to turn his keys over to the governor several days ago, which he did."

Charles nodded. It was the same thing he would have done.

"So when the rumors came about that hundreds of new muskets had had their locks removed, rendering them inoperable, the council couldn't confirm the truth. You see, if we confront His Lordship, we fear to give offense by falsely accusing him. I would hate to be blamed for the sitting House being dissolved again."

None of this explained what the mayor was doing in the office of a couple of young barristers. "That is quite the predicament," Charles said. "What can we do for you?"

"We're asking men of good character to keep watch. I'd like to put you two down for the evening of April twentieth. You'll be relieved at midnight."

Setting a watch over the magazine could be seen as an insult to the authority of the royal governor, but it was the *Williamsburg* Magazine. The mayor was within his authority to oversee its continued security. And if a watch could prevent more false rumors from taking flight, it could only help.

He nodded. "I'll do it, sir."

"And you, Mr. Morris?"

"Aye. I'll stand with Johnson."

"Thank you. Now, we don't expect any trouble, but I suggest you come prepared to defend yourselves."

"Just ourselves?" Quill asked. "No' the magazine?"

"Yes. We're trying *not* to start a war."

"Understood, sir," Charles said.

The mayor took his leave, and Charles secured the door.

"I didna wish ta speak for ye."

"You didn't. When the mayor comes 'round, telling you to serve, then it's your duty to serve."

"Ye dinna see a conflict between serving the mayor and the governor?

"Why should they be in conflict with each other? It's as absurd as pitting our militia against...well, the Royal Navy. We all serve the same king." Serving together might show Quill what he meant better than a lifetime of argument.

Forty-Nine

FLIRTING WITH FRIENDSHIP

SUNDAY, APRIL 9, 1775

Susan pocketed her prayer book. Offering to walk a lady home from church was one thing. Offering to walk her *to* church was...unconventional. "I'm ready." She tucked her hand in the crook of Charles's arm and together they stepped out into the sunlight.

Clouds feathered against a blue sky. Daffodils nodded. Tulips pierced the dark earth with their green blades. Rose bushes were awakening, stretching slender red shoots toward the sun. There had never been such a beautiful day.

In a few weeks, it would be May. That would make one full year since they had arrived. In the beginning, she had dreaded that year, but looking back, she could only think about it with fondness. The seasons were bringing her back to where she had begun. Soon, she would see the roses bloom and taste the raspberries again. But there would be no honeysuckle pergola for her this August. She wouldn't watch the oak outside her window greet fall in scarlet majesty. She wouldn't provide a yule cake and kiss Charles under the mistletoe ever again. She wouldn't see Polly or Emmeline marry and their children grow.

This July, she would leave Virginia, never to return. A year ago, she had wanted nothing more than to return Isaac home as soon as possible. Now, she cursed the ocean that separated her dreams from her duty.

"Is something on your mind?" Charles asked.

"Nothing. It's just—I want it to be spring forever."

"Your first summer in the south is always the worst. At least, that's what people say. It might not be so bad this time." Just like when she had found the pea in her Twelfth Night cake, he spoke as if she would be here forever.

"I won't be here this time," she said bitterly. "Isaac plans to leave in July. Remember?"

He gave her a long, searching look. "We'll see," he finally said. His uncharacteristic optimism was contagious. She pushed aside her worries and enjoyed the sun on her face and his strength beside her. They passed the next several minutes in companionable silence. As they crossed the Palace Green, he said, "Has the Committee of Safety given you and your aunt any trouble?"

"No. They've visited twice, but my aunt knows the members. They believe her when she says she is honoring the ban."

"Good." He covered her hand with his. "Let me know if they ever give you trouble."

"What about you? Have the patriots been giving you trouble?"

"No," he said a little too quickly.

"What is it?"

"Nothing. It's nothing."

"No more secrets. You promised."

"I never promised. I've just been following your orders."

A smile warmed her face. "Then follow my orders again. Tell me what's going on."

He pulled her to a stop and looked about them. Carriages drove around the green. Families and couples trod over it. But no one was paying them any mind. "It's just a little thing, but it needs to stay quiet so it doesn't become a big thing. Understand?"

"I'll keep it quiet. Just tell me."

He glanced around again, then spoke in a low voice. "Mayor Dixon is posting a watch over the Williamsburg Magazine. Morris and I will take it a week from Thursday, in the evening."

"Why?" A chill crept up her arms.

"Some firebrand started a rumor about the muskets being sabotaged. By keeping a watch, it gives the mayor witnesses to prove that nothing has happened."

Susan had heard that rumor over and over that past week. A lot of people believed it. A lot of people were distressed by it—distressed enough to threaten action. Even if the rumor was false, Charles couldn't have chosen a more dangerous place to be.

She looked up into his gray-blue eyes, only to realize how very close they were standing. She dropped her gaze to the buttons near the top of his waistcoat. "It's just for one evening?"

"Just until midnight."

She knew better than to dissuade him from his duty. He had been firm in supporting Isaac's choice last summer. He would only be more stubborn about this civic duty. "Then I'll pray for you—until midnight."

Inside the chapel, he escorted her to Aunt Dorothea, then withdrew to his usual pew. She bowed her head and prayed silently. *Dear Lord, may Charles and Mr. Morris be safe while they stand watch. And may I have the strength to make the sacrifice thou hast required of me.* The looming sacrifice grew heavier each day. She needed some of Charles's stubborn conviction. Otherwise, she wasn't sure she would have the strength to leave him once July came.

The Reverend Mr. Price chose that moment to read the banns. She squeezed her prayer book until her knuckles turned white. Church had a way of bringing hurts to the surface. She clenched her teeth and smiled the kind of tight smile that formed a dam to hold back a flood of tears.

Mr. Price's voice rang through the chapel. "I publish the banns of marriage between Mr. David Smith of Cannington and

Miss Lucy Pryor of Eversley." Susan whipped around. It couldn't be. Lucy hadn't seen that navigator since last May. Or had she?

"Is that your Lucy?" Aunt Dorothea asked.

Her Lucy was smiling as though heaven had come early. Susan turned away, stunned. "My Lucy," she said softly.

There was no hope after that announcement that she would hear the sermon. Lucy had been with her since before her coming out. She had been rather young, younger than Emmeline, when she had persuaded her father to hire Lucy after her old mistress died. She had proved her devotion through years of conscientious labor, and again in following Susan to Virginia. After all they had been through together, she hadn't expected Lucy to leave her.

Susan had given up much of her life to provide for the comfort and happiness of others. But at least she had had Lucy. She couldn't believe she was losing her. The banns would be read the next two Sundays, and then she could be married. After all they had been through together, why hadn't Lucy told her of her plans first? It hurt to hear an announcement over the pulpit that should have been shared in person.

Once the service was done, she found Lucy and Dave outside with Charles.

"Patience," Dave was saying to him. "Humility. A good kiss or two."

Lucy turned scarlet and took three prim and proper steps to the side.

Dave laughed and swung an arm about her shoulders, pulling her close. "We're about ter be married, Love. Even the reverend wouldn't be scandalized ter hear that."

"Congratulations," Susan said with an enthusiasm she didn't feel. "Where will you live?"

"Somerset," Dave said, "near my sister's family."

"You'll be near the sea?"

"I don't need ter be. I'll be a surveyor. And if that don't work out, I'll find something local. I'm not going ter sea again if I can help it now that I've got me a wife."

Lucy turned a radiant face toward the former navigator. Charles caught Susan's eye. He jerked his head away from the lovebirds and offered his arm. Susan took it, eager to escape the awkwardness of the situation and to pass another lazy Sunday afternoon with him.

She ignored the hypocrisy. They were just friends, after all. As long as they both understood that, there was no harm in favoring each other's company. They only had a few months left before she would leave him and her other Williamsburg friends forever. A familiar ache filled her heart. The thought of going home made her homesick. Hypocrisy though it was, she would cherish their friendship until the day she couldn't. Meanwhile, she would pray that when that day came, she would have the strength to make the sacrifice she knew was right.

Fifty

THE BAILEY'S SEAL

FRIDAY, APRIL 14, 1775

"Charles!" Henrietta leaned over the picket gate and waved. "You got a letter. It came all the way from England."

The cheery words were like lightning out of a blue sky. He stopped in his tracks.

"Didn't you hear me, Charles? You got a letter." She waved it over her head.

He grabbed it. "I heard you." An ornate monogram swirled across the blue seal. B for Bailey. His heart beat a tattoo, louder than the militia's fife and drum. The letter was thicker than he had expected. Was that good or bad? All he knew was that the post had been expensive. "How much do I owe my uncle?"

"I don't know. I wasn't here when it arrived. I was planting carrots, and I got all muddy, and Mama was going to dump a whole bucket of cold water on me if I didn't wash up proper. Say, aren't you going to open that?"

Charles had known the fright that accompanied a letter with black sealing wax. This was the first time he had been afraid to break a common blue seal. The drum in his chest beat the call to retreat. "I will. First, I need to put something in my room." His feet thundered up the steps, but fear stayed at his heels. This letter could be the end of everything. He threw his hat on the bed and paced the room, holding his future in his trembling hands. Why would any father sacrifice his daughter to a man he had never met? If he said no, what were the consequences of eloping? She was of age. The law would be on their side. But it was a shabby thing to require of her. She might never see her family again. Susan deserved her father's blessing.

At last, he broke the seal.

> Mr. Johnson,
>
> I received your letter two weeks ago. Forgive me for not replying immediately. I had no desire to prolong your suspense; however, much caution and delicacy must accompany a request of that nature. I am unwilling to subject my daughter to an unhappy life because I replied in haste one way or the other.
>
> We do have a partial record of your dealings with our daughter, as written by her hand and published throughout the neighborhood.
>
> My first business, therefore, was to better acquaint myself with your character through a careful rereading of the lengthy letters she has sent home, compared to your manner of presenting yourself. The result was not unfavorable in your direction, but I am not a man of hasty conclusions.
>
> Having business in London shortly after the receipt of your request, I extended my visit in order to interview the contacts you graciously included in your correspondence, as well as several additional ones I

discovered you had. They all painted a picture consistent with the opinion I had been forming: that you are a steady, sober, reliable man who always keeps his word.

The only person of import I regret being unable to interview is my daughter. Though she has written often of you, I cannot tell from her letters (which were intended to be public) how strong an attachment there is on her side, or even whether she is willing to stay in Virginia.

Therefore, you have my permission to propose marriage to my daughter. If she says yes, you have my blessing. Enclosed are two copies of the marriage contract. As you are a man of the law, I won't explain the details. Send one signed copy with Isaac when he returns.

Your servant,
Mr. Jas. Bailey

Charles reread the letter twice, unable to believe his good fortune. An obstacle he had feared would be insurmountable had shrunk so small that he held the victory in his hand. He looked at the marriage contract. Writing such documents was the work of an attorney, not a barrister, but the legal cadence had a comforting familiarity to it, comforting until he got to the specific terms. The paper slipped from his hand. He picked the priceless document off the floor and reread it carefully. He had never asked Susan or her family the specifics of her dowry. He had only hoped her father's disappointment with the marriage wouldn't deny his daughter any of the comforts she deserved. With such a substantial settlement, she could have fine gowns and hire servants for a lifetime.

Provided, of course, that he purchased their house and earned enough to cover all of their necessities. He fell back on the rope bed and stared at the canopy without seeing it. After months of wondering and waiting, her father had given his blessing. There was only one real question left.

What would Susan say?

She liked him. He was assured of that. But did she love him enough to sacrifice the home and family of her youth to be the cornerstone of his home and family? There was only one way to find out. His hands were clammy in anticipation, fumbling as he unlocked his trunk and removed his lockbox. There was what he had managed to save over the last year. He had done better than he had anticipated. If not for unexpected expenses, like Jenny's indentures or that bolt of fabric, he would almost have had enough to purchase a respectable house in town. As it was, he had several months of work before him before he could offer her a home.

For a long moment, he considered showing her the generous marriage contract first. It might give her the confidence to accept him while he was still saving for a house. But no. He didn't want her to think he was marrying her for her dowry. He put the contract in the lockbox for safekeeping, burying it in the old trunk under books and clothes. Then he turned the key and pocketed the letter from her father. That was where the blessing was.

In the cool of the evening, he set out on foot for the Blue House, finally ready to make his suit.

Fifty-One

BEFORE THE TULIPS

Charles wiped his clammy palms on his breeches and moved his hat from one hand to the other, as fidgety as the crickets leaping inside him. At last, he heard a door open. He looked up and froze. She was coming down the stairs, smiling like sunshine and starlight. *Lord, have mercy on the undeserving.*

"Charles. We weren't expecting you."

"Susan." Her precious name caught in his throat. A thousand memories were tied up in that name: her hands adjusting his cravat, her voice coaxing secrets, her making him ginger tea and licorice pastilles when he was ill. He craved a lifetime of those moments: of comfort and laughter and building a home together and falling asleep every night with her hand on his chest. Every night. "Have you heard from home recently?" Her father's letter was in his jacket, the family seal pressed against his heart.

"About a month ago. Anne, my sister, wanted to know when we will be having her ball. We postponed it until I can be there." There was a wistfulness in her voice. She really did miss her family.

This should have been the moment to tell her he had just received a letter from her father. But something didn't feel right.

He couldn't propose that she leave her family for his the moment she had shared her homesickness.

"Aren't you going to invite him in?" Mrs. Evans called from the parlor.

"We're coming," Susan said, taking his arm. She guided him to one end of the settee, then sat beside him, looking far more comfortable than he felt. Mrs. Evans was a proper chaperone, her eyes on her embroidery, but still firmly in attendance. It was hard enough to speak with Susan alone. He couldn't propose marriage with witnesses. How did men do this? Asking for a few minutes alone was as good as announcing his intentions, and he wasn't quite sure Susan would accept him. He barely heard what she was saying—something about a sick neighbor—until she frowned at him and asked, "Are you feeling quite well?"

"Yes. No." He pushed down on his knee to stop the involuntary bouncing. "That is, I was wondering if," he swallowed. "If you would like to take a turn about the garden." The words came out in an anxious rush.

Mrs. Evans glanced up from her embroidery.

Susan looked out the window. It was gray and gloomy. A line formed between her brows. "I suppose."

He jumped to his feet. Did all men make a fool of themselves when about to propose, or was he special? "You'll want a wrap. It's cool this evening."

"I'll get one."

He sat down again.

Mrs. Evans watched him over her spectacles. "The tulips won't bloom for a few more days at least. There isn't much to see in my garden unless you are an admirer of boxwood."

Charles opened his mouth. When no words came out, he shut it.

Mrs. Evans trimmed her thread. "But you didn't come to see my tulips, did you?"

"I—no." There was no point in denying something so obvious. He cleared his throat. "Excuse me." He met Susan in the foyer. He could think of nothing to say as they walked out the back door and then into the formal gardens. Nothing was blooming. Last June's roses were unrecognizable. The boxwood around them was trimmed and trained into overlapping diamonds. If Charles had been an admirer of boxwood, he would have been impressed. Instead, he watched Susan crouch beside the tulips. A fat brown curl fell forward against her neck. Her cheeks bloomed in the chill. The tulip buds held tightly, but the color bled through the outer petals as though ready to burst.

Susan rose. "They'll bloom any day now. There's nothing to see today."

"I didn't come to see the tulips." He held her gaze until she blushed and turned away.

"What did you come for?"

"I wanted to discuss the future." He'd wanted to say *our* future, but that seemed premature. First, she needed to know what he had to offer. "This last year has gone better than I expected, though I must credit my early success in the courtroom to you. I've had steady business and have been able to set aside more than half my increase." His confidence rose as he spoke. She would know he wasn't a treasure hunter. Her father had commented on his steady character. That would see him through. "Of course, I must pay my share of office rent, and I have some expenses, but I have endeavored to keep them modest." He paused, wondering if he should explain his hopes to buy a house before or after confessing his love.

Susan gave him a weak smile. "I understand."

"You do?" He hadn't said half of what he had planned to.

"I do. You've put a lot of work into your career. Your father must be proud."

Charles blinked. He had been more interested in impressing *her* father. "I suppose."

Susan clasped her hands so tightly that her knuckles turned white. "But there are limits to how far a bachelor can take his career."

"I—" He stopped, confused. She was hinting at his marriage state, but something felt off about the way she combined his career with it.

"You need someone with social poise. A notable housekeeper." Her face twisted in a painful smile. "And it wouldn't hurt if she were pretty." The wistfulness in her voice, even as she described herself, frightened him. If she had guessed his purpose for coming, why wasn't she happy? "And she should own land as a *feme sole*."

With every word she withdrew, and Charles didn't know how to follow.

"Miss Ray is the perfect choice." She smiled weakly. "I'm happy for you."

"I'm confused. Who is Miss Ray, and why do you say you're happy when you're obviously not?"

"Miss Priscilla Ray. From New Kent. She was here for a fortnight this winter. She's beautiful, an excellent conventionalist, and is heiress of twenty acres."

He stared at her anguished face. "You can't think I want to marry her."

"What's wrong with her? She's the best we've had all winter. Mrs. Underwood couldn't help you socially, Mrs. Kemp was missing teeth, and Miss Ingram had an obnoxious laugh. I despaired of finding anyone, but then we met Priscilla."

Like tumblers of a lock, the clues fell into place. "You've been trying to find me...a wife?"

She nodded. "Isn't that what you wanted to talk about?"

Yes. No. Not like that. "I had no idea you were doing that."

"I should have told you first. But I wasn't sure it would work."

It hadn't worked. "But...why?"

She pulled an embroidered handkerchief from her pocket. Its twin was tucked in Charles's lockbox with his life savings. "Because I'm leaving in a couple of months." She sniffed. "And I want to know you'll be happy when I'm gone."

Leaving. She said it with the finality of a door slamming in his face. He stared. Her eyes were red. She didn't want this any more than he did. She didn't mean what she said. But Susan never hurt someone without a very good reason. That truth was as solid as a brick wall.

He turned back to the dead roses. She had noticed his admiration, a passion she couldn't return, and offered to soften the blow the best way she knew how. He had placed his happiness in her hands. In her attempt to pass it to another, it slipped and broke. The pocket with her father's letter burned against his skin. What would she say if she read it? If she knew he had been so foolish in his hope that he had written to her father? A strangled laugh escaped. He should throw the letter in the fire with both contracts and every other reminder of his foolish hopes.

"Charles," she spoke his name uncertainly.

"It's fine." He blustered, backing away from her and the prickly remains of rose bushes. She wouldn't see him being torn asunder from the inside. "Later." He wasn't sure if he could see her again. There wasn't much of him left.

He kept his head down as he rushed through town, dodging acquaintances and the awkward questions they might ask. He beat a hasty retreat to solitude—but it couldn't be at the Gardiners'. They knew he had received a letter from London. He wasn't ready for their questions. He would seek solitude at Johnson Hall. Since his mother's death, no one there had ever questioned his heartaches.

Fifty-Two

SHATTERED PEACE

Susan paced the garden with the ferocity of a caged tiger. Her silk petticoats snagged on the shrubbery. Why had he spoken? Why couldn't he have continued holding his peace like he'd been doing for months? She had thought they had an unspoken understanding of sorts—an understanding that they would cherish the little time they had together and not pain each other by speaking of what could never be.

Now everything was ruined. They couldn't enjoy their remaining months together. It would be impossible to forget the look on his face when she had rejected him. Hurting Charles would haunt her for the rest of her life. It was little consolation that she hadn't turned down his proposal. She had cut him off before he'd had a chance to speak, just like she had done every other time she had rejected a man.

But it had never hurt like this before. He was no mercenary. He had saved a year's income. Had that really been for her? Her vision blurred. How many comforts had he denied himself to do so? How many times had he thought of her when he had made those sacrifices?

Tears fell like raindrops on the garden path. She had only dreamed of being loved like that. He didn't see her and her dowry as an easy path to comfort. He had taken the hard road, giving up comforts to reach her when he couldn't have known what her dowry was. She would trade all her jewels and even that dowry for the proverbial love in a cottage—if love truly looked like that. But was she selfish enough to trade her family?

She had made so many little promises about the future to Anne that she could never fulfill without returning. She was the only one who could manage her mother's health—at least, she had thought she was. Every letter assured her that Mama was fine. She wasn't sure if that was true. It seemed the sort of thing they would write, so she wouldn't worry. She had expected to manage the home, including the family's community responsibilities, until Isaac matured enough to choose a wife.

Suppose he did so in five years. Lucy would have forgotten her. Aunt Dorothea would be too far away to ever call on. Anne's ball would be in the past. Possibly her wedding and its accompanying arrangements as well. Mama would be no better. And the management of Bailey Manor would belong to Isaac's wife. In the confining solitude that followed, how often would she think of Charles? Constantly. She would wonder how quickly he had recovered from today's disappointment, and whether his evenings were now spent whittling toys for his sandy-haired children. She would wonder who his happy wife was. And she would be alone.

"Susan?" Aunt Dorothea called. "Are you out here?"

She patted her face with a handkerchief, trying to reclaim her dignity.

Her aunt's expression went from worry to disappointment to compassion faster than a hummingbird in flight. She let herself through the garden gate. "Oh, my dear." She wrapped her in a motherly hug. "You told him no?"

Susan's throat was too tight to form words. A pitiful whine was all that escaped as she clung to her aunt. Her soul was shattered. Pierced anew by the shards was a lonely little girl who had slept fitfully in a neglected chamber of her heart. The child woke, and it was only yesterday that she had burned day and night with a fever before anyone noticed or cared. It was just last week her dolls had been shunted to the nursery where they wouldn't pester Mama, and the week before that her childish hopes and troubles had been brushed aside so she wouldn't wake the baby. She had spent the rest of her life being so kind and helpful that people would always make room for her. But despite all her efforts, she was still a needy little girl, sobbing on her aunt's shoulder.

The man she adored had offered her the most beautiful love in the world, and she had pushed it away. She wasn't free to accept. She had been telling herself that for years. But now Charles had left her, and she didn't know whether she still blamed God or if she blamed herself. All she knew was that making the biggest sacrifice of her life hadn't filled her with pride or peace. She was as empty as a shelf at the general store—and she was the one who had rejected the shipment. She was the one who had placed the ban. But it was too late for regrets. No self-respecting man would offer again for a woman who had hurt him like that.

Her aunt patted her back and led her through the gate. As they passed the kitchen, she called, "Maurice, we could do with some tea before supper." Then she led her inside to a chair at the dining table.

Susan scarcely noticed her aunt unlocking the cupboard in the narrow passage that led to the parlor until she removed her precious tea chest. As their stores had gotten lower, they had used them less and less, until real tea was only served once a week, and only with discerning company. There was still no talk of lifting the ban. And there was no company to impress. Her aunt was wasting precious tea on her. Maurice brought in a copper kettle of steaming water and poured it into her aunt's china teapot.

As her aunt prepared the tea, Susan braced herself for questions. The more she waited, the more tense she became until at last she broached the subject herself. "You think I was foolish."

Aunt Dorothea gave her a piercing look. "Do I? Or do you? It isn't fair that your entire life hinges on one choice. Do you give up home and family for the man you love, or do you give up the man you love for home and family?" She handed Susan a cup.

She took a wobbly sip. "You don't understand what it's like. Mama hasn't been able to do anything since I was pulled out of school at fourteen to take her place. Papa tries, but he doesn't understand the details it takes. When he hosted my coming-out ball, he forgot to arrange for flowers. And he let the kitchen maids plan the supper. Some of them had never even attended a ball. So we had rustic, country dishes, which wouldn't have been so bad, but there wasn't enough food for all the guests. If I'm not there for her, Anne will have to endure the same embarrassments. And it isn't just the occasional ball. It happened every day at every meal until I persuaded him I was old enough to manage the kitchen, not just Isaac and Anne. I'm needed there. I only came to keep Isaac safe. I didn't come to stay. I can't stay."

"I suspected as much when your mother took ill. I used to lie awake at night, wishing I had stayed in England so I could have helped. I considered selling the Blue House and returning. In the end, I wrote your father, inviting you and Isaac, and Anne to grow up in my care. Isaac could have attended William and Mary here in Williamsburg and visited often. You wouldn't have had so much responsibility forced upon you at such a young age. But your father wanted to keep you close. He turned me down. So I've been inviting you to visit ever since."

"I didn't know." Ten years ago, her aunt had offered to mother her—her aunt who didn't need her at all, yet somehow wanted her anyway. They only had a few months left together. She had given up her aunt when she had rejected Charles. But the thought of leaving had never felt so wrong. Her country wasn't where she was well. Her home was. And home was built with the people you loved. When she left Williamsburg, she wouldn't be going home. She would be leaving it.

~

Charles crossed the bridge leading to Johnson Hall. Then, before anyone saw him, he took cover in the trees around the ravine. Sharing the secrets of his heart was what had brought this hurt and humiliation upon him. He wasn't about to repeat the folly. He picked up a stick and threw it, end over end, until it landed in the creek, bobbing like a boat.

His mind replayed every situation, every moment with Susan as he threw rocks in the water like a child pulled petals from a flower. *She loves me. She loves me not.* Every interaction was neatly sorted into two little piles labeled hope and dismay. But when he got to today's declaration—that she had been trying to find him a wife—he swept every hope away. Not even the memory of kisses could take the sting of that away. It was absurd, and she couldn't have meant it—not with those white knuckles and anguished face —but no woman would say such a thing if she wanted a man for herself. He had once thought of Susan as a miracle. He should have known then that they wouldn't be together. Miracles had never been for him.

He threw a rock as big as his palm five yards. He didn't aim. He didn't calculate. He just threw, then seized the next stone and threw again. Movement among the downstream shrubbery caused him to pause. Someone was watching him. Anger surged. He didn't need witnesses to his hurt and humiliation. He just wanted to be left alone while he licked his wounds. A man came out of the trees and made his way toward him. It was Marcus.

The irrational anger mellowed into resentment at the intrusion on his privacy. He braced himself for the idiotic question that was bound to come: Are you feeling well? Men who felt fine didn't hurl rocks into the creek like cannon fire at an enemy's ship. Marcus stopped ten feet away, picked up a rock, closed one eye, and threw it squarely at a tree on the other side of the ravine. "Woman troubles?" He asked the question casually, as if it was the only obvious reason a man would be out of his head with distress. As if men every day experienced the same hurt and disappointment.

"I—" He almost denied it. But he had grown accustomed to confiding his secrets. The secrets he had shared with Susan had become half as heavy. This distress couldn't be shared with his usual secret keeper. She was the cause. And somehow, he knew that even without an explanation, Marcus would understand. "Yes." He picked up another stone, aimed it at a branch, and threw it. The solid sound of impact was vaguely satisfying.

They took turns choosing targets and throwing rocks until their shadows waved like giants across the ravine. He didn't have his traveling pistol and would prefer to return home before dark. "I should pay my respects to my father before I go."

"He ain't here," Marcus said.

"Oh. Do you know who he's visiting?"

"Some widow up north." Another *feme sole*.

Charles snorted.

Marcus' brows rose. "Is that...funny?"

"Funny?" His voice was dry and bitter. "That my father thinks he has any idea what kind of woman I want is hilarious." He dusted his hands on his breeches. "I'll just see my grandmother."

"Chawz?" Marcus threw one last stone into the creek.

"Yes?"

"I hope you find a woman who 'preciates you."

"Thanks," he said. But he didn't want just any woman to appreciate him. He wanted it to be Susan. "I'm glad you found one."

He walked up to the great house and knocked on the door like a stranger, not the future master. There were voices and shuffling inside. Visitors had not been expected today.

At last, Gideon opened the door. "Master Charles! Are you here to see your father?"

"I heard he wasn't home."

"You heard correctly."

"Then I'll just pay my respects to my grandmother and be on my way."

His grandmother sat in a chair by the window. Slivers of dull blue splintered through lavender-gray clouds. He didn't have long. Sunset was coming. He greeted his grandmother with a kiss on the cheek. "Granny! How are you today?" He spoke with false cheer, confident she wouldn't see through his charade.

The woman turned clear blue eyes on Charles. Her wrinkled forehead creased in confusion. "Who are you?"

"Your favorite grandson, Charles." There was a long silence. He glanced around the room. Kitty was standing by the door, her eyes on the floor. "Does Kitty keep you good company?"

"I don't like cats." Granny's voice warbled.

"Not cats. I meant her." He gestured. "Kitty."

The girl's eyes met his, then returned to the floor.

Charles gave up. If he stayed any longer, he would have to introduce himself again. He stood and bowed. "Until next time, Granny. Kitty."

When he stepped into the foyer, Gideon was waiting by the door. "Is that all for today?"

Charles hesitated. There was one question that nagged at him every time he visited, though there had never been a good time to ask. Now was as good as ever. If anyone knew, Gideon would. After all, he was Kitty's grandfather. "Kitty is Abah's girl, but Abah is gone. What about her father? Does he live nearby?"

Gideon's face clouded. It must have been difficult for him to see his daughter sold. Charles cursed himself for prolonging his time in London. He might have prevented it if he had been here.

"Have you been raising her alone?"

"No, sir. Not exactly."

"I'm glad to hear that. Who is her father? Anyone I know?"

Gideon's jaw hardened. Charles followed his gaze to an old family portrait above the parlor fire. It had been painted when he was a boy, not much older than Kitty. His mother smiled sweetly, a songbird perched on one finger. His young self looked as somber as a clergyman. And his father—his stomach dropped. His father had the same broad forehead and narrow chin as Kitty.

He was having trouble breathing. It couldn't be. She was too old. His mother would still have been alive when—no. It was unspeakable, unthinkable, even for his father. He'd had a terrible temper and no sense of justice, but surely even he wouldn't have betrayed such a trust—fidelity to his wife and a duty to protect anyone else under his roof. Then again, he had witnessed other injuries to Abah before. To have done this, and then to have sold her away from her child... He felt ill.

"She doesn't know," Gideon said in a low voice. "There's no sense in telling her."

There was no sense in staying, either. This wasn't a cabin to be re-shingled. As a barrister, he couldn't even bring the crime against his father. Virginia's laws had been written by slave owners. He'd sinned against heaven, but not the law. There was nothing Charles could do, and he couldn't stand another moment staring helplessly at the victims of his father's transgression.

He slammed the door behind him and walked home in the gathering darkness.

Fifty-Three

TIPPING THE SCALES

SATURDAY, APRIL 15, 1775

Susan pulled her coverlet to her chin and stared morosely at the happy couples printed on the draperies about her. The sun was up. The house was awake. For an hour, she had lain in bed, listening to the muffled sounds of people beginning their day. For once, she had no desire to join them.

There was a soft knock. "It's me, milady," Lucy said as she let herself in, a breakfast tray on her hip. She arranged the tray on the desk. "There's a letter for you."

"A letter?" Susan sat up. News from home was just the distraction she needed.

"Mmhmm. It was delivered this morning with the *Gazette*. The newsboy said a ship brought in a whole bag of letters yesterday, and they're working to get them all delivered."

Yesterday. What a bitter word. Yesterday morning, she had believed their friendship would last forever. Yesterday, he had tugged at her heartstrings, as hopeful and anxious as a man could be. Yesterday, she had pushed him away. More hungry for cheer than food, she took the letter. To her surprise, the direction had been written in her father's hand. He hadn't written to her in months. Everything had come from Anne. She turned it over and broke the family seal.

Dearest Susan,

I have long suspected your attachment to a certain Virginian, an account of whom has made it into every one of your many letters. You may find it of interest, then, that I have just returned from London, where I was able to make a close study of his character. The accounts I received do credit to your judgment. All his former associates agree he is a steady and honest man. My only regret is that his home is so far removed from ours and that his gain must be our loss.

I fear I have made the two of you wait a painfully long time, but I could not in good conscience give just any man my treasured girl. Even so, I won't blame the poor boy if he gave up on ever receiving my blessing and spoke prematurely. Nor would I blame you for accepting him. The vast distance between us makes a strict observance of the usual customs impractical.

Either way, I have sent the relevant legal papers to the direction he originally provided. If you are already married, they need only a few signatures to be legally binding. If I have misjudged the situation and you have no interest in a union, then you need not worry about it. They can only be binding if you, of your own free will, marry him before God *and man.*

We shall miss you dearly, but to paraphrase scripture, therefore shall Susan leave her father and mother. I kept my little girl for longer than I deserved. If this man has your love and respect, then your union has my blessing. We shall do our best to get along without you, though I hope you will always be a steady correspondent.

Love,

Your Papa

Susan was stunned. Whatever she had expected her father to write about, marrying Charles Johnson was not it. His name didn't appear once, and yet she could think of no other man she had consistently mentioned in her letters. But surely she had said nothing that would have given her father reason to suspect an impending marriage.

The direction he originally provided. She pressed a hand to her heart. At some point, Charles had corresponded with her father. He hadn't proposed marriage on a whim. He had written her father for permission ages ago and had been waiting all this time for a proper blessing. But she had only gotten her letter this morning. If her father had written both of them—

"Lucy, when did you say the post bag came in?"

Lucy was laying out her clothes. She glanced over her shoulder. "Yesterday, miss."

She groaned. What cruel fate had delivered his letter first? If only she had received hers with time to think about it. She, who was blessed with the talent of seeing so quickly what others wanted, was often blind to her own desires. She hadn't known how badly she had wanted to kiss Charles until she had successfully dodged all the mistletoe on Twelfth Night. She hadn't known how badly she had wanted to marry him until she had thrown away her one opportunity. When they had first met, her love for Bailey Manor and her family there had far outweighed every other affection. Over time, her love for her family hadn't lessened, but her love for Charles, her aunt, and everything in Williamsburg had increased.

Her stubborn heart had been blind to the magnitude of the change, but tears had cleared her vision. Only now did she see that the scales had tipped in his favor. Now that it was too late, she had her father's encouraging words. Now that it was too late, she saw that Anne would surely release her from all her promises, especially if she wrote detailed instructions to her father on how to care for her. He did quite well with lists.

Susan threw back the covers. The ship hadn't sailed yet. They had nearly three months left together. Surely they could reach an understanding by then. All she needed was a good plan. She placed her feet on the solid floor and stood, casting her eyes about the room for inspiration. In a little basket beside the desk was her unfinished embroidery. She picked it up and looked it over with critical eyes. By dinner on Tuesday, it would be the most beautiful pocketbook the world had ever seen. A gift that grand, coupled with something akin to an apology, and surely he would forgive her. No self-respecting man proposed twice, but he hadn't proposed yesterday. She hadn't let him. Given enough time and encouragement, he might try again.

SUNDAY, APRIL 16, 1775

Charles went to Sunday service out of habit, not holiness. For months, the anticipation of Susan's smiles had been enough reason to worship. Today, his soul was as empty as the world before creation.

"Ye look like the devil," Quill said amiably.

"What?"

"Stop scowling at the rector or the rest of us are going ta suffer for it."

Charles slouched lower in the pew and dropped his eyes. He couldn't stop scowling, not with the rector punishing him with news of another couple's felicity.

"I publish the banns of marriage between Mr. David Smith of Cannington and Miss Lucy Pryor of Eversley. This is the second reading."

The rector should have been announcing the marriage of himself to Susan. He could almost imagine it as the voice droned on. "I publish the banns of marriage between Mr. Charles Johnson, Sr., and Mrs. Mary Underwood."

Charles's back straightened as quickly as musket fire. He must have misheard. He must have imagined.

"What?" Quill voiced Charles's stunned disbelief. "Ye didna tell me—"

"I didn't know." Charles let out a long breath. "Senior. Tell me you heard him say Charles Johnson, *Sr.*"

"I heard senior." Quill's eyes twinkled. "Ye're getting a new mother."

Charles dropped his head in his hands. That obnoxious widow was only a little older than he was. He could never consider her a mother. He couldn't even hold a civil conversation with her. And she would be family.

After the final amen, he followed Quill outside. Susan startled at the sight of him, then offered a false smile. "I suppose I should offer my congratulations." Her eyes shone with unshed tears.

He stared at her, wondering that she should care so much and yet not care enough.

Quill clapped Charles on the back. "I think a diversion would be preferred. Mr. Johnson, *Jr.* was not anticipating that announcement."

"Junior?" Susan's eyes darted between them. "Then you're not the one—"

"Didn't I tell you I was named after my father? He's the one marrying Widow Underwood."

The relief on Susan's face was unmistakable. If Charles hadn't known better—

But he did. He gave Susan a bitter smile. "Thank you for introducing me to my stepmother."

She laughed nervously. "You can tell me all about it at dinner on Tuesday. Unless," she suddenly looked hopeful, "you wanted to call this afternoon."

Blast. She was trying to put everything where it was a week ago, before hope had turned to hurt. He couldn't pretend friendship was enough. Not today. Not ever again. "I'm afraid I'm otherwise engaged. If you'll excuse me." He bowed and walked away.

Fifty-Four

HOT CIDER

THURSDAY, APRIL 20, 1775

He had made it nearly a week without telling Morris what had happened. He blamed his low appetite on indigestion. He talked even less than usual, but he had a lot of briefs to keep him busy. So many that he had been unable to attend dinner at the Blue House. Quill had conveyed his regrets, but since then, whenever Charles's attention strayed to the window, he had found his friend watching him. It should have been easier to confide his disappointment in a friend he saw daily, but Quill might tell Polly, and she would surely tell Susan, who already knew more than was good for any of them.

And now there was more than Susan to distress him. Had his father been drunk? That seemed likely. Had Abah been beaten? It had happened before. Had his dying mother known what his father had done? He sighed and bent lower over his papers.

"There's a storm brewing." Quill was looking out the window. "We're in for a long night." Men held onto their hats as the wind tore at their cloaks.

"Lucky us." Charles stacked his papers neatly. Major storms were expected in October and through the winter. To have one in mid-April was exceptional. "Do you want to meet at the magazine?"

"If ye can promise me some cider, I'll be happy ta meet ye at the Gardiners' in an hour."

Charles swung his cloak around his shoulders. "My aunt is visiting Johnson Hall, preparing it for a new mistress," he grimaced, "but Emmeline will get us some if I ask her."

Quill frowned, his hand on the doorknob. "Are ye alright, Charles?"

"What do you mean?"

"Ye've been in low spirits since the banns were read. Seeing yer father remarry, 'tisn't easy."

Charles was relieved Quill had such a plausible explanation for his mood. "How old were you?" He didn't need to ask. They had been boarding together when Quill's mother had passed and his father had remarried.

"Nine." Quill yanked the door open.

Dark clouds scudded across the sky as gusts of wind tore pink blossoms and chartreuse leaves from the trees. Quill was locking the office when his tricorn took flight. Charles chased it as it tumbled along the sandy road, catching it when it blew against a wagon wheel.

He dusted the hat as he walked briskly back. "Looks like we're in for a foul night."

"Aye," Quill said, latching the shutter closed against the storm. "I believe we drew the short straw, keeping watch at night and in such weather."

"Are you quitting, Morris?" Charles handed him the hat.

"Nay," Quill's eyes twinkled. "I'll not sleep tonight wondering if ye're helping the governor's men raid the magazine."

"First of all, I'm a Tory, not a traitor. Secondly, we have no proof that the locks were removed from the new muskets. It may be an idle report."

"It may be an honest man lied."

"An honest man will lie before I undermine Virginia's constitution."

Quill raised his brows. "Strong words. I thought ye left all your loyalties in England."

"Don't be ridiculous. But I'm only standing watch to protect the truth."

"Then we're in this together."

"We are. Meet me at the Gardiners'. And bring your canteen."

Quill replied by whistling a jig, which he danced as he crossed the street.

Charles set off for home. Despite himself, his head turned as he passed the Blue House. After all the turmoil of the past week, he was getting jittery about the watch. He wanted to forget everything that had happened, to run to the Blue House and kiss Susan like he was going off to war, but he ordered his feet to march homeward. With all his world turned upside down, it was more important than ever to prove Lord Dunmore's innocence.

The shutters were already secured when he reached home. He just needed to get supper, cider, and warmer clothes before Quill arrived. As he closed the door behind him, Emmeline skipped down the stairs, her face barely visible above a stack of blankets. "Welcome home. It's just the three of us tonight." She swept into the front room, arranging one blanket on each of three chairs arranged in a semicircle, facing the hearth. "I was thinking that after supper we could read by the fire and drink hot cider." She smiled up at him, blissfully unaware of his prior engagement.

He had kept everything to himself this week. He cleared the guilt from his throat. "I was hoping for a canteen of hot cider. It's stormy—"

"I know!" she said with the delight of a child receiving a toy. "It's perfect for *The Tempest*. You can be Ferdinand, and I'll be Miranda, and Papa will be both Prospero and King Alonso. We can draw straws for the other characters."

"I'm sorry, Emma. I have to be somewhere tonight. Some other time."

"Oh." Her face fell. She glanced at the hearth, which was neatly built up with sawdust and wood shavings in and around a cluster of branches. "It's nothing. Supper is on the table. I'll get my father." Subdued, she went out the back door.

Charles followed her as far as the table. Steam rose from the pork and each mug of coffee, and beside the apple pie was a bowl of something creamy. He dipped a finger to get a taste. It was ice cream, or as near as one could get without ice. He had expected cold meats and stale bread for supper. By comparison, this was a feast, and he suddenly had the appetite for it.

When Uncle Rob came in, he was equally impressed, and Emmeline brightened under their praise. After grace, Charles set about fortifying himself for the dreary evening ahead. He needed to remain alert until midnight. After clearing his plate for a third time, he excused himself and went up to his room.

A week ago, Aunt Charity had told him to move his warmest clothing into his trunk. She was a notable housekeeper. Johnson Hall would be more than ready for Mrs. Underwood to become Mrs. Johnson. Charles frowned. Mrs. Johnson had been his mother. Her name had lain dormant for years. He had been dusting it off like a family heirloom to be given to a bride. It was unfortunate to see it given to Mrs. Underwood.

He unlocked the trunk and removed a heavy jacket and woolen stockings without touching the cold metal lockbox beneath them. He had avoided it ever since the day he had secured the contracts within it. The contracts were useless now. Every time he thought of it—only a dozen or so times a day—he told himself he would burn it as soon as he got the chance. But every time he got close, something held him back. What man destroyed the last hope of the miracle he had been praying for? It might be nothing more than a castle in the clouds, but he wouldn't be the one to sweep it away, not when his shared name would be read over the pulpit again this Sunday. He would cherish hope until its last dying flame.

He pulled the woolen stockings over the cotton ones he had worn that day and buckled the leather garters.

Quill's father had remarried the same year he was widowed, providing his young children with a mother and additional siblings. Their family had grown together. Charles had long been hardened to the possibility of his father remarrying. His choice of bride was distasteful, but she could hardly make Johnson Hall less bearable. The insult to his mother's memory was far more repugnant. His father had conceived a child by another woman while his mother was dying. That was unforgivable.

He buttoned his heavy jacket and collected his weapons with a shiver of anticipation, but this was no different than carrying a pistol when he traveled at night. It was just as unlikely that anything would happen.

His thoughts returned to Johnson Hall. Kitty was stuck there. Did Mrs. Underwood know about her? Surely not. What man told such self-incriminating things to a woman he was courting? Not his father. Kitty would stay in the house, minding Granny as well as Mrs. Underwood's precious children. She would live a life of toil and neglect, until Mrs. Under—Mrs. Johnson—found out. Whatever Kitty's prospects, whatever abuses she endured now, could only get worse under a jealous mistress. He had lectured Isaac on brotherly responsibility. He had treated Emmeline as if she were his sister. Now he had a sister of his own and had no idea what to do with her.

Distantly, he heard a door open, followed by a murmur of voices. Morris was here. He yanked a knitted sailor's cap on his head, grabbed his cloak, and hurried downstairs. He found them in the front room watching as flames in the hearth leapt from shaving to shaving under a copper kettle. If that was the cider, they would have to wait a spell before leaving.

Emmeline turned and stared at the knife hanging from his belt and the pistol on his hip. "Where are you going? What are you doing?"

"It's nothing," Charles said.

"Nothing?" Emmeline's eyes flashed. "You don't leave the house on a night like this—dressed like that—for nothing."

"Ye didna tell her?" Quill's disbelief irritated even more than his cousin's indignation.

Charles threw his cloak on, covering the offending weapons. "The whole point is to prevent rumors, is it not?"

"And ye fancy sneaking about and keeping secrets from yer family will prevent rumors? The lass deserves ta know why she's being left alone on a stormy night."

Emmeline frowned at him. "I'm not afraid of the wind."

"Nay, but I am," Quill said lightly. "As for where we're going and what we're going—the mayor asked yer cousin and I ta stand watch at the magazine tonight."

Charles scowled. While Mayor Dixon hadn't said the watch was confidential, secrecy was obvious and essential. Now, Quill had told his cousin everything.

She couldn't have looked more stunned if they'd told her the kitchen had burned down. "It's happening," she said in a hushed voice.

"What's happening?" Charles asked.

"It was never just about Boston. Parliament won't stop there. Williamsburg is next."

He scoffed. "We're just going to stop rumors before they start. Don't let your imagination invent new ones. King George isn't a tyrant. We're a free people. Nothing will happen."

"The Romans were free," she said earnestly. "They were a republic for hundreds of years. And then there was that series of civil wars, and Julius Caesar became dictator for life. And then he was assassinated, and his nephew became the emperor. So after hundreds of years, the Roman Republic fell, and once it became an empire, only the emperor and the nobles in the senate had any power. The common citizens lost their vote. They lost their council. They lost everything."

For a long moment, firelight flickered across their faces as they stared at each other. At last, Quill said softly, "An excellent point, Miss Gardiner."

Fear turned to irritation. "Thank you for the history lesson," Charles said dryly. The British Empire was the only modern nation that could compare with the greatness of ancient Rome. It couldn't fall. It wouldn't. "Please excuse us. We have to relieve the afternoon watch."

"We have time," Quill said, moving to a wingback chair with a book on the seat. He picked it up. The faded gilt title caught the firelight. "Ah, *The Tempest*," he said, sinking into the chair. "Are ye reading that, Miss Gardiner?"

"Not exactly," she said, sitting across from him. "I had thought we would do that together this evening, but I didn't know Charles had other plans."

"Shakespeare is meant to be read aloud," Quill said, thumbing through the book. "I regret we have a prior commitment."

Emmeline smiled and pulled a quilt across her lap. "I had planned to be Miranda, my father of course, would be Prospero, and Charles would be Ferdinand."

Quill looked up from the book. "Nay, fair Miranda, Charles is no' cheerful enough ta be your prince." He chuckled. "See? He's glowering at me right now. Make him the monster."

The teasing was going too far. Charles pulled his cloak to the side, revealing his knife and pistol. "You do know I'm armed right now."

His friend ignored him.

Emmeline spared him a disinterested glance, then looked back at Quill. "Ferdinand isn't cheerful. He's been shipwrecked and thinks his father is dead. His character is wrestling with deep and complicated emotions."

Quill turned pages in earnest, then stopped and held it up to the light as he read, "The wreck of all my friends, nor this man's threats," he gestured to Charles, "ta whom I am subdued, are but light ta me, might I but through my prison once a day behold this maid." He rested the book on his knees. "Under similar circumstances, Hamlet would have been brooding about death. Romeo would have dueled Prospero on sight. Ferdinand says he'll be happy so long as he can see a pretty lass once a day." He smiled, a mischievous light in his eyes. "For my part, I think Ferdinand had it right."

Charles pushed aside the Windsor chair they had left for him. "Is the cider hot? We need to get going."

Emmeline stood. The keys on her mother's châtelaine clinked with the movement. As the quilt slipped from her lap, she caught it and tossed it on the chair behind her. "Do you have your canteen ready?" Without waiting for an answer, she wrapped her hand in a rag and lifted the kettle from a hook over the fire.

Charles uncorked his pine canteen. Uncle Rob had made it himself, coating the inside with brewer's pitch to make it watertight. He held it steady as she poured the cider. "Stop!" he cried as the scalding cider overflowed. He corked it quickly and shook his hands, as though the burning sensation could be shaken off as easily as cider droplets.

"Sorry!" she cried and set the kettle back on the hook.

Quill raised his tin canteen. "If 'tis no trouble, Charles may have promised me some of the famous Gardiner cider."

"It's no trouble at all," Emmeline said. This time she poured the cider slowly, checking often to see that it wouldn't overflow. Once it was corked, she said, "Wait a moment." Then she unwrapped the rag from her hand and tied it around the canteen. "That should keep it hot longer."

"What about mine?" Charles asked, tugging his gloves gingerly over his hands.

"Yours is wood," she said. "Wood doesn't change temperature half as quickly as metal."

"True. Well, we must be off. We need to be at the magazine by eight to relieve the watch."

"When do you get relieved?"

"Midnight," Quill said, lifting the canteen strap over his head. "Until then, be sure not ta open the door ta any monsters." He handed her the book. "After then, I suppose ye'll have ta let Charles in."

Charles elbowed him mid-bow. "Stay safe, Emmeline. I'll see you on the morrow."

"Aye. Dinna worry about us," Quill said, heading to the door. "Thank ye for the cider."

Charles glanced back before closing it. Emmeline was cocooned in a quilt and a wingback chair, reading Shakespeare by the fire, safe inside on a stormy night.

If only he and Quill would be half as comfortable.

Fifty-Five

KEEPING WATCH

The sky was a deep, velvety blue, smudged with charcoal clouds, which skittered across the waning moon. Charles regretted not bringing a lantern. He had reasoned it would be nigh impossible to keep one lit in such foul weather, but as the dark pressed in on them, he began to think it may have been worth the effort.

Quill hastened to keep up with Charles's long stride. The tin canteen, wrapped in Emmeline's rag, jostled against his cloak with every step. "Thanks for invitin' me ta meet ye at the Gardiners'. I'll need something ta keep me warm tonight." He harbored no guilt for sweet-talking another female he had no interest in.

"Don't quote Shakespeare to my cousin."

"Dinna be prudish. Even the rector quotes Shakespeare from time ta time, and Miss Gardiner likes the bard, herself."

"Don't you see? That's why it's a problem."

"Because she likes it? Honestly, dinna ye know yer proverbs? 'A merry heart doeth good like a medicine.' I'll no' apologize for raising her spirits."

Charles sighed. Quill always meant well, but he had never courted a woman longer than a fortnight or two before losing interest. He couldn't understand what it was like to love a woman for a year and want her for a lifetime.

"I expect we'll have a quiet night," Quill continued. "The storm should keep all the troublemakers home."

"If there were any, which I doubt," Charles said. "But it's after dark, so I came armed like the Mayor told us to be."

"Aye, I saw ye did."

"Didn't you?"

"I brought two knives and a slingshot."

"A slingshot?" Charles repeated in disbelief. "You brought a toy for defense? Where's your pistol?"

"It looks like rain. Wet gunpowder is useless, so I left my pistol with Polly. She has her own, but she favors mine." Leaves skittered across the road like it was a blustery October night, not April. "And the mayor just told us ta defend ourselves. That's easier done with a slingshot than wet powder that won't fire."

He made a fine point, but Charles had tucked his powder horn under his shirt, trusting that the layers would keep everything safe and dry.

Ahead, the brick capitol building blurred against the evening sky. They turned left onto Duke of Gloucester Street. Instinctively, Charles put a protective hand on his head as a gust of wind tugged at his cloak and pulled strands of hair from his queue, but the knitted cap stayed tight. He would rather be on land than at sea in such weather. This gale reminded him of the storm that had rocked the *Minerva* and driven him to bed. He had scarcely known Susan, but she had nursed him through it with ginger tea and broth. If love had a beginning, for him, it was there. That day, the seed had been planted. It had then surprised him with its rapid growth, nurtured by each encounter with her. The wind stung his eyes until they watered. Where was she now? He had confided the watch to her. He hoped she cared enough to worry, at least a little bit. If he hadn't been fool enough to propose marriage, he could have seen her this evening and heard her concern.

Now it was all over.

Quill filled the silence with cheery nonsense that failed to lift Charles' spirits. He had more important things on his mind than the havoc one escaped piglet could wreak in an apothecary. His mind bounced back and forth between Susan and Kitty like a shuttlecock between two unfailing battledores. *Susan is lost. Kitty is doomed. Susan is lost. Kitty is doomed.* His throbbing head ached for rest.

As they neared the magazine, the door to Chowning's Tavern opened, spilling the fragrance of hot food into the night air. It was good that he had eaten a large supper. Chowning's was across the street from the magazine, beside the courthouse. They would be teased by the aroma of stew and coffee until midnight.

The tall octagonal tower of the magazine had been a landmark in Williamsburg since his grandfather's boyhood. It was strong. Stable. Enduring. Virginia had withstood Frenchmen and pirates, ferocious animals, and fierce storms. The wind could howl all night. The magazine would still stand. During the French and Indian War, a ten-foot-tall perimeter wall had been built around the magazine. Leaning against that wall, on either side of a solid wood gate, were two men. As they neared, he recognized one of them as an old schoolmate.

"Ingram," Charles called over the wind, "I haven't seen you since the last drill. Are you the watch?"

"Yes, sir. Are you here to relieve us?"

"Aye," Quill said. "We have the next watch."

"You'll be here? Tonight?" Nathaniel Ingram's forehead creased. "You didn't leave her alone, did you?"

"She has many friends," Quill said coldly. "She's safe. That's all ye need ta know."

Ingram began examining the lock on his musket, an impractical business to be about after sunset with not even a lantern for light.

When no one expounded on the riddle, only two of them seemed to understand, Charles asked, "Have you seen anything unusual today?" He wanted to be assured that tonight was going to be as uneventful as he had told himself it would be.

The guards looked at each other.

"What is it?" Quill asked.

"It's probably nothing," Ingram said, "but earlier I thought I saw someone watching us."

The wind knifed through Charles's cloak. "Watched? By whom?"

"I can't say. It might have been nothing. I never got a good look, but it's been hours. He's probably gone."

"If you'll 'scuse us," said the other man, "It's been a long afternoon and I've got me a supper, a wife, and a warm bed a-waiting."

Ingram coughed.

"You're excused," Quill said, "ta go straight home, the both of ye." He took his place before the gate, standing as tall as nature allowed. Charles stood beside him. The afternoon guards went their separate ways.

Once they were out of sight, Charles asked, "What was that about?"

"What was what?"

"You and Ingram. Something happened between you since we were in school."

"It's nothing." Quill fixed his gaze on the courthouse opposite.

"Nothing? You criticized me for not telling Emmeline about my evening plans, yet you refuse to tell me this."

Quill shook his head. "I tell ye my own secrets, no' the ones entrusted ta me."

Was Kitty's secret one he had been entrusted with, or was it his to share? It might be his, at least in part, but he was too ashamed to admit to even his closest friend what his father had done, so he stood silently beside him, watching the road. The tall brick wall sheltered them from the worst of the wind as it howled around the magazine. Charles would have welcomed a springtime chorus of frogs and crickets, but the gale had canceled nature's music, rattling buildings and moaning through trees instead. Wind made the evening colder than April had any right to be.

For the first hour, they faced the courthouse across the street, as the previous watch had done. The portico, doors, and shutters glowed white in the flickering moonlight, making it easy to pick out shadowy figures against them. Most people didn't spare them a glance, and those who did hurried on by, eager to be out of the weather. No one was watching them. The next hour, they took turns pacing the perimeter wall, in case someone thought to sneak up from the quieter South Street. They fell into a rhythm: facing the courthouse, then walking the perimeter into the wind and away from it. Then, taking another swig of cider and facing the courthouse while the other walked the perimeter.

Taking turns like this made it easy to keep his own lonely counsel. He had done so for much of his life, but this past year, he had grown accustomed to having someone to confide in. He had learned, later than most, that heavy worries were lighter after being shared with a trustworthy friend. And if Quill could keep whatever his secret with Ingram was from him, he could at least keep Kitty's secret from others.

Charles completed another circuit of the wall. Quill was standing by the gate, hurling pebbles into the road with his sling-shot. He glanced at Charles. "This wind is making it dreadful hard ta aim." He pocketed his toy.

"Wait." Charles held up a hand before he could start the next perimeter check. "Can you keep a secret?"

"Aye. What is it?"

"Before I tell you, you must swear to speak of this to absolutely no one, not even Polly."

"Ye havena entangled yerself in anything illegal, have ye?"

"No," Charles said firmly. "Do you swear it?"

Quill narrowed his eyes and studied Charles. Then he raised his right arm. "With God as my witness, I swear it."

Charles looked about. The road was clear. He faced his old

friend. "I have a sister." The wind caught the words and wrapped the secret around them.

At last, Quill said, "Born on the wrong side of the blanket?"

'Ye-es," Charles said slowly. "You might say that."

"Well, your family's not the first. Best to send her off to a distant aunt to be raised. Be sure yer father writes her into his will. While illegitimate children may no' have a full share of the estate, it's easy enough ta give them a proper start."

"I wish it were that simple."

"Why shouldn't it be?"

"She's a slave."

Quill let out a low whistle. "That does complicate things a bit."

"A bit?" Charles scoffed. "Thanks to that blasted Act of 1723, it complicates everything." It was liberating to shout over the wind what he had long been afraid to whisper. "Her mother was a slave, so she is too." He pounded a fist against the gate. "My own sister was born a slave, and there's nothing I can do about it."

Quill stared at him, his usual levity gone. "How old is she?"

"Too old! She was born a few months after my mother died."

Quill's mouth and eyes went round, but he moved past the shock more quickly than Charles had. It wasn't his mother or nursemaid who had been hurt. "So, about eight. Ye've met her?"

"Every time I've been to Johnson Hall this past year. I had no idea. She hides in plain sight, spending her days caring for my grandmother." In the distance, thunder rumbled. "Oh. *Her* grandmother."

"I dinna believe ye can convince Dunmore that an eight-year-old caring for her grandmother has done a meritorious service worthy of manumission."

"I know!" This was why he had wanted to speak with Quill. He didn't have to explain the laws to him. They both knew no slave in Virginia could be freed without the sanction of the royal governor. Kitty was born a slave in her father's household. By law, she would always be a slave. But by blood, she was a closer relation than Emmeline and Henrietta. "As her half-brother, I feel a responsibility for her, but what can I do? Even if she had a lady's education, she will never have a lady's opportunities. What can a woman who is almost a lady do?"

"I believe the usual answer is ta be a companion for a crotchety aunt, tutor children, or be a governess."

"That's it." Lightning flashed. For a second, the empty street was illuminated. Then the darkness returned. "If she has any aptitude for book learning, she could be a governess," Thunder rumbled about them. "Even without that impossible manumission, she could be a governess. But the Bray School shut down last summer. Susan told me all about it. How do I find a teacher for her?"

"Is it no' obvious? Ask yer cousin. There's no more enthusiastic reader in the English language, and she has such an understanding of the Roman Empire. She could teach." Quill was right. The answer was so obvious he couldn't believe he hadn't thought of it first.

"There's one more thing that worries me."

"Only one?"

Charles ignored the jab. "I don't like the idea of her living at Johnson Hall after my father marries."

"Then move her," Quill said as if this were obvious. "The Gardiners could take her, though they already have ye and Jenny. There's that cousin down in Norfolk ye never talk ta. Or ye can bring her ta yer own house once ye're married if the missus approves." He winked.

Charles faced the courthouse. "That won't be anytime soon."

"Oh, I'm sorry. Did her father refuse? Ye said ye were waiting on his answer."

"He approved. She didn't." There. He had said it.

"Ye asked her?"

"Last week. She was really upset. That's why I couldn't go to dinner this week."

"But she was upset ye hadna come ta dinner. 'Tis plain as day. She wants ye."

"She wants me to be friends. I want more."

"Why did ye no' tell me sooner?"

"Because Polly is bound to ask questions, and she'll tell Susan. Please keep this one to yourself, too."

"As ye like. But 'tis a puzzle why she turned ye down. Polly says she fancies ye."

It had never occurred to Charles that he might be on the receiving end of the Morrises' confidences with Susan. Hope flickered a little brighter among the ashes. "I thought she did. But not enough. She turned me down before I even asked."

"Nay, how is that possible? How could she know ye were going ta ask before ye did?"

"Why else would I have asked for time alone with her? I'll wager half the household knew what I was about. Susan thought to spare me the embarrassment of rejection by speaking first."

"But before then, had ye ever hinted at it? Did she know ye had written her father? Did ye ever hint at a future together?"

"I wanted to be sure of her family's approval. But I've given her flowers. I called at least twice each week for months. It was obvious I was courting."

"Ye're discreet ta a fault. It may be that she was still surprised. With enough time ta think on it, she may regret her hasty answer."

"Do you think so?"

"Aye. Give her time, but dinna give up hope."

It was with considerably better spirits that Charles paced the perimeter wall for the remainder of their watch. There was something he could do for Kitty, and he wouldn't give up on Susan. He would give her space, then try again. After a week of being tortured by what had happened, he at last saw a path forward—a path that had been discovered by sharing a confidence with a friend.

The moon was high in the sky, seeking refuge behind scattered storm clouds, when he joined Quill by the gate, waiting for their relief. Their canteens had long been empty.

Quill stretched his arms above his head and yawned. "Bed ne'er sounded so good."

"Indeed," Charles said. After four hours in this weather, even his lonely mattress would be paradise. "I hope our relief comes soon."

A stray dog pawed against a cellar door before slinking between the courthouse and the tavern. The lower lights of Chowning's glowed faintly, welcoming weary travelers. Then the heavens opened, and the wind was armed with a thousand needles. They turned their backs on the rain and watched for their relief.

"Should no' they be here by now?" Quill asked.

They should have been here an hour ago. "I don't believe they're coming," Charles said.

"While I canna blame them for wanting ta be out of this weather, 'tis hardly fair ta expect us ta take their watch as well as ours."

"I don't like the idea of leaving the Magazine unwatched."

"We canna stand watch if we canna see," Quill retorted.

Rain trickled down Charles's face and into his collar. It would ruin his gunpowder. He pressed his back to the gate and held his arm against his forehead, shielding his eyes. The lights of the tavern still shone. "What if we watch from Chowning's?" They would see the road better from the other side of the tavern glass.

"I thought ye'd never ask."

Together, the loyalist and the patriot fled their posts, racing across the street to shelter.

Fifty-Six

GOD'S WITNESS

Charles latched the door behind them. After hours of hearing the wind howling through his ears, the quiet of the empty tavern echoed in his ears. He wiped his face with a damp handkerchief. The dying fire cast a red glow over the dark space. A bleary-eyed man in a nightcap and banyan came from a back room. "Are you travelers in need of a bed?"

A clock above the fire told them it was half past two, and nothing sounded more reasonable than to collapse on the nearest bed and sleep until noon. "We don't want a room," Charles said hastily before he could succumb to the temptation.

Quill smiled at their reluctant host. "Just a hot drink and a seat by the window, if ye please."

The tavern keeper, a man who had succeeded the original Mr. Chowning, turned toward the kitchen, grumbling something that sounded like, "Pesky parsimonious pirates." He clearly didn't think the effort of getting out of bed in the wee hours to boil water was worth the small payment he would receive.

Quill prodded a log in the hearth. Charcoal fell off in flakes, and cinders leapt into the air where they floated lazily before winking out.

"We're not sitting by the fire," Charles said, carrying a spindle-back chair to the window nearest the magazine.

"I know," Quill said with more longing than resignation. He picked up another chair and followed Charles to the window.

The rain dashed against the glass. "I can't see anything," Charles said. Their one excuse for moving into the tavern was that they would be able to see better. The combined efforts of rain, night, and distance made it impossible.

"We couldna see anything when we were out there, either. It may be better when the rain passes."

Even if Charles had the heart to suggest to Quill that they go out in the driving rain, he couldn't in good conscience leave Chowning's before they'd paid for their hot drink, so they sat by the drafty window, watching the raindrops run together until his vision blurred and his head grew heavy. He nearly dozed off a dozen times before jerking upright again. A minute or an hour later, Quill shook his shoulder, waking him. "Here." He handed him a heavy stoneware mug of coffee.

Charles yawned and stretched. He took the mug and stood, leaning against the glass. After a scalding sip, he noticed the rain had dried up. He could see the gate again. Once they finished their coffee, they should resume their posts until the next watch relieved them. If that failed, one of them would go to Mayor Dixon at daybreak. As the coffee cooled, he drank even more slowly, savoring the common comfort of four walls and a good roof.

"Do ye see that?" Quill asked.

Charles squinted. There was nothing by the gate and nothing on Duke of Gloucester Street, but beyond the magazine on South Street, he could just make out movement. "Is that a wagon?"

"Aye. Seems a wee bit early ta be going ta market."

"It does." Charles pressed his forehead against the glass. His breath fogged it. He rubbed it with his sleeve. "It's turning off the road." The horse and wagon were cutting across the green from

South Street to Duke of Gloucester Street, right beside the magazine, followed by about a dozen men.

Charles slammed his mug onto the windowsill. Quill stood so fast his chair tipped over with a clatter. Charles kicked it out of the way and beat him to the door. They stopped on the step, hidden by the darkness of the night.

"What do we do?" Quill asked. There were only two of them. They couldn't take on a dozen men.

"The mayor doesn't want a fight." He had thought the mayor wanted secrecy, but that wasn't what he had said. He wanted men who could witness to the truth. He and Quill made two, but if his time in the courtroom had taught him anything, it was that more witnesses were better. He hesitated as a man in the uniform of the Royal Marines unlocked the gate. They were the king's men, and only the king's governor could have given them the key. Who did he owe his loyalty to: the mayor and his fellow citizen-soldiers in the militia, or the king and his men?

He didn't have a week or a month to worry it out in his mind. Now was the time to act. *Lord, the city is counting on us. What do we do?* Like the moon showing its face on a cloudy night, a simple thought illuminated his mind. If it was possible to protect Kitty while being loyal to his father, then it was also possible to protect his country while being loyal to the king.

"We need to wake the city."

Quill took the steps in a single leap and ran west past the courthouse. Charles rounded the east corner of the tavern and loaded his pistol, praying the damp powder would fire. He aimed it at the starless sky and pulled the trigger, but nothing happened. He slapped the side of his firearm to settle the powder and tried again. And again. He had prayed for a miracle, and nothing had happened.

He thrust the pistol back into its holster and ran east, the wind at his back, banging on shutters and doors as he passed. "Wake up!" He banged on the next door. "Wake up! Get up!" Then he ran to the next house, not waiting for the doors to open.

The urgency was too great. They needed witnesses before the Marines got away.

He had made it two blocks when he froze, his knuckles raised to rap on another door. Over, under, and around the whistling wind came a deep metallic gong that rumbled through a body like thunder. Somehow, someone had rung the church bell.

Windows flew open. "Where's the fire?"

"What's going on?"

"Get to the magazine!" Charles shouted. "There's trouble at the magazine!"

He ran down the street, shouting answers over questions until he faced the brick wall of the capitol. He paused with his hands on his knees, gasping for breath. The street behind him was filling with people. Out of the nearest door came a Black freeman with his militia drum, beating the call to arms. It was enough. Once he caught his breath, Charles ran back. Militia men and college boys, housewives and young maids gathered outside the magazine. Quill ran up to him. "Did ye hear it? Did ye?"

"The drum? I was there when he—"

"Nay, the church bell."

"I'll wager all of Williamsburg heard that. Who rang it?"

"Me."

Charles stared. "You? How?"

Quill waved his slingshot and grinned.

"That's impossible," Charles said. "The bell tower's too high and the window's too small and you yourself said you can't aim in this wind."

"I didna think I would make it, but I did."

"That's wonderful, but what happened? Where's the wagon?" For the first time, he doubted what he had seen. The whole town would think he had cried wolf if the culprits had vanished before the witnesses were gathered.

"They were frightened," Quill said. "They each grabbed a barrel, loaded it in the wagon, locked the gate, and left before anything else could happen."

A barrel each. That was at least a dozen barrels of gunpowder at a time that hardly anything made it into Virginia's ports. He walked over to the gate. Would that have happened if they had stayed at their posts through the wind and rain? They would never know.

"Morris. Johnson." Mayor Dixon strode up to them, his cloak billowing. "What are you doing here? Where's the watch that was here when it happened?"

"They never came," Charles said. "We stayed out here for several hours, but it started raining and we couldn't see anything, and since our watch was over, we moved to Chowning's to keep an eye on things."

Quill added, "We never imagined this would happen."

"What happened? How much did they take?"

They explained everything that had happened. In the end, the mayor groaned. "And we still can't verify the damage because they still have the key."

Charles lifted the heavy lock in his hand and felt something slip. "It isn't locked," he said.

"Yes, it is. I saw them lock it," Quill said.

Charles pushed on the gate, which creaked under his hand. "Then why is this open?"

"They must not have turned the key all the way," Mayor Dixon said. "Let's take an inventory."

Fifty-Seven

DRUMS IN THE NIGHT

Susan woke suddenly, her ears ringing. It was still dark, but if her fitful dreams were any measure of time, it had been hours since she had fallen asleep. When Mr. Morris had left Polly at the Blue House on his way to stand watch, Susan had intended to stay up with her friend until he returned a little after midnight. But at half past ten, she couldn't help yawning, and Polly had insisted that she go to bed. It only took one person to answer a door.

Susan had swallowed back her objections. It would be pitiful to admit that the reason she wanted to stay up was because she hoped Mr. Morris would bring news of Charles. It had been humbling enough planning an apology. It was humiliating that he was avoiding her so effectively that she couldn't give it, and was instead reduced to begging news of his health from the Morrises.

If she had been asleep for hours, then Polly had already left. She wouldn't have any news of Charles and the watch until morning. So she pulled her covers to her chin and listened to the wind whistling down the chimney and rattling the windows in their frames, desperate to escape. Branches clawed at her shutters. It must have been a dreadful evening to stand watch. At least it was over now.

The next time she had a word with Charles, she would give the contrite little speech she had planned. Then in another week or two, she would give him the pocketbook she had made. That gave them several months of proper courtship before Isaac arranged their return ship. But Charles had other plans. From what she had seen, they all involved avoiding her. She might have to swallow her pride and call on him.

The oak tree creaked and moaned as she considered her strategy. She could call on him at his office or she could meet him at the Gardiners' home. The office would allow her to see him first thing in the morning. The Gardiners' might afford more privacy, especially if she could coax him into a country walk.

There was a deafening crack, a scraping and crash, then glass shattering. She threw back the covers and parted the bed curtains. Her windows and shutters were intact, but all possibility of sleep was gone. Somewhere in the house, a window had broken. She lit a candle and dressed as quickly as she could without help, struggling to tie her petticoat in back. Doors and footsteps sounded. She was eager to join the excitement, but her haste in tying her bed jacket made her clumsy. After three attempts, she succeeded and carried the candle downstairs.

From below, Isaac yelped like a child. Susan stumbled on the stairs, almost dropping her candle. "Are you all right?"

The response was as inarticulate as it was indignant.

"He'll live," Polly called.

Susan followed the flicker of candlelight to the dining hall, where Isaac was cradling a hand, dripping blood onto his feet. Shards of glass glinted in the candlelight. A branch of the oak tree protruded through the window. A breeze stirred her petticoat and snuffed the candles out.

"Isaac, stand still and, for heaven's sake, don't touch anything. Polly, what on earth are you still doing here?"

"Quill never came. At least, I dinna think he did. I fell asleep and didna wake until this happened."

Aunt Dorothea came in, wearing her late husband's banyan. "What's going on?"

"I don't know," Susan wailed. "Mr. Morris never came back from watch. Anything could have happened. Someone needs to find out. We need to check the magazine, their apartment, the surgeon, and the apothecary. He may be injured."

"Not to be dramatic," Isaac interrupted, "but I am bleeding all over the tablecloth."

"Right," Susan said. "Aunt Dorothea, get some wine and a bowl. I'll get bandages. Polly, see if you can give us some light." She left her candle on the table and followed the handrail upstairs. Reaching blindly under her bed, she found the medicine bag. When she got downstairs, Graves was building up the fire in the parlor. The shadowy face of the clock read half past four. Whatever had happened to Mr. Morris and Charles had delayed them by four hours. One of them had needed a surgeon. The only question was which one.

The fire in the dining hall had been lit but was flickering wildly from the chimney draft. Polly and Isaac were discussing the branch protruding from the hole in the window. His hand rested in a bowl on the table.

"Is there glass in the cut?" Susan asked, rummaging through her bag.

"No," Isaac said. "I pulled it out."

Aunt Dorothea slowly poured wine over the wound. Isaac inhaled sharply. The blood washed around his hand and pooled into the bowl.

"I'm surprised it wasn't your foot," Susan said bracingly. "What did you think you were doing?"

"I don't know if you've noticed, but there's a branch in the window. I was trying to get it out."

She patted his hand dry. "We should call a surgeon. You need stitches."

"It's not that bad," Isaac said through his teeth.

Susan began wrapping his hand. "You say that because you

don't want stitches." Isaac's injury could wait until morning, but it would give them the excuse she needed to find out whether an injury—violent or otherwise—was what was keeping the men. She tied off the fabric.

"I think—" she began.

Polly interrupted her. "What's that sound?"

"What sound?" Isaac asked.

Polly leaned toward the broken window, tangling her hair in the twigs. "Outside." There had been curious noises all night, all caused by the wind. It was foolish to make a fuss about it.

Aunt Dorothea frowned. She walked carefully around the glass and unbolted the back door. Susan followed her. Outside, what remained of the oak tree still scratched at the house, but when she listened carefully, she could hear something else.

Drums.

Her heart quickened in time to the beat. She had heard that sound before, on days the militia was drilling. But it wasn't daytime, and the militia wasn't drilling. There was no good reason for a drummer to be practicing in the dark of night.

"Something happened," Polly said in a strained voice, "at the magazine." If Morris hadn't come to get Polly, then he and Charles might still be there. And if something had happened, they were in the thick of it.

"We have to go." Susan ran into the house. With shaking hands, she put the remaining bandages back into her medicine bag.

"You can't go," Isaac said flatly.

"Don't you understand? Charles and Morris were standing watch tonight. They never came home. They're in the middle of whatever is happening."

"Which is exactly where you shouldn't be."

"If it bothers you, bring your rifle and come along," she said, buckling her bag.

Isaac snorted and held up his bandaged hand. "Do you think I can shoot with only one good hand? I can't protect you."

"Don't worry about that. Polly has a pistol. Don't you?"

Polly was pale under her freckles. "Aye, but ye heard the drums calling. We'll be outnumbered."

"Don't you care that your brother is out there?"

"Aye. I'll come with ye."

In a few minutes, they were hurrying down the street. Isaac carried a lantern in his good hand. Susan passed her heavy bag from one hand to the other. She had never carried it so far. They were joined in the street by men and women who had thrown cloaks over their nightclothes. *Make haste! Make haste!* The drums cried. Charles was in danger, and she still hadn't apologized. He might already be dead, and would never know that she loved him. Why had he asked before she was ready?

Half the town ringed the magazine. Lanterns bobbed like starlight on the water. Shadows flickered on shadows. How was she supposed to find him in such a crowd before the steady light of dawn? Her eyes fell on the open gate that led to the magazine. That's where he would have been standing watch. Her best chance at finding him was to press to the front of the crowd. Muskets, some with bayonets attached, rested over men's shoulders, glinting dangerously in the flickering light. She dragged Polly through the crowd, batting muskets and bayonets aside with her medicine bag.

Polly pulled back on her hand, stopping their progress. "What do ye think ye're doing?"

"I'm trying to find our men."

There was movement about them. Lanterns raised and voices hushed as three men came through the gate and blinked in the light. Lanterns lowered again and voices raised, but not before Susan identified the mayor, Mr. Morris, and Charles. The latter looked rather wild—his hat was gone, and his windblown hair was loose, but she had seen him in that state before. More importantly, he didn't appear to be injured, though she couldn't be certain without closer inspection.

"There they are!" She released Polly and cupped her hands

around her mouth. "Charles!" Her voice was drowned in the commotion.

Mayor Dixon raised his hands for quiet. The drums silenced, and the people hushed. He spoke in a carrying voice. "We will resolve this without bloodshed. The Marines have not fired, and neither have we. Do not seek them out. We will send a delegate to meet with Lord Dunmore to arrange for the return of what has been taken."

A woman asked, "What did they take?"

The mayor hesitated, then gave a short nod. "We just did an inventory. Fifteen half-barrels of gunpowder are missing."

Angry shouts surrounded them.

"Do not act in haste!" The mayor yelled over the crowd. "We will resolve this peacefully. We will send a member of the House of Burgesses to the palace at daybreak. The speaker of the house is just the man—"

"Henry! Send Patrick Henry!" The cry was taken up by the crowd, who roared for Henry. Susan didn't care who the delegate was, so long as Charles was safe. The crowd shifted, and she pushed to the front, mere feet from him.

In the flickering light of a thousand lanterns, his eyes widened. She stepped toward him. He closed the gap, put a hand on her shoulder, and pulled her within the perimeter wall, away from the harsh lights and shadows, sheltered from the roar of the crowd. For one breathless moment, she was charmed by his protectiveness. Then he spoke, and his voice was tainted with anger. "Do you have any idea how dangerous this is?" He waved an arm toward the crowd beyond the gate. "What are you doing here?"

His anger stirred a fire in her heart. She had left the house in the dead of night and pushed her way through a tumultuous crowd to get to him. She had carried her heavy medicine bag all this way until her fingers were numb from the weight. The least he could do was thank her. There was heat in her voice as she replied, "I know it's dangerous. I came to find you. To see if you were hurt."

He didn't answer. Didn't argue. Didn't do any of the things she might have expected from him. In one swooping motion, he pulled her to his side and wrapped his arms around her, his cloak encircling her, protecting her from the wind that whistled through the gate. Her fire went out like a candle. He wasn't angry with her, just worried. His wool cloak rubbed her cheek, smelling of coffee and rain. She had never been embraced like that, not even under the mistletoe. She soaked it in, wondering if she was brazen enough to return the embrace when he abruptly released her and stepped away.

"Forgive me," he said hoarsely. "It's been a long night."

"No." She fisted his cloak in her hand, restraining him from putting more than one step between them. She resented his apology. She resented any words that divided them, especially her own. "It's been a long week. I need to tell you—" She broke off, unable to remember a word of the pretty little speech she had prepared. "I'm sorry," she said, with pathetic simplicity. There was a long silence. His shadowed face was unreadable.

At last, he said, "For what?"

Her cheeks burned. She wanted to put this behind them, not revisit her foolishness. "For what I said last week. I didn't mean it." Her throat tightened. He might not have heard right, and it was so important that he understood her that she repeated herself. "I didn't mean any of it."

A ragged breath tore through him—she felt it through her hold on his cloak. He had been aching to hear those words. "Good," he said, and for once that common word was glorious enough to encompass all of creation, from the sun and the moon to man and woman. Slow and deliberate, like everything he did, he pulled her into his arms again. Coming from Charles, the action was a promise. She unfisted her hand and slipped it around his back. She had promises of her own to make.

Words would come in time—some twilight evening when the

roses and honeysuckle were in bloom. There would be questions to ask and answer. Letters to compare. Vows to make. All she needed tonight was the assurance that that day would come. She rested her head on his chest, savoring the steady rise and fall. She had found her country, here with him.

And it was good.

After the beautiful rhythm of his breathing had repeated a hundred times, she remembered the concern that had brought her here. "You still haven't answered my question. You're not hurt? Not even a little? I brought my whole medicine bag." She hefted it with her free hand—the one that wasn't wrapped around him.

His chest shook again, this time a low chuckle that rumbled through her. Once it steadied, he shook his head and said, "I love you."

She was so surprised to hear him speak those precious words that she dropped the bag. No longer grounded by its weight, she gazed up at him. He pressed a kiss to her forehead. Fireworks illuminated her heart. How had she ever thought him incapable of feeling?

She closed her eyes. Buried in the deepest chamber of her heart and in need of a good ironing was her reply. "I love you, too." The words trembled like a flag in the breeze. After this, they would be stored more carefully, ready for the next airing. She tipped her face higher and smoothed his hair back as he lowered his head, slow and deliberate. Unable to stand the wait, she rose on tip-toe to meet him halfway. Their lips had scarcely brushed when Morris' voice interrupted.

"Johnson!"

She took two hasty steps back, her cheeks burning. Charles caught her hand as he turned to face their intruder.

"The mayor wants ta lock the gate. Ye better come out."

Susan grabbed the medicine bag, which Charles promptly moved to his free arm. Then they slipped through the gate, just another shadowy couple in the thinning crowd. In time, he would ask her again. He would just be slow and deliberate about it. And she would try to bear the wait.

Fifty-Eight

ISAAC'S DEMAND

Susan glanced up at Charles as they walked. "Thank you for seeing us home. You must be exhausted."

He shook his head. "I couldn't rest not knowing if you were safe, especially on a night like this." The wind tousled his unbound hair. Her fingers itched to smooth the silky strands. That was a privilege she would claim daily as his wife. Her lips parted. If only the dark street were as private as the magazine had been. Morris had interrupted them too soon.

Isaac's lantern bounced up the steps to the Blue House. He set it down and tried the door with his good hand. "It's locked," he said indignantly. He rapped on it, the sound echoing in the dark street.

"Who's there?" Graves's muffled voice asked.

"Who do you think it is?" Isaac didn't mask his irritation. His wound must have been bothering him more than he had admitted. "It's us. The Baileys. Let us in."

The door swung open. "Apologies, sir." Graves nodded to Isaac. "We didn't know when to expect you."

"Isaac, there you are!" Aunt Dorothea embraced him in the foyer. Once she released him, she saw Susan and Charles standing together in the street. "Lord be praised," she murmured. "Mr. Johnson, thank you for keeping our girl safe."

Our girl. Susan hadn't heard that endearment since she was small, many years ago. It was not the sort of thing one called a plump fifteen-year-old with all the womanly responsibilities that came as the lady of a manor house. It also wasn't what one called a matronly twenty-five-year-old who had hastened across town in the dark of troubled night to bind her love's wounds.

Charles walked up the steps with her and set the medicine bag on the floor inside the door. "I was just returning a favor. After all, she came prepared to save me."

"Thank heaven that wasn't necessary," Susan said.

"Then you weren't injured? Do come in and tell us all about it. I'll get us some tea."

"I'm afraid I must decline your hospitality. I've been up all night and would be miserable company. Another time." He bowed and made his way down the dark street.

Graves secured the door. Isaac's lantern cast eerie shadows on their faces.

Aunt Dorothea clutched the banyan at her throat. "I'm glad to see Vina's boy is safe, but I cannot rest until I know what happened tonight."

"The Marines took the gunpowder from the magazine," Susan said. "Though I'm not sure why."

"I am," Isaac said. "You would be too if you'd spent five months in Lord Dunmore's company. His manners are open and friendly until he decides you're no longer a friend. Once he decided the Shawnee were enemies of Virginia, there was no more talk of peace and compromise. That's what this is. He's decided Virginians are enemies to Virginia and is taking action."

"That's ridiculous," Susan said. "You can't be your own enemy."

"I'm not saying it's sensible," Isaac said. "I am saying there will be no more compromises. From now on, everyone must choose a side. If you're not the governor's friend, you're his enemy."

"Neither of you is Virginian," their aunt said. "There's no need for you to be involved in this."

"He knows me," Isaac said, pacing. "And he is the king's appointed governor. If he ordered me to deliver a message or tell a lie or smuggle gunpowder out of another magazine, I'd have to do it or face treason." He stopped pacing and faced Susan. "We have to leave."

"Leave? We can't leave. I told everyone we would be here until mid-July." That was the plan. Everything depended on that plan. She clung to the plan like a sailor to a ship's rigging.

Isaac ignored her. "As soon as the sun is up, I'm going out to find us safe passage. If it's leaving today, so be it. We need to be gone by the time the dust settles and anyone thinks to look for me."

"This is too sudden," Susan said. "I have friends here and—" She stopped. Despite her certainty that she would marry Charles, she could not yet claim there was an understanding between them as the words had not been spoken. It was only a matter of time before everything was settled, but time was a luxury Isaac was determined to deny them. She appealed to her aunt. "Talk to him. Tell him things like this happen. It will blow over soon. No one was hurt tonight. Well, except for Isaac, but that was just broken glass. There's no need for us to leave so suddenly."

Aunt Dorothea shook her head. "It's too soon to tell what will come of this. It may blow over, or it may blow up. He makes a valid point. The governor relied on his loyal assistance during the frontier trouble last year. If his lordship finds himself doubting the colonists' loyalties, he may demand Isaac's assistance more. If the trouble blows up, that would put your brother in the middle of it. Do you want that?"

"Of course not. I want him to be safe. I begged him not to accompany Lord Dunmore last summer. If he had listened to me, the governor would have no reason to request the services of a boy whose hand is so badly injured he can't even buckle his shoes."

"*He* can hear you," Isaac cut in. "And *he* has crossed a mountain range, scouted the wilderness, canoed down a river, and come back alive—without you. Stop treating me like a little boy."

Without you. The rejection stung. It carried no gratitude for the many sacrifices she had made for him. Even if he didn't need her, would it hurt him to admit he appreciated her?

"Hush," Aunt Dorothea said, as though soothing a restless babe. "We're all tired, and it's not yet sunrise. Let's get some rest and discuss this civilly after breakfast."

"Yes, ma'am," Isaac said in a subdued tone.

He was halfway up the stairs when Susan said in a fierce whisper, "If he tries to make me leave today, I'll run off to the frontier myself." Then she trudged up to her chamber. To her surprise, the bed curtains were open and the bed was made, ready for the day. Lucy's service had been erratic ever since her banns had been read. She hadn't joined them during the nighttime emergency, but she had made the bed neatly in their absence. Susan threw her cloak on the chair and knelt beside the bed, her spirit too burdened for rest.

"Dear Lord, an hour ago, everything was perfect. I want to spend the rest of my life with Charles, who finally confessed he loves me. I had a perfectly reasonable plan to make that happen. Now Isaac is threatening to leave today, but I need more time. I've sacrificed everything for him. Not only won't he say 'thank you,' but after all these years, I ask him one favor, and my ungrateful brother won't even consider it."

She was ashamed, complaining about her brother to God himself. Surely God expected greater compassion from her. Yet who else remembered how she had cared for Isaac through childhood fevers? Who else had seen the letters sent when he was at Eton, counseling him in painstaking detail about the care of his linens? The Lord knew she had tried. She had loved her brother with all her heart, and he was pushing her away.

She rested her face on the coverlet. Her eyes burned from lack of sleep, but there was another weariness inside her. She was weary of her life of unrequited service. The harder she worked for others, the more they took it for granted that she would do whatever they asked. Most neglected to return favors, or even to thank her for her sacrifice. They only noticed if she took a rest. Was she doomed to spend the rest of her life serving family and neighbors, begging for crumbs of gratitude like a stray dog?

She should be proud to be the notable Miss Bailey, respected and admired in communities on both sides of the Atlantic. But behind that facade hid a little girl desperate for love who knew she was unlovable. "I'm sorry," she murmured into the coverlet. Sorry for her failures and her follies. Sorry for her pride in appearing selfless. Sorry for fighting with Isaac when she had gotten herself into this mess by rejecting Charles the first time. Sorry she was so unlovable. "I'm sorry."

She was five years old. An older girl had dared her to climb into the loft of the neighbor's barn. She wasn't allowed to go past the flower garden without her nurse, but she wanted a new friend. The girl teased her for being slow and clumsy as Susan tried to climb the tall ladder. As soon as they were in the loft, her new friend insisted they jump into the hay below. Susan jumped out of the loft.

She landed even more clumsily than she climbed, and pain shot through her leg. She couldn't stand. She lay in the hay and cried. Her friend ran away, leaving Susan alone. With all the certainty of five years, she knew she would never get home again. She couldn't walk, and she had disobeyed her father. She was still sobbing in the hay when he found her. He picked her up gently and carried her home. He gave her a stick of candy and held her while the surgeon set her bone.

Susan had scarcely thought of that day in years, but now she remembered it like it was yesterday. A feeling like a warm blanket spread through her. Her Father loved her even when she was foolish and fractured. She hadn't earned that love. It had been there all along before anyone had needed her for anything.

And if He loved her, then it didn't matter who didn't.

Her soul surrendered to a deep rest she hadn't known she needed. She unbuckled her shoes and climbed into bed. The mattress cradled her as she drifted into a series of hazy dreams with white swirling fog, colorful gowns, and children's laughter.

Hours later, she woke, wrapped in heavenly peace. When Lucy arrived with the breakfast tray, her mind reluctantly returned to her earthly tribulations. As she ate her buttered toast, she lighted on a compromise: she would ask Isaac for one last fortnight to say their goodbyes. If Charles was too slow, she would meet him halfway.

Fifty-Nine

SHORT ON TIME

TUESDAY, APRIL 25, 1775

Charles's stomach rumbled again. Anytime now, and Mrs. Evans's carriage would arrive. It had been ages since he'd seen Susan—last Friday, before dawn. On Sunday, he had ridden out to Johnson Hall to speak with his father about Kitty. Gideon had said he had left that morning and would be back sometime in the afternoon. When twilight had come, Charles had left, frustrated that he had wasted a day he had hoped to enjoy with Susan.

Especially now that they were on kissing terms.

It had taken restraint not to see her outside their customary times since their moments together by the magazine, but he feared her love for him was still fragile. Though she had welcomed his embrace and met his kiss, only a week before, she had rejected him. She might yet need time to think things over. So he had waited anxiously for their usual dinner at the Blue House.

He was locking his desk when there was a knock on the office door. Quill answered it.

Charles glanced up, surprised by a familiar face. "Marcus?"

The man had been looking over Quill's head, considering the

410

office with its oil paintings and law books. "Master Chawz," he drawled. "How d'you get on?"

"I'm well, thank you. And you? What brings you here?"

"Gideon sent me. Said you'd like to know your father's home, and in a fine mood. Thought you'd be wanting to come home for dinner and have a talk with him."

"Now?" Mrs. Evans's carriage had rolled to a stop just beyond the window. Susan would think he was avoiding her—again. But it would only become more difficult to get his father alone once he was married. He was running out of time to have this conversation the way he had planned.

"Yes, now," Marcus said.

Charles sighed. "Quill, tell Miss Bailey that I have important business with my father."

"Two weeks in a row?" He shook his head. "She willna like that."

"You know I need to do this. I'll call on her this evening. Actually, on the morrow. That way if things run late with my father, I won't disappoint her again. Yes, I'll call on the morrow. Tell her that for me." He grabbed his hat and followed Marcus out the door.

After they'd walked a couple of blocks, Marcus observed, "You ain't as troubled as last time I saw you."

Charles shrugged. "I don't think Morris would appreciate me using his mother's paintings for target practice."

Marcus laughed but didn't press him for details. Instead, he passed the time entertaining Charles with humorous stories from the neighboring plantations. The walk passed so quickly that Charles was surprised to see the bridge to Johnson Hall ahead of them. His old playmate left him there, using the cover of trees to return to his work.

Gideon met him at the door, greeting him as though nothing could have surprised him more than seeing him this afternoon. He excused himself to get dishes to set another place. Charles let himself into the dining room.

His father was sitting alone at the end of the long table, reading the *Gazette*. He glanced up in mild surprise. "Ah, Charles. Strange goings on these days. Did you hear the governor threatened to free all the slaves and burn Williamsburg to ashes?"

"From several reliable men." Gossip was spreading like a field fire in an August drought. So was truth. The trouble was telling one from the other. For his part, he repeated what he had done and witnessed at the magazine with no embellishments. Gideon set dishes before him, then retreated as silently as he had entered.

His father shook his head and folded the paper. "Strange doings. Speaking of which, what brings you here? I thought you worked on Tuesdays."

"I do. However, I needed to speak to you man to man about your affairs and thought it best to do so while you are still free of feminine distractions."

His father chuckled. "I'm quite looking forward to some of the feminine distractions, but I see your point. What's on your mind, boy?"

"The first matter concerns your will. As a barrister, I wanted to assist you in making the changes you will need as you take on a second family." Wills and other documents were typically left in the hands of attorneys, but Charles knew all the laws surrounding them, and if he wrote it himself, he might persuade his father to more conscientious terms than were legally necessary.

His father nodded, pleased. "And the second?" He scooped up a forkful of pie.

Charles spoke with the confidence of a man about to play his winning hand. "I wish to discuss the education of my sister."

Mr. Johnson, Sr., dropped his fork.

Susan paced the parlor, as anxious as Isaac, but for different reasons. An hour ago, he had returned with the news that he had secured their return passage. They would leave on

Friday. That was half the time Susan had compromised on, and she still hadn't seen Charles since just after Morris had interrupted their kiss. They had a lot to discuss.

"Ah, there they are," her aunt said.

Susan went to the window and watched Morris help Polly and Emmeline down. They approached the house together, without Charles. He had missed last week. She hadn't seen him at church on Sunday. He was missing again. She couldn't meet him halfway if he wasn't there to meet.

When the front door opened, it stirred the air in the parlor. She shivered, but her aunt had declared the sunny spring day too warm for a fire. When Graves announced their company, she gave Morris a where-is-he-and-how-dare-you-come-without-him look.

Morris shifted uncomfortably. "Charles had important business with his father. He wished me ta send his regrets and tell ye he would call on the morrow."

"Business with his father?"

"Aye. Ye ken he's getting married soon. There was some business his father needed ta attend ta before the wedding."

In any other circumstance, it would have been a reasonable excuse. "Well, you can tell him if he doesn't come tomorrow, I may never see him again."

Polly's brows rose. "That's a mite harsh."

"I didn't mean it that way. What I mean is—" She rubbed her forehead. There was a dull ache behind her temples that had been increasing all day. "We sail this Friday."

The Morrises cried out in alarm. Emmeline frowned.

Just then, Isaac strolled into the room. "It's true. I made the arrangements with the captain this morning."

"But," Morris said, "ye were no' planning ta leave afore July. Why so sudden?"

"If you haven't noticed," Isaac said, "Lord Dunmore is in a state of supreme anxiety. No one knows his zealous diplomacy better than I, having spent close to half of last year in his company. I refuse to be dragged into his political affairs again. I'm going home."

Voices jarred in response. Susan sank onto the settee and tipped her head back, eyes closed. Firstborn sons of gentlemen always knew where their home was. Life was more complicated for firstborn daughters. Bailey Manor had always been her home. Now, Virginia was—or should be. What a time for Charles to be elusive. She couldn't bring herself to join the conversation and only opened her eyes when dinner was announced.

The dining hall was darker because the broken window was boarded up, awaiting repairs. As plates were being passed around, Mr. Morris entertained them with the full tale of their watch at the magazine. "Did ye hear the bell?" He turned to Emmeline, a look of self-satisfaction on his face. "That was me. Ye see, I had my slingshot—"

"Mr. Morris," Emmeline interrupted, "I would not tell your tale in that manner if I were you."

"Oh? And how would ye tell it?"

"The gunpowder would never have been taken if you had kept your post. I would be ashamed of myself for betraying my country for a little comfort."

Mr. Morris' face fell. Polly gave a shrill, breezy whistle. Susan's head pounded. She rested her forehead in her hand.

"Susan, dear, are you feeling well?" Aunt Dorothea asked.

"It's just a headache."

"You don't look well. You should lie down."

She couldn't lie down. This might be the last time she saw her friends. If she and Charles didn't have an understanding by Friday morning, this was truly goodbye. Her eyes watered.

A hand was on her forehead. "She's burning up," Polly said. "Mr. Bailey, help me get her upstairs."

She tried to tell them she could walk on her own, but the words got lost before they were spoken, so she was forced to accept their assistance. The stairs were too narrow for three, so Isaac walked beside her, a supporting hand under her elbow and another on her back. Polly followed them into the bedchamber and turned down the covers.

"Where's yer maid?"

"She got married just yesterday." Aunt Dorothea's voice was far away. "Run along. I'll help her."

In a few minutes, she was dressed down to her shift. She shivered violently as her aunt tucked her into bed and drew the curtains, blocking out the harsh sunlight. Susan hated being sick. Nothing was lonelier than the hours spent tossing and turning, but there was no help for it. She had to rest. She had to get better.

Sleep came in fits. She returned to Bailey Manor and found it empty. A cool cloth was on her forehead. She was cradling her first child. He had sandy hair, just like his Papa. There were footsteps. Charles fell overboard and drowned. Someone sat her up and helped her drink something bitter. They were boarding the ship when she remembered the pocketbook and ran to the magazine to give it to Charles, but he wasn't there. A man was speaking to her aunt. He doubted whether an English-born lady had the strength to survive the seasoning. After he bled her, she slept soundly.

Sixty

PRIVATE CONVERSATION

FRIDAY, APRIL 28, 1775

The room was quiet save for the faint scratching of a quill. Her left arm was snugly bandaged around the elbow. The bed curtains had been pulled back, allowing sunlight to warm her face. Someone was sitting at her desk, silhouetted against the window. She hadn't been left alone in her time of illness. She was loved, even when she was doing nothing to earn it. Lulled by the soft sound of writing, she slept.

Susan blinked, fumbling toward consciousness. The sun had moved behind the oak tree. Spring leaves bounced in a gentle breeze. Sunlight danced across the coverlet like light upon the water. Cupped in her right hand was a wooden dolphin, small but lifelike. Her mind, heavy with dreams, struggled to make sense of it. Papers ruffled. A man still sat at her desk, a dark blond queue tied between his shoulders. She blinked in confusion, but the image didn't right itself. Charles was in her bedchamber.

She yanked the coverlet to her chin and gasped at the sharp sting inside the crook of her left arm.

Charles looked over his shoulder. "Susan?" He turned his chair so that he was facing her. "You're awake."

Was she? Her fingers curled around the dolphin. His voice had been in her dreams, soothing her restless sleep. His hands had placed cooling cloths on her fevered forehead and smoothed the blankets when she had shivered. His strong arms had helped her up to drink her medicine. She untangled the hazy memories from her dreams. "You came."

"Every day." His hand covered her forehead. Relief washed over his face. "Your fever is down. It was so high. The doctor said—well, never mind that. He was wrong."

Another time, she would have demanded to hear all about the doctor, but something else tugged at her curiosity. "Every day? What do you mean?"

"You've had a high fever since Tuesday. I came the moment Quill told me about it and didn't leave until your aunt sent me away. Then I came back at first light. Your aunt had been up all night, watching over you. Since then, we've been taking shifts."

She had surrendered her blinding pride to God's love. In her humility, she could see the concern of her family and friends. They, too, loved her for who she was and not just for what she had done. Their love was an imperfect earthly shadow of a heavenly form, but she was an imperfect earthly creature. To her, it was beautiful. Her body, worn down by fever and bloodletting, was too weak to contain her joy. Hot tears flowed unchecked onto her pillow.

"Oh, Susan, darling." His voice was full of compassion. He tugged his chair forward with a scrape until his knees pressed against the mattress and patted her face dry with his handkerchief, catching the tears before they moistened her pillow. "There, there. The fever's not so bad, now. You'll be better soon."

"It isn't that." She sat up, ignoring the pang in her arm, and held the coverlet securely above her bosom. "I'm just happy that you came."

"Of course, I came. I told you I love you."

"I was afraid I'd never see you again. Isaac—"

"Is going nowhere while you're sick," Charles said firmly.

"And not for a few days after that. We had a long talk, and agreed that you and I have a lot to discuss." He gave her a wry smile. "I didn't cross an entire ocean with you only to have your brother steal you away before I—" He stopped abruptly and sighed. "I'm doing this all out of order, and you're not even helping me."

"Helping you? What do you mean?"

"You haven't once demanded I confide in you the nature of the business I was attending to on Tuesday."

"Oh," she said, surprised and disappointed by the turn in conversation. His father's business affairs didn't tempt her curiosity as much as what Charles hoped to do before Isaac left. "What was it?"

"I recently made a startling discovery." He stood abruptly and looked out the open door. Then, to her exceeding surprise, he closed it. There was nothing scandalous about having a concerned caller visit a sickroom, but she would have preferred to be clothed in more than a shift and a blanket now that she was well enough to be sitting up. She trusted Charles, but the room felt much smaller with the door closed. Her cheeks were feverish as he returned to her bedside. She avoided his eyes, running her fingers over the dolphin's fins.

He continued in a lower voice. "It is a matter of great delicacy and confidentiality. You remember Kitty, the little girl from Twelfth Night who asked if you were a queen?"

"Yes," she said. It was the kind of compliment a lady never forgot. "What about her?"

"I only recently discovered the true nature of her parentage. She's my sister—born on the wrong side of the blanket." There was a long pause. "I tell you this because I have a duty to her. She cannot continue to live in my father's house, especially now that he is marrying again. I hope to buy a home in a few months. When I do, I want her to live with...with me."

Susan was certain he had almost said, "live with us," but she was too stunned by the revelation to appreciate the near-slip.

Discovering the family she had hoped to marry into had such a secret was disconcerting. How did she know Charles would be faithful to her? Could she trust the son not to be like his father? She glanced at him. He was watching her, so wide-eyed and anxious, her heart melted. He had trusted her with a distressing family secret. He was hoping for her approval of his plan and had taken the risk of rejection by telling her before renewing his suit. If he could be loyal to his unexpected sister, he could certainly be loyal to a wife. "You want her to live with you, not as a servant, but as family?"

"As family," he repeated, "though I've promised my father to guard his secret." He took Susan's hand, wrapping his own around hers and the dolphin she held. "I don't know how we'll explain—"

Just then, the door swung open. The sudden breeze blew several papers off the desk. Isaac glowered at Charles from the doorway. "I thought I heard voices. Are you feeling better?"

"I suppose," Susan said, annoyed by the untimely interruption.

Charles stood, taller than the tester that stretched above the bed. He folded his arms and looked down at Isaac. "She's far too ill to travel."

"Is she?" Isaac sat on the foot of the bed and patted her leg. "What do you say, Sue? If we pack you in one of the trunks now, we could still sail today."

"Today?" She had lost all track of time.

"Yes, today. It's Friday, didn't you know?"

She gaped at him in horror. "We can't leave today."

"You're not," Charles said firmly. "He's just teasing. He agreed to postpone his plans."

"Yes, well, I also only agreed to let you sit in here if you kept the door open. It's funny how you forgot that clause the moment she woke up."

"How are we supposed to have a private conversation with the door open?"

Isaac stood and matched his posture. "You have no business doing anything in private with my sister."

Charles reddened.

"We were just talking," Susan said. "Stop making a fuss."

Isaac shook a finger at her. "Until you are well enough to dress and act like a lady, there will be no more private conversations. Johnson, your services are no longer needed. You can call on the morrow and see how she's doing then."

Charles looked extremely put out but gathered his papers. He didn't face her again until he was in the doorway. "Until tomorrow, Miss Bailey," he said, with impeccable formality. "I hope you're feeling better by then."

"I will be," Susan said. She would be well enough to dress in all her layers and meet him alone in the parlor or the garden. Nothing would keep her from continuing their private conversation.

Sixty-One

LOVE & LOYALTY

SATURDAY, APRIL 29, 1775

Charles stared blankly at a list he was making of arguments that might be made against his client. He was determined to take on as many briefs as possible to hasten the time he could buy a home. Yesterday, it had seemed prudent to bring a brief home to work on, but three wagons had passed under his chamber window since he had sat at his desk, and the page was still blank. The only legalities on his mind this morning would be performed by the rector if Susan agreed to stay. He drummed his hands on the desk. A week ago Friday, before dawn, he was certain she had changed her mind in his favor. Today, he would ask.

Isaac's determination to leave might not allow him another opportunity.

He corked his ink jar. His mind was too restless for his usual work and would be until after he called on Susan, but the sun was still low in the sky, and she was recovering from a serious illness. He wouldn't be the one to wake her. He shrugged his jacket on and went out to his uncle's workshop. If he could keep his hands busy, it might calm his mind.

Emmeline's voice carried through the open door. She was clutching the *Gazette* with both hands. "To all friends of American liberty," she read with feeling, "be it known that this morning, before break of day, a brigade consisting of about one thousand or twelve hundred men landed at Phipp's Farm, at Cambridge, and marched to Lexington, where they found a company of our colony militia in arms, upon whom they fired without any provocation, and killed six men, and wounded four others."

"When was that written?" Charles interrupted.

"Wednesday morning," she said, "but the report is from New England, so it must have been the week before."

Then it had happened two mornings before the incident in Williamsburg, when a dozen of the king's men had entered the magazine and Williamsburg's militia had gathered, but no one had been killed. Virginians could be rational in any crisis. It was too much to expect from a town situated near Boston. "Why was the Lexington militia drilling before dawn?"

Emmeline frowned at the broadside. "I don't know. It doesn't say."

"Why were a thousand regulars marching on Lexington before dawn?" Uncle Rob countered. "This is an express. We won't have the full story for at least a week or two, if ever."

"Six deaths, was it?" It would be another Boston Massacre for the firebrand patriots to cry over. It was far too small to be called a battle, nothing like what Isaac had witnessed.

"Only at first," she said. "The action continued. Fifty militia men were killed and about a hundred and fifty regulars."

Charles dropped onto a three-legged stool. Two hundred casualties, and three-quarters of those were the king's men. It would be a long time before Massachusetts saw peace. The rest of the colonies would be wise to unite quickly with the mother country. "I don't always agree with our burgesses, but they have kept peace in Virginia, something Boston has failed to do." If they lived up north, he would be begging Susan to flee to safety, not proposing marriage, but even the magazine incident had been resolved without violence.

Uncle Gardiner's foot rocked back and forth on the treadle. The spindle on the lathe began spinning, slow at first, but soon so fast it blurred. "You and Mr. Morris did your part to keep the peace."

"I suppose we did." In many ways, the night had not gone as he had hoped, nor even as he had prayed. "I tried to wake the town with my pistol, but it had been raining, and the powder was wet. Then Morris hit the church bell with his slingshot." He shook his head. "I still can't believe he did it."

"Like David and Goliath," Uncle Rob said. The Biblical David had won a swordfight with a slingshot.

"A miracle?"

"I suppose you could call it that."

There was no other word for it. It hadn't been the miracle he had prayed for. It had been even better. If he had succeeded in firing, he might have been fired upon. It wasn't the first time he had received better than the short-sighted intervention he had prayed for. On the *Minerva*, if he hadn't been seasick, he might never have allowed Susan to get close to him. He had been blind to God's mercy. It was only when he looked back with the distance of time that he could see the wonders that had been too big to comprehend when they were right in front of him. His life was full of miracles.

An hour later, he allowed himself to call at the Blue House. To his surprise, he was redirected to the garden. The tulips were blooming, but Susan wasn't in the little formal garden. He heard the crunch of shell and saw her in the pergola, framed by spring leaves on the honeysuckle vines.

She smiled as he approached her. "Where have you been all morning?"

"Letting you sleep."

"I couldn't sleep, knowing you were coming."

"Then you must be feeling better." He reached into his waist-coat pocket. "I made something for you."

"The dolphin? I didn't get a chance to thank you yesterday. It's lovely."

"There's something else." He opened his fist. In the palm of his hand was a simple carving of a heart.

She gave a little gasp and took it, turning it over. "I made something for you, too," she said. Her mouth curved into a pout. "But I left it in my chamber."

"Then I'll have to come again another time. Do you know what I carved this out of?"

"No."

"It's ginger root."

"You carved ginger?"

"Yes. You can smell it."

Susan closed her eyes and inhaled slowly. "Why ginger?"

"You remember that first storm on the *Minerva*? I was so sick I wanted to die. Then you made me ginger tea."

"I remember. We had just met. You wouldn't tell me anything about yourself that first day. I couldn't sleep that night. The bed was painfully narrow. I was afraid I would roll straight off. It was the longest night of my life, but I wasn't alone. You were on the other side of that thin little wall, having a worse night than I. I'll never forget how miserable you looked that morning. I would have done anything to make you smile."

His voice was husky as he said, "There's something I've never told you about that day."

"What's that?"

Charles could no longer hear the birds or the horses or the carriages. All he could hear was his heartbeat, loud and slow. "That's when I fell in love with you."

Her face lit like sunrise. "From the very beginning?" She shook her head. "You hid it well. I thought you despised me."

"Never. The first moment I saw you, something felt familiar, like I had always known you. Like I could never forget you. I don't have much to offer. It will be a few months, at least, before I can buy us a house. It won't be grand, but I'm hoping we can make it a home." The words tumbled out, like coins spilling from an upended lockbox. At this rate, he wouldn't have any secrets left, but his trust had found its sanctuary. "Dearest Susan, would you do me the honor of becoming my wife?"

Her fingers curled around the ginger heart, and she wrapped her arms around his chest in a fierce embrace. Her breath warmed his throat.

"Is that a yes?"

She tilted her face up. "Yes. A thousand times, yes." A breeze meandered through the pergola. She shivered, and with her arms still around him, he felt the tremble right to his bones. She had been waiting for him in the garden for too long. He smoothed her shawl over her shoulders and down her arms, his fingers tingling. The fire in his chest was warm enough for two. He tugged her against his beating heart and kissed her with the tender passion of June roses and the constancy of the Pole Star. She had claimed his everlasting loyalty.

A raindrop fell on his hand. He might never be the provider she deserved, but he would be a good protector. He pulled back. "There's a fire in the parlor. Let's get you inside."

She rested her head against his chest. "You don't need to fuss over me."

"Says the woman who fusses over everyone." Only two days ago, the doctor had suggested she might not survive the seasoning. Her health was still delicate. She needed time to recover. He tucked her against his side, trying to shelter her from the coming rain with his arm as they made their way to the back door.

Musingly, she said, "I wonder what Isaac will say."

"Isaac? He already knows. I had to show him your father's letter before he would agree to wait."

"Do I get to read it?"

"If you like. It is about you, after all."

"I'd like to hear you read it."

"Me? Wouldn't you like to see it yourself?" They climbed the back steps together, which was at once clumsier and more comfortable than going one at a time.

"Yes, but I love the sound of your voice."

He opened the door and waited for her to enter. "Is that why you're always trying to get me to talk?"

"One of the reasons."

Mrs. Evans was waiting for them in the over-warm parlor. She looked at them shrewdly and said, "Do you two have something to share?"

He dropped his hat on the harpsichord and looked at Susan, who looked back at him like they were the only two people in the world. He couldn't suppress a grin. "We're getting married."

"Lord be praised," Mrs. Evans murmured. "When's the wedding?"

"We haven't decided," Susan said. *We.* It was a good word. Solid and cozy. Whatever the future held, they would face it together. She shivered again.

He led her closer to the fire. "After I buy a house in town. Probably sometime this fall." He glanced at Susan.

"Nonsense." Aunt Dorothea dismissed his plans with a smile. "Isaac should be here to give his sister away. If the rector reads the banns tomorrow, we'll have you married in under three weeks. Surely Isaac can delay his plans long enough to attend his sister's wedding." Her tone of voice did not allow for the existence of dissenting opinions.

A three-week engagement. Three weeks and he could kiss her every night and share her bed, and even—a thrill like fire ran down his spine. Even that. It was with great effort that he turned his mind to icy logic. "I cannot buy a home in three weeks, and we will not live at Johnson Hall. I regret that Isaac will be unable to stay for the wedding, but it cannot possibly happen before September."

Mrs. Evans fixed him with a stern look. "Swallow your pride, boy. You can work and save for a house just as easily living here as you can at your uncle's."

He had swallowed his pride many times in the past year. It still tasted bitter. "I would hate to impose."

"Impose?" Her eyebrows raised scornfully. "I invited you." The welcoming words were spoken through clenched teeth.

"Yes, but—"

"Your poor, dearly departed mother. How she would have loved to see you married. To see you having children of your own. But you would postpone that indefinitely for pride? Too long have these rooms been barren. Too long have I waited to hold a babe of my own flesh and blood. No. You are not that cruel. Life is too short and too precious. You will live here and take all the time in the world finding that house you speak of."

Susan said, "Might we have a few minutes alone to discuss it?"

"Of course. I need to speak with Maurice about dinner. If you'll excuse me." The door closed softly behind her.

Dazed, Charles turned to Susan. "Now we know how your aunt feels about it."

"I suspect she's felt that way since the day we arrived together. It's impressive she's waited so long to make her feelings known."

He kissed her forehead. It was warm, but not feverish. "I like your aunt. I'm glad you'll have your own family here in Virginia." He kissed it again. "But I want to marry you and take you home to our house."

"You'll do that eventually, whether we marry now or later."

"I will, won't I?" He sighed. "I love you. I've already waited a year. What do you think?"

"I think," she straightened his cravat, and his heart pounded under her fingertips, "it would be nice if Isaac could attend the wedding. I think my family would like that, too." She kissed the tender part of his throat, just under his chin.

His lips tingled, anticipating her nearness. "But what do you want?"

"What do I want? Charles Johnson, you need to understand

one thing as clear as crystal, or this will never work." Her serious-ness was as sobering as a sermon.

He straightened. "What is that?"

"I love you, and marrying you will be the most selfish thing I have ever done." She folded her fingers into the lapels of his jacket and tugged him toward her, greeting him with a passionate kiss that melted his resolve. Susan could turn any place into a home. There was no need to wait for a house.

"You make a persuasive argument." He reached for his tricorn.

"Where are you going?"

"I need to tell the rector to publish the banns."

She pulled him over to the settee, the gold flecks in her eyes dancing in the morning light. In a velvet-soft voice, she said, "We have a few more minutes." Her petticoats draped across his knees as she sank into his arms.

The banns could wait.

Sixty-Two

EPILOGUE

A crisp fall breeze blew through the house, clearing the air. Susan removed the dust cloth from the settee in her new parlor. The previous occupants, in their haste to leave the colony, had left most of their furnishings to be sold with the house. She had persuaded Charles to allow her to supplement his savings with a bit of her dowry to cover the cost of furniture.

The front door opened again. Jenny scooped Timmy up before he was trampled by Charles and Mr. Finlay carrying a trunk. She set him by the parlor window with a willow basket of toys and caught his attention by turning a Jacob's ladder over, the blocks cascading down in a mesmerizing rhythm.

"Where do you want this one?" Charles asked.

"Kitty's chamber." She and Marion had spent weeks preparing the contents of that trunk. The activity had been an unexpected source of peace when she had sorely needed it. For the past month, she had been eagerly looking forward to moving day, when she could put everything in its place. She hastened up the stairs but froze outside the nursery door. It had been propped open for airing. The nursery was the only room still draped in ghostly white dust cloths. A small basket of unfinished baby clothes was tucked in the cradle.

Charles's heavy footfall stopped just behind her. His familiar arms wrapped around her waist. She closed her eyes and savored the steady rise and fall of his chest. After a long minute, she whispered, "We should close the window."

Wordlessly, he walked over to the heavy window and pulled it shut. He stepped back into the hall and closed the door behind him. "I could send Finlay to Johnson Hall. He can drive the wagon. I can stay." He was fussing over her again. His concern warmed her heart more than dozens of roses ever could.

"I'll be fine." She fiddled with the top button of his waistcoat, sliding it in and out of the buttonhole. Teasing her husband was delightfully easy. "It's a beautiful day. I feel better today than I have in a month—all summer, really. I'd offer to go with you, but I want to be sure Kitty's room is unpacked before she gets here." She abandoned the button, went on her tiptoes, and kissed him. "Thank you for bringing me home."

He had taken such pride in buying a house for her. The worry line on his brow softened under her appreciation. "Don't work too hard."

"How could I, when I have so much help?"

"I'm grateful the Finlays are here."

"As am I, though I still don't understand why he refused his family's freedom." A little of her dowry had gone toward purchasing their indentures.

"He didn't refuse, love. He wants to earn it himself. Some men are like that. For now, it is enough to have all his family under one roof, safe at last." He squeezed her shoulders. "Is Granny's chamber ready?"

"Yes. Marion and I aired the mattresses and made the beds before dinner." She had suggested converting the study off of the parlor into a bedchamber so his grandmother wouldn't have to climb the stairs anymore. A tester bed was now pushed up against the interior wall for warmth and safety. Jenny would sleep in the trundle. "Hurry home."

He bowed and kissed her hand. "I'll be home as soon as I can."

She turned into Kitty's chamber. Cheery red-checked curtains framed the bed. Brightly painted figurines of every animal to ever board Noah's ark lined the windowsill. Resting against the pillow was a doll with a carved mahogany face, wearing a pink gown. Susan couldn't help smiling as she unpacked a matching gown from the trunk, trimmed with ruffles. She and Marion had copied the design from a French fashion plate. She hung each new gown on a row of pegs—white linen frocks for summer, colorful cottons and wools for the rest of the year. All in a row, they looked like friends waiting to welcome Kitty home. There were more pegs than gowns, so she added the red cloak for cold days, and a child's string of coral beads, to be worn daily for good health. Her sashes, fur muff, and embroidered mitts went in the clothespress.

It was the first day in their new home, and already, there were children who belonged here. God had been good to them in the most unexpected ways.

She found Thomas Finlay in the kitchen house, putting away a barrel of fresh cider the Gardiners had sent that morning. The weaving looms Mr. Gardiner was making wouldn't be done for another day or two. With imports so difficult, even Charles had agreed that it would be prudent to allow Marion a way to use and teach her skills as a weaver. He didn't like Virginian homespun any more than she did.

"Finlay, could you move Kitty's trunk to the rafters? I'm done with it."

"Yes, ma'am."

The gardens around the kitchen were overgrown and thick with weeds. Finlay had suggested digging out large sections and planting afresh. After listening to a wearying lecture on the properties of domestic plants, Susan had told him he could do whatever suited his fancy in the gardens, as long as he kept the old rosebush and left room for the pergola Charles planned to build with some help from his uncle.

She joined Marion, shelving books in an upstairs chamber they were converting into a study. The previous owners had allowed them to purchase their entire library of books. The only thing the house lacked was a music room. Eventually, they would buy a harpsichord. Every home needed music. But for now, she enjoyed having an excuse not to practice. After half an hour of work, they were interrupted.

"Mrs. Johnson, you have callers," Finlay said. "A Mr. and Miss Morris."

"Excuse me, Marion." She gladly left the dusty piles of books and went to greet her friends. They were the first in an hour-long flurry of late callers. The dining table was soon laden with gifts—smoked meat, fresh bread, and garden herbs. So many dinner invitations were exchanged that they wouldn't eat alone for at least a month. She was sitting at the dining table planning menus when, at last, she heard Charles's voice echo in the foyer. He had come home like he would every evening forever after.

She found him in the parlor, pushing a wingback chair up to the window and helping his grandmother into it. Timmy toddled over to Granny and climbed on her lap as though he had known her his whole life.

"Who are you?" Granny asked.

"I 'immy."

Granny accepted the introduction and pointed a shaky finger toward the window. "There's a horse out there."

"Horsey!" Timmy exclaimed.

Charles shook with silent laughter.

"What is it?" Susan demanded.

"Who would have thought they would go so well together?"

"Well, that leaves us with one person to get situated." She looked around and found Kitty standing in a corner of the parlor, clutching what looked like a bundle of rags. "Good afternoon, Kitty. Do you remember me? We've met before."

She nodded. "You're the other Mrs. Johnson." That was correct, though it did nothing to explain to the child why she would now be living with them, not as a servant, but as family. The men in Kitty's life had agreed that it wouldn't do her any good to know the truth, but Susan doubted it was healthy for a child to be moved around with no explanation.

In her best hostess voice, Susan said, "Would you like to see where you sleep? It's upstairs."

Kitty followed her. So did Charles.

"This is your chamber." Susan gestured for her to go first.

Kitty walked around the bed, frowning at the floor, then got on her hands and knees to look under it. There was nothing there but a plain white chamber pot. "I—I thought I got a bed," she faltered.

"You do," Susan said, confused. She patted the coverlet. "This is your bed."

"You want me to share with Granny?"

"What? No." She glanced at Charles, horrified by the misunderstanding. This was what came of keeping secrets. She had half a mind to tell Kitty everything right now. "She sleeps downstairs. This is your chamber. You get this bed all to yourself. Everything in here is for you. This is where you'll wash up each day." She showed her the washbasin. "Charles made these toys for you." She pointed to the animals in the window. "And the doll, but Mrs. Finlay and I made the gown."

"A princess doll?" Kitty stared in awe. Susan almost corrected her. A princess doll should have a rhinestone tiara and a fur cape.

"Yes, a princess doll," Charles said. "This new house is our castle. Mrs. Johnson is the queen. You get to be the princess."

Now, Susan stared. Charles was the last person she had expected to tell fairy stories. But his fiction at least attempted to explain Kitty's new role in her new house, without divulging heavy secrets.

"A princess? Really?"

"Really," Susan said. "See, you get a princess gown, too." She picked up the matching gown, showing the ruffles to advantage. "It's your best gown, so we'll save it for Sundays."

Charles squatted so he was at eye level with Kitty. "There are some rules to being a princess. Are you ready? Princesses have to mind their manners, wash their hands before meals, learn their lessons, and," he glanced at Susan, "always listen to the queen. Can you do that?"

"Yes, sir," she said eagerly.

"I thought you could. That's why you get to be our princess." He straightened. A rare smile was on his face. "Oh, and one more thing. There are some rebels in the street. They don't like the monarchy, so don't tell anyone you're a princess. It has to be our secret."

"Yes, sir." Kitty climbed on the bed and picked up her doll.

"We'll let you get acquainted," Susan said, pulling Charles into the hall. She lowered her voice. "Speaking of rebels in the street, I don't think you have time to return the wagon and make it home before curfew. The light's fading already." She didn't like the wild look of the men from Culpeper assigned to guard the city each night.

"It's already taken care of," Charles said.

"But, how? Did you send Finlay to return it?"

"No. I picked up Uncle Rob on the way back from Johnson Hall. As soon as we unloaded, he left. Since he was only going one way, he had plenty of time."

"I must admit, I'm relieved. If you didn't make it back in time, I would be up all night wondering if you were safe."

"And I would be doing the same thing. Come, I want to show you something." He covered her eyes with his hand. Through the cracks in his fingers, she could see their big tester bed as they went into their bedchamber. The door latched quietly behind them. With his other hand on her stomacher, he pulled her against his chest. They squeezed past a stack of trunks at the foot of their bed. He stopped in front of the window and uncovered her eyes. "There."

She gasped. Their house was deeper and a little taller than the neighboring ones, allowing them to see much farther than one usually could in town. Sunset had painted the western sky lavender with luminous pink clouds.

"I promised you would see sunsets," he said.

She turned toward him. "When was that?"

"In the beginning, when I first fell in love with you."

"That, my dear, might be the most romantic thing you've ever said." She tugged his hair ribbon loose, like she did every night. Fine, dark blond strands fell about his face. She smoothed it back, twining her fingers in it. She went up on tiptoes, but just before her kiss reached him, he said something even sweeter.

"Welcome home, Susan."

Author Notes

We never wanted to move to Virginia. The Navy first stationed us in Charleston, South Carolina, where my husband taught at Nuclear Power School. The area was beautiful, but it was on the opposite side of the country from our families.

When our time in Charleston was almost done, we were asked where we would like to be stationed next. There was an opening in western Washington that would put us close to family again. There were exciting overseas locations. Then there was Norfolk, Virginia. It wasn't exciting. It wasn't sunny. It wasn't close to family. It was the last place we wanted to go.

The Navy moved us there.

And so I experienced the soothing thrum of cicadas, the tropical storms common in September and October, and sweetgum burrs sprinkled across the front walk. Snow was rare, but winters were cold in our drafty historic townhouse. I had a December baby. The first few months of his life were spent in the warm upstairs bedrooms. Downstairs, the kitchen and living room sometimes dropped to fifty-five degrees Fahrenheit (thirteen degrees Celsius).

A couple of blocks away, I could see across the water known as

Hampton Roads to the town of Hampton. Sometimes we took the HRBT (Hampton Roads Bridge-Tunnel) to Williamsburg. We walked the roads George Washington, Thomas Jefferson, Peyton Randolph, and Patrick Henry frequented throughout their lives.

Somewhere along the way, a story began.

The whitewashed Powell House, where my children built with blocks, played shut-the-box, helped with household chores, and stitched lavender sachets, became the Gardiners' home. The big maples, oaks, and sweetgum trees I watched herald each season were theirs.

But Emmeline's story wasn't first. Her serious cousin in the bedchamber across from hers had something to say, and that something didn't begin in Virginia. It began in England, where many ideas about human rights and government began.

That story led to the Magazine Incident. Thanks to a ship's log, we know the weather that night was stormy, with gale-force winds. Lost to time are the details of who alerted the town and how they did it. I imagined two possibilities—a militia drummer and the bell of Bruton Parish Church.

The 450-pound bronze Tarpley Bell was cast at the same foundry as the Liberty Bell. It rang to celebrate the repeal of the Stamp Act, the signing of the Declaration of Independence, and the 1783 Treaty of Paris that ended the war. It seemed appropriate for "Virginia's Liberty Bell" to wake Williamsburg the night they lost faith in their beloved king.

Beloved? Yes. As I read through the 1774 and 1775 issues of the *Virginia Gazette* (miraculously preserved all these years, scanned, and uploaded to the internet) I was amazed that time and again Virginians demanded their rights and in the next breath praised their king. That Twelfth Night toast? It came almost verbatim from one recorded in a two-hundred-fifty-year-old newspaper.

I didn't want to move to Virginia any more than Susan

wanted to visit it. But as I look back, I can see that a misfortune I blamed on a dispassionate military bureaucracy was one of the greatest miracles of my life. God continues to be the author of my faith and my life.

Acknowledgments

I owe my deepest gratitude to Keira Dominguez. When I had hit a wall and was ready to give up on my first draft of 20,000 words, I sent the clumsy and confused story to her. She was kind and creative enough to find something to praise. By doing so she gave me hope that I could wrestle an intimate love story out of scattered and impersonal morsels of historical facts. That was three years ago. It has been a long wrestle.

My other alpha reader is my mother, Debra West, who has always been willing to squint past the scaffolding and tell me if a coherent story is in progress.

Several people kindly offered to beta-read *The Lady and the Loyalist*. This was a great act of faith and service, as none of these readers had ever read anything by me when they volunteered. Thank you, Erin Rigby, Angela Glover, Abby Santos, Cordelia Fitzgerald, and Kendall Hoxsey. Many adjustments were made following their feedback.

Thank you to Samiat, my sensitivity reader, for giving me the courage to address some heavy issues in what was supposed to be a light and sweet romance.

Thank you to Lady Carstens of Almack's Historical Dance Society for your delightful instructions on historical dance. It was your voice Charles heard counting out the steps.

Thank you to Melissa Rivers and the members of Write Over Here for quiet evenings and vocal support at the public library.

Thank you to Emily Poole at Midnight Owl Editors for your insights into the developing story.

My gratitude also goes out to the many passionate historians whose work is freely shared on YouTube and websites, including those who scanned and organized fragile copies of the *Virginia Gazette*. There were so many historical details gleaned from so many places.

If any readers are curious to know everything historians can say about the events on the frontier in the summer and fall of 1774, I highly recommend *Dunmore's War: The Last Conflict of America's Colonial Era* by Glenn F. Williams.

About the Author

Stephanie McRae is a descendant of American patriots, including one soldier who died at Valley Forge. She is also the wife of a US Navy veteran. While their family of seven was stationed in Virginia, they took many opportunities to visit Colonial Williamsburg. It was during one of these trips that the seed for her first historical novel was planted.

Also by Stephanie McRae

Heart of the Revolution

The Lady and the Loyalist

The Hero and the Patriot

Novellas

Wager for a Kiss

Novelette

(Free for Newsletter Subscribers)

Marry Me at Willow Haven

www.ingramcontent.com/pod-product-compliance
Lightning Source LLC
Chambersburg PA
CBHW022255310726
48973CB00001B/73